Rufus Pike

Making Of A Mountain Man

A carefree life in New Orleans is disrupted by one quick act that puts a young man on the run.

James Oliver Virmala

Edition 1

Cover Photo By James Oliver Virmala

"Popo Agie in Sink Canyon"

ISBN: 978-1-7340021-4-0

ACKNOWLEDGMENTS

To those who had the wisdom to create the national parks that provide us a glimpse of what the original travelers saw as they traversed the wilderness of our great nation.

CONTENTS

BOOKS BY THE AUTHOR

Oli's Gold Book One
Search For Oli's Gold Book Two
Return To Oli's Gold Book Three
To Be A Mountain Man
Trouble On The Kansas Plains
Frontier Justice
Return Of The Mountain Man
The Tall Man
The Prospector
The Green Valley
Twilight Of The Mountain Man
The Mother Lode
Quest Of The Mountain Man
Journey's End
Rufus Pike
Rufus And The Pup
The Winding Trail Home
Rufus The Lost Years
The Kankakee Kid
Bogus Island
Tyler Tomas The Brothers' War
War of 1812 The Choice
Kyle Oliver The Next Horizon

CHAPTER ONE

Thomas Wallingford was born mid-summer in a small room above a New Orleans saloon. His mother Ruth was married to the piano player and faro dealer, Allen Wallingford. The year was 1806 and the president was Thomas Jefferson. Lewis and Clark began their journey home after exploring to the Pacific Ocean. Andrew Jackson fought his second duel, killing Charles Dickinson. Zebulon Pike saw a distant peak on his second expedition which would eventually be named after him.

Needless to say, the birth of Thomas Wallingford was not a noteworthy event that year. Just three years earlier, New Orleans had become part of the United States with the Louisiana Purchase. The city's population was under 10,000 people, and it was the major port for export of cotton and other goods to France and New England.

Ruth lay in the hot and humid room, nursing her newborn in the light of a smoky lamp. She told young Tom, "Some day you will be a great man. You will attend school and go to England for college. You will be a lawyer like your grandfather."

Ruth's father was a respected lawyer in Philadelphia. She had fallen in love with Allen, a musician, to the objections of her family. The two young lovers had run away and traveled from town to town through the South. Allen made enough for them to live on playing piano in saloons and brothels. He had also become quite proficient at dealing faro and learned to manipulate the deck.

The couple and their young son moved frequently, often ahead of a mob that was intent on hanging Allen for cheating at the faro table. While his father was working in the taverns or saloons, Ruth would read the Bible to young Tom. The boy would fall asleep in her arms, listening to her stories and the piano music that came up from the establishment below.

Tom was a happy child and by three years-old was the darling of any place his father was working. He would often sit on his father's lap and giggle as his father's fingers glided over the keys. His mother would sit at one of the tables and sip on a glass of brandy as she enjoyed seeing her favorite two men together.

While Ruth waited patiently, Allen kept telling her that their big break was just around the corner, once they were rich he'd take her back to society in Pennsylvania. By the time young Tom was five, Ruth had become disillusioned with the future and chose to solve her disappointment with the ever-ready brandy. The young boy was still her pride and joy. She would, in whatever squalid room they called home, tell him about her childhood. Ruth told him that he would be starting school after the next move. Her hopes always hinged on the next move.

The young wife did not see her son's sixth birthday. It was a Monday in October 1811 when she fell ill with a cough. Allen had taken them north, hoping to become partners with two men who were laying out a town and had offered to build him a grand saloon to run. The family had been living in a troop tent waiting for materials to be brought upriver.

With young Tom in tow, the couple had walked along the Mississippi River and had planned their future. Allen was going to be a part of a great venture that would bring men with means who were traversing the river to his saloon to spend money. He would offer the finest rooms and a fancy dining room that would encourage visitors to spend a few extra days. Those days would be spent in his saloon losing money.

The damp, chilly nights had been blamed for the cough. A week later, burning with fever, she went into a coma and passed shortly after. Young Tom had been taken to another tent and was being watched by one of the partners' wives. Allen remained by Ruth's side until the end. Blaming himself for his wife's death, he became resigned to being a piano player and dealer. Allen took the young boy back to New Orleans.

Nobody told young Tom about the death of his mother. When he would ask his father, Allen would just say, "She is gone, son."

Little had changed for the young boy. Instead of being watched over by his mother, the task went to one of the ladies working the rooms upstairs. Young

Tom would be asked to sit on the steps when they entertained a customer. He always received a treat for being good, when the lady was finished. Often a happy customer would press a coin into the young man's hand.

It was during these times that young Tom met a new best friend; Rufus the son of one of the Creole women. He was a year older than Tom and became his first mentor. Young Rufus knew his way around the saloon and brothel. The area he was allowed to wander went from the livery back all the way to the waterfront.

Allen watched the two young boys playing and was thankful his son had found a friend. Now, Rufus was not only a year older, but he was also smart. His mother had taught him some writing. Rufus even had a folding knife and would carve his name into posts and planks, claiming they became his territory.

Not to be undone, young Tom wanted to claim some territory. "You can't claim it unless you put your name to it," Rufus told him.

"Can you show me how to write Thomas?" the young boy asked.

"That's too long a name to put on a post," his young friend said. "You is also called Tom. I will show you how to carve that."

With the help of Rufus the young boy was soon adding his name to posts and planks. Once finished, he would say, "T-O-M. That's my name, Tom."

Once Rufus asked Tom what his last name was. "It's Wallingford," the boy told him.

"You don't want to be carving that," Rufus told him. "You'd be all day on one plank."

Learning how to write his and his friends names was the extent of young Tom's education. There were just too many other things to do. Rufus showed him where to find partial bottles of liquor, where to spy on the ladies working, and how to make money offering to take customers horses to the livery. That worked well. They would often make a few cents bringing them, and again when getting them.

CHAPTER TWO

The years went by and life was easy for young Tom in New Orleans. By the time he was 15 he had a regular job, hawking customers into the saloon and brothel named La Maison. He worked the front of the saloon like a general. There wasn't a post around that didn't have "Tom" carved in it.

Wearing his linen shirt, string tie, wool trousers, ankle-high boots, and a tattered, low-top hat that had been left by a prior inebriated customer, the young man lured the hesitant passerby into La Maison while keeping the porch in tip-top shape. His shoulder-length, light brown hair had a bit of curl in it. Being tall for his age, Tom realized that most people found him handsome.

He quickly learned that there were benefits in helping ladies out of their carriage and arranging boards to walk on when the street was muddy. Every one of them had his name carved in it. Nobody borrowed young Tom's boards.

His father was spending most of his time playing piano. He tended to get into trouble dealing faro and had to move due to the mistakes. His friend Rufus had left after his mother was beaten by one of her customers. Young Tom couldn't be sure, but he learned some time later that the man's body had been found floating in the Mississippi, and he was some cut up. Tom figured that his friend had found something other that a plank or post to carve.

Starting early in the morning and continuing until after dark, young Tom worked the front of La Maison. His voice was often hoarse by the end of the day. He did not mind the hours because he always had money in his pockets. He no longer had to find partial bottles to drink. Most of the time he had a pint in his pocket and used it to sooth his throat.

One afternoon he was sitting on his stool at the side of the building, counting up his money. There was shouting from inside the saloon. Soon the batwing doors burst open and a stocky customer flew out, rolling into the street.

The man slid to a stop and seemed to be looking for something in his pockets. Appearing to give up the search, he rolled over and sat up. After an impressive outburst of cussing and threatening was over, the man slowly struggled to stand. Hurrying over, young Tom gave him a hand. He carried a small whisk, usually reserved for dust on men's cuffs and shoes. The young man quickly whisked the dirt from the man's coat. He did not expect a tip for his services, but he was standing and blocking the view of a pistol that had fallen from the man's pocket. Finishing brushing him off, Tom turned the man and headed him down the street. As soon as the ejected patron turned the corner, Tom picked up the pistol and stuck it inside his shirt.

His prize was a U.S. 1819 Simeon North Flintlock Pistol that shot a .54 caliber ball. While young Tom didn't know it, this was the same pistol that the military carried. He hurried back to his stool and looked around. The street was empty. Normally he would be disappointed because there was no money to be made, but right now he had something more important to look at.

He cocked it and check the pan. There was no powder in it. Sliding the rod into the barrel, he was fairly sure that it was loaded. Young Tom had an excellent relationship with the hostler at the livery. The man knew things and Tom was able to sneak bottles and bring him one every so often. He checked in his small cupboard near the stool and took out a full pint.

There was a young helper named Jacob who Tom was mentoring to take over his business in front of La Maison someday. He found Jacob sitting on the stoop at the back of the building. He made loose change directing customers to the little house and then providing a wet cloth to clean their hands.

"Jacob," Tom called. "I need you to watch the front for a while."

The young man came on the run. "Sure will, Tom," the boy said. "Will you be gone long?"

"About an hour," he told him. "Take and sweep the front porch while I'm gone."

With the instructions finished, Tom hurried toward the livery. The hostler was named Damas. He had a French father and a Creole mother. Damas had been a pirate aboard the ship captained by Jean Lafitte until 1815. It was during this period that he'd learned much of his fighting skills that were needed for hand-to-hand combat. When the French captain joined the Americans in The Battle of New Orleans, Damas left the life at sea and joined the army of Andrew Jackson. The battle had been waged just five miles southeast of his livery.

After the battle ended with an American victory, news came about the Treaty of Ghent, that had been signed December 24, 1814, which officially ended the War of 1812. While the Battle of New Orleans needn't have been fought, this postwar victory by Jackson propelled him all the way to the presidency.

After the war, Damas used the earnings he'd gotten as a pirate to purchase the livery. Tom had met his dark-skinned friend in 1819, shortly after his father had come to work at La Maison. Damas had taught the young man boxing, knife throwing, and had talked a lot about his time as a pirate and about being in the war. Tom was sure he'd be able to fill him in on this prize.

Damas saw him coming and smiled. "What you in such a hurry for?"

"I got two things," Tom told him. "One is a bottle for you, and the other is I need information on something I found."

The 15 year-old boy's eyes were shining, and Damas couldn't help but laugh. "You is some excited."

Handing the pint to his friend, Tom said, "Let's go inside. I don't want anyone to see this."

Shoving the bottle into his pocket, Damas' face became serious. "You didn't go and steal some of the ladies' jewelry, did you?"

"I don't steal," the young man said. "If I find it, it ain't stealing."

"That's a fine line you are talking," his friend said.

Sitting near a dusty window, young Tom took the pistol out of his shirt. Damas' jaw dropped. "Where did you get that?" he asked, his eyes wide and somewhat scared.

"They threw a troublemaker out of the saloon and he dropped it," Tom said. "I helped him on his way and he didn't pick it up."

"Was he able to see where he dropped it?" Damas asked.

"That's not important," the young man said. "I just need to know how to shoot it."

Hesitantly, the hostler took the pistol. He slowly looked it over. "It's got a little dirt in the frizzen."

"Frizzen?" Tom asked. "What the hell's a frizzen?"

"It's what makes it fire," Damas replied. Using a stiff piece of hay, the Creole dug and blew on the pistol. "That's better. I got it out."

"Are you going to tell me what I'll need to shoot it?" the impatient young man asked.

After a short debate with himself, the hostler replied, "You will need a powder horn with powder, some, let see, .54 caliber balls, and some greased patches."

"Can you get these for me?" Tom asked.

"I can," Damas said, "I have friends that carried one of them in the war. But if you are going to do any amount of shooting, you better get a mold and some lead. You'll also need a little pot to melt the lead and a dipper to pour it into the mold."

Concern showed on the young man's face, "What is that going to cost me?"

"Less than you think," he told Tom. "Just keep the bottles coming."

"Can I leave the pistol with you?" he asked.

"Why? So, I can be found with it and end up in jail? There ain't too many of these pistols around and it would be hard to explain coming by it," Damas said.

"You got plenty of places to hide it," Tom replied. "In the saloon or brothel, folks got their hands in everything and they might find it."

"What you going to say if the man comes back looking for it?" the hostler asked.

"Well, after I tell him you got it, he'll probably give me a big tip," the young man said.

"Well, I'll keep it loaded for when he comes for it," Damas said, laughing.

The man never did come back looking and for two dollars and the promise of several bottles, Damas got Tom what he needed. The hostler also gave the young man a possible bag to carry everything in.

He then showed the young man how to clean and load the pistol. The weekend brought the best tips, so it was another three days before Tom had Jacob watch the front. He then got the possible bag with the pistol and walked up the river to a secluded bend.

He had already cast a small leather bag of balls and had a full horn with a cap for measuring the powder. Pulling the pistol at half-cock, he put powder into the pan and then closed the frizzen. Damas had set the flint for him, so all was ready. Bringing the pistol to full-cock, he aimed it toward the river. His hands were shaking with excitement.

Gripping the stock tightly, Tom pulled the trigger. There was a flash and smoke as the pan lit, followed by the discharge of the pistol. Fire and smoke belched from the barrel and the recoil caused the young man to react, knocking his hat off. He could only assume he hit the river. He did not see the results.

Walking in circles and exclaiming, "Wow!" the young man held the pistol close to his chest. He could smell the spent powder. Firing the pistol was everything he had expected. It was great!

Placing his hat firmly on his head, Tom loaded and fired twice more. He chose a short stump as his target. He missed both times. Seeing the dirt being kicked up right alongside the stump was enough. He looked around and saw that he was still alone. The sound of a shot often drew people in to find out what you might have been shooting at.

"One more time," Tom mumbled as he poured a measure of powder into the cap. Placing a greased patch over the end of the barrel and a ball, he then pressed it in with his thumb. Removing the ram rod, he tamped the ball into place.

Squaring his shoulders, the young man looked at the stump. "This time, you are mine."

Holding the pistol out in front, Tom lined the brass front sight with the oval rear sight on the stump. Calming himself as best he could, the young man pulled the trigger. His whole body flinched as the flint hit the frizzen . . . nothing happened.

Tom's heart sank. Somehow, he had broken the U.S. Model 1819 pistol. Pulling the pistol to half-cock, he suddenly blushed. In his haste to shoot again, the young man had forgotten to prime the pan. After a quick look around, making sure no one was around to see his mistake, he poured powder into the pan and closed the frizzen. Then pulling the pistol to full-cock once again, he addressed his foe, the stump.

* * *

The young man stuffed the possible bag into the small cupboard. He had missed the stump every time and was concerned that the sights had been damaged when the man had dropped the pistol. Damas would be able to check it out.

Stationed back in front, Tom began hawking those passing by, attempting to get them into La Maison. He always liked seeing a regular. There would be a bit of friendly conversation and often a tip. Up the dusty street, he saw a small buggy pulled by a tired brown horse.

As the animal plodded toward him, Tom smiled, "Good afternoon, Doc. It looks like you've driven a long way today."

Hurrying to take the reins near the horse's head, Tom watched the old man climb out of the buggy. "I was up most of the night delivering a baby east of here."

"I will put your horse into the shade and give it some water," the young man told the Doctor. "Will you be here long?"

"Long enough to slake a powerful thirst," the old doc said.

Doc Randle was a frequent visitor at La Maison. He felt it was his job to make sure the ladies were in good health and the whiskey was tolerably good. Tom had never seen him play faro or sit at a poker table. Another thing was he never tipped, but the young man still looked forward to his visits.

Leading the horse around back of the saloon, Tom tied it under a large oak. He then got a bucket of water for the animal. As it was sucking up the refreshing liquid, the young man rubbed its shoulder.

"Some day I'm going to have me a horse," he said. "It won't be as old as you and won't be pulling a buggy. When I ride through town, folks will take notice."

Returning to the front of the saloon, the young man heard the piano playing. That meant his father was up. He and his father had a room above La Maison. It was small and to the back. His father played late into the night and would then join some of the ladies for a drink. Despite the heat, it was best to sleep during the day. The bumping and groaning in the rooms next to theirs made sleeping difficult.

Many a night, Tom would bring a bottle to Damas and spend the night in the hayloft. After a few drinks from the bottle, the young man found he slept just fine. As darkness set in, it was Tom's job to clean and light the lamps mounted to the front of La Maison. His plan was to go to the livery once things quieted down. He had much to tell Damas about shooting the pistol.

The night was late and he had moved his stool onto the porch, mostly watching the customers leave. Tom was waiting for the doc to finish. He would then head for the livery. Finally, the old gentleman exited the batwing doors.

"My horse, young man," he said as he steadied himself against one of the porch poles.

Tom trotted to the back and untied the animal. Leading it to the front of the saloon, he asked, "Did you find everything satisfactory tonight?"

"I am pleased to inform you that two of the ladies are in excellent shape." Then, staggering to the buggy, the old doc attempted to climb in. After falling back at his first try, Tom stepped up and assisted him.

As the young man watched the buggy drive away, he heard footsteps behind him. The piano had stopped playing, so he knew it would be his father. "Did you get anything to eat?" the voice behind him said.

Turning, Tom looked up at his father. "Damas had some stew, so I had a bowl with him."

Allen Wallingford was showing his age. His hair was a dirty-gray and he was stoop-shouldered from years of playing the piano. They had been at this location for two years, which was a long time for his father. "I talked to Tully," the man said. "When you are ready, he will teach you how to deal faro."

"I been doing pretty good right here," Tom told his father.

In the lamp light, the young man could see a shine in his father's eye. "You think your doing well out front, but son, if you do well at dealing, there is no limit for you. You could buy your own place and not be answering to anyone."

While Tom couldn't read a book, he knew how to read cards. When business was slow, his father had taught the young man to play poker. Truthfully, it was something that Tom enjoyed, but most often it just took money out of his pocket and put it into his father's. The young man just didn't have the head for keeping track of the cards.

"You'll have the room to yourself tonight," his father said. "I'll be with Sadie."

The middle-aged woman had been at two of the prior establishments that his father had played at. His father had kind of taken a fancy to her and wasted a good part of his pay on the woman. It seemed that the only nights she had time for him was when she had had a bad one with other customers.

"The room will be empty, father," Tom replied. "I'll be at the livery tonight."

"You best be careful son," Allen said. "They watch the whiskey pretty close and I've heard rumblings about missing bottles."

"I figure it is just part of the pay," Tom said, smiling. "I bring in a lot of customers for just tips. The front of La Maison has never been cleaner. I don't think they want me moving my business across town."

Allen looked at his lanky, sandy-haired son. He liked the boy's spunk and was sure that someday he would be an owner. When it happened, Allen figured he'd be able to retire and live the good life of whiskey and women.

"Just don't become greedy," his father said. "A few missing could be due to spillage. A lot becomes a problem."

"Say hi to Sadie for me," Tom said as he watched his father go back in. "Maybe we can play some poker tomorrow."

Without turning, his father waved to him. The young man knew his father would need some money after the night with Sadie. Losing money to his father felt a lot better than having him need to ask.

Now in a hurry, Tom moved his stool back to the side of the building. He grabbed his broom and swept the porch. He then got his possible bag and a bottle he had hidden in the cupboard. Slipping it into his pocket, he went back to the front of the saloon.

Tully came out and stood on the porch, looking at the sky. "Sure, could use a little rain to keep the dust down."

Standing beside the owner, Tom said, "Rain would be good, but that makes mud and dust sweeps better than mud."

Both chuckled over the thought, and then Tully said, "Your father told me you would like to learn to deal faro."

"He thinks I could make a good living doing it," Tom replied.

"Those that make a good living often get shot or hung," the owner said, laughing.

"I have been doing okay out front," the young man said, "and I don't have to worry about being hung."

"Had a man ask me about a pistol today," Tully said. "He had a friend that was in here and he said it was stolen."

Suddenly the U.S. Model 1819 felt very heavy in the possible bag. "Where did he think it was stolen?" Tom asked.

"I believe it was a man that we bounced out of here last week. He was harassing the ladies and in general being a bad ass," Tully said. "We showed him the door, but never saw the pistol. If we had, we'd have put the clubs to him."

"It is probably better that a man like that doesn't have a pistol," Tom told him.

"Maybe so," Tully said, and as he turned, he took a pint out of his pocket and handed it to the young man. "Now you and Damas don't have to share a bottle."

As he walked up the street to the livery, Tom opened one of the bottles. Taking a swallow, he winced as the liquid burned his empty stomach. The stew had been over 12 hours ago, and had worn pretty thin. Approaching the bay doors, the young man took another drink. With the empty stomach, he began to feel the effects.

"You still awake, Damas?" Tom called.

The Creole came out from the tack room. "I was just thinking of going to sleep."

Lowering his voice, the young man hung his hat on a wooden peg and said, "I shot the pistol today." He then handed the partial pint to the man.

Damas took a drink and held it out for Tom. "That's for you," he told the hostler. Like I said, I shot the pistol today, but I think the sights are off. Out of four shots, I missed the stump every time."

"Every time?" the hostler asked.

"I got close, but it was shooting to the right," the young man told him.

The hostler took another drink. Hitting the cork tight with his palm, he asked, "Are you flinching when you shoot?"

"What's flinching?" Tom asked.

"It's kind of hard to explain, but if you thought the pistol was loaded and you pulled the trigger, would you jerk back expecting the pistol to kick back?" Damas asked.

Remembering how he jerked when he forgot to put the powder in the pan, Tom said, "Yes. It happened once today."

"Was it a flash in the pan?" the hostler asked. Seeing the blank look from Tom, he explained. "That's when the pan burns, but doesn't get any flame into the touch hole. Then the gun don't fire."

Or if you don't put powder in the pan, Tom thought, but he said, "Yes, like that."

"It could cause you to shoot to the right," Damas told him.

Suddenly excited, Tom exclaimed, "I was shooting to the right."

The hostler shook his head, "We are going to have to work on you to stop that."

There was a bit of the stew left sitting on the potbelly stove. Tom ate that right out of the pot while Damas talked to him about shooting. He had the young man hold the pistol and draw down on a post supporting a near stall. The pistol was empty and needed cleaning after the day's shooting.

"We'll heat some water come morning and clean it proper," the hostler told him. "Think about what I showed you. Now I am going to sleep."

Damas lowered the flame on the lantern near the bay doors and then headed for the small room where he slept, near the tack room. Climbing the ladder, the young man went into the loft and sought out the dusty blanket that he'd spread over the hay.

Curled up on the blanket, he took the bottle from his pocket. Pulling the cork, he swallowed a mouthful of the amber brew. Tom liked the warm feeling in his stew-lined stomach. "That's better," he mumbled, staring out from the darkened loft.

Suddenly there was rattling on the shingle roof. It was raining. Tom smiled, "Less dust and more mud tomorrow. I'll drink to that."

The clanging of metal on metal brought the young man awake with a start. "It is full sun outside and you're still snoring in the loft," Damas called to him.

The young man sat up quickly and then groaned. His head was pounding and his stomach felt ill. Beside him lay the pint bottle, with only a swallow left in it. Memories of lying on the hay and listening to the rain came back. "I listened too long and drank too much," he complained, to no one particular.

Sliding the bottle into his pocket, Tom crawled to the ladder and climbed down. The smell of coffee came from the potbelly stove. Handing a cup to his ill-looking boarder, Damas said, "Looks like you were holding out on me. There was another bottle, weren't there?"

"I was saving it for you, but the damn rain put me in the mood to drink," Tom said, trying to explain.

"Yes, Mr. Tom. I imagine it did," Damas replied. "Course, some time it is the wind, maybe the sun, or maybe just the darkness that can cause it."

Giving his friend a half-smile, Tom said, "Thank you for the coffee."

"I got a pot of grits on the stove," the hostler said. "Grab you a bowl and et some."

Heading back toward La Maison on the muddy street, Tom had all but forgotten the hangover. Damas was going to show him how to stop flinching tomorrow. The hostler would let him ride one of the horses so they could be well away from folks. Jacob could watch the front while he was gone.

Rounding the side of the building he saw that his cupboard hung open. "Damn!" he snapped. "Ain't nothing safe around here."

The only thing of value in the cupboard was a partial pint of whiskey, which was gone, and a bar of lead, which was still there. His rags and whisk broom were lying on the ground, soaked by the rain. A small jar of sticks used to light the lamps had been dumped into the dirt. His money was safely in a small bag hung around his neck and tucked under his shirt.

Tully came to the end of the porch and looked at the mess. "I got some dry rags under the bar. Take what you need," he told Tom.

"I would put a lock on the cupboard, but then they would just break off the doors," the young man told him.

"Do you want to put your possible bag inside the saloon today?" Tully offered.

"No." Tom said quickly. "No, I think it will be safe out here. Not much anyone could get out of it anyway."

"Going to be a lot of mud to scrape and sweep today," the owner said, looking at the street. As he turned away, he commented, "Made the air smell nice and fresh."

Wringing out the rags, Tom hung them over the stool. He then placed his bag and the bit of whiskey into the cupboard and closed the doors. Things would be safe in the cupboard during the day, but he best not leave anything overnight.

Tom decided to have Jacob work the morning. It was generally the slowest part of the day. Even though he knew this, the young helper was happy to do so. He had hopes of someday claiming the front for his own.

His father came out shuffling a deck of cards. "Shouldn't be anyone coming for a bit," Allen said. "Want to play a few hands?"

It was seldom that Tom saw his father up and about this early. The young man figured he must really be tight for money. Maybe Sadie gave him some credit. "I'll start watching the front right now," Jacob offered.

It was already warm and steamy out near the street. The coolness of La Maison felt good to Tom. He always enjoyed playing with his father. They would talk about the good days when his mother was still alive. Allen would tell his son about the dreams the two of them had had.

After about an hour, he father threw in his cards and said, "I best try and get a little more sleep. I got a long night ahead of me."

It had been a good time playing with his father. Tom had won a few hands and his father had won a few more. He had noticed at least once his father had dealt from the bottom, but that was okay. He knew his father had debts to cover.

Tully had put a tray of cheese and bread at the end of the bar for patrons who would be coming in for a mid-day drink. Tom made himself a thick sandwich before going out to take over the front. He thanked Jacob and gave him half of the sandwich. Thanking Tom, he headed back to his station in the back.

The hot sun quickly dried the street, cutting down on the amount of mud tracked onto the porch. The day seemed to go slowly as the young man called to the passersby, hoping to steer them into La Maison. Tom noticed that every time he drank, his voice would sound raspier. Damas had told him that someday it would stay that way permanently from all the calling.

La Maison was crowded that night. Tom was kept busy helping folks out of their carriages and bringing them around back. Many of the patrons needed their shoes brushed and the dust whisked off their trouser cuffs. He noticed that his father had a bounce in his playing tonight. No doubt there was Sadie to thank for that.

As the night wore on, the saloon became warmer with all the bodies, and some of the ladies came out to the porch to cool off and help calling to those going by. One of the ladies was quite young and had blond hair. Miss Fanny always smiled at Tom and would make small talk with him. He always felt sad when she would go back inside. He would even offer to get his stool for her to try and keep Fanny on the porch for a bit longer.

Unfortunately, there was no money to be made by the ladies out front, so after a bit of fresh air, they went back in. Sometimes it was with a customer whom they had attracted off the street. On busy nights when a customer that had a carriage or buggy in the back came out, Tom would call to Jacob to bring the rig around. He would then split any tips received with the young helper.

It was well after midnight when he heard the piano stop. That was the signal that there were only a few patrons left and most of the ladies had retired with a customer, or just to get some sleep. Grabbing the broom, Tom gave the front one more good sweeping. He then went inside to dump the spittoons. Doing so most often got him a pint from the bartenders.

Coming back out, he went around the side . . . the cupboard was open! He saw the shadow of a man running along the alley. His possible bag was missing! Like a shot, the young man was off, his hat falling behind him. Tom knew the area beyond the saloon and the open area beyond. There were few choices of where the thief could go.

Again, Tom caught sight of him as he ran past a lit window. Now the young man knew he had the bugger. There was a fenced-in garden just ahead. The creak of the wires being impacted was loud. By this time, the young man was only a dozen steps behind the thief. Seeing only shadows moving in front of him, Tom launched himself at them.

An elbow of the flailing man knocked across Tom temple as he tackled the robber. The force of the two bodies propelled them through the fence and into the garden. There were shouts and screams between the buildings as the young man pummeled the thief. Tomatoes, cornstalks, and cabbage was sent flying as the two fought.

Hours of boxing and wrestling with Damas definitely benefited Tom. He was landing solid punches while the robber scratched and bit, trying desperately to escape. Suddenly there was light on the fracas, as the homeowner came around the back with his lantern.

"What in all that's holy are you scallywags doing!" he shouted. "Get the hell out of my garden and take your fight to the street!"

The light gave Tom a clear view of the thief's face and he swung hard. Driven by anger, he sent some of the man's teeth flying as he landed the final blow. The struggles of the robber ended. Still shaking with anger, the young man slowly got up. Seeing the possible bag among the uprooted vegetables, he picked it up and turned to the homeowner.

Gasping for breath, Tom tried to explain, "This . . . this bastard stole. He stole my bag here."

Suddenly the man's wife came out, clutching a Springfield Model 1807 musket filled with shot. "Look at my garden!" she screamed.

By this time Tom recognized the homeowner. His name was Willard Ames, and he often stopped by La Maison for an afternoon of drinks or whatever. The young man did not call him by name and by this time the man recognized Tom.

"Put the shotgun away, Martha," Willard ordered. "This is a fighting matter, not a killing matter."

Again, Tom explained, "This man stole my possible bag, sir. I am sorry that we ended up fighting in your garden."

Patting Tom on the shoulder, Mr. Ames said, "Don't you worry about it. I understand, he stole from you. Just get him out of my wife's garden."

Grabbing the thief by the collar, Tom dragged him to the street, past the front of the house. Behind him he could hear the wife giving her husband all kinds of hell while he defended Tom's tackling the man in the garden.

A few houses down, Tom left the man near the edge of the street in the ditch. He had seen him around La Maison before, but had never learned his name. The robbery wasn't something the young man could take to the police, because the possible bag contained the more or less stolen pistol.

Drained from the experience, Tom gave the unconscious man one more solid kick in the ribs before leaving him. He walked the long way around, on the streets back to La Maison. His father was on the porch talking to Fanny.

He stepped into the light of the lamps. Fanny looked over and smiled. The smile suddenly turned to concern. "What happened to you!" she said rushing off the porch.

"I got into a bit of a fight with a thief," he told her.

"Come in and let me clean you up," she said, taking his arm.

Keeping the possible bag close to him, Tom sat at a table while she washed the cuts on his face. He told them about the thief robbing his cupboard and then chasing the man down. "You should have let him have that old bag," Fanny said. "It certainly wasn't worth being hurt over."

Her gentle hands cleaning him up gave Tom a caring feeling he hadn't had since his mother had died. His father sat across the table with a smile on his face. "You're liking that, ain't you son?" he said.

"She is just making sure I don't have any problems with the cuts," the young man told his father. "Old doc would have done the same if he was here."

He could feel the warmth of her body and smell the gentle perfume she wore. Too many of the ladies put on a heavy scent that would almost make your eyes water. Unable to come up with anything better to say as she finished, Tom told her, "I will owe you for this kindness."

Without saying a word, she gave him a kiss on the cheek and headed for her room. Blushing bright red, Tom sat looking at his father. "Ain't you going to follow her?" his father asked.

"No," Tom said firmly. "She don't want nothing more to do with me. Fanny was just being helpful."

Laughing his father said, "I best get some sleep. Don't be getting into no more fights tonight."

Tom went out front to get his hat and take care of the few things he still had to do. The bit of whiskey was still in the cupboard. He drank that and tossed the bottle. The inside of his mouth was on fire as the liquor contacted cuts from the fight.

His right eye was beginning to feel thick. He blinked several times and it didn't seem to help. With the last of the chores finished, he headed for the livery. It was after three in the morning and Damas was sleeping. Climbing into the loft, Tom collapsed onto the blanket, the possible bag still hanging by his side. Despite the cuts and bruises, the young man was quickly asleep.

* * *

"You awake?" a voice said. It was Damas looking at him from the ladder.

Rolling over, his body ached and Tom groaned. "It's too damn early," he mumbled.

"Are you hungover again?" the hostler asked. "A man can't shoot worth spit when he's been drinking the night before."

Crawling over to the ladder and dragging the possible bag, the young man said, "I ain't been drinking. I was robbed and had to fight the thief."

Once down from the loft, Tom walked into the morning light. "Damn!" Damas exclaimed. "Your shooting eye is almost swollen shut."

"I think it come from his elbow when I caught him," Tom said.

Looking the young man face over carefully, the hostler said, "Looks like you were fixed up okay."

"Miss Fanny doctored me," he told Damas. "She had gentle hands."

"She done all that for you and you come back here to sleep?" the man said. "What was you thinking?"

Again, Tom blushed. "You got some coffee?" he asked.

After the coffee to clear his head, and a quick trip to the saloon to get Jacob covering the front, Tom hurried back to the livery. Damas had two horses saddled and ready to go. Looking at the young man in the sunlight, he laughed. "It is a good thing you don't have a mirror to look in. Your face is a mess. Scratches and teeth marks all over it."

"The bastard was a biter," Tom said. "Now let's go do some shooting."

About three miles upriver there was a small clearing. It was well off the road and away from any homes. Damas had a stake with a piece of board nailed to it. This he pounded into the ground. He then paced off a distance of 45 feet.

"Given time and something to rest against, that pistol could kill a man at 50 paces. It is seldom you'll have those conditions, so I would figure killing range would be closer to 15 paces, or maybe a couple more," Damas told him.

Looking at the target, Tom realized he had been half that distance when he had missed the stump. For the next hour, the hostler would load the pistol and hand it to Tom. The young man aimed and pulled the trigger. Sometimes the pan was without powder, sometimes the pistol was empty with just some powder in the pan. And then there were the times when the U.S. Model 1819 was loaded and ready to fire.

Damas told Tom to assume the pistol was always loaded and be prepared for recoil. When there was a flash in the pan, or none at all, he was to concentrate on remaining as still as if the pistol fired. He told the young man, "The pistol firing should be no more of a surprise than when it misfires."

Once the hostler was satisfied with Tom remaining steady, he told the young man they would work on hitting the target. Drawing down on the target, the young man shot low the first couple of times. Once he was hitting the target, he hit it consistently.

The hostler told him this type of shooting would be used during a duel, where you would turn, draw down on the opponent and fire. A quick shot would most often go errant. Just after that, Damas said, "Now I want you to fire on command. No matter what direction you are facing, when I say shoot, you will turn to the target and fire."

Accuracy was much less when he had to turn and fire quickly. This his mentor told him that would take lots of practice. "Once you work at it, the hand will naturally line the pistol with what you are looking at. If it is a man, look at the center of his chest, not his head."

"A head shot would be much deadlier," Tom replied, confused.

"And the target is a hell of a lot smaller," Damas told him.

The two men rode back from the clearing after three hours of shooting. Tom's ears were ringing from the shots. His right hand was aching from the repeated recoils. He continued to ask the hostler questions about shooting pistols or muskets. Damas told him that much was similar between the two, but in each case, practice made the difference.

While helping the hostler put the horses up, Damas said, "If you would like to try shooting a musket I got, we can take it next time."

"Did you use it in the war?" Tom asked.

"I got it when I joined," Damas said. "They let us keep the muskets as part of our pay."

Putting the saddle on the rack, the young man asked, "What kind of musket is it?"

Closing the stall, Damas said, "It's a Springfield flintlock Model 1812. It shoots a .69 caliber ball."

"My God," Tom exclaimed. "That would be big enough to take a man's arm off."

"It may not take an arm off, but it will put a hurt on a body," the hostler said, laughing.

The young man hurried back to La Maison. He needed to take a bath and change clothes before working the front. One benefit of the brothel was that there was plenty of hot water to bathe and he could get his clothing washed for doing a few favors.

Jacob was disappointed when Tom took over the front. He had hoped to have the whole night and all the tips. Thanking his young helper, Tom put his bag into the cupboard. He had noticed a few clods of mud on the porch, so he took his broom and began to sweep. While he should have pointed the dirt out to Jacob, he decided not to. Tom would be needing the young helper in the near future so he could go shooting.

The summer heat and humidity were ruthless through August. It slowed the business and cost Tom the much-needed tips. He and Damas did get out shooting several times. Tom found shooting the pistol to be much more fun than the musket. He had started to become quite accurate with both and had began betting with the hostler. He had managed to stay almost even with the ex-pirate.

Fanny had taken to coming out onto the porch each evening and make small talk. He liked the look of the slight flush on her face and the hint of perspiration on her temples. The night of his 16th birthday, she made a big thing of it. Tom's father had always treated a birthday as just another day. Secretly, the young man figured it was because his father never had money to buy him something.

The night of his birthday was slower than usual. It was hot, humid, with the threat of rain. Most of the customers stayed home on their own porches, trying to keep cool. Tom was giving the front a final sweep when Tully came out.

"It's been a damn poor night," the owner complained.

"Maybe we'll get some rain to make sleeping bearable," Tom told him.

Tully began to turn down the lamps. He would leave just enough light to help any customers that spent extra time with the ladies to find their way out. "By the way, I think Fanny bought you something for your birthday. I was supposed to tell you earlier, but it slipped my mind."

"Has she gone to her room for the night?" Tom asked.

"I believe she has," the owner said. "Give a knock on her door before heading to your room. She might still be awake."

Then Tully reached into his pocket and took out a bottle of whiskey. Handing it to Tom, he said, "It ain't much, but it might make your day a bit happier."

Thanking the owner, Tom put his broom away and closed his cupboard. He had stopped keeping the possible bag in the cupboard to prevent it being stolen. It was safely in the hayloft of the livery. Some nights he would carry the pistol in his shirt and put it to the back of the cupboard. When business was slow, he could take it out. The young man liked the feel of the pistol.

With his chores finished, he debated whether he should sleep at the saloon or go to the livery. He had just bathed and had clean clothing on. He decided to sleep at La Maison to keep the horse smell out of them. Their room was to the back on the first floor. As he entered the saloon he headed for the room. Then he remembered Fanny's present.

He looked toward her room on the second floor. He really just wanted to go to sleep, but he also didn't want to disappoint Fanny, who had become a friend. Taking the stairs two steps at a time, he climbed to the second floor.

Tapping lightly on her door, he waited. After a second tap, he was about to leave, not wanting to wake her in case she was sleeping. He heard light footsteps from within. The door opened a crack and she looked out.

Recognizing the young man, she opened the door and said, "I was afraid you wouldn't come up."

"I'm sorry to be so late," Tom apologized, averting his eyes. "It wouldn't be right, you having a gift, if I didn't show up."

"Come in," she said softly.

Everything about the room was soft and warm, like the young lady. The lamp had some kind of shade that gave splashes of color and shadows on the wall behind the bed. He saw a pitcher with some type of drink sitting on a small table with two padded chairs.

Standing awkwardly just inside the room, he tried not to look at the woman. It is evident that she had just gotten ready for bed and he had disturbed her. "Have a seat," Fanny told him. "I have made a special drink. My mother used to make it for me on every birthday."

Realizing that the drink was his present gave the young man some relief. Taking a seat, he watched as she poured a tall glass for him. Fanny then dropped some slices of lemon into the glass. She then poured one for herself. Sitting opposite him, with her seat slightly turned to the right, she held up the glass. "To your birthday."

Tom had seen people toast before, so he touched her glass before drinking. Then he almost choked. Covering his mouth, he coughed. Concerned, Fanny said, "I didn't make it too sour, did I?"

Trying to clear his throat while looking away, Tom thought, *Her robe just fell open and I saw . . . everything.* She pulled the robe around her and stood near the young man. "Does it need more sugar?"

"It is just fine," he struggled to say. "I . . . I just drank too fast."

Leaning her warm body against him, Fanny purred, "Are you uncomfortable, Tom?"

The young man had urges surging through every part of his body. He knew it was no time to lie. "I don't know . . . I think that . . ."

She shushed him. "I'm sorry. I am going too fast. Let me get you something a little stronger than the lemon drink."

Suddenly there was no doubt in the young man's mind. Years back, he and Rufus often spied on men and women in the back rooms. Tom knew what was going to happen. He just prayed he didn't mess up.

Smiling, Fanny brought two glasses and a bottle of brandy. "Take a drink of this and it will help you relax."

The young man tossed down a shot and then poured another. "You're going to tell others of how nervous I was."

She led him toward the bed. "When a girl is kind enough to give herself to a man, he should be gentleman enough not to tell his friends. That works both ways."

The robe slipped off, exposing her soft, inviting body. She sat and slowly removed Tom's clothing. At that moment, he knew he was the luckiest man alive, but fear made him wish he was someplace else. Then Fanny slowly pulled him down onto the bed.

Later lying in the dark, basking in the glow of what had just happened, Tom listened to her soft breathing and realized he had just experienced something that would lure him for the rest of his life. In all of his young years, he had never experienced the like.

CHAPTER THREE

Nothing in life lasts forever. Or so it was for the young man. After a year of special nights with Miss Fanny and spending a good part of his tips, she announced that she was getting married. Upon hearing the news, Tom sat on his stool and stared at the ground. Inside he was torn by the realization that he was losing her.

At the age of seventeen, Tom was no longer a boy and had even contemplated asking for her hand himself. As it turned out, a customer from her past had been keeping in contact with Fanny. His wife had died over the winter and he had two children to raise. Evidently, he and Fanny had been rather close, with only the wife standing in their way. After a proper six months of mourning, he was ready to get on with his life.

Tom heard the sound of her trunk being placed on the porch. He could hear the other ladies wishing her well and fussing about missing her. One of Fanny's frequent customers was coming by with a carriage to take her to the stage station. The young man knew he had to go around and wish her well. He was fearful that his voice might crack.

Reaching into the cupboard, he took out a pint and took a large drink. He hoped that would dampen his emotions. Tom had grown to full height by now and was just shy of six feet. His frame was still lanky, but with time he hoped to put on more muscle. He saw the carriage turning into the street.

Getting up, he walked to the small gathering. Fanny looked at him, her eyes bright and smiling. "I thought you were going to hide from me," she said.

"I don't much cotton to long goodbyes," he told her.

Moving close to the young man, her head reaching the top of his chest, Fanny looked up at him. "Can I get a kiss goodbye?"

Still very awkward at displaying affection, Tom steeled himself and smiled. "Yes."

Her tender lips met his and sent a surge of feelings throughout his body. If he lived to be 100, Tom knew he would never forget her kisses. "Would you like to ride with me to the station?" she asked.

"I would, but . . . I . . . I can't. I got . . ." he stammered.

"I understand," Fanny said. Then she whispered in his ear, her soft breath caressing him, "I will always remember our special time together."

Then, that was it. The carriage arrived and he found himself helping to put her trunk onto the back. The ladies surrounded Fanny, hugging her and wishing her well. Tully came out and called to her, "If he don't treat you well, you are always welcome back here."

The man with the carriage took her hand and helped Fanny into the seat. He then climbed in and the carriage pulled away, taking Miss Fanny out of Tom's life. After a bit more waving from the ladies, she was gone and everyone went back into the saloon to start their day.

Standing alone in the street for a moment longer, Tom stared at the corner where the carriage disappeared. For a second, he thought of running and catching her and asking her to stay with him. But he knew better. He had nothing to give her and the man she was going to would offer her a home.

The young man was not in the mood to work. Tom needed to do something that would take his mind off Fanny. He needed to go shooting. He saw Jacob coming to La Maison. "Would you like to work for me for a couple of days?" he called to the young helper.

"I would indeed," Jacob called back.

Tom went into the saloon to get a few things. He saw his father sitting at one of the tables playing solitaire. "I didn't see you outside saying goodbye," he told his father.

Looking up with tired eyes, Allen replied, "It is a scene I have witnessed repeatedly over the past 15 years. A place like this offers no future. The truth is, son, the only one that comes out ahead in this business is the owner. The rest of us just survive."

"Why do you stay, father?" Tom asked.

"Somewhere along the road of life, I lost the will to do more," he told his son. "Am I happy? No. Can I change things? Probably not."

With that, his father continued to play solitaire and Tom went to get his things. With a small bundle under his arm he stopped again near his father. "I will be gone for a couple days," he said. "I think I'll do a little fishing on Lake Pontchartrain."

As he stepped away, his father said, "With her gone, you will have more money in your pocket."

Without comment, the young man headed out of the saloon. He did not begrudge his father's words because it was the truth. He had been spending much of his spare money on Fanny.

Damas was shoeing a horse when Tom walked into the stable. "Do you have some kind of tent?" he asked the hostler.

"I got the one I had in the army," the man said. "It got a few holes where the mice got to it."

"I am going fishing for a couple days and need a tent and to rent a horse," Tom told him.

"I see you are working on getting over Fanny," the hostler said. "It's a good plan. Do something that allows you to think of other things and get your mind off it."

Setting down his bedroll and the bag holding his frying pan and coffee pot, Tom said, "I figure to do some shooting while I'm there."

"Then you best go north along the lake," Damas told him. "Ain't no folks living that way."

"Which horse should I saddle?" the young man asked.

"See the one to the back?" the hostler asked.

Tom replied, scowling, "You mean the mare with bad knees?"

"That's the one," Damas replied. "You ride it easy and it will take you where you want to go. That horse I can let you use for no charge."

Being low on cash money, the horse suddenly sounded good to Tom. "Can I take the musket too?"

"Damn, boy. You want everything," Damas said. Then he laughed, "Go ahead, and take the saddle with a scabbard to put it in."

Leading the horse near the bay doors, Tom placed the blanket on its sway back. Placing the saddle on the animal, he flipped a stirrup onto the saddle and tightened the cinch. Damas had brought the tent over and the young man put his gear behind the saddle. Stepping back, he shook his head. Tom had never seen such a sorry sight as the old horse, with a scarred saddle, and a disheveled pack.

After a stop at the mercantile to get some side meat, coffee, and a few other items, Tom rode north out of New Orleans, on his way to get his mind right. Behind him, tied with his blanket, was a threadbare coat, just in case the weather changed. The tent and ground tarp draped down each side of the old nag. As he rode out of town, the looks people gave him were nothing like he had always imagined.

It was about 15 miles to the area he wanted to go. His father had taken him there once when he had to hide out from some angry cardplayers. He remembered a place on the water with an oak tree that leaned over, almost making a bridge between the shoreline and the point next to it.

After an hour of riding, Tom led the old horse. He smiled, thinking that the old doc's animal was far better than this horse. As he rested and chewed on some jerky midday, he had to admit that the animal had a good temperament and a smooth gait. Of course, he'd only been able to keep it at a walk.

Just before sunset, Tom arrived at his destination. There was a clear area near the tree-lined shore with a spring flowing into the saltwater lake. It would be perfect for setting up his tent. The mosquitoes were already out in force, which meant he'd be sleeping with his blanket over his head.

After building a smoky fire, Tom put up the tent. Smiling, he looked at the sides that were well-chewed by the mice. The wind began to pick up, which would help with the biting insects. The canvas tent fluttered in the wind and the waves off the lake broke on the shore. The sound of the water was soothing.

After roasting and crushing some beans, he added them to some steaming water in the coffee pot. With the sun down, it was too late to try and catch any fish, so he sliced some side meat for his supper. The old horse cropped grass close to the tent as Tom ate his meal. The young man enjoyed the peace of the lakeside camp and wondered why he hadn't done this before.

Before turning in, Tom watered the mare in the spring and then moved it to fresh grass. He spent extra time, liking the gentle nature of the animal. He should have taken a grooming brush with him. The moon was near full and gave a gentle light to the area. With the fire banked, and his supplies put out of reach of wildlife, he crawled into the tent.

Setting the musket next to him and the pistol under the saddle, Tom pulled the blanket up over his head to keep the mosquitoes away. The sounds of the night, with the breeze, the waves, and two owls calling to each other, lulled him to sleep.

The screech of an early morning hawk woke the young man. The inside of the tent canvas was covered with mosquitoes. Some were plump with blood, having gotten to his exposed skin. Tom looked out from the tent and froze. Not 20 feet away was a gator. It was only about eight feet long, but from his point of view it looked like a monster.

The coffee pot and frying pan were in the tent, so the young man struck them together in an attempt to send the reptile running. It worked and the alligator slipped away into the lake. Tom knew it probably came from the area swamps. The gator would not want to stay in the salt water.

After getting the fire going and setting the coffee pot to heat, he got out his line and hooks. Cutting a sapling, he fashioned a rod, using a piece of cork for a bobber and a stone for a sinker. He cut a sliver of side meat for bait and tossed the line into the lake. After a few minutes Tom was rewarded with a strike. He pulled in a fat catfish. A half-hour later, he had two more and was ready to make breakfast.

Tom had a 10-inch skinning knife he'd gotten from Damas. Touching the edge up with his whetstone, the young man cleaned the fish. While he could broil them over the fire, he decided to use a bit of side meat and fry them. It would be fast and save him having to find sticks to use for broiling.

The coffee was done, so he drank a cup while the catfish snapped in the frying pan. He had a tin plate and a three-prong fork to eat with. Damas had told him stories about having only his knife to eat meals. Tom thought about trying it and then realized that the 10-inch blade was still covered with blood from cleaning the fish.

The young man had tossed the guts and discarded parts of the catfish well away from his camp and was sure that the gator would discover and eat them. He set up a 12-inch target after cleaning up from the meal. While loading the pistol, he talked to the mare, warning it that the pistol would be rather loud. Knowing that the animal wouldn't understand him, he still felt it only fair to warn it.

Standing 15 paces away, he fired several shots, hitting the target near the center. He then tried a few quick shots and still managed to hit the target, but more towards one edge or the other. It was obvious that the old horse had been used in battle, because the sound of shooting brought its head up but did not appear to scare it.

While taking a break from shooting, he went to the animal. "You looked a little younger when I start firing. I think it reminded you of days gone by."

Suddenly the scars on the old animal gained new meaning for Tom. He was sure they were battle wounds. It gave him a new respect for the horse. "You were a warrior, weren't you?"

His time at the idyllic camp went by quickly. Tom felt regret as he took down the tent. The hectic pace at La Maison was his way of life. It had been his life for as long as he could remember. Out here near the lake was a different world. He could fish or hunt for his food and spend time listening to nature around him. It was unlike the saloon, where he'd have to rush around hustling for tips.

Tom was just riding away from the lake when he spotted a whitetail button buck feeding in a meadow. Climbing off the mare, he slid the musket out of the scabbard. Keeping his eye on the deer, he poured powder down the barrel and rammed down a patch and ball. Expecting the deer to run at any time, he pulled the musket to half cock and put powder in the pan. Closing the pan, he pulled the musket to full-cock.

The button buck was about 75 paces away. The smoothbore musket was effective at that distance so Tom knew as long as he was steady, the deer was well within the range. He raised the heavy musket, putting the sights on the deer. The horse snorted, no doubt anticipating the shot. The deer's head came up.

Controlling his breathing, Tom pulled the trigger. The flint struck the frizzen, lighting the powder in the pan, and the musket fired, sending a .69 caliber ball at the young deer. Through the smoke, the young man saw the button buck bound away, its white tail flashing as it disappeared.

"I sure as hell didn't miss at this range," Tom muttered as he ran toward the spot where the deer had been feeding.

There was no sign of blood. He saw the deep tracks of the deer taking off in the damp soil. Following them a short distance, he swore and came back to the place where he'd seen the button buck. His eye caught sight of a split sapling in front of a bald cypress. Beyond the sapling was a hole in the cypress where the ball had embedded itself. The height was right for hitting the deer.

"How in the hell did I miss?" he exclaimed.

Thinking over the shot in his mind as he walked back to the mare, he clearly remembered the deer being in his sights as he pulled the trigger. "That must have been a damn ghost deer."

The young man was still complaining when he arrived at the livery hours later. Damas saw him coming and met him at the bay doors. "So how did the old nag work out?"

Smiling at his friend, Tom replied, "This ain't no nag. It is a war horse."

"You figured that out, did you?" the hostler said.

"I have a question for you," Tom said. "I had a deer dead in my sights and shot. It appears I missed it clean. Could the musket be off?"

"Was this deer looking at you?" Damas asked.

"The horse snorted and it did look up," the young man replied.

"You should have waited until it started eating again," the hostler said. "It saw the flash of the pan and was gone before the ball got there."

"They can do that?" Tom asked, surprised.

"They sure as hell can," Damas replied. "The mare probably snorted to warn the deer because it didn't want to carry anymore weight." The two men laughed at the thought and led the animal into the livery.

While Jacob seemed happy to see Tom coming down the street from the livery, the young man believed that if he had never come back his young helper would have been delighted. "Anything new?" Tom asked.

"Business has been good," Jacob said. "Was a pretty good fight yesterday," the helper told him. "Some furniture broken, and a few heads. Four more men that aren't allowed in anymore. Mr. Tully can tell you who they are."

Taking some items out of the cupboard, Jacob headed for the back porch. Tom took the broom and gave the front a good sweeping. It was late afternoon, and once the men were off work the streets would be busy for a while. Tom needed a bottle. Going into La Maison, he visited with one of the bartenders named Sam.

He noticed his father coming out of his room after a break to start playing. Allen looked pale and hollow-eyed. His father needed more sun. Tom promised himself that he'd try and get his father out tomorrow.

Traffic in the streets was picking up and the young man said, "How about it, Sam? One bottle and I'll catch the spittoons tonight."

Being a little difficult the man said, "That's two bits a spittoon. It's a pretty high price for dumping a little chew."

"Make it one bit and I'll dump them tomorrow also," Tom said, a bit of edge in his voice.

Nodding, Sam replied, "You can pick the bottle up at the end of the night."

Feeling a slow burn, Tom went outside to his station. He saw Jacob peeking around the building. Waving him over, he said, "Get me a bottle and I'll split four bits of tips with you."

He watched as they young helper hurried around the building. The was a small window in the back that Tom used to squeeze through and snitch whiskey. As he grew, the avenue closed. Jacob was still small enough.

Tom began to hawk passersby, offering cheap drinks, an honest faro table, and warm women to accompany them. When a carriage or buggy came, he would help the people out and then bring the rig around back.

On one trip, Jacob was waiting, breathless from his assignment. "I got the bottle," he said. "Sam was watching for you but he didn't see me." Then he put his hand out for his reward.

"Thanks," he told the young helper. "Now get a bucket of water for the horse."

Back in the front, Tom did his job, but his heart wasn't in it. The number of tips began to show this. While he called out to the men, he was thinking about the camp. He was thinking that next week would be a good time to go again. He even wondered what Damas would sell the war horse for.

Doc came out of the saloon. He didn't have his normal load on. "I'll go get your buggy," Tom said.

"Just a minute son," the old gentleman said. "I am worried about your father. Has he been acting sickly around you?"

"He is looking a little tired," Tom admitted.

"Have him come and see me tomorrow," the doc said. "Now get me my rig."

Even though Tom had got there late, the night seemed long. He managed to keep a smile on his face, and with the help of a couple pulls from the bottle, he laughed some. Tully came out and stood on the porch for a few minutes.

"Too many of them are getting away," he said. "Kick it up a bit. Make sure they notice you."

Finally, the piano went quiet. In another hour, Tom should be able to call it a night. He made an extra effort helping the customers as they left, hoping to get a few extra tips. He caught a glimpse of someone and turned quickly. It was his father.

He was carrying a drink. "You always told me that you didn't drink when playing. You said it affected the music."

"Son, those bastards don't care. Most don't even hear me."

Changing the subject, Tom said, "Doc wants you to come by tomorrow."

"I ain't got the four bits," Allen told him.

"I got it, father," the young man said. "I'll get you up tomorrow in time to go."

"How was camping?" his father asked. "Did it help you get over Fanny?"

Even the sound of her name tore at Tom's feelings. Keeping his voice steady, he replied, "She is already forgotten. I caught some nice fish and almost got a deer."

Nodding, his father went back into the saloon. He would often sit at a table playing solitaire and wait for Tom. Then they'd play a couple of hands of poker. The young man watched him toss the drink down and head straight to the small room.

Looking at the star-studded sky, Tom said, "Fanny. I sure as hell could use you tonight."

* * *

With time, Tom got over Fanny and the work routine fell back into place. It was getting near to Christmas and the weather was getting colder. Tom often had to wear his threadbare coat. It was getting a little small for him. Tully kept promising to bring one of his old ones in, but always seemed to forget.

His father's visit to the old doc had not gone well. Doc told him he had something in his chest and was making it harder to breathe. He wasn't coughing up blood, so the old doc wasn't too concerned. He gave Allen something to rub on his chest that put off vapors and told him that it would clear the lungs. The only problem is it had an awful odor and his father could not use it when playing.

Tully had brought in a second piano player. He would spell Allen for part of the evening to allow him to rest. Unfortunately, his father would look for Sadie or play poker rather than rest. He had little money for either and would often hit Tom for a loan.

One would think men would stay with family during Christmas and New Year, but it wasn't so. Business at La Maison was brisk and the tips more generous. Tom started having Jacob cover one day a week so he could take his father away from the saloon.

Damas gave him a deal on a buggy if Tom would polish it. He took his father out in the country, and they always carried the musket in case they came across any game.

It was the middle of January 1823 when his father started coughing up blood. The doc said he had consumption. By mid-February, his father could no longer play piano. Tully, being the business man that he was, took Tom aside and handed him the old coat. It was in better shape than the threadbare coat and fit him well. The owner then told him he needed his father's room for a new girl. A moment of anger flashed through the young man, but he caught himself before saying something he couldn't take back.

"Can he stay there for a little while until I find a place for him?" Tom asked.

It was obvious that Tully wasn't happy with the request, but he finally said, "How about a week, two at the most."

When Tom went back out to the porch, he put on the coat. It had a few small holes from moths while in storage. It also had a musty smell that would soon go away. He noticed a note posted near the door. While Tom couldn't read it, he knew that the last one had been for a piano player. He adjusted his top hat and went for his broom to sweep the porch.

The sound of a buggy coming down the street caught his attention. To his surprise it was the old doc. As he pulled up in front, Tom called to him, "You're here kind of early."

"A kid west of town fell and broke his leg," the doc said. "I will be there most of the day and figured to check on your pa before going."

"Want me to take your buggy around back?" the young man asked.

"No, that won't be necessary," he replied. "I won't be long."

The doc took out a lead rope with a weight on one end and a clip on the other. He snapped it onto the horse's bridle and dropped the weight to the ground. The animal was set to stay. Tom busied himself with a few things while waiting for the doc to come back out. He had no expectation that his father would improve, but he wondered how much worse the doc thought he'd gotten.

Business was slow in the cold weather and Tom was nervous. He even polished the lamp glasses to keep busy. Finally, he heard the old doc coming out. He was talking and laughing about something with Tully. His smile disappeared when he stepped onto the porch.

Hitching his pants up, his moustache twitched back and forth. "It don't look good, son," he said, a solemn look on his face. "Truth is, I don't expect him to see the summer."

Tom stood listening to the news with a lump in his throat. Not trusting his voice, he stood looking at the doc for a moment. Then he mumbled, knowing he should say something. "We got to find a place to stay. Tully needs the room for a new girl."

"Yes," the doc said. "I saw the note saying they need another hostess."

Tom walked off the porch with the old man and picked up the weight for him. Unsnapping the rope from the bridle, he placed them in the back of the buggy. Slowly, the finality of the news from the doctor was sinking in. His father was dying.

Then he turned his head quickly and looked at the note. "You say the note is about looking for a hostess?" Tom knew it often took over a month to hire a new girl.

"Yep," the doc said as he flipped the reins to start the horse. The young man watched the buggy disappear around the corner. It was obvious that more than needing the room, Tully wanted his father out, with him being sick and all.

Most of the next day was spent sitting on the stool, watching an empty street. It gave the young man far too much time to think. One conclusion he did come to was that he would be moving on once his father died. He was getting too old to work the front and Tom had no desire to deal cards. If he was going to deal, it would be when he was playing.

Damas came to the rescue on a place to stay. He knew of a Creole family that had a small cabin near their house. It had been used by the family's uncle that worked on the riverboats. He had drowned just before Christmas and the cabin was still empty. The hostler offered to put a word in for them to get Tom a better price.

"Will they have to know my father is sick?" Tom asked.

"Oh, they'll know," Damas said. "The woman is some kind of a voodoo queen, taught proper by those coming from Africa. Many folks go to her with illness. She makes amulets to keep bad away, or gris-gris charms. She even has powders that got magic in them. Maybe she can make your father feel more comfortable."

"So, she'll just look at my father and know he is sick?" Tom asked. Truthfully, he was quite skeptical of voodoo.

"She already know," the hostler said. "I already told her when I was dickering the price. She be wanting $5 a month. That will include any powders or spells."

The rent for the room would really cramp the young man's lifestyle. He would be giving up the pints for four bits and the ladies for a dollar. Tips were scarce this time of year and he didn't have a big nest egg.

Tom decided he was not going to wait for the week or two to go by. It was time to take his father out of the dingy room in the back of the saloon. A customer named Carter offered to take his father and their belongings to the cabin. The cabin was near the waterfront, about a mile from La Maison.

Damas offered Tom the war horse for his ride to the voodoo queen's place to make arrangements for the cabin and to pay the first month's rent. The small dwellings on the waterfront were connected by narrow streets and had even narrower alleys between them. Between the cluster of houses were the warehouses, stock yards, auction stands, taverns and brothels along the waterfront. The latter businesses were frequented by the dock workers.

During the day, the area was bustling with business being conducted and it was safe to travel. Come night the rougher element came out and one had to be careful in the dark alleys and streets. The cabin for rent was next to a clapboard house, several streets up from the waterfront.

Tying the mare to a post next to the house, Tom stepped onto the small porch and knocked on the door. He could hear singing inside. It wasn't anything he recognized, but it had a pleasant sound to it. The door opened and he realized he was at the wrong house.

Standing at the door was a slim, olive skinned woman, with a gingham dress, her black hair pulled back into a bun. She looked up and smiled, "Is there something I can do for you?"

"I'm sorry," Tom replied. "I was looking for the home of Miss Camille."

The woman looked at him, a curious look on her face. Tom continued, "I was told she was a . . . a voodoo queen . . ."

A broad smile came to her and she laughed. "What would a young man like you be looking for a . . . voodoo queen?"

"I'm sorry," Tom said, and he started to turn away.

"I am Camille," the woman said. "Some come to me for things they need, and I help them."

"Damas sent me to you about a cabin to rent for my father," Tom said, now realizing that he was at the right place.

"Did he tell you it was $5 in advance?" Camille asked.

"He did," Tom replied. "I have the money with me, but would like to see the cabin first."

Looking him in the eye, she called, "Gabrielle."

Tom began to get a strange feeling inside. He wondered if she wasn't casting a spell on him right now. He wanted to look away, but couldn't take his eyes off her. Someone came from the back room. Out of the darkened room, walked Gabrielle. She was absolutely beautiful. The slim young girl had large eyes and perfect features. She had on a dress that clung to her shapely figure.

"This is my eldest daughter and she will show you the cabin," Camille said, stepping aside.

The daughter passed close to Tom as she went by. She was wearing some type of fragrance that stirred the young man to the quick. Suddenly remembering that the mother was probably a witch, he thanked Camille and followed the girl.

The cabin was more than suitable for what Tom needed. It had two comfortable rooms. The front was a kitchen and sitting room. The small table had three chairs. There was a pump at the sink for drawing water. A six-plate stove would be used for cooking as well as heating the cabin. A curtain covered the doorway into the back room, which had two cots and a side table with a pitcher and bowl. An oil lamp was on a stand between the two cots. Pegs were fixed into a plank mounted onto the wall that would be used to hang clothes. There was a back door that led to the outhouse, which was shared with the main house.

Leaving the cabin to pay Camille the rent, Tom realized that what he'd just looked at was better equipped than any place he'd ever lived before. As he followed Gabrielle back to the house, he couldn't keep his eye off the way she walked with a gentle sway. Knowing the mother was a voodoo queen, Tom did not want to be in the same room as the daughter any more than he had to.

Guiding the horse through the narrow streets, Tom rode back to the livery. Swinging off the mare, he led it into the building. Damas was pitching hay into the stalls. "I rented the cabin," he called to the man.

"What did you think of Camille?" he asked.

"I kind of told her she didn't look like a voodoo queen," Tom told him.

"You what?" he exclaimed. "You don't be telling her she's a voodoo queen. You be lucky if she don't put a spell on you to make your manhood fall off."

"Well, I mentioned it," Tom said. "I don't think I really called her a . . ."

The hostler began to laugh, "I can see you are going to be walking on eggs near that place. She got three mighty good-looking daughters. They can all cast spells."

"I sure as hell know that Gabrielle can," he said more to himself than to Damas.

His father got upset when Tom told him that Carter would be bringing him to his knew home in the morning. "I am staying right here!" he shouted. "This is my home and you ain't going to take me out of it!"

Tom ached inside as he looked at this gaunt father, whose normally clean-shaven face now bristled with whiskers and dried blood on his chin. "I already paid a month rent for a cabin," Tom told him. "Tully is kicking you out of here, Father. He has someone coming to stay in this room."

His father grabbed a stick he'd been using to walk and threw it across the small room. "I worked hard for Tully. How can he do that to me?" His voice weakening toward the end.

"We are family," he told his father. "I will be taking care of you. You are going to like the cabin. It has water at the sink. No going out to the well."

For the next hour he talked with his father and was able to make him see reason. That time had taken Tom away from the front and was costing him tips. Tom was afraid to just leave his father in the room angry about leaving. He feared he might hurt himself. Satisfied that his father had accepted the move, the young man hurried out to the front to send Jacob to the back.

Carter was prompt and Tom had his father and their belongings packed and ready to go. Tully was nowhere to be seen. The was no grand farewell to the man who had played piano for him the past three years. Tom would have been happy had he just come out and wished his father well.

Carter complained about that area they were going to and about the narrowness of the streets. Tom assured him it was safe during the day. "And another thing," he said, "I got a voodoo queen that will cast a spell on anyone that bothers us."

Camille heard the buggy coming and met them. She approached the wagon and reached for Allen's hand. "Once you get settled in, I will come by and see what I can do to make you more comfortable."

Watching her leave, his father whispered to Tom, "That wasn't an offer of sex was it? I don't think I'm in any shape to . . ."

"Don't worry father," the young man said, grinning. "I think she just wants to make sure you like the place. You might want to watch out for her daughters, though."

CHAPTER FOUR

Allen Wallingford was most comfortable in the cabin. Camille came back and brought him something to help the pain in his chest. She mixed a bit of it in some water and had him drink it. He had to cough after the final swallow and quickly brought a hankie to his mouth. The cough left flecks of blood on the white cloth.

The woman took his kerchief and looked at the flecks and frowned. Without saying anything, she left, still carrying the hankie. "Do you think she is going to conjure something up with my blood?" he asked his son.

"If you see a mist floating around above your head tonight, I wouldn't be looking at it," Tom said, laughing.

After a couple of minutes, his father said, "You know, the chest does feel better."

"That's good," his son said, although Tom did notice a bit of a slur in his father's speech. The young man decided that he would accept anything Camille did because it couldn't be blamed for killing his father. The consumption was going to do that.

Things had changed at La Maison. The note was still posted outside the door. The small room remained empty and Tully didn't come out on the porch to visit any more. When times were slow, Jacob would come around front and sit with Tom. He was quick to get up when a carriage stopped in front. Tom no longer minded, because soon the front would be his young helper's.

The young man knew it was time for him to move on. It would be another couple of months before business picked up. Tips were down, and after food he was barely making enough to cover the month's rent. Even the bread and cheese tray had been moved from near the door to the far end of the bar. When Tom went in to get some, Tully would watch him and frown.

The fact that the owner never said anything told Tom that Tully still found value in him. Once that was gone, the front would be closed to him. Two weeks after his father had moved out, the young man decided that it was time to go.

He came to work as usual and waited for Jacob to arrive. The young helper always stopped to talk for a bit. "There is something you have to do Jacob," Tom told him.

"Tell me what it is and I will do it," the energetic helper replied.

"You have to find someone to cover the back," Tom said.

A horrified look came to the helper's face. "You letting me go? Is it because I been beating you to the carriages some times? I won't . . ."

Tom stopped him. "As of today, you are in charge of the front. I am leaving. That is why you have to find someone for the back."

Jacobs jaw dropped. "You are leaving? You're just giving me the front?"

"I don't own it, and neither will you," Tom said. "Just keep Tully happy and he'll let you work until the day you die."

Turning to leave, he heard Jacob ask, "Can I keep the stool and cupboard?"

"It is yours, and everything in the cupboard," Tom called back as he headed for the livery.

When he told his friend that he'd given up the front, Damas said, "That's a fool thing to do. We ain't but a month from busy times."

"I'm going to find some work on the waterfront," Tom told him. "After father dies, I will move on."

"Move on," the hostler snorted. "Like you got someplace to go."

"It is a big country," he told his friend. "I plan to try and see some of it. Maybe find a job that pays enough to have a family."

"You never struck me like the family kind," Damas said. "I see a wanderer in you."

Looking at his old, single friend, Tom smiled, "I might become a pirate. It gave you your start."

"Get the hell out of here," the hostler said. "I taught you everything I know, and you still don't know nothing." As Tom left, Damas called after him, "Say hello to your father for me."

Finding work on the waterfront was easier than Tom thought it would be. Two days after leaving La Maison, Tom was dealing faro at a seedy place near the water. The pay was regular and he made a little on the house winnings.

He was surprised to see how much money the dock workers had to waste on cards, whiskey, and women. Most of them lived in the boarding houses that held up to 10 in a room. They could get a bowl of some kind of soup and a slice of coarse bread for a nickel from the street vendors, and in many cases that was their only meal of the day.

When somebody died, everyone was encouraged to join singing in the funeral dirge and a decent spread was normally served after. Frequent funerals saved many a dock worker his nickel. The dock laborer earned between 75 cents to a dollar for 10 hours work per day. At the faro table, Tom was making as much as two dollars a day for his 12-hour shift.

There were women who did laundry, and Tom would bring his dirty clothing to them once a week and have them cleaned and pressed for two bits. Unlike working the front at La Maison, there were several rules on the waterfront. If you saw something happen that was against the law, you said nothing. If something needed to be done about the incident, there were men on the waterfront that would take care of it. It often ended up in another free meal.

Each night a man would come into the tavern and sit near Tom's faro table. After a little small talk, Tom would shake his hand and give him four bits, which protected him for that day. Each night he would weave through the buildings on his way to the cabin, knowing that if he was attacked, the long arm of the waterfront would deal with the attacker.

One night, he entered the cabin and found Gabrielle sitting in the front room, reading. His heart leaped just a little at the sight of her. "Your father is having a bad night," she said.

Tom looked at the curtain. "He is sleeping right now," Gabrielle told him.

There was a pot of coffee on the box stove. Pouring himself a cup, Tom sat at the table. "Did your mother give him something to help him sleep?"

"She did," the girl said, shifting slightly on her chair. As though she couldn't have looked prettier, the move made her even more beautiful.

To be polite, Tom said, "You can go if you want to. I will watch him."

"I don't mind staying," Gabrielle replied.

That night, something happened that scared Tom to death. He found himself lying in the second cot with the beautiful Gabrielle while his father lay in an opium stupor on the cot next to them. There was no way in hell he was going to survive the spell her mother was going to put on him.

For the next several days, Tom was unable to look into the eyes of Camille and would avoid her if at all possible. He knew she would read his mind if he looked at her and then his life would be a living hell.

It was early morning a week later, and Tom was helping his father back from the little house. In a weak voice, Allen said, "I would like to have coffee with you."

Helping his father to a chair, Tom got two mugs, filled them, and placed them onto the table. He added some honey to his father's and gave it a couple of stirs. "I had a dream last night," his father said.

"Good dream or bad dream?" his son asked. Tom had heard that opiates could give a person nightmares.

"It was good," he father replied. "An angel told me it would not be long."

"How did you know it was an angel?" Tom asked, making conversation.

Allen stirred the coffee a couple of more times and then, with shaky hands, took a sip. Setting it down he said, "The angel looked like Camille."

A flash went through him. *Had the voodoo queen told him that she was going to end his life?*

"How do you know it was an angel and not Camille?" he asked his father, afraid of what the answer would be.

His father smiled, "When I said it looked like her, I meant it looked beautiful like her."

Accepting his father's explanation, Tom got out some cards and dealt them out. For an hour they played, Tom slowly losing money to his father. Unable to help himself, the young man said, "I will miss playing with you."

"So will I," Allen said, laughing. He then winced from the pain in his chest and coughed.

The door opened behind him and Tom saw his father's eyes light up. "You caught me playing cards," he said.

Turning, Tom stood quickly. It was Camille. "I didn't think it would hurt him to play some cards."

"It is good for him to be up," she said, taking his cup and rinsing it in the sink. She then put water into the cup and mixed in some powder. Setting it down in front of his father, she said, "Drink this slow."

She went into the bedroom and began to straighten the bed. Following her in, Tom said, "I was planning to do that."

"I don't mind," Camille told him. "You work long hours. The other night Gabrielle sat up with your father and you got in very late."

"I will try not to let that happen again," the young man said, blushing.

"It happens," she said. "You should try and spend time with your father. He doesn't have long."

She went back to the table and talked briefly with his father. Then, placing her hand on the side of Allen's head, she smiled and left the cabin. Tom sat back at the table. "Did you want to lie down father?"

"How about a couple more hands," he said. "I got a hot seat here."

Tom dealt the cards and looked at his hand. He had three, fives. As he looked as his cards, his father said, "I had another dream a couple nights ago."

"You did," the young man said as he tossed in three cards.

"I dreamt that Gabrielle was in our room and in your bed." Allen threw in two cards.

Avoiding his father's eyes, Tom dealt him two and took three himself. "Was she an angel too?" Both checked.

"It didn't sound like she was being an angel," his father said and laid his cards down. "I have a pair of queens."

The young man threw his cards down and pushed the pot to his father. "I hope you don't tell these crazy dreams to Camille," Tom said.

His father smiled, "I better lie down now. The medicine is making me sleepy."

True to the dream, a couple of days later, a young Creole came to the tavern and told Tom he needed to come home. Tom's hands were shaking as he apologized to the players and put the cards into the box. Following the young Creole through the alleys, Tom feared his father had already passed.

The lamps were lit in the cabin and Gabrielle was sitting at the table. "My mother is with him," she said.

Camille was sitting on a small tool near the head of the cot. She was talking or chanting to his father. Hearing him come in, she stood up, placing her hand on his father's chest. With almost no expression on her face, her eyes burned into Tom's. "He is ready to go to that good place."

As the voodoo queen left the room, Tom expected to see his father already dead. Relief flooded over him as he saw his father's open eyes looking at him, while his breathing was labored. Sitting onto the stool, Tom knelt close to his father and said, "I am here."

"Did you know she can open the gates to heaven for you?" he father whispered.

"That is a good thing," Tom told him.

For the next half-hour, they spoke quietly, much of it about his mother and how much his father missed her. He heard Camille at the doorway. Tom looked up and tied to smile. "He is gone," she told him.

Confused, Tom looked back at his father. In just seconds, he had slipped away. Unable to move, tears filling his eyes, Tom sat looking at his father. Camille took the sheet and put it gently over his father's face. It had been only four months since he'd first coughed up blood.

"Gabrielle will stay with you," she told him. "Your father is now with your mother. He no longer feels any sadness or pain."

Still numb from the loss, Tom had to make plans for the burial the next day. The body would remain in the cabin until everything was finalized. Tom would have liked to have buried his father with his mother, but she had died many towns ago, and he wasn't even sure what town that was.

Thanks to the men who ran the waterfront, there was a proper funeral dirge for his father. Tom found out that the food provided after was not free and he owed those who ran the waterfront. Three days after his father died, he was back dealing faro. Each day a dollar was taken from his pay to help cover the funeral expenses.

Unable to sleep next to where his father had died, Tom spent a week in the hayloft of the livery. Up the street he could see Jacob working the front of La Maison, hawking customers and sweeping the porch.

Tom's shift was from 2:00 p.m. until closing which was always after 2:00 a.m. He stretched on the blanket in the loft and sat up. He could smell the coffee. "It's about time you got up," Damas called from below.

"What time is it?" Tom called back.

"Half past getting up time," he friend kidded him.

Feeling stiff from a long night standing at the faro table, Tom climbed down the ladder. Damas stood waiting with a cup of coffee for him. "I dun drank the first pot waiting for you."

The Creole made good coffee. "I see that Jacob is already in the front," Tom observed.

Looking out the bay doors, Damas replied, "He's like a river hawk, protecting his territory."

"I got to stop by the cabin today and give Camille the rent," Tom told him.

"It don't make no sense," Damas said. "You got a perfectly good bed in that cabin and you be sleeping in the loft."

"It would save me a long walk each day," he told his friend. "If I don't come back tonight, you'll know I stayed in the cabin."

"It'll save me a whole lot of coffee," Damas pointed out.

It was midday when Tom walked the mile to the cabin. He went inside, expecting to find someone new had moved in. The front room was neat and orderly. He pushed aside the curtain and went into the bedroom, half-expecting to see his father still lying there. The cot was gone!

Looking around the room, he noticed that the furniture had been rearranged, more to suit one resident. There were fresh curtains on the window. He and his father's bags were neatly lined up where the cot once was.

He turned as he heard the door open. It was Gabrielle with clean sheets for his cot. "I saw you come and figured I best get the bed made in case you needed to rest."

"I have the rent for your mother," he told her.

"You'll find her in the house," the girl said. "We are doing laundry today, so leave your dirty clothes in the room and I'll come and get them."

She bent to put the sheets on the bed and Tom caught his breath. She was beautiful. Not wanting to stare too long, he went to settle up on the rent. Camille had the curtains closed and incense burning in the room. She was working on a charm for someone.

"Just set the money on the stand next to the door," she requested. "The room is clear of bad spirits and this will protect those that wear it."

Placing the $5 on the stand, he quietly left the house. He could hear her chanting something in a tongue he did not recognize. For a few minutes he stared at the door in wonder. Turning to leave, he felt foolish. There stood Gabrielle, watching him with a sly smile on her face.

"She makes an amulet for you," the girl told him.

"A charm for me?" he asked. "I don't need one."

"Mother had a dream that danger would come your way and this amulet will protect you." Gabrielle explained.

A chill went through Tom. Camille's dreams generally came true. She had known his father was ill before he'd told her, and she had predicted the day of his death. Of course, he also knew she was giving him stuff for the pain and could just as easily have given him something to end his suffering.

Once back in the cabin, he felt safe. Things that when on in and around the house made him feel uncomfortable. Gabrielle always made him feel in danger. The attraction he felt for her was not healthy. It was as though she had cast a spell on him. As Tom dug out clean clothes, he looked at the cot. *Had she put something on the sheets to control him?*

"Damn fool," he muttered. The church bell rang in the distance, letting him know that it was noon. He had two hours before needing to be at the tavern. Suddenly he found himself talking to his father. "I don't know how, but she seems to know things. I best make a quick trip back to the livery."

That afternoon, Tom showed up at the tavern with his possible bag. Inside was the pistol, loaded and ready. He did not feel there was danger in the tavern, but the trip to and from could hold peril. Tom had paid up the funeral expense and now kept all his pay except for the four bits the man giving protection charged.

It was after three in the morning when the owner gave him the nod to leave. Tom put the possible bag over his shoulder and headed for the cabin. He was glad that he'd decided to move back. It was a much shorter walk than the livery. A lamp was burning in the front room. Tom slid his hand into the bag, gripping the pistol. Then, shaking his head, he removed it. Trouble in the cabin would have waited in the dark.

Slowly he opened the door and saw the smiling face of Gabrielle. "You worked late tonight," she said.

The next day, Tom walked to work thinking about her warm embrace and tender lips. She was trouble. He sure needed that amulet Camille was making in the worst way to break the spell the girl had on him. Rather than send her home with a stern warning as he should have, he'd taken her hand and led her right into the back room.

As he cut through an alley, staring at the ground, muttering and scolding himself, Tom didn't notice when two ruffians suddenly stepped out in front of him. One of them had a club raised to strike him. Too late to jump clear, he put up his arm to deflect the blow.

It did not come. The two thugs suddenly stepped back, recognizing Tom. "We didn't know it was you," one of them said as they disappeared around the building.

Sliding his hand into the possible bag, he felt the pistol. "I'm glad to see I'm getting my money's worth from the protection," he called out.

His pounding heart hadn't settled down yet when he got to the tavern. He knew of the danger presented on the waterfront, but it was seldom he came face-to-face with it and Tom found it unsettling. He decided that he would be moving on as soon as he had a little money saved up.

For the next month Tom stayed away from whiskey and saved as much of his money as he could. Gabrielle took care of his need of warmth and comfort. Most days the 17 year-old would walk to the livery and have coffee with Damas, mostly to make sure he didn't run into Camille. When she looked at Tom, it was like she was looking into his heart.

It was mid-May and the heat of summer had already engulfed New Orleans. Damas had poured a measure of whiskey into the coffee, and as Tom walked to the tavern he had a warm, comfortable feeling inside and was sweating on the outside.

Entering the tavern, the young man noticed that Ben, who was the casekeeper at his table, was at the bar nursing a whiskey. The casekeeper was most often paid by the players. He would keep track of the cards played using abacus beads on thirteen strings. As the cards were played, bettors would watch the case to see what cards were still available in the deck. That way they knew what cards were available to be bet on.

Mopping his face with a hankie, Tom frowned, knowing that when Ben had too many drinks he tended to make mistakes tracking the played cards. Too often Tom would have to settle with the unruly players at the end to prevent turmoil.

As the night progressed, Tom was thankful that Ben was doing a decent job with the case. There was one problem he'd noticed. Twice he could have sworn that chips on a losing card had moved when he looked up to collect the losers. He suspected one of the players had a horse hair tied to his bottom chip and was pulling it back.

This cheat was most often tried when the deck neared the end and the betting became frantic. Tom had narrowed down the player he thought was cheating. He noticed that the fat player had placed a copper or penny on top of his chips, which reversed the winning and losing cards that were turned up.

Turning up the first card, or the house card, Tom saw that it was not the one that the cheater had played on. When he turned up the second card it made the cheater's bet with the copper a loser. Tom saw that the penny was gone and the fat man shouted, "I win!"

Stopping the play, Tom said, "You pulled your copper."

"The hell I did!" the man snarled.

"Ben, you saw the copper on the bet?" Tom asked.

With fear in his eyes, the casekeeper said, "I was moving a bead."

Suddenly a flintlock pistol came out of the man's boot. Tom had the U.S. Model 1819 on a shelf under the table. He grabbed it as the man fired. The ball burned across Tom's neck, knocking him back. As he fell, he fired at the center mass, putting a .54 caliber ball into the man's bulging gut. Hitting the wall behind him, Tom slid to the floor, clutching the wound on the side of his neck.

All hell broke loose. Tom sat, his head spinning from the ball and wall impact, with blood oozing from between his fingers. Players were grabbing money and running from the table, while the fat shooter lay on his back screaming for help.

Suddenly, rough hands grabbed Tom, dragging him forcefully across the filthy floor. Whoever had him tossed him into the street. His head was clearing and he saw that it was the man who he paid protection to. The man tossed his possible bag at him.

"That's the end of your protection!" the man snapped. "You shot the wrong damn man!" Then he hissed at Tom, "Run for it and you just might live to see morning."

By some miracle the pistol was still in his hand. Stuffing it into the possible bag, Tom got to his feet and began to run. "You shot the wrong man," kept running through his mind. "The man shot me!" Tom hollered.

Those at the tavern knew that he lived in the cabin, so Tom couldn't go there. He thought of the small room at the back of the La Maison. If someone came looking for him there, Tully would turn him over in a minute to prevent trouble. Staying in the shadows, Tom arrived at the livery, gasping for air, and bloody.

He went into the back door that was used for cleaning the stalls. Creeping inside the livery, he stood in the dark. Next to him the war horse snorted. "I need help," he whispered.

Exhausted, Tom slipped into the mare's stall. He slid down onto the hay in the back corner. Suddenly, Tom began to shake. Fear went through him. Had the wound been more severe and was he bleeding to death? In the dark, he began to pray. Over and over, he asked God what else could he have done. The man had tried to kill him.

The horse looked back and gently nudged his shoulder. Coming in contact with the blood, it snorted softly shaking its head. "That bad, huh?" he whispered to the mare.

Tom dozed fitfully waking to any sound, his neck was throbbing, and there was sticky blood down his shoulder and on his hand. He had nothing with him to fashion a bandage. It was still dark when he heard voices. Someone was shouting for Damas.

The lamp near the bay doors was turned up and Tom could hear some muffled conversation. The hostler sounded plenty angry. "Check the damn place from top to bottom. He ain't in here!" Damas snapped.

Knowing they would check the stalls, Tom crawled under the war horse, which was standing close to one side. Huddling beneath the animal, he could hear the searchers climb into the loft. He could hear their stomping and cussing as they search through the hay. Tom heard them climb down the ladder. They would now search the stalls. As one of the men stopped at the war horses stall, it reached out its head and tried to nip him.

Jumping back, the man said, "The damn animal is a biter."

"Been that way as long as I've had it," Damas said. "If it weren't such a good riding horse, I would have sent it out for glue."

The men went back to the front and checked the tack room and Damas' small sleeping quarters. Tom heard the hostler snarl as the men left, "Now get the hell out of my livery! You disturbed my sleep and I got lots of work to do tomorrow."

Tom had crawled back to the corner of the stall and sat, feeling absolutely miserable. His eyes were getting heavy and he was about to doze when someone speaking brought him wide awake. "I said, is that you in the stall, Tom?"

His mind was muddled, and he wasn't sure what to say at first. Trying to move toward the horse, Tom was unable to stifle a groan. "It is you, ain't it," Damas said. "You got to get up and open the stall. The old mare is protecting you like a newborn foal."

Using the wall to steady himself, Tom stood up. The mare whinnied and sniffed him. Placing his clean hand on its neck, he whispered, "I'm okay now. Damas is a friend."

Raising the rope loop, Tom pushed the stall door open and looked at his friend in the dark. "I feel just awful."

"When I get you to the light, I'm betting you look like hell too," hostler said, pushing the stall door closed and patting the horse on the head. "You done good, horse."

Steadying Tom, he guided him to the tack room. The dusty window had a grain sack hanging over it. Leaving him in the dark room, Damas went out and then soon returned with a candle. Pulling the door shut to prevent anyone from seeing the light, the hostler got his first good look at Tom.

"Good God!," he exclaimed. "You got blood all over you. How many times was you shot?"

Tom closed his eyes due to the brightness of the candle. "Once," he said. "I am pretty sure I was shot just once. It is on the side of the neck."

The hostler placed the candle on a crate and looked at the wound. "Damn," he said. "An inch over and you wouldn't have had any more worries. Now sit right there and let me get something to clean your wound."

Sitting on a keg, Tom looked down at himself. There was blood from his shoulder all the way to his boot. His left hand and forearm were coated with dried blood from stanching the wound. Any move he made with his head caused a tearing pain in his neck.

Damas quickly came through the door of the tack room, splashing water from the bucket. "I should have shielded the candle before I went out. That light can be seen all the way up the damn street."

Setting the rags and bucket down, the hostler began to attempt to wash some of the blood from around the wound. "Blood be a funny thing," he said. "Just a little will make an awful mess. Now you got more than a little, but it is less than you think."

As he worked on the young man, Damas kept talking softly. "I ain't going to worry about the shirt and stuff. Right now, I got to get something on the neck to stop the bleeding. Every time you move, some blood comes out. What you need is the doc, but if I get him, I may as well kill you myself. There are men that would follow him and make short work of finishing the job the man in the tavern started."

"How do you know where it started?" Tom asked, trying to move his jaw as little as possible.

"Them that came here looking for you told me," Damas explained. "You shot an important man."

"I shot a man that was cheating," Tom said. "And that was after he shot at me."

"He was the brother-in-law of a man that is very powerful on the waterfront," the hostler informed him.

"He weren't dead when they threw me out," Tom replied. "He was screaming like a stuck pig."

"It will take a day or two," Damas said, "but that gut shot will surely kill him."

A flash went through Tom, realizing that he had killed a man. At a young 17 years-old, that was a heavy burden to have laid on him. He closed his eyes and tried not to think of it, while his friend put the bandage on his neck.

He heard the cork come from a bottle. "Have a drink of this."

Tom looked at Damas, who was holding a pint of whisky out to him. Taking the bottle, the young man took a large swallow. Coughing, he handed it back to his friend. "I needed that," he said in his raspy voice.

"I put some sacks on the floor for you to lay on," Damas told him. "Try and get some sleep and we'll figure what to do come morning. By the way, I didn't see your possible bag."

Tom was carefully lying down on the sacks and replied, "I think I had it when I came in the barn. Then again, maybe I dropped it."

Due to the effects of the whiskey and the exhaustion, Tom was almost sleeping when Damas blew out the candle and left the tack room. There was worry on the hostler's face. By daylight every street would have someone watching for the young man. Those on the waterfront would not be happy until Tom was dead.

CHAPTER FIVE

Tom woke in the dark tack room. He lay still, feeling the beat of his heart throb in the wound on his neck. A sliver of light came from under the door. Slowly he pushed himself to the sitting position. The bulky bandage that covered the wound made it impossible to turn his head.

Reaching up, he pulled the sack from the window. While the cobwebs and dust made it impossible to see out of, it let some light in. Tom was able to see his possible bag next to him. He reached in and felt around. The pistol was inside.

He was having trouble putting together the events of the night before. All he was sure of was that he had killed a man. Much of the rest was a blur. Tom's mouth and throat were dry and he sorely needed a drink of water. Moving his tongue around did little to stimulate saliva.

He took the pistol from the possible bag. There was no way that Tom was going to leave the tack room without the Model 1819 being loaded.

Expending a great deal of effort, he loaded the pistol and then sat breathing heavily in the middle of the room. His neck was throbbing with pain and even the thought of moving seemed impossible.

Suddenly the tack room door opened. Tom's head jerked up and he brought the pistol to bear. "Put that damn thing down," Damas said. "I got some coffee here for you."

Unable to see the man through the pain of moving his head, Tom reached up with a shaking hand for the coffee. "I got a plan. Drink this here coffee and I'll be back in a few minutes and let you know what it is."

Tom's tongue was so dry and thick, he couldn't reply. Unable to see through his tear-filled eyes, he felt the hot cup in his hand. While it burned, there was no way he was going to let it drop. As the door closed, he got the cup to his cracked lips and felt the sting and burn as the strong brew hit his tongue.

Sitting alone in the dusty room, Tom slowly drank the coffee and wondered what plan his friend was talking about. He wished that Damas had left the bucket of water in the room. Tom would have liked to wash the blood from his left hand and arm. Just having done that would have made him feel better.

Damas came back into the tack room. He had the coffee pot and a bowl. "I got some porridge here in case you can eat." Setting the bowl onto the crate, he refilled Tom's mug and then set the pot next to the bowl.

Finally able to talk, Tom asked, "What is the plan?"

"I've been promising to deliver some hay to Camille for her chickens and goats," the hostler told him. "You'll be hidden under the hay, and once I get you there she'll figure how to get you out of New Orleans."

"Why am I leaving New Orleans?" Tom asked.

"Damn, boy," Damas said. "I know you got shot in the neck, but it shouldn't have scrambled your brains. You couldn't survive walking across the street in this city. They got a $50 reward on your head, and it ain't to bring you in alive."

The full realization hit the young man. The life he'd been living was gone. He would be lucky to live long enough to even get out of town. "Where will I go?" he asked.

A sad look came over the hostler's face. "Some place far from New Orleans where nobody knows you."

Damas left to get the cart ready while Tom sat alone with his thoughts. He looked at the bowl of porridge. Suddenly he realized, that he hadn't eaten since yesterday's nickel bowl of soup. He was hungry.

After what seemed like a long time, Tom heard his friend say, "Get your stuff ready. It'll be only a minute or so."

The hostler had a two-wheel cart loaded with hay, parked in the livery. As single mule was hitched to it. "You climb into the back and get under the hay," he told Tom.

The dusty hay made the young man sneeze, sending stabbing pains through the wound. Damas climbed onto the cart and slowly drove out of the livery. Tom lay crouched under the hay, the loaded U.S. Model 1918 against his chest. If someone discovered him under the hay, it would be the last thing they'd find, he vowed.

It was a mile to Camille's and the cart ride was slow and bumpy. There was a shout and the cart stopped. "You got anything under that hay?" a boisterous voice asked as the man started poking the hay with a rod.

"You put bad juju on Miss Camille's hay and her chickens get sick, she'll put a spell on you that you'll regret the rest of your days," Damas threatened the man.

Suddenly, the probing stopped. "I'm sorry, I . . . I didn't know it was for her." There was the sound of footsteps as the man ran away.

Tom recognized the familiar sounds around the cabin as Damas pulled into her yard. The barnyard behind the house was where Camille did her magic, so few people dared to even come near it. It was said she could conjure the bad spirits and make a man a babbling fool for just looking at her wrong.

Lying under the hay, he heard her voice, "Put it into the barn and throw a little for the chickens to scratch."

Then he heard Damas talk to him, "Climb out and go into the house."

Pushing the hay back, Tom sneezed again. "Damn that hurts."

The barnyard was enclosed by stone and plank walls, providing the seclusion Camille wanted for her conjuring. Tom saw Gabrielle standing near the back door. "Hurry," he heard her say.

The young woman held the door open for him and he ducked into the house. Stopping suddenly, Tom said, "I forgot to thank Damas."

"Do not go outside," a sharp voice said. It was Camille. "You will do everything I tell you if you want to live. I can make bad things happen to the man that might kill you, but I can not stop a fool from trying."

Tom found himself in a spotless kitchen. His clothing was covered with dust, manure, and blood. And worst of all, his rushing into the house had started the wound bleeding again.

"Empty the bag and then remove all of your clothing," she instructed him.

Hesitating, Tom looked at Gabrielle smiling at him. "Did you want me to step into another room and do that?" he asked.

Camille gave him a hard stare. "And let you dirty my entire house?"

Opening the possible bag, he removed everything and placed it onto the floor. He then lay the pistol next to the powder horn. Slowly, Tom began to remove his clothing. There was a woven basket and he was instructed to put the bag and clothing into it. Once down to his bloody long johns, he stopped and looked at Camille imploringly. She said nothing, but the look she gave him let Tom know she meant everything.

Dropping the last item of clothing into the basket, he stood totally naked and blushing brightly. "You didn't tell me he was so shy," Camille said to

Gabrielle. Then she said, "Take the basket and burn everything."

Grinning at the embarrassed man, the young girl took the basket and went to the fire pit in the barnyard. Like the cabin, this kitchen also had a pump near the sink. Camille told him, "Do not touch the neck, but wash all the blood off yourself."

Partially filling the sink, he took a cloth and began to soak and wash the blood. Several times he had to drain the red water and refill the sink. Finally, he got to his hair. The ends near his wound were stiff with blood. Camille, who had sat watching the entire process, said, "I will help you with your hair. Have a seat."

He saw that she had placed a stool, much like the one he'd had at the La Maison, in the middle of the room. Tom sat wondering what other indignity she had for him. He saw that she had scissors in her hand. Quickly, his long locks fell to the floor as she snipped. Once she had finished the bloody ends were gone as well as most of his hair.

"There is a bath in the next room and some clothes. Wash well and then get dressed," Camille told him. Then she added, "Keep the water away from your neck."

Thankful to get out of the kitchen, he closed the adjoining door. Before it closed, he saw her carefully collecting his hair. The water was warm and soothing. There was some type of soap that had a pleasant smell. Before he finished, Gabrielle came in and helped him wash his hair. Her tender hands sent sensations through Tom.

She then removed the bulky, bloody bandage Damas had put on, and washed the area near the wound before putting a clean bandage on the angry gash. Then, standing near the tub, she said, "The clothing was my uncle's. He was about your size. After dark, we will bring your items from the cabin so you can go through them."

Sitting in the now cool water, he watched her leave the room. Alone, Tom climbed out of the tub and dried off with a coarse towel. He then put on the long johns, the dark wool trousers and a shirt. He pulled on the wool socks and the low heeled boots. The boots fit well.

Walking back into the kitchen, he looked around. It was as though he had never been there. Any evidence was gone and the room was again spic and span. Camille called him into the sitting room. She had him sit in a chair with good light.

As she started to remove the new bandage, Camille said, "You look good in my brother's clothes."

"They fit well," Tom said. "I will give them back when you bring my stuff from the cabin."

As she tenderly probed and swabbed the wound, she said, "Everything but a few personal items will be burnt. All evidence of Tom Wallingford will be gone."

Her careful cleaning of the wound caused Tom to wince several times. What she had said was spinning through his mind. Wanting to explain his concerns, he said, "My father has letters and things from the places we lived. There are names and addresses from mother's family back in Philadelphia."

"Do you read?" she asked. "I was told you did not."

Feeling a bit of shame, Tom admitted, "I do not. Someday I might learn."

"You are a very smart young man," Camille said, "but I doubt you will ever need the information in your father's pack. I will read each item to you before it is burnt. Now, have you been thinking of what name you will be using?"

"I have a name," Tom said. "I can spell it and everything."

"Thomas Wallingford is well-known by the men on the waterfront," she said. Then she challenged him, "Can you spell Wallingford?"

The young man was beginning to get angry. Refusing to answer her question, he said, "I can move to another town and take my things," he said rather tersely.

"You can," she said, "but if that is your plan, it is hardly worth me taking care of your wound. You will be dead long before it can go bad on you."

Tom did not have the benefit of years of wisdom. What he had learned from his father was that if you got in trouble in one place, you just moved to another and started over. It had worked for his father, it should work for him.

Confused by what she was saying, he tried to explain. "Tonight, I will go east and live in another town, or maybe I will go upriver. Those looking for me will be here. I will be far away."

"You will not make it out of New Orleans," Camille said. "If that is your plan, I will need money to pay for your funeral. Of course, they might hang your body on the waterfront and let the birds pick at your bones."

Finished cleaning the wound, Camille placed a bandage on his neck and then went to another room. Gabrielle had been in the sitting room for part of the discussion. She moved near Tom. "What she is telling you is true. Those that rule the waterfront control a wide area and will have men looking for you all along the river and in every town all the way to the ocean in the east."

"What should I do?" he asked the young girl.

She smiled, "My mother can get you out of New Orleans. You will need a new name and, in every way, become a different man. Dealing faro or working for a saloon will have to be in your past. These are the kind of places they will watch."

He liked her and trusted what Gabrielle was saying. "What name should I choose?" Tom asked.

"How many names can you spell?" she asked.

Tom hesitated before telling her, "Two. I can spell two names. Tom and Rufus."

"Rufus," she said. "Who was Rufus?"

"When I was young, we were best friends. He taught me to spell Tom.," he told her.

Camille came back into the room. She had something in her hand. "Rufus would be a good name, and you can spell it." Camille said. "I have finished the amulet to protect you. It will guide you on a safe path."

Suddenly he remembered her telling him she was making him one. But that was days ago! How would she have known he'd need it?

She held it in her palm, nestled in a bed of his hair for him to see. The two-inch oval amulet reflected light as it moved. "It has a mountain etched in it for grandeur, or strength."

"My father told me that I was born the same year that Zebulon Pike saw the high peak in the Rockies," Tom said.

Laughing, Gabrielle asked, "Do you think you could learn to spell Zebulon?"

Having listened to their exchange, Camille suggested, "Pike. It has four letters and you could learn to spell that. You do know your letters, don't you?"

Again, embarrassed by what he didn't know, Tom said, "I know most of them."

Standing and holding the amulet above her head, she chanted for a while and then, slowly lowering it and locking eye contact with the young man, Camille said, "From this day forward, your name is Rufus Pike."

If Tom was expecting a loud thunder clap, or the earth to shake, it did not. The three of them alone, in the sitting room, experienced the young man being reborn.

Camille carefully removed the amulet from his hair, and put on a silver chain, before hanging it around Rufus Pike's neck. She then turned to Gabrielle. "Show him how to write Pike."

Alone again in the sitting room, Gabrielle got some paper and a pencil. She wrote the letters on the paper. The young man was thankful that he recognized them. "Why do I have to know how to spell my name?" he asked.

"It is how my mother is going to get you out of New Orleans," she said. "You will be working on a boat going north on the river. You will have to sign your name in the boat's log. There are people that know you can not read and write. If you had to put an 'X' for your name, they may look closer and recognize you."

Slowly, Tom, now Rufus, was realizing the peril that he was in. Those around him were risking their own safety by helping him and it was important that he do everything they asked. For the next hour, the young man sat at the table and wrote his name. It was a good name, and the friend of his youth was a fond memory.

When looking in the mirror he saw that the transformation they had attempted had been complete. He did not look anything like the young man who had come into the house. The bandage on his neck would be a problem. He was sure that those in the tavern had seen the blood running out of the wound.

The young man stayed away from the windows and he'd look at the paper with his name, wondering if he could ever learn to read. He hadn't noticed that it had gotten dark and was surprised when Gabrielle came in with the packs from the cabin.

All of the clothing was immediately discarded. He kept a pair of low boots and a belt. He found a leather pouch in his father's pack. He thought of all the years he'd seen his father holding the pouch. Allen had always told him, "Our whole life is in this here pouch."

Slowly the pouch was opened. It contained several letters and notes. The young man had no idea what any of them said, but as promised he and Camille sat in front of an open box stove and she read each letter and note to him before burning them.

There was a lock of hair in a folded piece of paper. The note inside said: "Ruth's hair, given to me on our wedding day." The note was burned, but the hair was put into a clean piece of paper for the young man to keep. In as second compartment there was some money that made the young man's jaw drop. His father had talked about the insurance he'd had, but never said what it was. It must have been the money, which totaled just under $100.

He and Gabrielle spent time together that night saying goodbye. She kept calling him Rufus, to help the young man get used to it. She was softly fanning him in the hot and humid night as he fell asleep. When Camille woke him to leave in the morning, the young woman was gone.

* * *

The sun was just coming up when Rufus Pike approached the *Marybelle* tied up at the waterfront. The steamboat had a high-pressure steam engine and was outfitted with a single stern paddle wheel. Rufus was listed on the crew roster as a stoker. How Camille accomplished that, he did not know.

Rufus had the collar up on his shirt that covered most of the dark-colored bandage. He had a neckerchief around his neck to wear over his face while shoveling the dusty coal, and also wore a wool cap with a narrow brim on the front.

His gear was in a sea bag tied with loops at the top. A leather tag had his name scratched into it and then it had been worked over to give it a worn appearance. The sea bag contained a second set of clothes, the boots, items from his possible bag, the powder horn and the pistol. It also had a blanket, ground cloth, and the pouch with the lock of hair and money.

As he approached the riverboat, Rufus could feel the weight of the amulet against his chest. He whispered, "Okay charm. Do your stuff." Rufus knew that the next few minutes would be the most dangerous of the trip and he would need all the guidance he could get.

An old riverboat man named Homer sat near the gangplank, smoking a pipe. He looked up as Rufus stepped onto the boat. "I'm one of the stokers," the young man said.

Picking up the roster, Homer asked, "What's the name?"

"To . . ." Coughing, he said, "Rufus Pike."

"Okay," Homer said. "Sign the log or put your mark here," his tobacco-stained finger pointing to the logbook.

He suddenly felt relief and a kind of pride as he signed Rufus in the book. Other than carving his first name on a whole bunch of things, he had never signed something official. "Take your gear aft and stow it in the boiler gang quarters. Choose a hammock, but don't make too much noise. There's a couple guys sleeping off a good time in town."

Rufus was thankful that the man had pointed to the back when he said aft. There was much that the young man didn't know about a boat, and the terminology was one of them. He walked toward the back and saw the boiler and the coal storage. Just beyond he saw an open area with several hammocks strung from poles supporting the upper deck.

Setting his sea bag down, he sat and waited. Finally, a couple of more men came and chose hammocks and hung their bags from wood pegs fixed into the posts. Rufus followed suit and chose his hammock. One of the men, with blue, smoky eyes, watched him get settled. He then put out a hand. "My names Johnson."

Having learned a lot about names the night before, the young man said, "Just Johnson?"

Nodding the man said, "Yes, just Johnson."

"My name is Rufus Pike," the young man said, liking the way it rolled off his tongue.

The other man who had come in with Johnson had gone to the rail and was having a chew. "Is that your partner?" Rufus asked Johnson.

"Don't know him," the man said. "We just come on at the same time."

A man who appeared to be the mate of the boat came to the compartment and said, "We need to make steam, boys. Turn to."

Rufus was thankful when Johnson took him under his wing. Right off he said, "My guess is you ain't tended too many boilers."

Looking around quickly, the young man said, "I pretty much worked loading the boats. I was told I could make more money as a stoker."

"You can also get yourself burnt, or blown up," his new acquaintance said. "It is pretty simple, just shovel coal into the firebox."

Feeling dread as he followed Johnson to the boiler, Rufus wondered if he had already blown his cover. Who was this Johnson, anyway? He had cold, smoky eyes and could be hiding his true reason for being on the boat. Rufus saw some gloves stacked near the shovels. Pulling on a pair, he adjusted the neckerchief over his face and grabbed a shovel.

His job as a stoker was not difficult to learn. Two men used wheel barrows bringing coal from the storage and dumped them into a box near the boiler. Rufus shoveled the coal into the firebox. The job was dusty and hot. Two other men adjusted the water and lubricated the linkage and piston.

Black smoke billowed out of the stacks as the whistle blew twice, signaling that the boat was about to depart. A few of the passengers or crew hurried up the gangplank. A load of freight for St. Louis arrived at the last minute, and men all over the boat were tagged to help load it.

Running down the aft cargo plank, Rufus grabbed sacks of grain and carried them to the cargo hold. He could hear the captain complaining about the delay, and shouting at everyone to hurry. Grabbing the last bag, the young man ran up the cargo ramp just as it was pulled in.

Tossing it onto the pile in the cargo hold, he leaned against the pile, gasping for breath. Dealing faro had not conditioned him for this kind of work. The boat mate came by and snarled, "Ain't you supposed to be shoveling coal?"

"Yes sir," Rufus replied and headed for the boiler. As he walked aft, he caught sight of the paddle wheel churning the water and the boat pulled away from the landing. The young man stumbled a bit due to the movement of the boat. He got back to his station and picked up his shovel, to a grateful smile from Johnson, who had been working alone.

Every four hours the workers were relieved. There were three crews, so Rufus was on for four and off for eight. Other tasks were often assigned during the off hours, including cleaning the boat, moving freight for better balance, or setting out torch baskets for night navigation.

Arm weary the end of his first shift stoking, Rufus followed Johnson to an area where the crew was fed. It was little more than benches near the paddlewheel to sit on, and a pot of some kind of stew ladled out by a greasy galley worker. A line quickly formed at the buckets holding drinking water.

Sitting with his thin bowl of stew, Rufus slowly ate. He listened to the excited talk nearby. A passenger that said he was out for air, talked of a killing in New Orleans. Some faro dealer shot a man just because he was winning. He said that there was a poster near the quarter deck that offered $50 if someone found this man. The talker said he believed that the reward had gone up to $100 by now.

When someone asked what the shooter looked like, the man gave a decent description of Rufus before the change in clothing and the haircut, and he also said that someone got a shot off at the killer and believed he'd been wounded.

Rufus tried to make himself as small as possible as he sat staring into his bowl. There were probably men on every steamboat spreading the same story. The young man would have liked to jump up and shout, "The bastard was cheating and shot me first!" but that would have ended his escape very quickly, and no doubt his life.

With his stew gone, Rufus wanted to get away from the talker. He wandered toward the bow and watched the leadsman toss the lead line over the side and call out the depth to the pilot house. The line was marked in fathoms. Mark one was one fathom, or six feet. Mark twain was two fathoms, or 12 feet. The steamboat required a minimum of two fathoms to safely navigate.

This was a job that Rufus would have liked to have been assigned to. Given time he could learn all the marks on the line. A standing line was used, which had a pipe filled with lead fastened so that when it hit bottom, the weight was standing upright.

There were footsteps behind him. "Pike, I got something to keep you out of trouble," the mate said. For the next hour, he hauled garbage from the galley and dumped it near the stern. Rufus quickly learned that if you were away from your assigned job, you best be sleeping in your hammock, or hiding so the mate didn't find you. There was always more work than hands, and he was always looking for someone to do it.

The galley turned out to be a good place to change the bandage on his neck. Camille had made up several coated with something she said would help the wound heal. Carefully pulling the old bandage off, which tended to stick to areas of the wound, he then used a rag to clean it as best he could. Then unrolling and unfolding the bandage, he placed it around his neck. Whatever she had put on it caused the wound to sting. He then put the coal-dust covered kerchief back on to hide the bandage.

One day the command came down to pour the coal to make steam. The were running abreast of another steamboat and the race was on. Soon the boiler was at max pressure and climbing. The head boilerman knew how far he could push the system before catastrophe, and he was flirting with it to make sure his captain won the race.

Anyone could see the strain on everyone's faces as the boat shuddered and the boiler groaned. The stokers expected the boiler to come apart at any time. Rufus just kept shoveling the coal and shaking the grates to let maximum air get to the fire. There was a cheer from the passengers as the *Marybelle* pulled ahead.

Once the pressure was lowered to the safe level, Rufus scraped the cinders and ash into the ash chute, which dumped the spent coal into the river below the boat. He was covered with the black dust and sweat, and was looking forward to going to the rail and breathing clean air.

The young man wasn't the type to hide, and he really didn't mind doing various chores. The trip upriver would take just over a week and keeping busy made the time go faster. On the fourth day, they were running in a section of river that was predictable and had good depth.

The mate had learned that the best place to find help was near the leadsman and that help was Rufus. Talk of the killing in New Orleans seemed to be a popular topic, so the young man avoided groups of gossiping deckhands and found solitude forward near the leadsman. Rufus would watch the line and whisper the mark before it was called out.

He saw the burly mate coming forward and wondered what task he'd be sent to do. "Chester, here needs a break," the mate said. "Toss the line for a bit. Make sure you call the depths out clearly."

"Yes sir," Rufus said, anticipating his first throw.

"You don't have to call me sir," the man said. "Jake is the name."

Chester told Rufus that he was throwing every couple of minutes with this being good depth. It had been running between quarter-three or half-three, which is 20 feet give or take. "Just make sure you toss it out enough so the weight is standing when it goes by."

Taking his position at the rail, Rufus tried a toss. He left too much slack in the line and did not get a good reading. Twice more he tossed before managing to keep the weight standing as he went by. He called out in his gravelly voice, "Mark Three!"

"Mark Three," was repeated by someone in the pilot house and then a head came over the side. "Where's Chester?"

"He'll be back in a bit," Rufus called back to the man.

"Just make sure the marks come out clear," the man said as he pulled his head back in.

For the next hour Rufus called out the depth, enjoying the breeze and sunshine. Chester came back still chewing on some bread. Rather than taking over the line, he sat and watched for a while. "You're reading just a bit deep," he said, "but not bad. I'll tell the mate you done good."

As they approached the confluence where the Ohio River flowed into the Mississippi, there was an ever-changing bottom, with unexpected sandbars and snags from downed trees washed down in the spring floods. The captain wanted a leadsman on each side of the boat. Rufus was assigned to the starboard side, with Chester on the port.

The two men tossed the lead line alternately and called up the depth. The difference in the two men's voices made it easy for the pilot house to know which side the reading came from. Rufus was in his glory, finally getting away from the boiler.

A week of healing and whatever Camille had put on the bandages had done a remarkable job on the wound. It was well-scabbed over and even itched a little as the gash healed. While tossing the line, Rufus left the bandage off, letting air get to the wound. He still wore the neckerchief when near the other crewmembers. He didn't want to have to explain how he'd been injured to anyone.

One evening he got to his hammock and noticed that his sea bag had been gone through. Panic went through Rufus as he thought about the leather pouch and his pistol. Setting it onto the deck, he kneeled down and started checking to see if anything was gone. Feeling around inside the bag, he looked around to see if anyone was watching him.

He felt the pistol and powder horn. Then he found the cloth bag that held items from his possible bag. Through the cloth, he could feel the mold, dipper, and other bigger objects. At the bottom, he felt the pouch. He could not tell if the money had been taken, but doubted that the culprit would have left it had they found the pouch.

There was a half-dozen men in the hammocks. It was doubtful that anyone would have tried stealing from the sea bags while others were around. The only time that the compartment was empty was during the midday meal.

The next morning Rufus told Johnson about his bag being dug through. The smoky-eyed man agreed that the midday meal would be the only time the compartment would be empty. Rufus heard comments from others that their sea bags had been gone through. He did not let anyone know about his. He had a plan.

There was a locker for storing rope and other docking items behind the compartment. While it did not have a window, it did have a grill to let in air. Rufus made sure he was at mess early so he could grab some bread. Fishing a potato out of the soup pot, he folded the bread around it. It would have to do for his meal.

He then went to the compartment, walking quietly, just in case he caught anyone in there. It was empty. He climbed into the rope locker and sat on some coils and pulled the door closed. He was just at the right height to see out the grill. There was the smell of tar and turpentine in the locker.

The potato wrapped in his bread was a little under-done. That was a good thing, because it allowed Rufus to chew longer on his sparse meal. While he watched, twice men had entered and left the compartment. One placed some extra bread under his blanket. The other reached into a sea bag and brought out a twist of tobacco, took a chew and put it back.

The next day found Rufus back in the rope locker. Tomorrow they would reach St. Louis and he would be on his way. The young man had gotten lucky. He'd fished a piece of meat out of the stew. He bit into bread and had a shock go through his teeth. The meat was mostly bone. He was trying to pick the meat off the bone when he saw movement.

The man with all the stories about the shooting came in. Looking around quickly, he went to one of the sea bags and started looking through. Not finding what he was looking for, he cut across the compartment heading for the next row of hammocks and bags. As he walked by the rope locker, Rufus violently pushed the door open knocking the man over into a post.

Stepping out of the locker, Rufus was ready to take a toll from the intruder. The man looked up, blood running from his nose. Like a flash, he was on his feet and gone. Rufus remembered that the man was a passenger, not ship's crew. If he had chased him, Rufus, not the man, would be in trouble.

Looking at the blood near the post, the young man had to accept that that would have to be enough punishment. No doubt the man was looking for evidence of the New Orleans man's killer, and Rufus' sea bag hadn't given him any.

CHAPTER SIX

St. Louis was one of the fastest growing ports along the Mississippi River. In 1823 when Rufus stepped off the *Marybelle* onto its docks, St. Louis had just recovered from the Panic of 1819. The port lacked the present trade found in New Orleans, but had a promising future, being the most northern port on the Mississippi and having the bounty of the western frontier to exploit.

Before he'd gotten off the ship, the mate had talked to Rufus about remaining as part of the ship's crew. The truth was, the young man found traveling the river exciting and would very much have liked to continue, but that would put him in constant danger of being discovered by those who wanted him dead.

He stood on the dock with his $15 pay. It was good wages for a week's work. The best part was that he hadn't had to give part of it to a thug offering protection. In the distance he could hear a sawmill cutting boards from logs floated down the river after the spring thaw. He saw signs of new construction in several places.

The existing docks were filled with stacks of cargo, some of it waiting to be loaded onto steamships to be shipped south. Rufus looked at several piles of brown hides. He wrinkled his nose at the unpleasant smell.

"Those are buffalo hides," Johnson said as he set his sea bag down next to Rufus. "They are money on the hoof. All you have to do is go out on the plains and harvest them."

"Have you hunted them?" Rufus asked.

"Not yet," Johnson said, "But I come here to join a group that will be heading out in August. Each of us will put in something for the company and then we split whatever we get for the hides."

"How much can you get for a hide?" the young man asked.

"The bull's hide pays the most," Johnson said, appearing to have full knowledge of buffalo hunting. "You can get $3 for each. Maybe a little more. These hides will be shipped to New York or Boston. Some all the way to Europe."

It made little sense to Rufus. If the buffalo hide was worth so much, and there were many of them, why weren't more people hunting them? The young man did not realize that the steamboat was the first step for mass hunting, providing a way to ship the hides. Until the railroads went west, bringing the hides east from further on the plains would be difficult.

The man who had talked of the New Orleans killing went by, glaring at Rufus. It was obvious that his nose was broken and one of his eyes was still blackened. The young man knew that the word of the killing and the reward offered would soon be spread around the saloons and gambling houses of St. Louis.

"Are the men you're joining looking for anymore partners?" Rufus asked.

Johnson looked at the young man with his smoky eyes. "Maybe. It would be as a skinner though."

Rufus had never skinned anything bigger than a rabbit, but he figured that a buffalo is just a big rabbit. "I would be interested in joining the company, but right now I have to find a place to sleep and buy a horse," he told Johnson.

"I was told there's a boarding house that charges two bits a night and offers breakfast," the smoky-eyed man said.

"Sounds like my kind of place," Rufus told him. The two men picked up their sea bags and headed into the city of St. Louis.

The sign on the weather-beaten building said: "Two Bits a Night." No name. Rufus followed Johnson inside the first room that served as a lobby and dining room. A large woman in a sweat-stained dress was peeling potatoes next to a door, which appeared to lead into her kitchen.

"Welcome to Ma's," she said. "Looking for a place to sleep?"

"We are," Johnson said. "Might need a room for a couple weeks."

"Ain't got no rooms, but if it's a bed you need, it's two bits," Ma said. She pointed to a tattered ledger.

"If you will be staying, put your name or mark in the book. Two bits in advance."

The men handed her the two bits and signed the book. Again, Rufus was proud to see his name written. They went through the curtain to the back. The Two Bits boarding house was an old army barracks with wooden bunks and hay tick mattresses. The large back room had about 20 beds. In past day's as a barracks, two soldiers would have slept in each bed.

By the looks of the gear scattered about, the bunks were about half-occupied. They chose two toward the back and put their sea bags on the beds. The room smelled strong of sweat, with a hint of urine. A door in the back led to two outhouses. Rufus noticed a barn and wondered it he'd be able to keep a horse here.

"I could go for a drink," Johnson said.

"A drink, and then a bath," Rufus said. "I got to get rid of this coal dust."

The young man picked up his sea bag. "Ain't you going to leave it?" his friend asked.

"I got to get a possible bag and take important things out before I can leave it," he told Johnson.

The large woman watched Rufus with his bag slung on his back. "You ain't staying?" she asked. "Ain't no refunds."

Looking at the distasteful woman, he said, "I will be back."

They walked up the rutted dirt street and stopped at the first saloon they passed. It had the familiar smells that Rufus had grown up with. The scarred bar had seen years of business, probably back to the days the Spanish and French.

The two men ordered a bottle and sat at a table made of rough cut lumber. The whiskey was laced with pepper, giving it a bite after being diluted with water. It made Rufus long for the La Maison. Tully had always served good whiskey.

After a couple of drinks, Rufus got up. "I got to find a few things, including a bath."

Johnson looked up at him. "When you get done, come by here to see if I'm on the floor passed out, or dead from all this pepper."

Laughing at the man's humor, Rufus went out into the streets of the city. He found a mercantile that was more of a trading post and walked around looking at the goods. A balding man, with a thick beard, watched him.

"You off the boats?" the man asked, leaning on a small counter.

Unsure of how to answer the questions, Rufus continued to look at the goods. "Most of what I got here is useful for those going out on the plains or to the mountains," the man said. "Men off the boats usually find goods closer to the waterfront."

Deciding that the man might be honest, telling him of another place to buy stuff, Rufus went to the small counter. "The name is Rufus Pike. I am not sure what I need. I think I will be going buffalo hunting. Right now, I could really use a bath to get the coal dust off me, and a possible bag."

Looking at the unlikely candidate, the man asked, "You ever hunted buffalo?"

"No, I haven't, but folks tell me I'm a fast learner," Rufus told him.

The man went toward the back of the room and came back with a leather bag with a flap that had ties. It had a strap to go over a shoulder. "This bag is used by mountain men that come through here. If you run into any, tell them you got it from Andre LaRue and they'll all say you got a fair deal."

Rufus spent some time looking it over. Two dollars seemed like a lot of money for a bag. Seeing his indecision, the man said, "Why don't you get that bath and then come back? I'll put together a few things you might need and then we can talk price."

The young man really liked the bag. It had a good feel to it. "Put this in with the stuff. Now where can I get a bath?"

He was sent to a barber and bath a few streets from the trading post. The man offered a cold water bath. "Ain't got hot water this time of day. You wouldn't need a shave, would you?" he asked. "I can give you a good price on both."

They settled on a bath and laundering of his extra clothing. Once the bath was finished, Rufus looked in the mirror. His chin whiskers had grown and he was developing a decent moustache. Rubbing his hand over his chin, he liked the feel. With all the coal dust that had been in them he hadn't noticed them growing.

He looked at the wound. There was still bruising around the neck, mostly moving down on his shoulder. He gently pushed on the scab. As long as he didn't have something poke it, the wound should heal nicely.

The barber had shaken and brushed his clothes, removing most of the coal dust. The ones being washed would be ready the next day. Feeling good about the day's accomplishments, Rufus headed back to the trading post.

Andre had a good amount of stuff put out for him. It even included some wool socks and long johns. Rufus took the long johns, socks, and the possible bag, placing them on the counter. "Do you have a skinning knife?" LaRue asked.

"Not yet," Rufus said. The man took two and a whetstone and put them on the counter.

"How about a rifle?" Andre asked.

"I've got a fine pistol," the young man told him.

"That will work well for shooting a rabbit to make yourself a hat," the storekeeper said.

Recognizing the sarcasm, Rufus was distracted by a hat in the stuff. He picked it up and tried it on. It fit well. Leaving it on his head, he said, "I guess I will need a rifle."

"The Hawken brothers are your best bet," LaRue said. "They build plains rifles, good for shooting buffalo and grizzly bears."

Rufus then notice the knife sheath. He added that to the counter. "My funds are limited. I still have to get a horse and saddle."

Picking up the underwear and socks, Andre placed them in front of Rufus. There was also a small tin of salve wrapped with strips of cloth. "You can take these now. Give me a couple days and then come back. I'll see what I can do to help you out."

"You don't want money for these before I leave?" Rufus asked, his eye on the possible bag.

LaRue looked at the bag for a moment and then handed it to him. "Like I said, come back in two days."

Leaving the trading post, Rufus walked along the street and then found a tree to sit under. Opening the possible bag, he put his pouch, flint, steel, lead, mold, and the other items into the bag. The pouch had over $100 with his pay from the boat. He also set the pistol on top of every thing for easy access. He then hung the powder horn onto the bag's strap and slung it over his shoulder.

Suddenly he realized that he had the hat on. It was another item he owed the trading post for. The strap scraped the wound, causing him to grimace. Rufus thought about the salve. Andre had seen the wound. He carefully removed the bag and put it on the other side. While the pistol would now be on the wrong side, the strap wouldn't be on the wound.

Figuring that he'd found a good man in Andre LaRue to do business with, Rufus headed for the saloon where he'd left Johnson. Finding his friend gone, the young man turned to leave. "Is it the place or me that you didn't like?" a feminine voice called out to him.

Glancing back, Rufus saw a pretty girl sitting at the back of the saloon. Walking toward her, he smiled, "I would never walk away from you."

She was slowly shuffling a deck of cards. "I was just thinking about having a drink, but I do hate to drink alone."

"I would never deny a lady having a drink," Rufus told her, slipping the bag off his shoulder.

He had barely sat when the bartender came over with a bottle and two glasses. The woman began to deal them hands of poker. Bets were kept small as the two of them played and worked on the bottle. Running into the lady had been an unexpected pleasure. She told him that she was partial to sailors and that she had a friend who might join them. Sitting there with a nice glow from the peppered brew, he wondered how she knew that he was a sailor.

* * *

The morning sun coming through the cracked window woke Rufus. His stomach felt sick and his head was pounding. He was alone in the room, in a sagging bed that could have used its straps tightened. Swinging his legs out of the bed, he sat holding his head in his hands. Getting up on unsteady legs, he walked over to the sideboard and poured water from the pitcher into the bowl.

Splashing water on his face did little to help how he felt. Bits and pieces of last night came back to him. He had played cards, drank whiskey, and enjoyed the pleasures of the women, while forgetting all the worries he'd been carrying.

Coming back to the bed, he pulled his sea bag and possible bag out from under the bed. Opening the possible bag, he saw the leather pouch lying on top of the rest of the contents. With shaking fingers, he picked it up and looked inside. Over half of the money was gone. It was the money he'd planned to buy a horse and rifle, along with the other gear he'd need to go buffalo hunting.

What the young man didn't realize was that in the past he had always spent everything he'd earned on his favorite three pleasures. When he'd awoken broke, it hadn't mattered. He'd just go back to the La Maison, or even the tavern where he'd dealt faro and earn enough to for the next day's fun. Now, having real money for the first time and making plans for his future, old habits of spending had cut the legs out from those plans.

Sitting on the sagging bed, Rufus couldn't believe he'd spent so much last night. He'd lost some playing poker, and he had bought a few drinks. The cost of the room couldn't have been too much. It had to be the two women he'd spent time with. While one had his full attention, the other was probably in his money pouch.

From the silver chain around his neck hung the amulet. Holding it up, he asked, "Where the hell were you last night?"

Stumbling down the stairs, Rufus looked at the empty saloon. There wasn't even the bartender to complain to. "It wasn't his fault that you were stupid," he muttered to himself.

Dragging into Ma's, the first person he saw was Johnson. "Hey Rufus!" he called. "Join me for this fine breakfast of thin porridge."

The thought of eating almost made the young man nauseous. "She got any coffee?" he asked.

Dropping his bags and taking a seat, he saw the heavy woman come from the kitchen with a mug of coffee and a bowl for him. "You just made it," she said. "A few more minutes and you'd have missed breakfast. I don't give no credit for another day."

Pushing the bowl of gruel away, Rufus tasted the coffee. It was much like the rest of his morning, a disappointment. Johnson gave him no break and immediately began to talk of all the things that had to be done before the hunt. His smoky eyes were dancing with excitement as he talked of being told that herds could stretch all the way to the horizon.

Hardly listening, Rufus was just hoping that the coffee stayed down. His mouth and throat were raw from all the pepper he had drank with the whiskey. Ma came back out to collect the dishes and snorted when she saw that he hadn't touched his porridge. "If you two are staying another night, I will need the two bits now."

All Rufus wanted to do was go into the back and lay down. Johnson said, "I got to find a place to buy stuff for the hunt."

Remembering that he owed Andre LaRue for the things he'd already gotten, he said, "Give me a minute, Johnson. I found a place that has everything a hunter would need."

After putting his sea bag into the back, he and Johnson headed for the trading post. Andre looked up as they walked in, "I didn't expect you until tomorrow. Don't worry though, I found what you need. Come out back."

The two men followed LaRue to the back door. Tied just outside was a saddled sorrel. "The owner just rode it over and says if you are interested, the animal and saddle can be had for $45. The horse has a few years on it, but it is a good, solid animal."

Rufus' heart sank. It was a good horse and the price was very good. Yesterday he had had the money in his pouch for not only the horse, but probably a rifle and the other supplies. This morning, he had enough for supplies.

"I am going to have to say no on the animal . . ." he began when Johnson interrupted.

"I would be very interested in the animal. Now, that was with the saddle?" he asked.

All Rufus could do was watch as Johnson made the deal on his horse. He saw Johnson pick up saddle bags and place it onto the counter. When Johnson was finished, he had everything a hunter would need except a rifle. Andre told him about Hawkens and that would be the next stop.

Going through the pile of goods that LaRue had laid out for him, Rufus eliminated everything except items that he absolutely needed, which included one skinning knife and sheath. Once he had settled up he had less than $30 left. He had to still pay for the laundry and then he and Johnson would head for the Hawken brothers' place.

All the rifles manufactured by the Hawkens were made to order. At this early date the parts were still not interchangeable from rifle to rifle, but the fit in each was excellent. The prices started at $25 for a reconditioned rifle and as much as $50 for a new one. Some of the reconditioned rifles were Kentucky rifles and Harper Ferry Models.

All Rufus could do was look on while Johnson made a deal for a reconditioned Harper Ferry Model. A new one could take as long as three to six months to get. Johnson was in a great mood. "Let's go to the saloon and drink to buffalo hunting."

"I might need you to back me if we run into some folks I met last night," Rufus warned him.

Raising the Harper Ferry rifle above his head, Johnson said, "Let them come. I am ready."

There was only the bartender in the saloon when they walked in. He was balding on top and had what hair remaining slicked back with some type of grease. His moustache tended to drop over his upper lip and he would chew on it while waiting to take an order.

Johnson ordered a bottle with two glasses. Rufus asked if he could get some food to settle his burning stomach. The burn now was more due to hunger than what he'd drank the night before.

"Bread and ham be okay?" the bartender asked. "One bit unless your partner is hungry."

Joining Johnson at a table, Rufus accepted a drink and left it sitting in front of him. "I got to eat a bite before drinking."

The slick-haired bartender brought over the ham and bread and hesitated after setting it down. "You ain't here to play more cards, are you? Them damn women picked you clean."

Taking the bread and meat, Rufus told him, "I'd like to meet them ladies again."

"Don't know them. I think they come in on the boats," the bartender said. "I couldn't believe it when you cut the deck to see which one you were taking upstairs." Walking away laughing, he added, "Then they both followed you up."

"It sounds like you had a little trouble last night," Johnson said. "Is that why you didn't buy the horse?"

"I thought I'd hit pay dirt and the two beauties buried me," Rufus replied. "They left with a good bit of my money."

"You got enough to buy into the company?" Johnson asked. "We are each putting in $50."

"I don't appear I'll be going then," the young man said. "I got enough for a skinning knife, some jerky and beans."

"We'll need skinners," the smoky-eyed man said. "It won't be for a share, but you'll get something for every buffalo you skin."

"How long before we go?" Rufus asked.

"A week, might be a bit less," Johnson said.

After eating the food and having a couple of drinks, Rufus got up to leave. "I'll see you at Ma's."

Walking toward the river, the young man wrestled with the knowledge that he would be going as a skinner and not a partner. One night of drinking and card playing had changed his whole summer. He thought about the women. They had stolen from him, but at least he had sweet memories of them.

Rufus found himself at the waterfront. He had his possible bag, a broad belt around his waist that held his skinning knife in its sheath, and could also hold the pistol if he wanted. Downriver he saw a steamboat fighting the current as it headed for the docks. A small group of men waited to offload the cargo. He overheard someone say they paid $5 for two hours work.

When the bow line was thrown, Rufus was there to catch it and secure it to a pilon. He then managed to get chosen to off load sacks of grain. The evening was hot and muggy and his shirt was wet with sweat by the time the job was finished. It had taken almost three hours to complete and the mate gave each man their pay.

About a dozen boats came and went each day, and most hired off the dock for loading and unloading. Rufus decided that he would be there every day and get on as many crews as he could. The young man quickly found that here, too, there were men who ran the waterfront. While the mate might give them $5, they had to pay $1.50 for the right to work.

After meals, a few drinks, and a night at Two Bits, Rufus cleared $6 a day. This he added to his pouch. When he got back to the boarding house on the fourth day, Johnson told him that they would be leaving in two days. Without having a horse, Rufus would be driving the hide wagon. Johnson had mentioned that there was some concern that he did not have a rifle. There was always the possibility of trouble with the tribes.

The next morning, Rufus went to Hawkens before reporting to the waterfront. He had seen a Kentucky Long Rifle hanging behind the sales counter. It would be heavier that the other rifles and would not have the range and killing power, but he might be able to afford it.

The clerk he spoke with also built the Hawken rifles. The man tried to discourage Rufus from buying the Kentucky Long Rifle for $20, but that was all the young man could afford. After an hour of discussion,

Rufus owned the .48 caliber rifle. He was told that when he came back they would take it in trade for a better rifle.

Having to head right to the waterfront, Rufus asked them to hold the rifle until the next morning. He would have time to pick it up before the hunting party was ready to leave. There were two boats at the dock being unloaded when Rufus got there. He pitched right in and worked with a positive attitude. He now had a rifle and felt much more a part of the buffalo hunters.

It was dark when the last boat was unloaded. With each boat, there were passengers arriving or leaving. Rufus had watched for the two women he'd met that first night. They appeared to have vanished from St. Louis. The word came that there was another boat coming that had had boiler trouble it would be midnight before it got there and would pay extra to anyone willing to help with cargo.

Most everyone headed for town to have some drinks or a meal. Rufus was arm-weary and decided to remain at the waterfront and rest. He also didn't want to take a chance that he had too many drinks and then miss the last chance for money working the midnight boat.

He sat touching up the blade of his skinning knife when he saw movement near the water. One of the dock crew had returned. Slipping the knife into the sheave, he leaned back on some grain sacks. Again, he saw movement to his right. Someone was moving between stacks of hides.

Feeling some concern, Rufus reached into his possible bag and touched the U.S. Model 1819. He knew it was loaded and primed. There had been talk of young gangs wandering the waterfront and robbing those they found.

He started to stand up when he heard footsteps behind him. Only this was not somebody sneaking. They were briskly walking towards him. Figuring one of the loading crew had returned, Rufus turned to warn him about what he'd seen.

"Hello, Tom," the shadowy figure said.

Hesitating for a second, he replied, "It's Rufus," The moon had just come out from the clouds and he saw the man, 10 feet away, and he also saw the pistol held in his hand. His heart pounding, Rufus tensed to leap for safety. Only he saw nothing he could put between himself and the man.

"You wondering how I found you, Tom?" the man asked.

"Who are you, and I ain't Tom," the young man told him.

"It was your voice. When you were calling out the depths, I thought the voice was familiar, but I couldn't place it. Just the other day it came to me. The brat that was hawking customers into La Maison," the man said. "I also remembered you came from there to the tavern and dealt faro. Yes, Tom. I know you killed the man and if I take you back, it will mean money for me."

Realizing the man wasn't just going to just shoot him, Rufus asked, "You ain't the snoop I hit with the rope locker door, are you?"

"You bastard," the man hissed. "I'll just haul your carcass back to New Orleans." Angered at the memory, the man pulled the trigger.

The flint hit the frizzen, giving a flash of sparks. Rufus tensed violently anticipating the impact of the ball. Then nothing. The man's pistol had misfired. "Damn . . ." the man swore as he cocked the pistol again, but his exclamation was cut short as Rufus pulled the skinning knife and charged.

Impacting the man, Rufus felt the man turn as the knife went into his side. The sound the man made as he flailed with the pistol, attempting to strike the young man while twisting and turning to get away, was more the sound of an angry animal than a man.

Breaking Rufus' grip, the man got loose and attempted to flee. The young man started after him, still clinging to the bloody skinning knife. Then the man collapsed onto the dock. There was the sound of running feet as the gang closed in to get what they could.

Rufus turned and ran between the cargo stacked on the dock. He felt the amulet hitting his chest. "You done your work today," he muttered.

Nearing the street, he looked back. In the moonlight he saw four boys stripping the clothing, boots, and anything of value from the man. Rufus felt no pity for the man and had no idea how badly he'd been hurt. He was not going back to meet the midnight boat and he would be leaving St. Louis come morning.

CHAPTER SEVEN

Rufus met Johnson and his partners near the livery. They had four horses hitched to the hide wagon and were just settling up with the hostler. They seemed pleased when they saw that the young man was carrying the Long Rifle.

Johnson, who was proudly sitting on the sorrel, introduced Rufus to his partners. A stocky man with a dark beard with streaks of gray said, "I go by Hank Hanson, and the redhead there is Wally Talbert."

The redhead was young, maybe as young as Rufus. He was missing some teeth from a fight and spoke with a southern drawl. He was covered with freckles, and lean and wiry. He was also carrying a new Hawken rifle.

"Johnson here says you can handle the team," Hank said.

Truth was, Rufus had driven carriages and buggies several times when bringing them from the La Maison to the livery, but the most he'd handled was two horses. Tossing his sea bag behind the seat, he climbed onto the wagon and said, "Shouldn't be no problem."

He was told that it would be his job to set up camp and take care of the team while out on the plain. Once the shooting was done, he'd help with the skinning and fleshing the hides. Rufus was thankful when Hank led the way out of town. The team would follow the riders, and once on the open prairie he could practice turning the team.

Other than flour, coffee, and some beans, they carried little else in supplies. They would be eating mostly buffalo tongue and backstraps. There also were several bags of salt to rub onto the green hides. Lacking control of the team, the first half day was a rough ride. Rufus was unable to avoid several jarring humps and bumps.

The others had fanned out in front of him and were more enjoying their rides than looking for buffalo. It would be a couple, maybe three days, before they found a herd large enough to start shooting.

After a short rest midday, the group continued southwest. Rufus was getting a handle on controlling the team and was able to avoid the worse bumps and washes. His back and bottom were aching when they finally stopped a couple of hours before sundown. Wally rode on for a bit to look for meat for supper.

Hank came to show him how he wanted the camp set up. It was simply a fly tarp extended off one side of the wagon to keep things out of the weather and for whatever fuel could be found for a cook fire. The harnesses were draped onto the wagon tongue and the team picketed near the camp.

"You had me a bit worried this morning," Hank said.

"How so?" Rufus asked.

"I was fearful that you would bust up the wagon before we got to the buffalo, but come this afternoon you seemed to do much better," the man told him.

They were getting the fire going when they heard a shot. "Too near St. Louis for Indian trouble. Wally got us some supper," Hank announced.

They heard Johnson toss his saddle near the wagon. "Did you work late last night?" he asked Rufus.

"No, I didn't," the young man said. "There was a ship coming in late, but I didn't stay. I wanted to be rested up for today."

"I was wondering. They found a body down on the docks," Johnson said. "Even his clothes were gone. I guess he'd been stabbed."

"Now I am glad I didn't stay," Rufus replied. "It might have been me that was robbed."

Walking to the stream to fill the coffee and cook pot, Rufus had mixed feelings because his knife had killed the man. The man knew that Rufus was Tom and he would have continued to spread the word and offer a reward.

Wally came back with a small doe. Hanging it onto the side of the wagon, he began to skin the animal. Hank had a large, blackened frying pan out to burn some steaks. The doe had eaten well and had plenty of fat to fry the meat. The liver went in first and the four men ate that while the steaks were added to the snapping grease.

While drinking coffee after stuffing themselves with venison, Hank pulled out a twist of tobacco. Each man cut off a chunk to chew. Rufus followed suit to be one of the hunting party. It was not the first time he had chewed tobacco, but had never felt a desire. He had hoped that a bottle of whiskey would be passed around, but he also learned that one of Hank's rules was no whiskey on a hunt.

It was quickly obvious that Hank was the leader of the hunt. He had been after buffalo since 1810. He talked of trapping in the Rockies one year and had little good to say about it. Traveling so far only to be wading in cold water for a couple of months made little sense. He said that most of the beaver pelts had come from trading with the mountain tribes.

After a few problems harnessing the horses, Rufus was finally ready to continue. He could see that Hank was not happy with the delay. The hot August sun blazed down on the men as they continued to the southwest.

They were sighting buffalo most of the day, but hadn't seen any larger herds. Wally kept asking the leader if he could knock down a few so they could load their first hides. Hank told him that it made little sense to shoot a buffalo here and haul its hide to the hunting grounds and back, not to mention the time lost to get the few hides.

On the third day in the early afternoon they finally spotted a large herd. Rufus pulled the team to a stop and stood on the wagon, marveling at the large number of buffalos. "Set up camp," Hank said. "Tomorrow we start shooting."

That confused Rufus. They were here and so were the buffalo. It seemed that they should shoot right now. By tomorrow the animals could be gone. Wally didn't seem bothered by the delay. He took care of his gear and then began to clean his rifle. Johnson just kept quiet. This was his first hunt and he didn't want to ask any stupid questions.

All night, Rufus lay in his blanket and could hear the wooly beasts grazing and grunting. Wolves howled as they followed the herd, looking for a weak or young animal to take down. He was excited and restless. Rufus hoped that Hank would let him shoot some. He was anxious to test the Kentucky Long Rifle on big game.

After little sleep, Rufus woke to find even more buffalo than the day before. Some of them were only 100 paces away. He thought about shooting at the deer in Louisiana. He wondered if the buffalo would jump when it saw the pan flash. He also thought that they should all fire at the same time so they'd be able to kill more animals before they could run away.

He ate his fried side meat and drank his coffee while waiting for Hank to tell him to get his rifle ready. It made little sense. Only Wally was getting his rifle ready. Rufus kept watching Johnson to see if he was getting his rifle ready, but the Harper Ferry Model remained in the scabbard.

After breakfast, Hank sat against a wagon wheel, chewing tobacco. Rufus was told to put harnesses on two of the horses. Johnson offered to help him. As they pulled the animals pickets, the young man asked, "Isn't Hank going to have us get our rifles ready? He hasn't even gotten his own out."

"I'll admit, I am new to this," Johnson said. "I am keeping quiet and watching. I kind of told Hank that you and me had hunted buffalo before. Otherwise he'd have hired me as a skinner and I wouldn't have been able to buy into the company."

Hank spat into the fire as Rufus led the horses into camp. "I figure we'll shoot 15 today. There will be some kinks in our process and we don't want to still be skinning hides after dark."

Rufus pulled the knife and touched up the blade with his whetstone. Smiling, Hank said, "You look anxious to get blood on your new knife."

"Yes," the young man said, thinking of the man on the dock. "Buffalo blood will be good on the knife."

While Rufus hadn't noticed it before, there was a type of sledge slung tight to the bottom of the wagon. It was no more than planks nailed to two shallow runners. One of the harnessed horses would be hitched to the sledge to haul hides to the wagon, and the other would be used to move or roll a buffalo that could weigh up to a ton.

Wally got on his horse and rode away to set up for shooting. Rufus noticed that Hank had gotten his Hawken out and was loading it. He called the young man and Johnson over. "I know you told me that the two of you had hunted buffalo before, but so far I have my doubts."

"I noticed that Rufus picked up driving the wagon pretty fast. When the shooting is done, I am going to show the two of you how I want a buffalo skinned. If I have to show you the second time, you'll be packing up and heading back to St. Louis."

It was obvious that Johnson was embarrassed being called out. The two of them watch Hank ride to catch up with Wally. "Did you ask him something stupid?" Johnson asked Rufus.

"Like you, I kept my mouth shut," the young man said. "Hank is a pretty smart fellow and I figure we weren't doing some things he expected an experienced buffalo hunter to do. What we can do is be the best damn skinners Hank has seen, and he will be glad to have us."

His words did not seem to satisfy Johnson. Heading for his horse, he snapped, "You were supposed to be the damn skinner. I come here to shoot buffalo."

Having Johnson angry at him bothered Rufus. The lecture from Hank had been due to things he'd promised, not Rufus. Figuring that anything he said would not salve Johnson's feelings, the young man planned to listen hard during the lesson on skinning and then do everything he could do to please Hank.

Rufus and Johnson were riding toward the closest point of the herd when they heard a rifle shot. The young man watched, expecting the herd to break into a run. To his surprise they didn't even stop grazing. As they came over a rise they saw Wally and Hank methodically shooting at the herd. Both rifles were being used, Wally would fire and Hank would load the empty Hawken.

Finally, Rufus saw several buffalo lying on the grass covered prairie. Other animals had moved around the downed buffalo as if for defense. Wally kept shooting and the buffalo just milled around. In less than 10 minutes there were 16 animals down.

It was almost 30 minutes before the herd moved far enough away so the hunters could go in. Hank chose one of the younger buffalos to use for instruction. Grabbing a front leg, he pulled it onto its back. His moves were precise and quick with the razor-sharp knife. He slit the hide up the stomach to the neck. He then cut up all four legs, joining the stomach cut. He then cut around the four legs and most of the way around the neck. Expertly he tugged on the hide, his knife flashing back and forth as he removed the hide from the legs and sides. Tucking the hide close on one side, he rolled the animal over to finish removing the hide from the back.

Pulling the hide away from the animal, hair down, he folded it to a size for the sledge. Rufus realized that it was no different than skinning a deer or cow, but when skinning the buffalo there was no care taken to makes sure that the meat remained dirt free.

Stepping back, Hank said, "Now get to it."

As they headed to their first animal, Wally put a hide onto the sledge. Rufus chose one of the larger buffalo. Straining on the front leg, he managed to get it on its back. His skinning knife had been properly honed and cut through the hide without a great deal of effort. With the stomach and front legs slit, he grabbed a back leg and pulled it a bit to get at the inner area. The buffalo rolled to its side, knocking him back.

Cussing and scolding himself, he managed to roll it onto its back again and finish the slits. Removing the hide on the first leg, he went through it twice with his blade. He had noticed that Hank hadn't done so once on the whole animal. Rufus felt awkward, and every step seemed to take much too long. Finally, he had the hide free of the carcass and was folding it for the sledge. For the larger hides, they would bring the sledge over to it for loading.

Without taking a moment's break, Rufus went to the next animal. When the buffalo had been skinned, he had removed the hide from three animals. All of Rufus' were on the large side. Johnson had skinned four and made sure he mentioned it within hearing of Hank. The young man noticed that all of Johnson's were on the sledge, which meant they were smaller buffalo.

There was still plenty of daylight when Rufus led the horse with the sledge toward the wagon. While he was bloody and covered with fat from wrestling the animals, he wished they'd shot more. Hank had cut the tongue and some tenderloins from one of the younger animals and promised a fine supper with them.

For some reason, Rufus figured that their days work was done. Little did he know there was fleshing and drying to be done to the hides before rubbing salt in them. Poles were leaned against the wagon and the hides were draped over them. Hank had two-handled scrapers for everyone and soon Rufus was scraping the excess fat and meat from the hides. He did one of Johnson's hides and found it full of cuts, or "button holes" from the sharp blade.

Hank worked on their supper while the other three men readied the hides to be spread out and dried on the grass. If Rufus had thought he'd gotten dirty skinning the buffalo, he quickly learned it was much worse when fleshing.

Exhausted, Rufus went to the stream and attempted to clean some of the blood and fat off his arms and clothes. He plunged his face into the cool water wishing it could wash away some of the memories of the day's slaughter. They had harvested about $50 worth of hides today and left tons of meat rotting on the prairie.

Hank had told him that there were more buffalo than man could ever kill. The few that would be shot during their hunt would make little difference to the number left on the prairies. Rufus could not argue the point. If the herd they were shooting was one of the smaller ones, he couldn't even imagine what the larger herd must be like. Wally told him that he'd spent a whole day once waiting for a herd to pass.

The buffalo meat made a memorable meal. "We took all the kinks out today," Hank said "Tomorrow we will shoot 20 buffalo. At that pace, we will be heading back for St. Louis in two weeks."

The hide wagon could carry two tons, which would be about 200 hides. The hides had to be scraped and dried. As the men went to sleep, there were hides staked out around the wagon. They would have to be turned each day. Time would be lost when the buffalo had moved on and they had to wait for hides to dry.

Both Hank and Wally wore buckskins and, according to the leader, the blood and fat just made them more waterproof. Rufus' wool trousers just felt sticky and uncomfortable, but he would have to live with the discomfort until they got back to St. Louis.

By the third day, Rufus couldn't wait to move on. They had hides staked out all around the wagon which only added to the rotting smell of all the carcasses a short distance from the camp. Wolves, coyotes, and fox wandered freely through the rotting animals, eating their fill.

Finally, the hides were dry enough to fold and load into the wagon. Hitching the team to the wagon, Rufus was anxious to move on. He had had all he could take of the rotting buffalo. It was another two days before they found another herd large enough to shoot. The smell that the young man had hoped to escape clung to the wagon and his clothing. He found no relief.

They made camp at a slow-moving stream. Hank was worried about their horses attracting Pawnee or Arapaho. Once the seven animals were picketed they ranged a distance from the wagon, making them easy to spirit away. Grain was carried in the wagon to supplement their diet, and if things worked out all the grain would be gone by the end of the hunt, leaving room for the hides.

One morning Hank stopped and watch Rufus cleaning his long rifle. "You any good with that thing?"

"I can't be sure," the young man said. "You haven't let me shoot it. I do normally hit what I aim at."

Laughing, the leader said, "Come morning, I'll let you help Wally. We got to shoot 30 buffalo to make up for lost time drying the hides."

Rufus would have liked to have expressed his excitement of shooting, but just beyond Hank he saw Johnson looking at him with a look that could almost kill. Instead he just replied, "I appreciate that."

The young man was up early and had his possible bag ready, and his powder horn slung over his shoulder. Hank had told Rufus that he'd be loading his own, while the leader would be loading for Wally. Once 30 buffalo had been shot, they would commence skinning.

Johnson sat drinking coffee as Rufus collected his gear to go to the shoot. Hank asked the smoky-eyed man, "Would you mind bringing the harnessed animals over so Rufus can ride yours?"

The young man wanted to shout "No! I'll bring the team!" but he kept quiet as Johnson said, "Sure. You can ride my horse, Rufus."

The morning had been cool, and clouds of breath were hanging over the herd as the men set up to shoot. "You work to the right. Don't shoot over 10," Hank told him.

The killing range of the Kentucky Long Rifle was 100 yards. The buffalo he'd be shooting at were just under 75 paces. Rufus chuckled, "So many. I don't know which to aim at first."

"Keep a few things in mind," the leader said. "Bulls bring more money than calves and cows. Cows are used for robes and we can carry more of them than bulls. Watch for a leader and shoot it first. The others will come to its aid and stick around. And most important, don't shoot at anything you can't kill. We don't want a wounded animal riling up the herd."

Wally fired first, sending a rush of adrenalin through Rufus. He was fighting down the buck fever he felt. Picking out a bull, the young man aimed at the shoulder. Fighting to breathe easy, he pulled the trigger. Fire and smoke belched from the long rifle, and the bull stumbled and began to run. After a few steps, it went down.

The fear he'd had that his shooting would disappoint Hank was gone. He was a killing machine. Loading the rifle, he took aim at the next target. The cow fell immediately when the ball hit it. Quickly, Rufus lost count as he kept loading and firing. He was ramming another ball down the barrel when he heard Hank shout, "No more shooting!"

His heart was pounding in his ears, as Rufus set the butt of the rifle down and looked at Hank. The leader was laughing at him. "You got 12 buffalo down there to skin. What the hell happened to 10?"

The fact that Hank was laughing let Rufus know that he wasn't in trouble. He was thankful that the leader had stopped him. The young man knew that he hadn't been counting and would have just continued shooting, hell, until he ran out of lead.

He saw the stain of the black powder smoke from the pan on Wally's face and knew that his was also stained. He fought the desire to leap for joy after the shooting because he knew that Johnson was disappointed. Instead, he slipped the rifle into the scabbard and hung his possible bag from the saddle horn. Near the herd, he saw Johnson leading the horse with the sledge.

They had 33 buffalo to skin, and working without break it would take the men about 4 hours. Then scraping and staking the hide's would take them right up to supper. Rufus began to skin buffalo that he had shot. There was one buffalo that had fallen on top of another. He used the horse to pull them apart before starting the skinning.

By the time the skinning was finished, he'd skinned all but two of the buffalo he'd shot. Hank said, "Pick some tender ones and get us a couple tongues."

It turned out that cutting loose a tongue was more difficult than skinning. He cut open the throat of one of the cows and tried to find the base of the tongue to cut it loose. He made one hell of a mess of the animal by the time he had the first tongue out. The second was much easier. Rufus had two fine tongues for their supper. Johnson had ridden the horse back to camp, so the young man walked, carrying their supper and whistling a tune his mother used to sing.

The four men sat near their fire after supper, drinking coffee and chewing tobacco. Rufus had begun to look forward to the nightly chew. Johnson was kind of quiet and sitting a bit away, messing with his Harper Ferry Model.

"How does the rifle shoot?" Hank asked him.

Quickly Johnson replied, "Good. It shoots good."

"Well tomorrow, I'll give you a chance to show me," the leader told him.

Suddenly, Johnson was all smiles and even joined in the small talk. Rufus was glad that Hank had asked him. The smoky-eyed man was the only friend he had in St. Louis and he didn't want Johnson mad at him.

They woke the next morning to find that the herd had wandered about a half-mile away. They already had 33 hides staked out and drying at the camp, so they weren't able to pick up and leave. While waiting for breakfast, Rufus and Johnson flipped all the hides and staked them. The leader figured three flips with the dry, hot weather and they'd be ready to pack into the wagon. Wally watered the horses and moved them to fresh grass.

Hank banged on a pot with a spoon to announce that the meal was ready. Johnson had his rifle cradled in his lap as he ate the side meat and frying pan bread. "How many do you want me to shoot?" he asked.

"Same as Rufus," the leader replied. "You shoot ten and we'll kill the rest."

As the young man got the harnessed horses ready, Johnson came by. "Didn't you shoot 12 yesterday?"

"Maybe," Rufus said. "I can't be sure. I know I skinned 10."

Because they were deeper into Indian territory, Hank wanted all the horses brought down near the shooting. Rufus was riding bareback on one of the team horses and leading the other three. The sledge bumped along behind on the rock-strewn plain.

It would take two trips back to the wagon to haul the day's harvest of hides. Much more than 15 hides in a stack would tend to tip or slide off of the crude sledge. The men had started shooting. Rufus could see the smoke from the rifle before he heard the report. From his point of view, he could not tell how many buffalo were down.

The shooting was over by the time he arrived. Hank was having some stern words with Johnson. Grinning, Rufus figured he'd probably shot too many. As it turned out, several buffalo had been wounded and had run, stirring up the herd. It appeared that Johnson had done the wounding. The leader telling him, "Once we skin these, you go out and bring back the hides from some of the ones that run."

Again, Rufus felt the tension as the men removed the hides. Once half of the buffalo had been skinned, Hank had Johnson haul a load to the wagon. By the time he got back, the remaining buffalo were finished. Rufus began loading the sledge.

Hank and Wally rode back to the wagon. Once they were out of earshot, Johnson began to cuss, "What the hell did they expect? They had me shoot at son-of-a-bitches that were damn near out of range."

"I'll go with you to hunt down the wounded," Rufus offered.

The cold look he gave the young man was different than the words that came out of his mouth, "I would appreciate that."

Once the sledge was emptied, Rufus told the leader that he was going to help find the wounded buffalo. Hank spat and looked up from the hide he was fleshing, "Take your rifles, but don't be shooting any more buffalo."

While he said it to Rufus, the young man figured it was meant more for Johnson. The young man rode the sledge horse and followed Johnson on the sorrel. The disruption of the wounded animals had moved the herd almost a mile away. Rufus could see several dark lumps on the grass, which he knew were buffalo that had run away before falling. He also saw two that were wounded but still standing.

As they dismounted near the first buffalo that had fallen, one of the wounded animals bellowed and charged them. Johnson's rifle was in his scabbard, and he jumped back onto the sorrel and spurred it away.

Still holding his rifle, Rufus realized there was no way he could get onto the sledge horse and escape. The long rifle was loaded and primed. As the angry bull bore down on him, he pulled the rifle to full-cock and aimed just above the lowered head.

The rifle recoiled, sending a .48 caliber ball, along with a prayer on Rufus' lips. The head went lower as the animal charged on, and then it dropped, rolling in the grass as it slid to a stop only 15 paces from the young man. He heard Johnson riding back.

"I moved away to shoot, but you and the horse were in my way," he explained.

Wanting to get the rest of the animals done, Rufus said, "Shoot the other wounded one. I'll start skinning."

Nothing was said about the buffalo charging when the two men got back to camp. Rufus had to believe that Johnson was trying to get clear, rather than abandoning him and running from danger. It was well after dark when the last hide was staked down. The day's harvest had been 37 buffalo.

While they worked, Hank had put on a pot of beans and the exhausted men filled their plates and ate in silence. They now had a half-load of hides. Three good hunts could fill the wagon. The herd had moved away from the camp and the leader had hoped to get one more shooting at this location. As long as the buffalo were within two miles, one more hunt could be done.

The next morning, Rufus crawled out from under the fly tarp and climbed up onto the wagon. In the early morning sun, he looked at the hides staked out around the camp. It was a sight to behold. Each hide represented $3 and he slowly did the math. Counting just those drying, it was over $180.

He looked across the prairie, in the direction of the herd. Between them and the grazing buffalo were the rotting carcasses of the past two days. The fat on the skinned animals glowed white in the sunshine. The buzzing of flies was a constant companion.

Rufus felt some excitement when he spotted some eagles pecking at the decaying flesh. The ever-present wolves and coyotes could be spotted. He even saw some fighting over a carcass with several more only a few feet away. Hearing Hank in the fly tarp, the young man climbed down to help with the fire. Breakfast would be warmed-up beans.

While the hunters rode toward the herd, they passed another buffalo that had been wounded and died during the night. Rufus was on the sledge horse and Johnson was leading the others. The young man slid off the horse and checked on the buffalo.

It had been gut shot. It had not been dead that many hours and nothing had gotten at the hide, so Rufus commenced to skinning it. The smell of the punctured intestines was disgusting and he tried not to get any of the liquids on himself. The shooting was over by the time he had the hide folded and on the sledge.

Johnson had not been asked to shoot, and Rufus had wondered if he would. All the wounded that they had skinned the day before had shown clear misses of the lungs. Rufus began to wonder if Johnson tended to flinch, or if his rifle shot to the right.

Once again, the men had a long day. They were all looking forward to a few day's rest while the hides finished drying. Hank had brought tongues and loins back to eat over the next couple of days. They now had over two acres covered with drying hides. In the morning, after the dew was off the hides, they would be folding and packing the first day's hunt into the wagon.

After filling themselves on buffalo meat, Hank brought out cigars. "Men, we are halfway to our goal. It is time to celebrate with a good smoke."

Rufus sat with the smoldering stogie clenched in his teeth and went through his possible bag in the fire light. Wally was watching him and asked, "You any good with that pistol?"

It made the young man wonder if everyone assumed that he couldn't shoot. "I can hold my own," he said.

"You ever kill anyone with it?" the redhead asked.

His mind flashed back to the tavern and the fat man. Forcing a smile, Rufus said, "I ain't never seen anyone die from this pistol."

Wally asked to see it and questioned if it was loaded. Rufus handed it to him. "It wouldn't make much sense carrying it if it wasn't loaded. If you want to shoot, you'll have to put powder in the pan."

"You don't mind?" the redhead asked.

Grabbing a chunk of wood, Wally set it about 20 steps from the fire. He then added powder to the pan. Cocking the pistol, he took careful aim. Blinding fire burst from the barrel and the pistol fired. The piece of wood tumbled with the impact of the ball.

Remembering his first attempts at the stump, Rufus asked, “You shot pistols before?”

“No,” Wally said. “I just have a knack when it comes to shooting.”

Puffing on the cigar, Rufus reloaded the U.S. Model 1819. Before going to sleep, he always added powder to the pan. Late into the night, the men made small talk and told stories. Johnson was the first to crawl under the fly tarp and go to sleep. Hank talked of past hunts and of trouble with the tribes he’d had in the past.

Talk of that made Rufus think of the horses so he walked out into the dark and brought them in close for the night. He stood near the sorrel, rubbing its neck. “I am sorry I got drunk and let the women steal my money. If I had not, you would be my horse.”

The next morning the men began to fold up hides right after a breakfast of fried buffalo. There were several wolves that had stopped their eating and lay watching the men. Rufus noticed them and figured that they had gotten spoiled on fresh meat and lay there waiting for them to start shooting.

With the morning chores completed, the men headed to the stream with bars of soap to try and get some of the stink off themselves. Johnson’s moodiness from the day before seemed to have lifted and he kidded with everyone else and they sat in the slow-moving stream. Rufus scrubbed his clothes and draped them on some bushes to dry. The clean set he put on hadn’t been used for skinning. He wanted something decent to wear when they went back to St. Louis.

Sitting with a chaw in his cheek, Hank said, "Them wolves down there are worth a buck each." With that thought in mind, he continued, "Did you know that a dollar is called a buck because it will buy a set of buckskins?"

Laughing, Rufus said, "When skinning buffalo, it is a buck well-spent."

Wally got up and came back with his Hawken. "I think I'm going to shoot me a new pair of buckskins."

The young man had his Kentucky rifle nearby and got it. "It sounds like a good idea."

The men noticed that Johnson seemed to be debating, but finally settled down to watch. Wally took the first shot. The wolves were just over 100 yards away. He scored a hit. They scattered, leaving the dead wolf lying near the rotting buffalo.

It was almost an hour before they came into sight again. It was Rufus' turn. He aimed his rifles and squeezed the trigger. The wolf seemed to dance, spinning around and went down. Wally smiled. "So far we are even."

For the rest of the day, the two men sat with their rifles, waiting for a shot. Wally was one up on Rufus when Hank finally said, "That's enough noise. Git on down and skin them wolves. I am sorry I mentioned the buck."

Laughing and poking at each other, the two men headed to skin their kills. They carried their rifles loaded and ready. Rufus also had his pistol in his belt. Not necessarily to be used against wolves, but being in Indian Territory they were never far from their rifles.

The wolves were quickly skinned and they were cleaning their hands and knives on the grass when the two men heard the snarling of a cat. It was a puma challenging a fox. The tawny paw lashed out at the fox. So intent on protecting its meal, the cat hadn't noticed the men. Eyes wide with excitement, Wally slowly moved toward his rifle.

The cat was near 100 feet from the men and its shoulder was exposed. Rufus drew his pistol, aimed, and fired. The .54 caliber ball impacted the cat, causing it to leap and roll, screaming and snarling. Mortally wounded, it lay crouching and growling as it life slowly ebbed away.

"Damn you," Wally said. "You shot my cat."

"I believe I shot my cat," Rufus said. "By the time you'd have gotten your rifle, we'd have been looking at it disappear behind all these carcasses."

"That was a hell of a nice shot with the pistol," the redhead said. "Was it luck or skill?"

Puffing up his chest, Rufus said, "Maybe a bit of both."

With each man carrying a bundle of wolf skins, and Rufus dragging the cat, they headed for the camp. There was no lack of excitement when they saw the tawny feline. Even Johnson seemed impressed. Hank looked the cat over. "You got a five, maybe ten-dollar skin here, and some fine meat for supper."

Hank offered to skin the cat while poles were gotten to stretch the skins. As the sun was getting low in the west, the frying pan was full of sizzling puma meat and the skins were stretched and leaning around the wagon. Wally suddenly exclaimed, "More wolves!"

"Forget it," Rufus replied.

CHAPTER EIGHT

A week later the men were camped near a pond with the last of their hides staked out and drying. It would take two weeks to make the trip back to St. Louis. The weather was good for drying, so the hides would take little time to be ready. Rufus noticed a gold color starting to come into the grassy prairie.

Hank had figured up the tally of hides and said they had 212, which was made up of 62 bulls, 133 cows, and 17 calves or youngstock. They also had the 9 wolf skins and 1 puma. For all the hides and skins, they would see something over $655. A dozen of the cows had been skinned, including the hide from their heads which made them worth a bit more because they would be used for rugs.

The spirits in the camp were high. Rufus was thinking of a bottle of whiskey and a soft woman. That would be his reward for the weeks on the prairie skinning buffalo. Wally and Johnson were cleaning the rifles, pouring hot water into the barrels. The horses were picketed just beyond the staked hides.

The constant buzz of the flies and the smell of the hide wagon had become a way of life. Rufus hardly noticed it anymore. He had just loaded his pistol and put it into his belt, when Hank said, "We best water the stock and bring them in."

The young man wanted to ask the leader about what his pay would be. He had skinned close to 60 buffalo and if he made fifty cents per hide, he would make $30. With his wolf skins and the puma, he would have close to $50. If that was what he got, Rufus decided he would be okay with it, but in his heart he hoped that Hank had seen more value in him.

His thoughts were cut short as they reached the horses. Their appearance had foiled the plans of a dozen mounted Arapaho. They had come up on the blind side of the camp and had planned to spirit away several of the animals. One of the braves already had the picket ropes of two horses in his hand.

Hank held his Hawken across his front and Rufus had pulled the pistol and held it at his side. The defiant Arapaho leader began to speak angrily in Algonquian, their native language. Hank replied in a broken version of the language, using his free hand to make his point.

After several exchanges, Hank spoke to Rufus. "They want some of our horses as payment for the buffalo, or many hides."

"Do they speak English?" the young man asked.

Shaking his head, Hank said, "I don't think so."

"I say we aim our rifle and pistol at them and tell them to get the hell out of here or some of them will die," Rufus said.

"Brave words, when you know they don't understand you," Hank replied.

Suddenly, Rufus had an idea. "Would they find value in puma claws and skin?"

"I believe they would," Hank said.

Remembering being told by his father that the voodoo practiced in New Orleans was not so different from the beliefs of many of the plains tribes, Rufus said, "Tell them that I have very strong medicine and with this small pistol, or whatever they call it, I killed the great puma. I will share the strong medicine with them in exchange for the buffalo hides we have taken. They can take Johnson's horse if they want."

Giving the young man a confused look at the last part of the statement, he asked, "You want to give them the puma skin and claws?"

"Yes," the young man replied. He also took the amulet out from under his shirt and displayed it for them to see.

When Hank finished speaking, there was a murmur among the braves. The Arapaho holding the picket ropes dropped them. Figuring he had nothing to lose, Rufus said, "Tell them that his charm around my neck blinds those that attack me."

"You're getting mighty cocky, considering these braves could ride away with our scalps," Hank warned him. "I think I told them enough. Go get the skin and claws. Also tell Wally and Johnson to stay put."

Walking back to the wagon, Rufus stepped around the back and whispered to the two men that there were Arapaho and they were to keep down. The shock was plain on Johnson's face. Wally began to load his Hawken. "I am giving them the puma. Hank thinks they will be happy with that."

Returning with a sack containing the paws and the tawny skin over his arm, Rufus placed them in front of the Arapaho. The sun reflected off the amulet as he bent down. Another murmur went through the braves. One of the Arapahos slid off his horse and picked up the sack and skin. Then in a graceful leap, he was back on his horse.

With cries of success, the braves wheeled their horses and rode away. The two horses that had their pickets loosened started to follow the braves and then stopped. "Damn," Hank said. "I thought we lost two horses on this deal. There is no way in hell I was going to follow the braves and chase the horses down."

The two men stood and watched the Arapaho disappear in the rolling prairie. Hank said, "I told them about your magic charm while you were getting the puma. I told them the cat had attacked you and when the charm blinded the animal, you were able to kill it with the small gun."

Pulling the picket ropes, the two men led the animals near the wagon. It was clear that the encounter had shaken Hank. What Rufus didn't know was that the leader had come across more than a few buffalo hunters scalped and mutilated in his years on the prairie. Ignorance had given Rufus misplaced courage, or had it been the amulet?

For the next two days they were an armed camp while waiting for the hides to dry. Wally and Rufus did some shooting with the pistol, betting a little of their hide money. The young man managed to keep ahead which impressed Hank. Johnson seemed bored by the whole thing.

There was a sense of urgency as Hank instructed them while loading the last of the hides. He had Rufus hitch the team to the wagon, then the leader wrapped rope around the wheel hub and had the wagon pulled forward, compressing the hides. Even after this process, the hides were still two feet above the sides of the wagon.

Rufus took his place on the wagon with the long rifle beside him and the pistol in his belt. Slapping the horses with the reins, he drove the wagon away from the camp, leaving behind a good deal of the smell of rotting meat and fat. Soon birds and wolves would move in and clean up the fleshing scraps.

The sledge bumped in its sling under the box and the heavily loaded wagon creaked and groaned as Rufus attempted to avoid the larger obstacles. The trip back to St. Louis would take more time with the slower progress of the hide wagon. Three days out, they joined an improved trail, which made travel a bit less difficult.

Rufus guided the team through the narrow streets of St. Louis to the waterfront. There Hank would make a deal on the hide and skins. Rufus Pike was basically broke as he followed Wally and Johnson to a saloon to wait for their money. They chose a saloon frequented by dock workers because the stink of the hides was on them.

Wally owed Rufus $4 from bets placed when shooting the pistol. As they sat down, he pushed the money over and said, "Pike, you can buy the first bottle."

"You should be buying me a bottle," Pike said. "I had a birthday while on the hunt. I am 18 now."

Laughing, Johnson said, "That means you buy the first bottle with the winnings and the second to celebrate your birthday."

It had been an hour and the first bottle before Hank joined them. He grabbed the remaining bottle and poured himself a good measure. Once he had finished drinking, he smiled. "Prices were up just a little. I got each of your shares figured."

He handed a sack of coins to Wally and Johnson. "I figure you will each find that satisfactory."

Hank then placed a sack that appeared much lighter in front of Rufus. "I put some in for the puma you gave to the Arapaho."

Having one more drink, Johnson got up and thanked Hank before leaving. The leader turned to Wally and Rufus. "I figured you two would have a woman on each arm by now."

"They come this way until they get a smell of us," Wally told him, "and then they run the other way."

Pike sat at the table making conversation while really wanting to get away and count his money. Anything over the $50 would be a bonus. The whiskey was starting to make him think foolish thoughts. There was a faro table and he was beginning to think he could place some bets and increase his earnings.

"Will you be staying at the Two Bit again?" Hank asked, breaking into his thoughts.

"If I don't get out of here right now," Rufus admitted, "I just might be sleeping in the street."

"Wally and I will be going on another hunt in three weeks," Hank said. "We figure the fall hides will be worth even more than the ones we brought in. You are welcome to join us. Set aside $50 and you'll get an equal share."

Making a promise to think about it, Pike left the saloon, with the sea bag containing his bed roll and dirty clothes over his shoulder and wearing his less dirty clothes. He had got a look at himself in the saloon mirror and he was looking pretty rough, with an unruly beard and moustache, greasy hair hanging over his ears, and a sweat-stained shirt. The only item that was respectable was his hat.

He headed for the barber and bath, with the last words Hank had told him rolling around in his mind. "Set aside $50." If there was enough to set some aside, his pay must have been quite a bit more. Rufus reached into his possible bag and felt the coins. He wondered if they were silver or gold. The saloon they had been in or the streets of St. Louis were not the places to count the money.

There was hot water for the bath. Seeing the shape of his clothes, the barber offered to send his wife out to purchase Pike a shirt, trousers, socks, and long johns. The blood and fat-covered clothing could not be brought back with any amount of boiling. Even his boots had to be discarded. Fortunately, Rufus still had the extra pair with his bedroll in his sea bag.

His hat rested on top of his possible bag, and his rifle leaned in the corner near the metal tub. He had carefully placed the amulet on the brim of the hat. The barber came in with the new clothing and offered to add some hot water to the tub. Pulling his legs back, Rufus let him dump some in.

Almost two hours after he'd gotten to the barber and bath, Rufus Pike left a new man. The smell was gone, his new clothing gave him the store-bought look, his hair was cut above the ears, and the beard and moustache were neatly trimmed.

While alone in the tub, he'd counted the money in the bag and was shocked to find that it held $105. He could only imagine what each man who had put into the company earned. He had pondered going on another hunt. It had its dangers, but the money a hunter made on a six-week trip would take six months to earn at most other jobs. It did bother him to leave all that meat rotting on the prairie, but hefting his earnings in the bag helped one forget about the waste rather quickly.

The hot bath had helped take some of the effects of the whiskey out of him. He wondered where Johnson had gone. Rufus had half-expected to find him at the barber and bath. With no place in particular to go, and few people that he knew, he finally headed for the trading post.

Andre LaRue was pleased to see him. "I thought you went buffalo hunting. You don't look and smell like a hunter."

Suddenly, Pike had a thought. "I have a favor to ask. Can I leave some money with you in case I need it for hunting or even a horse or rifle?"

"Do you know me well enough to leave money?" LaRue asked.

"To be truthful," Rufus said, "If I go into the saloons, the whiskey comes first, cards second, and if I have anything left, the ladies get it."

Andre laughed, "Sounds like my youth. I will do it only if you promise not to come back in a couple days wanting it for more of those pleasures."

"It is a deal," Rufus said. He then removed $50 from the possible bag and gave it to LaRue. "Now I have to find a place to stay."

"You thinking of Two Bits again?" Andre asked.

"I may have to start there," Rufus told him. "Later on, I will find something better."

"I have a small shack in the back that was my first home," LaRue said. "I could let you stay in it for $1 a week."

Skeptical of what condition the place was in, Pike replied, "That is less than the Two Bit."

"No breakfast," Andre pointed out.

Following the owner out of the back door, Rufus saw the shack. It was a well-built 8 x 10 shack. A small, cast iron stove with enough room on top for one pot was used for heat and cooking. A single bunk was built along one wall, to be used for sitting or sleeping. A sideboard with a basin for making meals or bathing was near the stove, and a small table with two stools was located near the door. Above the sideboard was a small window without a curtain.

Rufus Pike was sold, but not wanting to say yes too quickly, he walked around the shack and noticed a small lean-to for storing wood. "You say a buck a week."

"Yes," Andre replied. "Paid by the month or by the week."

"I will take it," Rufus said, not believing his luck. He placed the rifle into the corner behind the bunk and his sea bag on the bunk. Taking $4 out of his possible bag, he paid Andre for the first month.

Owning only the clothing on his back, the possible bag, and a rifle, Pike walked around the town. He needed to find work. The sound of the sawmill drew his attention. The stack of its steam engine sent black smoke into the blue sky.

He heard the whistle of a steamboat coming into the waterfront. Loading and unloading steamboats would be another option, but the gangs were always a problem, and like New Orleans, a pretty rough crowd controlled those who worked. One other thing was that at any time someone could step off a boat and recognize him.

The sawmill was on the water's edge. It consisted of a long, open building with a carriage that the logs were loaded and clamped on. The carriage with the log was then pulled, using block and tackle, through a reciprocating sash saw to make boards. It was much like the pit saw method, where one person manned the saw in the pit while the other stood above the log. It was dirty work for the man in the pit, but the method had made boards for thousands of years. In this mill the vertical blade was moved up and down by the never-tiring steam engine.

The logs arrived at the mill already hewed square by the camps using broad axes. Rufus watched men hoist logs from the river and swung them on to bunks to be dragged or rolled with cant hooks onto the table.

He saw a small building with the door open that appeared to be the office. A stocky, square-jawed man, chewing on a cold cigar sat behind a crude table made out of planks. Shelves behind him were piled with dust-covered stacks of paper. A potbelly stove stood to one side with a coffee pot.

The square-jawed man looked up when Pike entered. "You looking for lumber?" he asked.

Feeling a bit awkward, Rufus said, "I come looking for a job. The name's Rufus Pike."

"They call me Gus," the man said. "Have you worked in a mill before?"

"I worked some on steam engines," Rufus said. "I am strong and will do you a good day's work."

Standing up, Gus stuck the order he'd been working on onto the shelf. "Wrong time of year to be hiring. Sawing is almost done. The camps north will be hiring. If your good with an ax they'd be quick to give you work. If you go north, come back down with the logs and I can put you on in the spring."

Thanking the man for his time, Pike stood a while and watched the reciprocating saw bite through the logs. Once finished, the board would be grabbed by two men and put onto the stack with spacers, to allow air to flow through and dry the wood.

"Stack them tight and they mold," a voice behind him said. It was Gus who'd come out of the office.

To the side of the saw, Rufus notice a stack of boards that had been tossed into a pile. "What's wrong with those boards?" he asked.

"That's scab wood. We take that off to make a clean edge," Gus told him. "Some we burn in the boiler, most is bought up cheap by folks making shanties or rough outbuildings."

Walking back into town, Pike thought about his next move. Maybe a winter in the logging camps would be a good idea. His skills with an axe were nil, but he hadn't ever skinned buffalo before and he was able to pick that up in a hurry.

Walking past the livery, he stopped short. In the corral was a sorrel that reminded him of the horse he had almost bought. Walking to the bay doors, Rufus saw the hostler cleaning stalls. "Who do I talk to about buying horses?" he called to the man.

"That would be Johnson," the hostler called back, leaning on his fork. "I sold him my horse-trading business. There's a small shack he works out of and lives in on the side near the corral."

Johnson? Pike thought. Just this morning they were having a drink in the saloon. Walking around the side of the livery, he saw the smoky-eyed man sitting on a bench near the shack. "I understand you are selling horses now."

Giving Rufus a wide smile, Johnson replied, "I got some fine horseflesh here if you are looking to spend some of that skinning money."

There was a half-dozen horses milling around the corral. "Are you selling the sorrel?"

"I am," Johnson said. "You've ridden it and know it is a fine animal. I could let it go for . . ., maybe $35."

"You paid $45 with a saddle," Rufus said. "What would you be asking with a saddle?"

"Now, that saddle," Johnson said, "that saddle was the best part of the deal when I bought the horse. It's well-made and sits really good. Course you know that. I'd have to get $55 for the horse with the saddle."

"Why, that's $10 more than you paid for it!" Pike exclaimed.

"I got lucky," Johnson said. "The man that was selling it needed money. I'm selling now and a profit has to be made."

"I wish you well," Rufus said as he left. He really wanted that sorrel and that damn Johnson knew it.

Once back in his shack, Pike emptied his possible bag and took inventory of what he had. In the small bag, he had $57 and some small money. It was enough to buy the horse, if he and the animal didn't have to eat. He thought about the money he'd given to Andre. It was too soon to be asking for some of that back.

His options were to deal faro at one of the saloons, or handle cargo in the docks. Both would expose him to being recognized. His two other options were the logging camps up north, or buffalo hunting with Hank and Wally.

Rufus looked at the Kentucky Long Rifle in the corner. He could sell that back to Hawken and use it for eating money. Then he thought of the pistol. He might get $20 from Hawken for that. Pike's mind raced and he went over one scenario after another. The bottom line was he was short of cash to buy the horse.

It was getting late, and all Rufus had put down today was some jerky on the trail, and the whiskey in the saloon. He wondered what food items LaRue sold. Stuffing the items back into the possible bag, he crossed the yard to the trading post. His stomach growled as he smelled something good cooking.

On the potbellied stove sat a pot of thick, bubbling stew. Next to it was some steaming coffee. Andre looked over at Rufus. "Did the smell bring you in?"

"I come to buy some supplies," he told LaRue.

"I got a few items that trappers like and the mercantile doesn't carry," Andre told him. "I'll get us bowls and we can try the stew. It's got new taters in it."

As they ate the tasty stew, Rufus told Andre about the sorrel. "You had gotten me a good price and he bought it. Now he wants to profit selling the damn horse."

LaRue scraped the last mouthful of stew from his bowl. After swallowing, he said, "You can't begrudge a man wanting to make a profit. If he bought and sold for the same price, he would quickly be out of business."

While what Andre said made sense, Pike was still having trouble with it. He and Johnson had hunted together. He'd skinned some of the hides that had helped the smoky-eyed bastard buy the business. Rufus set his bowl down and glanced at the pot.

Giving him a half-smile, Andre said, "Have another bowl. I'll get us cups for some coffee."

When the meal was done, Pike grabbed a broom and helped LaRue sweep out his store. For just a second, it felt like old times at the La Maison. Placing the broom back behind the counter, he saw a small package.

"That is for you," Andre said. "A sort of welcome home gift."

Not wanting to take advantage of his new friend, Pike said, "I want you to keep track of the things you give me and I will settle up. I don't want you feeling like I cheated you."

Laughing, Andre said, "I will let you know if you owe me anything. If I was you, I'd go buy the sorrel tomorrow before the price goes up. Don't worry about the saddle. That can come later."

"Where would I keep it?" Rufus asked. "I can't afford to put it up at the livery."

"There's room in the back near your shack," LaRue said. "Maybe something can be built to keep the sun and rain off the animal."

Rufus Pike was excited while he walked to the shack, the package under his arm. It made sense. He could afford the $35 for the horse. Once he found work, he could buy a saddle. Then he remembered the scrap wood at the mill. It would be fine to build a place for the horse.

It was dark in the shack and Rufus hadn't considered borrowing a candle from LaRue. Feeling his way around the dwelling, he set the package onto the table and got his blankets out of the sea bag. The smell of the hide wagon hit him. His bedding reeked of it. He would need to purchase some soap and do his best to rid them of the smell. The night was warm, and he'd have little need of the blankets. Pulling his boots off, he lay fully clothed on the bunk.

Having some trouble falling to sleep with so much on his mind, he tossed and turned late into the night. Once he did, Rufus slept soundly. The sun was shining in the small window when he woke. Pulling on his boots, he headed to the little house. He then got his blanket and draped them over a rail fence to try and get some of the smell out of them.

Pulling the string from the package, he opened it. It contained coffee beans, salt, pepper, some flour and corn meal. It also had a few pieces of jerky and some hard bread. Rufus checked in the small stove. He had another surprise. It had kindling and some tinder waiting for him to strike his flint. Starting the fire, Pike took the wooden bucket from near the sideboard and went to the hand-dug well near the trading post.

The stove put off plenty of heat and Rufus kept the shack door open. Once the coffee was done, he poured a cup, took a piece of hard bread and went outside. There was a bench next to the door, which gave him a view of the prairie to the west. He took a seat and enjoyed his first breakfast in his new home.

There was a worn broom in the shack, and Pike used it to sweep out the dust and cobwebs before slinging his possible bag over his shoulder and heading for the livery. He had to see a man about a horse.

When he got to the livery, he found that Johnson had not returned from breakfast. The hostler's name was Billy. His shoulders were a bit stooped and he had tobacco-stained teeth. "I got some coffee on if you want some, and Esther sent me here with fresh biscuits."

Sitting in front of the livery while waiting for Johnson, Rufus drank the hostler's weak coffee and chewed on a biscuit, which had sweet butter on it. Billy came and joined him, his cheek bulging with a chew. The hostler spat and said, "I sold the horse business, but I don't figure the man will stay long. All he talks of is going and trap beaver. He's too late for this season. I showed him the ad in the paper from last year. It was in the *Missouri Republican* looking for men to trap for them for up to three years. I heard that over 100 men answered that ad."

Having little interest, Pike asked, "Who put the ad in the paper?"

"A couple of ex-army men named Ashley and Henry," Billy said. "They is trying to pick up the business of the Missouri Fur Company. The Blackfoot have kind of been tough on them the past couple of years."

Rufus heard a horse coming and looked up. It wasn't Johnson. Billy got up and took the man's animal into the livery. A few minutes later he came out with the tattered newspaper. "Here, read it for yourself."

"You pretty much sorted it out for me," Pike told him. "I don't know nothing about trapping." He wished he could read, because it would be nice to get a paper that helped a man keep up on things. And it might have ads for other jobs.

Finally, Johnson came walking up the street. He waved when he saw Rufus. "Have you come about the sorrel? I got two others looking at it."

Billy kind of shook his head and took the cups and headed back into the livery. "I saw it back in the corral, and could have sworn I saw it limping," Rufus replied.

The two men walked back to the corral, while Johnson talked of the demand for horseflesh and how he had some on order coming from New Orleans. Pike ignored what he was saying and looked at the sorrel.

"How old is the horse?" Rufus asked.

"About two months older than when I bought it," Johnson said.

A side door of the livery opened and Billy came out with a rope to throw a loop over the sorrel and bring it to the rail. "I knew the owner and he raised it from a colt. I believe it's around 10 years-old. I could look at the teeth if you want."

"That's okay, Billy," Johnson said, seeming a bit edgy. "I figure it might even be younger than that."

"You said $35 yesterday," Pike told the smoky-eyed horse trader.

"Now that was yesterday, before the demand picked up," Johnson said. "You were also talking about the saddle and I was almost giving that away."

Both men knew that Rufus wanted the horse, so the dickering could go south in a hurry. Pike reached into his possible bag and took out the $35. "I will talk to you later about a saddle."

With Billy watching, Johnson felt kind of trapped. A man is only as good as his word, and he had given a price of $35. "I'll tell you what I will do. I'll knock off $5 with the saddle. For $50 even the horse with a saddle is yours."

Rufus' heart was pounding in his chest. He had gotten Johnson to come down to a price he could afford. He would have to show up on the docks to work for food, but he would own a horse. The two men shook on the deal and Pike fished out $15 more.

"I'll have papers ready for you this afternoon," Johnson said. "It will be saddled and ready to ride."

Walking back to the trading post, Rufus realized that he now had only a few dollars left. Tomorrow he'd have to start working on the docks. With the horse came the expenses of hay, grain, and a shelter. Andre had gotten a delivery and was busy sorting through it when Pike got back to the trading post.

"Did you buy the horse?" he asked.

"That and the saddle," Rufus told him.

"I suppose you are going to need the money back now," Andre replied.

Shaking his head, Rufus said, "Nope. But I will be working on the docks again."

For the next hour Pike helped the owner put the purchases away. He like the smell of the leather, rope, and canvas in the trading post. He hung the metal traps on the wall, impressed by the weight. LaRue told him it was to keep the beaver under water so it would drown.

At noon, Andre made coffee and warmed up what was left of the stew. "The meal is for helping me," he told Rufus.

The horse was tied outside the corral when Pike got back to the livery. The first thing he noticed was that it did not have the original saddle. This one had seen better days. It also did not have a scabbard for the rifle.

Johnson handed him the bill of sale. "Look it over to make sure it says everything." Pretending to look at it, Rufus stuck it into his possible bag.

"You put on a different saddle," Pike told him.

"I hadn't planned to," Johnson said, "but a man come in and bought the other one. You'd be happy. What he paid made up the difference that I was losing on this sale."

Looking at the smoky-eyed bastard's smile, Rufus nodded and climbed onto the creaky, dry saddle. Riding away from the livery, he felt little joy from the deal. He should have stayed at $35 and ridden away bareback.

Rufus rode around the trading post and tied the horse near his shack. Climbing off the saddle, he ran his hand alongside the horses head. "You were a good deal, but I think I got taken on the saddle."

Andre came out of the trading post. "I saw you ride by. It is a fine horse, and it should carry you for many years."

"Not with this saddle," Pike told him. "He let me think I was getting the saddle he'd used and then switched it to this old hunk of leather."

The owner came over and took a good look at the saddle. “It is old and in need of some repair, but there is no reason we can’t fix it up.”

Hearing those words made Rufus feel good again. He pulled the saddle off and then the blanket. It had been chewed by rodents and was worn quite thin. Taking the receipt out of his possible bag, he handed it to LaRue. “Can you read this for me?”

“You don’t read?” Andre asked.

Uncomfortable with the fact, Rufus shrugged and said, “I been meaning to learn, but things have always gotten in the way.”

“Let’s see,” the man said, looking at the paper. “It says one sorrel horse, no brands $35. Then it has one saddle, $15. Oh, on the bottom he wrote: Blanket and bridle, no charge.”

Handing the receipt back to Rufus, Andre checked the teeth of the horse. “I been told you can tell the age that way. I can assure you it is older than seven years and younger than fifteen.”

“You can tell that just by looking at the teeth?” Rufus asked, impressed by LaRue.

Wiping his hands on his apron, Andre replied, “Some can, but not me. I know because the man that brought it to me said it was 10 years-old.”

The trading post owner headed back into the store. Then he stopped at the doorway and asked, “Have you decided if you are going on the next buffalo hunt?”

“I need money to build a shelter for the horse,” Pike replied. “I figure to go down to the docks and haul cargo right now. I got a couple of weeks to decide about the hunt."

"Come in and join me for coffee," Andre said. "I have something to discuss with you."

Sitting on a chair near the potbelly stove, Rufus took a sip and smiled. "You do make good coffee."

"Would you like to work for me?" the man asked.

"What could I do?" Rufus asked. "I ain't never worked in a store. If someone gave me a list to fill, I couldn't . . . I couldn't read it."

"You can work with numbers," LaRue replied. "You know your letters, don't you?"

"I know most of them, but when put together, they don't make words in my eyes," he told the owner.

"There are many things that you could do to help me," Andre assured him. "We'll try, and if it doesn't work out, you can go to the docks."

The years of working at the La Maison had taught Rufus more than he'd have guessed. He had a natural way of greeting and treating customers. He found out that many of the old timers liked to stop by the trading post and reminisce about things that they had experienced.

Pike learned the ins and outs from old trappers, about the rivers and various ranges that were best for beaver or hunting; the friendly tribes and those that were not; hunting grizzlies and elk, as well as a lot about dodging Indians while buffalo hunting. Most importantly, Rufus learned about the equipment and gear that the old mountain men used and how they survived in the high country.

With the help of a borrowed wagon from Billy, a trip was made to the mill to talk to Gus about the scrap wood. "It sounds like you won't be going to the logging camps this winter," he told Rufus.

"Right now, I am leaning at going on another buffalo hunt," Pike said. "When I get back, LaRue wants me to help him in the trading post."

Looking at the wagon Pike had brought, Gus said, "I can let you have two loads for a buck. Will that get the lean-to built?"

"If I stack the load high, that should do it," Rufus replied.

The scrap boards worked just fine, and within three days a decent lean-to was built on the south side of the shack. There was still enough wood to build doors that could close the open end during winter storms. The structure also had room enough for hay or another horse if needed.

Andre came out and liked the results. "It doubles the size of the shack," he said. "I'll have to take another look at the rent."

"I might have to hit my boss up for a raise," Rufus replied.

CHAPTER NINE

Hank and Wally were very pleased that Rufus was going on another hunt. They had hired a skinner named Luther. The man was a free black and had originally lived in New Orleans. When his wife and two children, who were not free, were sold and brought to northern Arkansas near Crowley's Ridge, he had moved to St. Louis to be closer to them and look for work. On the wagon with him was his mangy-looking yellow dog.

With the help of Andre, the saddle received with the horse had been brought back into shape. Billy had sold Rufus a scabbard, and along with his wool clothing Pike also had a set of buckskins. This trip he was a partner, having the $50 held by LaRue to buy in.

Riding up to meet the hide wagon, Rufus had a whole new look. Dressed in the buckskins, he had a broad belt around his waist that held the pistol, a short axe, and his skinning knife. The possible bag and powder horn hung over his shoulder. A haversack with his wool clothes, cookware, cup and plate was tied to the bedroll at the back of the saddle. The scabbard held his long rifle, and he also had a rope hanging near the saddle horn and he'd been practicing tossing a loop.

Looking up as Rufus rode up, Hank exclaimed, "Wally, come look! We got a mountain man hunting with us."

Feeling proud of the statement, Pike tilted his hat back on his head. Seeing the black man driving the wagon, he said, "My name's Rufus Pike."

"They call me Luther," the man said. "I was given the last name Washington, but don't tend to use it much." Luther had a long rifle similar to Rufus' leaning against the seat.

"What do you call your dog?" Rufus asked.

"Mean," Luther said. "Mostly mean."

Riding tall in the saddle, Rufus rode out ahead of the wagon. They crossed to the north side of the Missouri River and took the Boone's Lick Trail west. Boone's Lick was 150 miles from St. Louis. It had natural mineral springs, and by evaporating water, salt remained. The trail had been made to haul the salt to St. Louis to be sold.

Wally had told him they'd be hunting to the northwest this trip. With the empty wagon they would make good time and should start hunting in about 10 days. The hunting grounds were in the unorganized territory that would someday be Nebraska. The trip back with a loaded wagon would take two weeks. Figuring about two weeks to harvest the hides, they should be back in St. Louis in six weeks.

Rufus learned quickly that he had nothing to worry about regarding the mean dog. Those who had to worry were those who showed up in the camp unannounced. Luther had a nice head of salt and pepper hair and the dog would help him keep it.

The hunting party traveled about 10 hours per day, with breaks for the horses. Part of the time the dog rode with Luther, but it preferred to be running ahead, ranging back and forth, looking for a rabbit or bird to catch.

On days with good traveling conditions, the party could make 40 miles. On the fourth day they stopped to purchase a few supplies in Boone's Lick, settled by sons of Daniel Boone. This was where they crossed to the south side of the Missouri River. Talk was that steamboat traffic would soon be coming up the Missouri River and those hunting buffalo or trapping could sell their hides and furs there, saving the additional days of travel to St. Louis.

It felt great for Rufus to be on the trail. He had spent his whole life living in backrooms of saloons and taverns. Freedom of travel had always been limited to a few streets around the saloon. Here on the prairie, it was wide open and the opportunity for new places was unlimited.

They passed small herds of buffalo, prong horn, and whitetail deer. Often the horses were startled by ruffed grouse flushed out of their hiding places. Hank would ask Rufus to ride ahead and hunt for their supper. Most nights he'd come back with a prong horn. Once he'd stalked a whitetail.

The skins were saved and stretched using poles carried in the wagon. Knowing the discomfort of the wagon seat, Rufus would offer to drive and let Luther ride the sorrel. Reaching the point where they would ford the Kaw River at the confluence with the Missouri River, they found a scattering of dwellings. The Osage had an encampment with several teepees. The yellow dog stayed near the wagon and growled a lot. Hank had some beads, mirrors, and knives and did some trading with them for buffalo jerky.

After a day's rest, the party headed northwest, following the Missouri River. Hank intended to follow the river for four or five days before heading west. While Rufus did not question the leader, they had already passed enough buffalo to have made a load. He had heard Hank say that they were after higher-quality hides, but Pike figured a hide was a hide.

One morning, Rufus had ridden out to scout the area for the best route to take the wagon when cries caught his attention. Sliding off the sorrel, he knelt down and watched as 10 or more mounted braves rode hard toward a herd of buffalo. Most were armed with bows, leaning to shoot an arrow while holding on to their horses with their powerful legs.

When the charge was over, he counted six buffalo down on the prairie. Pike then saw a group consisting of women and children come from some trees lining a river and walk toward the downed animals to butcher them. While there was danger riding among the buffalo and shooting them with arrows, Rufus envied them the thrill they must feel.

Staying low to attempt not being seen, he led the sorrel away from the hunters. The wagon was taken south of the area to avoid coming in contact with the braves' hunt. Hank guessed that they were the Lakota who would come from the north to hunt.

Three days later they crested a rise and came upon a herd of buffalo that stretched all the way to the far horizon. Rufus just sat on the sorrel with his mouth open. Never had he seen so many animals of any kind. Hank announced, "We start hunting tomorrow."

That night everyone was in high spirits, anticipating starting the hunt. They had found a good camping site near a stream. They had plenty of firewood, and it was in a depression, giving them cover from those riding by.

The sledge was removed from under the wagon, and the fly tarp was put up. The herd was less than a mile from the camp and Hank hoped to hunt from this location for several days. The guns were cleaned and knives sharpened. Luther had a deer quarter roasting over their fire and some beans boiling in the pot.

Sitting around the fire that evening and eating their meal, Wally said, "We should start off with 30 animals tomorrow. We have a seasoned crew, so there shouldn't be any kinks to take out."

It was near October and the nights had become cool. Bad weather could affect the drying of the hides. Hank agreed that they should take the hides as quickly as possible. Everyone was up before daylight and having their morning coffee. There was frost on the prairie grass. Rufus had seen some cool weather in New Orleans, but never in October.

As they headed toward the herd, Luther said, "We gonna have buffalo tongue for supper."

One forgets the blood, the fat, and the smells of buffalo hunting when far away from it in St. Louis. The memories flooded back to Rufus as he skinned his first animal. He kept his horse close and used the animal to help turn the carcasses during skinning.

The yellow dog stayed near Luther mostly, but it made sure to grab scraps that had been tossed aside. Rufus noticed that the black man made sure plenty were available for his dog.

By the end of the first day, they had 32 hides staked out on the prairie grass. Rufus' new buckskins were covered with blood and fat. The big difference was that he did not feel it on the inside. Luther was roasting the buffalo tongues and singing a gospel song. Wally and Hank sat chewing while the redhead cleaned his rifle. After wandering away from the camp, the dog came trotting back and flopped down near his master.

While eating the juicy meat sliced from the tongue, Hank announced that starting tomorrow they would have two shooters. He would only load for Wally, but Pike and Luther would take turns with their rifles. After the meal, when they were alone, the leader told Rufus that he had wanted to do the same on the last hunt, but Johnson tended to wound too many. To spare hard feelings, he had Wally do most of the shooting.

One day blended into another as the men harvested hides. The smell was less in the cooler fall weather, but it was still ever-present. Twice, after the wagon was half loaded, the hunters had seen groups of braves ride to the rise above the camp and watch for a while before wheeling and riding away.

"They are checking out our horses," Hank said. "Two years ago, trappers had traded with the Blackfoot for beaver pelts and later had their horses stolen by the same braves."

"Are these Blackfoot?" Rufus asked.

"My guess is these are Cheyenne or Lakota," Hank replied. "They'd take our horses in a second if they saw the chance."

"Come dark, if you hear the dog growling, we best count our horses," Luther advised.

The next morning, the camp was moved to an area that would be easier to defend. Water would not be as convenient, but their horses would be easier to watch. It took most of the day picking up the hides and then staking them at the new site.

Finally, the hunt was finished, the wagon packed, and the men headed east. They all carried their rifles at the ready. Everyday they caught sight of braves riding in the distance and watching. One night Hank began to talk at the fire. "When they come, we don't want to be caught with our guns empty."

"You mean if they come," Rufus said.

"They will come. For the past three days they have been scouting us and that is too much time to invest to just go away," Hank said. "We got to stay close to the wagon. It will give us cover under all conditions. From now on, we have someone on top of the wagon at all times. With luck the dog will warn us if they come at night."

Rufus was sitting on top of the hide wagon in the early morning when the Lakota came. Twice the night before the dog had growled a warning. All of the men had come awake and pulled their rifles to full-cock. The sound of the rifles and the dog had saved their horses in the dark. The fear was that they'd sweep down on the camp and scatter the animals.

The sun was coming up in the east when they finally attacked. Rufus sat with his coffee on top of the hide wagon, watching for trouble. The dog smelled, or saw them first and started barking a warning. Squinting, Rufus dropped his cup and lay across the hides, trying to see the riders. The braves were riding low on their horses and coming fast.

Wally was the first to fire. Then, in desperation, Rufus aimed at the line of braves and fired. Loading his rifle as quickly as he could, he shielded his eyes and saw them clearly. They were close. He fired the rifle and saw one of the braves fall. Having no time to load the rifle, he pulled the pistol and lined up on a Lakota. Again, he scored some kind of hit with the shot.

The braves swept by with the dog charging their horses. Others were firing as Pike rammed another ball home. With his hands shaking, he put powder into the pan and pulled the rifle to full-cock. The braves were turning to come back. When he fired, he did not hear the other three rifles. A horse went down and two braves spun off their horses.

The Lakota hesitated. Wally fired, followed by Luther. Rufus was ready, and as he aimed he heard Hank fire. He waited a few seconds and then squeezed his trigger. The hunters had finally gotten into a rhythm that kept lethal balls flying toward the braves.

The attack broke and the braves rode away, disappearing into the rolling prairie. One of their horses remained down and the braves that had been knocked from their horses had evidently only been wounded, because they were nowhere to be seen. Rufus heard Wally holler, "They got one of our horses!"

It was one of the horses from the team. It had pulled its picket pin and run. "Try putting the sorrel in the harness," Rufus called to Hank.

A half-hour later, without even taking the time for more coffee, the hunters were on their way. Snowflakes began to fall. Despite the stress of the morning attack, Luther began to laugh. "The Lord sure do know how to lift the mood." Rufus just marveled at it. He'd never seen snow before.

The yellow dog had cut a pad during the attack and sat on the wagon between Luther and Rufus. They could make the crossing of the Missouri before nightfall if they kept the breaks short. Most of the day Rufus lay on top of the load, covering their backtrail.

At midday the men drank water and chewed buffalo jerky while the horses took a breather. Wally walked around the wagon. "They were after you," he called to Rufus. "Three arrows are buried in the hides."

After six weeks on the prairie, the hunting party returned to St. Louis. It was near dark and Hank decided to leave the wagon at the livery and have Billy give the horses some grain. Johnson came walking around from the corral.

"I see you put the sorrel in a harness," he said. "Did you miss riding on the wagon?"

The hunters ignored him as they pulled the gear off their horses. Suddenly he saw the feathers of an arrow sticking out of the hides. "I see you had a close call with some Indians."

"They were after the horses," Rufus said. "They hadn't figured on four crack shots defending them."

Pike was dead on his feet from the marathon trip back after the attack. Wally said, "I'm buying the first drink."

Shaking his head, Rufus replied, "I would not have the energy to swallow." Leaving the saddle on the hide wagon, he took the reins of the sorrel and walked toward his shack.

Billy came running from the livery with a bag. "Here's some grain for the horse."

Rufus had been concerned knowing that the horse had worked hard, with poor grazing. "I appreciate that, Billy," he said. "I'll be back to get the rest of my gear in the morning."

A strange feeling came over Rufus as he saw the shack. He had never had a home and the warmth he felt was the coming home feeling. After watering and putting the horse with its grain in the lean-to, he stripped off the buckskins near the door and walked into the shack. Even though it was cold, he did not light a fire. He simply crawled under the blankets and was soon snoring.

The sun was full up when there was a knock on his door. Groaning, he sat up on the bunk. "Come in," he called.

The door opened and Andre set the haversack near the table, along with a cup of coffee. "Wally brought this over last night. He'd had a few drinks and

I had no idea what he was talking about. It was something about being attacked."

"We had a little trouble on the way back," Pike told him.

Looking behind himself, Andre asked, "What are these rotten smelling things in front of your door."

Laughing, Rufus told him, "Be careful and don't get any of the smell on you."

* * *

True to his word, the hides were prime and Hank had a broad smile as he handed the bag of money to Rufus. "I couldn't believe it," he said. "We got $5 for the bulls. I even got a buck each for the arrows that were in the hides."

When he was alone, he counted the money. It was an unbelievable $250. Hank had told him he'd given Luther some extra and then, smiling, he said there was a bit to the dog for protection. Rufus realized that he was set for the winter. It had taken him $50 to buy into the company, so he had turned that $50 into $200.

He found Andre stirring some soup on the potbelly stove. "I suppose with your hide money you won't be wanting to work over the winter."

"If you would let me, I would like to work," Rufus said. "I also need you to hold onto some of the money."

"How much?" LaRue asked.

"It will be $200," Pike told him. "I will need some of it when I buy a Hawken rifle and maybe another pistol."

"Will that leave any for you?" Andre asked.

Smiling, Rufus said, "It will."

"Okay," LaRue said, "Have fun tonight. Be at work tomorrow."

By late afternoon, Pike had gotten his saddle from the livery, had a visited the barber and bath, and had bought some new buckskins. He then walked toward the Hawken brothers to dicker on a rifle. The first thing that caught his eye were a set of Kentucky Flintlock Pistols. He thought about the attack. I would have been nice to have had another loaded pistol.

He had the Kentucky Long Rifle with him and the U.S. 1819 Simeon North Flintlock Pistol. He had intended on adding to his current pistol, but to have a matching pair kind of took his fancy. By the time the dickering was done, he had a new Hawken, .54 caliber flintlock rifle on order. He also had the set of .54 caliber Kentucky flintlocks in his belt. Jacob Hawken told him that he could keep the long rifle until the new one was completed.

* * *

As winter set in, Rufus fell into a routine. He worked in the trading post six days each week, and for this he was paid a stipend and his rent and food were included. Most of his days off were spent getting over the hangover from the night before, and many found him still in the arms of a soft, warm lady he'd met.

Card playing was seldom indulged in. After a few drinks and some hands of cards, he had nothing left to purchase the favors of the lady.

During the afternoon of his day off, Rufus would saddle the sorrel and ride out onto the prairie in search of meat to add to Andre's fare. As the winter snows got deeper, his rides became shorter and frequently he came back empty-handed. Rufus had been excited with the first, lasting snow. If he wounded an animal, tracking it was easily done. As the winter snows deepened and the cold, miserable weather made doing anything outside harder, the fascination began to wane.

When business was slow due to foul weather, Andre showed Rufus how to make a set of saddle holsters for the pistol. The two leather holsters had flaps to protect them from the weather and were connected with a flat strip of leather with a hole that fit over the saddle horn. He was now equipped for three rounds of fire in the event he was attacked.

One advantage of the frigid weather was the need for firewood. Rufus had taken over that chore. He quickly became proficient with the axe, sending chips flying as he cut up the logs and split them for the potbelly stove. Andre had also gotten some of the scrap boards from the sawmill and these were cut to length using a bucksaw. Rufus found that these worked the best in his small stove to take the chill off in the evenings, warm the shack and make coffee in the morning.

It was late March when the snow started melting, and bare patches began to show out on the prairie. The mud in the streets reminded him of the rainy season in New Orleans. Nights were still cold and the mud and water would freeze in the rutted streets, making walking a challenge. A wrong step could leave a man with a sprained ankle.

In April, Johnson began to stop by the trading post. He spent time pricing traps and other items needed by a mountain man. He proudly talked of already being signed up for the coming year's beaver trapping with Ashley and Henry. All he had to provide was a horse and his rifle. The company would take care of supplies and pack animals.

When Rufus asked him what a trapper would make, Johnson was vague on that point. He said, "I've done some studying on it and a beaver pelt sells for $3 a pound and I hear the streams were loaded with them, so the pay has to be good."

"What will you do with your horse business?" Rufus asked.

Proudly the man said, "The price of horses has gone up with all the folks coming to St. Louis, so I'll sell it for a tidy profit."

Even though Johnson tended to be overconfident and brag a bit, Pike still enjoyed the man's company. He had taken him under his wing when they'd come up on the steamboat, and a kindness like that shouldn't be forgotten.

It was June when the trappers began to trickle back into St. Louis. Some had well-worn buckskins, others threadbare wool clothing. All types of head gear could be seen, from rabbit-skin hats, to coon-skin with the tail, wool toques, wool socks stretched over their head, or flat-topped leather hats with drooping brims.

A few men with great manes of hair wore nothing on their heads.

Most of the men had moccasins, from ankle to calf-high. Rufus laughed when he saw one trapper with the toe split open on one boot and the sole made a flapping noise with every step. One thing they all had in common was their destination when they reached the city. The saloons were noisy and full of drunken trappers as they attempted to quench the thirst for whiskey that had been built up during the long winter.

Most of the trappers would only spend a month in St. Louis, and then it was back to the Rockies. If their money was gone, they could depend on going with the "Company". The companies provided the supplies they'd need at high prices and were run under military rules, with the men eating in a mess and trapping in groups called brigades. They would report to a *boosway,* or head trapper.

Most of the men who worked for the company remained in debt and had no choice but to remain with the company. Those who managed to pay off the debt had the option of becoming a free trapper. Even when this happened, they often sold their furs to the company at a low price, in exchange for supplies at high prices, along with a little money for necessaries and whiskey.

Much of the understanding that Rufus gained about company men and free trappers came from Andre. LaRue never spoke harshly about the companies, but he did say they provided a service at a cost. Seeing all the mountain men and hearing about their lifestyle had excited Rufus. They did not have the workaday type of job. They had an adventure that lasted all year. It had risks, but it offered a way of life that Pike could adapt to.

Again, Rufus found himself looking to Johnson to find out how to join the company. He wanted to go trapping. Pike knew that Johnson had no experience trapping, yet had managed to sign up for the coming season.

After telling Andre of his plans and having the trading post owner attempt to discourage him, Rufus finally convinced LaRue that he was going. Andre went into the small room he called his office. A moment later he came out with a copy of the *Missouri Republican* and put his finger on one of the advertisements. "Right here, Rufus," he said. "They are looking for 100 men. You must own a rifle and have a horse. You can sign up for one to three years."

"I want to do it," Rufus said. "I should just sign up for three years."

Shaking his head no, Andre said, "If you insist on going with the company, sign up for one year. That way, if you do not like it, you can come back here and work for me. If you do like trapping, you will have the experience to become a free trapper. Just remember, everything they give you comes with a price. Nice knives, hatches, beads for the Indian women, new buckskins, all of it will cost you. Do not take anything you don't need."

Rufus hadn't thought about the women from the tribes. He had seen some of the trappers with Indian brides. They had come into the trading post and spent money on fancy things for them, things they called "foofaraw." There was no way Pike was going to add the expense of a wife when he went trapping.

He did take Andre's advice to heart. He had his own money and could purchase the extra things he needed right here at the trading post.

The trading post was busy with the mountain men purchasing items they'd need for trapping. Knives, sheaths, belts, moccasins, necessary clothing, hatchets, castor bottles, trading beads and hawk bells, tobacco, clay pipes, playing cards, flintstone, striking steel, lead bars, trade mirrors, trade cloth, and trade silver, fish hooks, line, and even a few possible bags and powder horns. Some of the free trappers also purchased traps and other items that otherwise would have been supplied by the company.

Representatives from the company also came and purchased stacks of goods and traps to pack west. Many of Andre's shelves were left bare when they finished. Much of it would be resold to the trapper at much higher prices. Rufus tallied most of the goods, fully aware of what they had paid.

The night before the company was gathering to go west, Andre talked of his early days trapping. Back then a lot of the furs were traded from Blackfeet and other tribes, but an enterprising man could trap the beaver and save the cost of items to trade. LaRue was one of those and had spent weeks in the chilling water.

He demonstrated how a trap was set for beaver and how to properly use a bait stick. He also gave the soon-to-be mountain man a set of clothes that he said would get Rufus some kidding. They were buckskin britches that came to the knee, long johns with the legs and arms shortened to the knee and elbow, and two pairs of moccasins.

"Add these to your gear and wear them putting out traps and retrieving them," Andre told him. "The men might think short britches are for children, but you'll be doing a lot less drying of your clothes."

"I can see how the shortened clothing will help, but why the moccasins?" Rufus asked.

"The bottom can have sharp rocks and broken sticks that cut your feet," his friend pointed out. "You wear these in the water."

It was late when Rufus went to his shack to sleep. He stayed away from the saloon, not wanting to have the misery of a hangover the first day on the trail. Little did he realize that come morning there would be a new way of life for Rufus Pike, the mountain man.

CHAPTER TEN

It was early July 1824 when the company was scheduled to leave. It was still dark when Rufus saddled the sorrel. He was somewhat concerned over the amount of added weight in packs that the horse would be carrying. His haversack, as well as an additional leather bag, were hung over the bulging bedroll.

Those going west were to meet near the livery. The area around the corral was littered with packs and pack saddles. To Johnsons delight, the pack animals, consisting of mules and horses, were held in his corral. Rufus wouldn't be asking the smoky-eyed man about the sale of his horse business. Johnson had planned to make a profit selling them to the company, but they already had all the stock they needed. Billy had bought it back at a bargain.

The sun was just coming up when the men began to arrive. One would have thought they were headed for church by the way they looked. Most were clean-shaven, with their hair and moustaches neatly trimmed. They had new store-bought or freshly laundered clothes. The hats they were wearing were the only items that reminded Rufus of when they'd come off the plains.

When the head trapper, Philo Becker, came, Rufus heard some of the men mumble, "Boosway." He walked among the men, speaking to several. The trappers he talked to headed for the corral and started packing the mules and horses.

Pike almost followed them to help, but one of the older trappers touched his arm and shook his head. "They get paid to handle the pack animals and set up the boosway's quarters."

Philo looked at the large group, appearing to be pleased with the response to the ad. "The first thing we have to do is break into brigades. If you have someone you want to trap with, pair up now."

There was a great deal of milling in the crowd as men looked up prior partners, or men they knew who had success trapping and wanted to be with. Johnson came over and stood with Rufus. Philo Becker then divided the men into brigades of 10, with a man of his choice as its head, or boss. He would only meet with the bosses of each brigade to relay information to the trappers.

Rufus and Johnson had hoped to be together and had gotten a two-piece troop tent. Half was carried by each man and at night they could be assembled, making a satisfactory shelter. A half would also make an acceptable fly tarp should they be separated.

The boss of their brigade of ten was named Alfred Woods. Alfred had been with Ashley for many years when the main source of furs was trading with the tribes. He was also an experienced trapper. Each brigade of 10 would travel and set up sleeping quarters together. In case of an attack, they would also fight together. To prevent food waste, the brigades ate in a common mess area. The company paid those responsible for the meals.

It was two hours before the pack animals were ready, and a meeting was held by the bosses. The trappers would ride two abreast with the caravan of pack animals following. Some of the free trappers tagged along and stayed to the rear. If that was not satisfactory to them, then they were invited to strike out on their own. They did offer some protection to those leading the pack animals.

It was very evident that discipline was important and enforced with threats of being cast out. In the event of thievery or killing of a fellow trapper, Becker was within the law to hand down harsher punishments, which included hanging.

The brigade Rufus was with was assigned to a position six back from the front. Alfred had told them that the trip to the Wind River Range was about 1,100 miles and would take a month. When they arrived at the range, a supply cabin would be built and trapping would start at the end of August. By sometime in November things would freeze shut and the trappers would build simple shanties near the cabin to stay in until April. Once the thaw started they would trap through May. Then the results of the season's trapping would be tallied at the cabin.

Ashley and Henry would be traveling out with the company until the men started trapping. They would then head back to St. Louis. Come spring, one, or both, would return to the Wind River Range to purchase the furs and pack them back to St. Louis.

It was then that the company trappers would be paid after settling up what they owed. Those who had signed up for more than one year would be given instructions about the following year's trapping, and a date and place to meet to get supplies.

Free trappers could also sell to the company on the Wind River Range if they wanted to avoid the long trek east. They also had the option of selling their furs to The Hudson Bay Company, or even take them to Santa Fe to sell.

The company would be traveling 10 hours each day, except for Sunday. It was a day to rest, wash laundry, repair gear, or just sit around the fire and tell stories. Philo had a clergyman who would give a service each Sunday, which was mandatory to attend.

The first half of the trip would be on the grass-covered prairies. As the elevation increased they would be on the more arid plains, with shorter grass mixed with sage and tumble weeds. The trail would start along the Missouri River and then follow the North Platte River. The Sweetwater River would be the last before reaching the Wind River Range.

Rufus sat loose in the saddle as they rode away from St. Louis. He had a chew in his cheek and spat at whatever object they passed, missing most of the time. Wiping the spittle from his chin whiskers, he smiled, thinking, *By the time we get to the range, I should be damn good.*

For the second time, Rufus rode west on the Boone's Lick Trail. The landmarks were familiar and he felt excitement knowing that soon he'd be beyond the areas he'd ridden before.

After four short breaks and many miles of travel, Becker called a halt near a stream and gave the order to take care of the animals and set up camp. The camp stretched out a quarter-mile along the prairie grass. Rufus saw a larger tent go up near the front which would house Philo, Ashley, and Henry.

Up and down the trail, horses were picketed and fly tarps and tent were erected. Several of the trappers chose to sleep under the stars and just spread a ground tarp and their blankets on the grass. Pots of soup and coffee were made over a large fire at the front. A triangle would be struck to call the men to chow. Each man was responsible for having something for eating the soup and a mug for coffee. If they didn't have one, it would be provided by the company and added to their account.

The two-piece army tent worked well for the two men. Both Rufus and Johnson were able to stow their gear in the shelter. Pike had a pan recommended by Andre that had three-inch-high sides and would be good for cooking in or eating out of. It had a single, rivetted handle that made setting it over the fire easy.

The cook scoffed when he saw the pan. "You'll get but a splash on the bottom of that damn thing," Sooky said. "I suppose you got a pannikin for a mug, too."

Holding out the pannikin, Rufus said, "I saw you looking them over at the trading post."

"Hell, that's where I saw you," the cook replied, smiling he put another ladle of soup into the pan.

One meal a day was provided, which included a slice of bread. In the morning there was always coffee and some hard bread. To the rear, beyond the pack animals, another fire burned. It was the free trappers. They had a young deer roasting on a spit. The smell made the bland stew a little less attractive.

The boss came back from eating with Becker and announced that there would be two-hour watches. Rufus was assigned to a watch from midnight until two. Watches were assigned from dark to dawn. At this point it probably wasn't necessary, but the company wanted the men to get used to them, and as they got into Indian Territory they would be needed to protect the stock.

An old army bugle blasted in the morning alerting them that the company would move in just over an hour. An hour and a half later, the bosses were shouting due to the delay, trying to hurry the men along. Rufus and Johnson were ready in plenty of time and sat drinking coffee near their saddled horses. Pike tossed the dregs out of his pannikin and hung it from his belt.

On the third day they reached the Missouri River crossing. It was Saturday and they would be camping on the south side of the river. An enterprising Missourian had set up a large tent with Kentucky whiskey on the sign. Several of the men made a beeline for the tent after setting up camp. Johnson had gone and gotten a bottle to bring back.

The village of Boone's Lick was only a couple of miles away, but the men had been ordered to stay near the crossing. The company feared that several men could forget that they needed to get back and there was no time to hunt them down.

The two men sat near their tent and enjoyed the bite of the Kentucky whiskey. "How much do you think we will make on the beaver?" Johnson asked.

"From what Andre said, we can expect to trap 80 to 100 beaver each. The company will keep their share and that will leave us between $300 to $375, that is if the price per pound stays at $5."

"I already owe them for a few things I needed," Johnson told him. "At the prices they're charging, a man could easily end up owing them money come spring."

Nodding in agreement, Rufus didn't bother telling the smoky-eyed man that Andre had warned him about that too.

It was noon before the Sunday services were done. Several of the men had heavy heads from the night before. Rufus had seen some of the men head to the shanties and teepees to look for other entertainment. He and Johnson planned to try some fishing after the services and scrub a few clothes on the rocks.

It was hot and sunny as the two men draped their wet clothing on some bushes and rigged their fishing poles. Several of the other trappers had the same idea. By the time the clothes had dried, several bullhead had been caught. Rufus cut several green sticks to use for roasting while Johnson cleaned the catch.

Three of the men in their brigade joined them to enjoy the fish. Otis Bass was an older, balding man who had been trapping for years, Harold Jones had brown hair and a ruddy complexion. This was his first year. Shorty Smith had hunted buffalo for years and had decided to try his luck on beaver.

After the meat had been picked from the bones, Johnson got out the remaining whiskey and poured some into each of the men's coffee. The brigades of ten would be split into two parties once the trapping started, and while drinking the coffee the five of them decided they would be one of the parties.

A week after the crossing, the company headed west along the North Platte River. Rufus looked at the slow-moving river, with its brown color and foul smell. As they continued west, he'd often see islands with small trees growing in the middle. Herds of buffalo were everywhere. Due to the pace the company was traveling, there was no opportunity to take advantage of the meat on the hoof.

While it was not a scheduled stop, the company spent a day in Ash Hollow. After crossing the South Platte River there had been the 240-foot rise onto the plateau between the North and South Platte Rivers, and then down the steep hill which would later be named Windlass Hill. The hollow provided lush grass for the animals and clean, clear water for the exhausted company after traveling the first obstacles of the trail and having had to drink water from the distasteful Platte River.

Two days after leaving Ash Hollow, the men marveled at the sight of Chimney Rock. It was Saturday and hunters had ridden ahead to shoot a buffalo for the Sunday meal. When the caravan reached them, they found that the hunters had shot four buffalo for their tongues and loin meat. The remaining meat had been left to rot. While the wasting of meat did not bother Rufus, he did regret that the hides were left.

The company camped in a scattering of trees along the river, with their stock picketed just outside on the shortgrass prairie in the blue grama and buffalo grass. With firewood being plentiful, many of the hunters went to the kill site and hacked strips of buffalo meat and built fires to broil it.

Come Sunday supper, Rufus couldn't believe it when he found that Sooky had made a stew out of the tongue and loins. Unable to help himself, Pike said, "You just ruined some tasty meat."

"Maybe so," the cook said, "but four tongues and the loins wouldn't have fed a 100 men. I was told to cook up a tongue for the headquarters tent and to put the rest into stew. It's got bagas in it."

Taking his portion of stew and bread, Rufus headed back to his tent. Johnson had gone out with others on Saturday to get meat to cook over their fire. He was busy broiling what he had left. The rutabagas tasted good in the stew, but the tongue and loin were tough to chew.

"I should have got us more meat," the smoky-eyed man said as he watched Rufus tear at a chunk from the stew.

After a disappointing meal and a day of rest, Johnson and Rufus had their animals ready to go and sat smoking clay pipes around a dying fire, admiring the beauty of the rock formations in the early morning sun. There were some shouts from the pack animal area where the men were just heading out to get the horses and mules. Then the sound of shots!

Leaping to his feet, Rufus grabbed his possible bag, pulled the Hawken rifle from the scabbard and stuffed the pistols in his belt. Thankful that the pistols and rifle were loaded for travel, he ran outside the edge of the trees. A band of Lakotas were attempting to steal pack animals while handlers were removing their hobbles. The men had left their rifles near the gear.

Dropping to one knee, Rufus raised the Hawken and pulled it to full-cock. Pulling the rear set trigger, he lined his sights on one of the charging braves. Touching off the hair trigger, the rifle fired. The brave's bronze body twisted and went backwards off the horse.

Something to his right caught his attention. As he held the powder horn to load the rifle he saw a Lakota brave riding straight at him, his arm back, holding a tomahawk. The brave had seen him fire and knew his rifle was empty. Reeling back, Rufus pulled a pistol and fired at the Lakota, now only seconds away!

Blood spurted from the brave's neck, spraying onto Rufus as the tomahawk slipped from the Lakota's grip. The look of shock was on the brave's face as his horse swept by. Moments later the brave slid from the horse, rolling on the grass.

Having no time to think, Rufus dropped the pistol and finished loading the Hawken. As he raised the rifle, there was a severe jerk on his possible bag. The second band of braves coming from the right had swung away as he fired at one of the trailing braves horses. The Lakota's horse stumbled and fell, spilling the rider.

While loading the Hawken again, Rufus watched the braves chasing the spooked pack animals, disappearing across the plain. Someone behind him said, "Damn foolish place to set up, but good shooting, Pike." Looking back, he saw boss Woods.

"They were after the packhorses," Rufus said. "I didn't see the riders coming from the west."

"They didn't get as many as they might have if those from the west hadn't been turned," the boss said. "Lucky you had the pistol. You were about to get your head caved in and my rifle was empty."

Without saying more, Alfred loaded his rifle and walked away. Rufus was unsure if he had done well or not. There was no doubt that the boss wasn't happy about him exposing himself.

Reaching into his possible bag for a patch and ball, he saw the arrow that had struck the bag. He realized that he had put himself out as a target. A chill went through him and his hands shook as he struggled to load the Hawken and pistol. He felt the amulet against his chest.

"Camille, your charm protected me," he whispered.

Johnson brought over the horses as Rufus pulled the arrow out of the possible bag. Tossing it onto the ground, he accepted the reins for the sorrel. "You mind if I keep the arrow?" his friend asked.

"It's yours," Rufus said as he led the sorrel towards the downed brave.

There was a large, bloody hole in the Lakota's neck. No doubt the jugular had been nicked, resulting in the spray of blood. The men came over from the pack animals. "You going to take the scalp?" One of them asked.

"No, I'm not," Rufus said.

"Mind if I take it?" the man asked.

Turning his blood-spattered face to the man, Rufus said, "I sure as hell do mind."

Upset, the man headed back to the pack animals. He heard the man snarl, "I could have got $10 for that scalp."

Riding in silence, Rufus dealt with the realization that he had killed another man. That made three in the last year. He wondered if that was to be his life from now on. Was he to travel this earth and take lives? Word had come up from the men leading the pack animals that two men had been wounded and one killed in the attack. Try as he might, Rufus couldn't convince himself that he was just defending the company and he had to kill to do so.

* * *

As the days of travel passed, the beauty of the plains brought his mood up. After the attack, new rules had been passed down. No man was to be away from his rifle at any time. When readying the animals in the morning, some would remain on guard, watching for danger.

Philo Becker had figured that the Lakota had watched the caravan for several days, noticing that the men had been lax when getting the horses and mules ready. They had come in from two directions, with plans to drive away most of the pack animals.

While not mentioning names, he had told the bosses that a few men had been prepared for such an attack and because of their quick action, only a few animals had been lost. After the bosses had come back with the new rules, Alfred had taken Rufus aside and told him that Philo was aware of his actions during the attack.

After passing the Red Bluffs, the company carried leather bags of water for the animals. The arid trail had several springs, but they had dangerous levels of mineral that would make the men and animals sick if drank. They would have some relief once they reached Willow Springs. It had good water and grass for the animals.

Arrival at the willows offered plenty of fire wood, so most of the brigades had fires going. Rufus spent time brushing the sorrel before putting it on its picket to graze. He wished he had grain for the horse. The days of travel with only grass to eat had taken a toll on the sorrel and the weight loss was noticeable.

One upside was that a lot of the extra supplies that had been carried were consumed and the pack on the horse had become lighter. Johnson was riding a buckskin and it being younger than the sorrel, the buckskin remained in better shape.

Alfred told his brigade that they were only about five or six days from the Wind River. A cheer went up from the men, knowing they were that much closer to preparing to start trapping.

When the company left Willow Springs, Rufus figured that they'd seen everything of interest before the Wind River. As they reached the Sweetwater River, they saw a large domed rock. Many travelers in the past had chiseled their names into the stone to mark that they'd been there. Pike also saw the large gash that the river ran through. One of the older trappers told Rufus that it was made by a large tusked animal that the local tribes had tried to kill. Angered the behemoth had used its tusks to rip the large opening and then escaped.

The Sweetwater River offered much better water than the North Platte River. The winding river was crossed several times before finally reaching the Wind River Range. Ashley and Henry chose a location to build the temporary quarters along a river that at one point disappeared into the ground which was called a sink. The area offered adequate timber and the Popo Agie River provided good water. Winter supplies and trade goods would be stored in the structure.

Several tribes also traveled the area and the plan was to trade for furs from the Indians and attempt to stay on friendly terms. A good amount of trade goods had been brought along for this purpose.

Rufus and Johnson had just finished setting up their tent and were sitting on the grass debating if they should make coffee. Otis came over and told them. "The boosway told Woods to send a couple men out to hunt for meat. Woods picked me and told me to take one more man."

As if sitting on a spring, Johnson stood up. "Let me get my rifle."

Rubbing the back of his hand across his mouth, the old bald trapper replied, "I appreciate the offer, but I was thinking of Pike."

Johnson's face fell, and he mumbled, "I . . . I was just . . ."

Inside, Rufus was thrilled to be asked. Outwardly he felt awkward as he collected his rifle and possible bag. "Should I take my pistols?" he asked.

"May as well," Otis answered. "They worked well for you with the Lakota."

Each man took one of the packhorses to carry the meat, should they have success. At Bass' suggestion, Rufus took his blanket roll. "We may be a couple days on the hunt."

Riding away from the company, Rufus had a feeling of freedom for the first time since leaving St. Louis. The strict structure was necessary to keep the trappers traveling to a schedule and ready for any problems. He followed Otis as they wound through the trees on their way to the valley below, with only one goal: Find some buffalo or elk wherever they might be.

Each man was carrying three days ration's and they were told to return to camp, with or without game in that time. Rufus knew that if they returned without meat, others would be sent out and they would have to live with failure.

Otis told him that the elk were in the high country this time of year, and buffalo would be grazing on the plains or valleys. "I know where we can find buffalo," he told Rufus. "We'll go after elk first. I like the meat better. If we have no success, we will kill a couple of buffalo and go back to camp."

Riding across the valley, Rufus saw dark clumps in the distance that he figured were buffalo. *Onward to find some elk*, he thought.

They worked their way to some of the high meadows. The vistas that they witnessed in all directions were breathtaking. Whenever possible, the two men rode abreast. Otis kept pointing out landmarks and commenting on areas he'd traveled in years past. They stopped in the trees next to a sheer granite cliff. Looking down, the men could see a long valley with a web of streams, dotted with ponds. The also saw some large-horned animals.

"There are our elk," Bass said.

"Can we get down there today and shoot?" Rufus asked.

Sitting there looking into the valley, Otis said, "It would be a shame to cut the hunt short. I figure we'll camp up here tonight and enjoy the view. Tomorrow we will stalk the elk."

Staying within the trees, the two men set up camp. Over a small fire, they made coffee and fried cornmeal cakes. By the time the sun was disappearing behind the mountains, the fire was out and they were enjoying a chew.

"I believe Johnson was disappointed when I asked you," Bass said.

"He kind of feels like my teacher," Rufus said. "When we come up from New Orleans, he took me under his wing and kept me out of trouble."

"When the Lakota attacked us, he hunkered down and didn't even shoot," Otis said. "I saw you out there taking the braves on. You might have been a little careless, but you weren't hiding."

"Woods did mention that I might have stayed behind some trees," Rufus said, smiling.

Leaning forward, Bass spat. "Maybe so, but I wanted someone with me that I could depend on in case we run into any hostiles."

Once the sun was down, it got cool in the high country. The two men spread their bedrolls out under the trees and were soon dozing. In the distance they heard elk bugling and wolves howling. Two owls called to each other with haunting hoots.

The men woke to face the chill of the morning. The trees behind them prevented the morning sun from warming the camp. Sitting with their blankets around their shoulders, they poked sticks into the small fire. Rufus took a piece of side meat and sliced it into the high-sided pan.

Otis watched him and said, "I like it. The pan is good for frying, or making beans."

"A man I worked for gave it to me," Pike said. "He used one like it when he was trapping."

Bass stirred up some cold flour and water for fried bread and added it to the pan. Looking down into the valley while the food was cooking, he said, "Lots of beaver in them streams."

"Will we start trapping there?" Rufus asked.

"If they let me," Otis replied. "Some of the others will have first say. Course, they might not know about this meadow."

With the meal finished and the sun finally warming their bones, the two men packed their gear and rode from the camp. Rufus looked back and hoped he'd have a chance to stay there again. It was a couple of miles to the northeast before they came to a place where they could descend into the valley.

Slowly the two men rode along the valley. They came to a rise and stopped. In the distance they could see several elk grazing. Most of them were females without horns, and a few males with impressive racks followed them. Rufus was impressed by the size of the horns. He had seen the whitetail deer in Louisiana, but their horns did not compare.

Grunting, Otis said, "It won't be easy getting close to them." After watching for a while, he continued, "Last evening they were moving to the north. Now they are slowly grazing south."

"When I bought the Hawken, they said it was able to kill a quarter-mile away," Rufus told him.

"That's true, if the wind don't blow, and if the land is flat. Also, it depends on sighting of the rifle. Have you sighted it in at that distance?" Bass asked.

"No, I haven't," Rufus admitted.

"I figure that we can both hit them at that distance," Otis said, "but if we wounded the elk, we'd spend the rest of the day chasing it."

Respecting what the old trapper was saying, he asked, "How do we get close?"

Pointing, Otis said, "You see that clump of brush, yonder there? I figure we ride south and then come up behind it. Then we wait for the elk to come into range."

Leading the packhorses, the two men rode to the south in the valley. The valley ran to the southwest.

Mountains rose to the north, and rolling hills and granite cliffs lined the south side. Over their left shoulders they could see the cliff where they had camped above.

Bass continued to point out all these things as they rode. Rufus realized that he was busy teaching him, so the next time he entered this valley he would recognize it. Suddenly, Otis stopped and put up his hand. He motioned for Rufus to keep quiet and get off the horse.

Moving close to Bass, he heard him whisper, "I saw horns just ahead of us. We got some elk enjoying the sunshine."

They tied the horses to some low bushes and took their rifles. Crouching, they moved in the direction Otis had spotted the horns. Rufus looked to the north. The elk they had hoped to intercept were standing with their heads up, watching them.

Stopping, Otis knelt down. Rufus moved close and heard him whisper. "They are just beyond the brambles in front of us."

Proceeding on their stomachs with the rifles in front of them, they moved using their elbows and toes. Rufus found it easiest to place the rifle ahead as far as he could and then move up to it. Pike saw the horns suddenly move. The bull was licking its side as the horns bobbed up and down.

He saw Otis hold up three fingers. He had spotted other elk. Rufus knew from their prior plan that he was to shoot at something on the right and Bass would be shooting at the elk on the left. Now as they moved, Rufus kept the rifle close, ready to put it to his shoulder at any time and fire.

Both men had their rifles cocked. They didn't touch the rear set trigger for fear that as they crawled something would contact the hair trigger, firing the rifle prematurely. Suddenly one of the females stood up. It was watching the elk to the north. It was on Otis' side and he had the rifle to his shoulder.

Then a bull loomed up in front of Rufus. He heard Bass whisper, "Fire."

With his heart pounding and his nerves screaming in his body, Rufus sighted on the bull and set the rear trigger. He then touched off the hair trigger. He never heard Otis' rifle. His whole focus was on the elk in front of him.

There was a crashing of brush as other elk that had been out of sight took flight. The bull followed the others. Rufus got up in time to see the male collapse. Otis' elk had fallen where it had stood after taking the well-placed shot.

"Fine shooting!" he heard Bass shout.

Coming onto the second herd had saved them having to wait for the slow-grazing elk. The excitement of the hunt was over. They now had the work of cutting up the animals. The female weighed about 450 pounds and the male over 600 pounds. Now they would have to discard everything they could to get them closer to 300 pounds each for the packhorses.

The two buffalo hunts had made Rufus an efficient skinner. After reloading his rifle, he took out the whetstone and touched up the knife edge. Otis came over. "We got us two nice-size elk to pack back to the company."

"Will we be skinning the animals and then pack their meat back in the hide?" Rufus asked.

"We won't be skinning them," Bass said, surprising Pike. "After gutting the elk we'll quarter them and discard head, legs, and most of the ribs."

"What about the horns?" Rufus asked.

"You might have to carry them on the sorrel," Otis told him. "You can't eat them and they weigh up to 40 pounds."

There was no way that Rufus was going to leave the horns behind. He led his horses to the downed male. After gutting the animal, he removed the backstraps and tongue. Rufus then removed the lower legs and quartered the elk. He had a canvas bag that he put the loose meat, into including the heart and liver.

He was unsure how the quarters should be packed on the sawbuck saddle, so Rufus waited until Otis led his loaded packhorse over. The heaviest parts of the elk were the hind quarters. Even these weighed just over 60 pounds each. In short order the elk was loaded onto the packhorse and a tarp tied around the load to keep some of the flies off.

It was early afternoon when the two men led the loaded packhorses from the valley. The elk horns were tied with the bedroll on Rufus' horse. Bass kept a continuous stream of chatter as they rode, pointing out distant landmarks as well as sign made by animals that lived in the valley.

Having a keen interest in what Otis was telling him, Rufus asked several questions. They stopped near a beaver pond to rest the animals. Taking advantage of the time, Bass showed Pike good places to set traps in the canals the rodents had excavated. Startled beaver slapped their tails on the water and dove out of sight.

Stopping just before dark near a babbling brook, Otis chose a spot to camp within some evergreens. They hung the elk quarters well off the ground in some tall pines. Bass built a small fire, pointing out that the branches of the trees would disperse the smoke, preventing someone from a distance being able to spot it. The fire was also kept small and shielded by the trees to attempt to hide it from others who might be camping in the area.

Rufus realized that when in Indian country it was prudent to do your best to be invisible to any passerby. He had noticed that Otis never rode in the open if there was some kind of cover. He also never skylined himself.

They ate the two elk tongues for the supper. Using Rufus' high-sided pan, they boiled the tongues and then removed the outer membrane. Then, using fat from the elk, they sliced and fried the meat, again using the same pan.

The two men stuffed themselves on the meat, and then sat back to drink coffee and have a chew. Bass noticed that Rufus liked to watch the flames flickering around the glowing coals. "Don't be looking at the fire," he said.

"I kind of enjoy watching it and poking the coals," he said, a satisfying smile on his face.

Dusk had set in and Otis could see a fox taking a drink a way up the brook. "You see the fox over there?"

Looking where Bass was pointing, Rufus said, "No I don't."

The fox finished drinking and trotted away from the brook. "I see it now," Pike told him.

"How long did it take your eyes to adjust before you could see in the dark?" Otis asked.

Frowning, Rufus said, "Not long."

Bass tossed out the dregs from his cup. "It took long enough that you would have been dead, had it been a Blackfoot or Shoshone coming at you. Never stare at your fire. Look beyond it at what's around you."

He did not take it as a reprimand, but rather as a lesson. Rufus respected the old trapper and was happy to learn everything the man was willing to teach him. Shortly after dark, they pushed dirt over the remaining coals. With a full belly after a successful hunt, Pike slept well.

After some coffee to wake up with, and left-over tongue, the two men loaded the packhorses and continued toward the company camp. The night had been cool, helping to keep the elk meat in good condition.

Cheers rose from those finishing the log building when they saw the packhorses loaded with elk. A couple of the trappers came and looked at the horns. "You planning to make a soup out of these, sonny?" an old-timer asked.

All of the men new to the high country were impressed with the horns. Johnson even made a positive comment about them. "We can put these on the front wall of our shanty when we build it."

Having over 100 men to keep busy and feed while waiting to start trapping wasn't easy. A lean-to was added to the back of the supply cabin for use by Sooky and his helpers to make the meals. For security, night guards were posted around the cabin and with the horses. All the free trappers had gone into the mountains to start trapping.

Finally, the word came down that the men were to draw their supplies and traps. Each brigade would be given horses or mules to pack supplies and furs. They were also told that Ashley and Henry would be talking to everyone.

Once everyone had drawn their supplies and traps, they stood by, waiting to hear what the owners had to say. Philo Becker, the booswav, came out first. He held up a bottle of whiskey. "Go get your mugs, men. There will be a drink to a good year's trapping."

Like a wave against the rocks, the men scattered, stumbling over each other, as they went to their packs to get a mug. Rufus watched Johnson run and smiled. His own pannikin was hanging from his belt.

Like any group of men that had spent over a month following military-like discipline, they quickly lined up for their share. Becker called out, "Don't drink until Ashley comes out and makes a salute to our success."

Waiting until the line got short, Rufus watched the men hold their cups out for their measure of whiskey. Sooky had a measuring cup that the liquor was poured into and then dumped into whatever container the men brought. Some held a hand under Sooky's cup to catch any spillage.

Ashley came out of the cabin just as the last measure was poured. He then held up a glass containing brandy. "First things first," he called out. "I want to wish everyone a successful fall and spring trapping."

If he had any more to say in the salute, the men couldn't wait. Most of them drank the contents of their cups in a large gulp. Rufus sipped his, enjoying the warm feeling in his throat and stomach.

With the salute finished, Ashley continued. "Next July the company will be having a rendezvous in the area of Burnt Fork and Birch Creek. The company will bring all the supplies you need and purchase your furs. This will save you spending months making the dangerous trip to St. Louis." There was a round of cheers from the trappers as they held their cups in the air.

Once the men quieted down, Ashley continued, "To make the trip out here successful, we will depend on all of you to spread the word about the rendezvous. I want to thank everyone for joining the company and again, wish you all good trapping."

After a quick wave, Ashley went back into the cabin. Becker said a few quick words of instruction and then ended the meeting. Moods were good, stomachs were warm and the group broke up to make ready to leave. Rufus watched some of the men go straight to their waiting horses and ride away.

Walking with Bass and Johnson, Otis said, "That man would make a good politician. He can stir up a crowd and then go away and let others do the work."

CHAPTER ELEVEN

Once Ashley and Henry left with Sooky and some other company men, Philo Becker and a half-dozen men would be staying at the supply cabin.

It was time to set up the teams to trap. Otis had chosen to trap with Rufus, Johnson, Harold, and Shorty. Alfred Woods took the remaining men. Bass led his party toward the valley where the elk had been shot. Woods headed with his men to a parallel valley. It was decided that each team of five would divide the catch into equal parts.

The company provided four packhorses to each group of five to carry needed supplies for two months and to carry the pelts back. If the weather held beyond the two months, one of the trappers could make a trip back to the supply cabin bringing pelts or getting additional supplies.

After two day's travel they arrived at the valley and Otis held a short meeting. "Come morning, I will show those that had never trapped how to set one properly. Each of us have four traps and these traps will be set every day except when we move. After the morning check of the traps, all those with success will skin their catch, flesh it and stretch it to dry on a hoop. Beaver meat will be eaten for our meals. We got side meat, beans, and hard bread to eat during bad trapping."

If a man had tobacco, he did not have to share it with others unless he wanted to. It could also be used for betting when playing cards. They would normally eat one meal a day, which was supper. Coffee was made in the morning and the men chewed jerky, if they had it, or hard bread.

A pot of beans was made for supper the first night while the men cut their stakes and sticks needed to place the traps. The traps had been boiled with oil at the cabin in preparation for being used. Bass laid out a trap set, giving some prior instruction.

That night, Rufus slept restlessly, anticipating setting his first trap. The next morning, he showed up at the fire pit wearing his short britches and moccasins. Pike got plenty of friendly ribbing about his getup. Otis did not take part, but rather said, "It looks like Andre dressed you."

The trapping would be done with the team working the same area. It was mostly for safety in the event of a problem. Otis led the men to the nearest pond. It had two lodges and he estimated that four to six beaver could be taken. Freshly chewed trees led the men to active canals.

Removing his boots, Otis took a trap, stake, and bait stick. Entering the water a short distance from the canal, he waded to it. Slipping the four-foot stake through the ring on the end of the chain fastened to the trap, he used the back of the hatchet and drove it into the bottom of the pond. He then strung out the chain and placed the set trap under water at the mouth of the canal. Sticking the bait stick above the trap into the bank of the canal, he then applied some thick, reddish-brown castor onto the end of it.

Sloshing some water around the area, he waded back to the point where he'd entered the water. "It is as easy as that," Bass said. "You don't want to leave your smell near the trap. The beaver will be drawn to the bait stick looking for another beaver. When the trap springs, it will swim back into the pond trying to get away. The weight of the trap will keep it down and it will be drowned."

After the demonstration, Johnson, Pike, and Harold set traps in the same pond. It did not go as smoothly as the one set by Otis. Traps were accidently sprung while being placed, and underwater obstacles caused the men to trip. In one case a hatchet was lost when dropped. While setting the traps was serious business and the men depended on it being done correctly, there were still several laughs as mistakes were made.

When coming into the valley, and from memory during the hunt, Bass sketched the layout of the near ponds. Two to three ponds could be handled by two men. Shorty Smith took off with Harold, shouting back a challenge that he'd trap the most beaver the first week. Otis would take care of the pond where the training was done, and Rufus and Johnson headed south along the stream to find ponds for themselves.

Bass figured it would take the team about two weeks to trap the valley. Once they had about finished the area, he would ride out and find another location. The beaver were plentiful, so Otis had no worries about keeping his team with traps in the water. Meantime, he started making hoops to stretch and dry the pelts.

Johnson had chosen the first pond they came to. Rufus selected one a quarter mile away. Swinging off the sorrel, he chose one of the traps wrapped in a ground tarp behind the saddle. He debated if he should take one of the pistols in his belt, but chose to leave them and the rifle on the horse.

He led the horse as he searched for a canal, or an area where the beaver came in and out of the pond. He saw a marshy spot that had a trail cut through it. Carrying everything he needed, he entered the water, feeling the mucky bottom ooze over his moccasin. It was the last week of August and the pond water temperature was tolerable. The water in the streams was cold year-round due to the source being in the mountains.

Unlike the first pond he'd set a trap in, this one was difficult to walk in. The water was above his knees and the beaver had stuck several branches into the bottom to be eaten come winter. Finally, he got to the water side of the path.

Rufus feared he had chosen poorly. Where he was the water was too deep. The beaver would swim right over the trap. As he moved between the cattails and reeds toward the bank, he knew that he was leaving scent on both sides. Once he reached the shallow water, he put the double-spring trap down and managed to set it.

Placing the trap into the pathway, he pondered the bait stick. There was no bank to poke it into. Taking care not to spring the trap, he stuck it into the pathway between the trap and the shore. It remained about five feet out of the water. This he applied the caster to. He then strung the chain out and secured it with the stake. This wasn't exactly how Otis had shown them, but it was the only way Rufus could see to do it.

The next three traps were easier to place. They went into the mouth of the canals. Climbing out of the pond after setting the last trap, Pike sat on the shore and let the water drip off his short pants. In the distance he could see one of the beavers working at plugging a leak in the dam. He was surprised that he hadn't scared the rodent.

The sun was shining and the valley felt peaceful. In the distance he caught the movement of an elk. In his mind, he relived the shooting of the large bull. He wondered if Otis would want to hunt for any elk. *Maybe when it got colder*, Rufus thought.

Johnson had already returned and was sitting near the fire when Pike got to the camp. Then his eyes grew wide. Hanging from a poplar was a beaver carcass. "Did you get that?" he asked the smoky-eyed man.

"I got it," Otis called to him. "It come to the first trap I set. I heard it get caught from here. I don't know if it was ready to fight or court when it smelled the castor."

Rufus soon learned that Bass was going to show how he wanted the beaver skinned and stretched after Shorty and Harold got back. "He said we will be eating beaver meat tonight," Johnson told him.

Harold was wet from head to toe when he got back. "I tripped over a damn log and took a dive," Jones admitted.

"You best be careful," Bass said. "If you get wet all over and swallow the pond water, you can get the fever. That's why we drink from the streams."

The fever he was warning about was beaver fever, caused by single-celled organism called Giardia lamblia found in beaver ponds. In his years as a trapper, Otis had seen more than one trapper come down with diarrhea after a season of wading waist-deep in the ponds.

With everyone back from setting their traps, Otis instructed them on the proper way to skin a beaver. It included a warning about laying a wet beaver on a frozen surface and pulling the fine hair off. It decreased the value of the pelt, or plew.

With keen interest, Rufus watched how easily the old trapper removed the skin from the beaver. Otis then removed the castor glands to add the reddish-brown castor to one of the bottles. He then carefully laid the skinned carcass on a log. "You are looking at our supper," he told them.

Once the hide was fleshed and stretched onto a poplar branch loop, Otis announced that it was time to start cooking. Taking his time, he cut all the edible meat from the carcass, including the tail. "I saw some wild onions growing yonder," he said, pointing.

Getting up and adjusting the pistol in his belt, Rufus wanted to look for the onions. Dressed in dry clothing, Harold followed him. "How do you figure beaver will taste?" the pock-faced man asked.

"I ain't never heard anyone say I wish I had some beaver meat to eat," Rufus said, "so I figure if it don't taste right at first, by the end of the season we will like it just fine."

Returning with a couple handfuls of onions, Rufus sat back to watch Bass cook. He had side meat snapping in a well-blackened frying pan. This he filled to the top with meat from the beaver. The tail hung over the flames on a green stick. Shorty had mixed up some bread dough and sat across the fire and fried it to eat with the beaver. Harold roasted some coffee beans and crushed them to put into the steaming pot of water.

Adjusting the pistol in his belt, Rufus sat down with his tin plate heaped with beaver meat, some of the fatty tail, and fried bread. His first bite of the beaver meat left him doubtful, as it was chewy, and it left a hint of liver flavor in his mouth. Hearing compliments from the others, he chimed in, figuring it must be what good tastes like.

With the meal finished, Rufus sat and looked at the beaver pelt stretched on the hoop. It was the first of the season. He was suddenly worried that he might have done something wrong when placing his traps. What if he didn't catch any beavers?

Taking the whetstone out of his possible bag and rubbing an oiled patch on the surface, he began to move his knife edge across it. He thought about the beaver that was working on the dam. It wasn't that far and he could have shot it. Then he would also have a pelt drying on a hoop.

He heard footsteps and looked up. Otis sat next to him. "What did you think of the beaver?"

"It is a nice-looking fur," Pike answered.

Laughing, Bass said, "You know I meant the meat."

"Are they all so tough to chew?" Rufus asked.

Switching cheeks with his chew, Otis spat. "It was a good-size beaver. You will find that older ones tend to be tougher. I thought you'd say it reminded you of liver."

"Oh, hell," Rufus said, "I like liver, but do all the tails taste fishy?"

"By the time the spring thaw comes, you will be fighting for the biggest chunk of the fatty tail," Bass said. "When we start having too many beavers to eat, we can keep just the back loins and every bite will be tender."

Otis handed his tobacco twist to him. Using the newly sharpened knife, Rufus cut off a chew and stuck it into his cheek. He was sitting and staring out into the dark. Suddenly he said, "The fox is back."

Rufus was up before the sun and had a pot of coffee on. He heard a groan and saw Bass toss his blanket aside. "You are up damn early," Otis grumbled. "There ain't no hurry to get to the traps. What you caught will wait for you."

"What if I don't catch nothing?" Rufus whispered to him.

"Then you check you traps and maybe move a couple," Bass told him.

The two men heard the others getting up. Johnson called, "Is the coffee ready?"

"It will be by the time you have visited the woods," Rufus said.

Pike needn't have worried. He had two beavers and a muskrat. It turned out that the muskrat had made the path. The only one who didn't have two was Johnson. He sat with his one beaver and skinned it in stony silence. The others talked and kidded each other.

A total of nine beavers and a muskrat was a big haul. Otis told them it was because the ponds hadn't been trapped for a couple of years and they had multiplied without the pressure. With so many beavers, only the tenderest meat was taken.

Once they had been skinned, fleshed and stretched, the carcasses were hauled a mile away by Rufus, Harold, and Shorty. Otis said he had something he needed to do with Johnson. Pike was sure he was taking him to check his trap sets. If the sets had to be changed, it was important to do so, because every beaver missed was money out of all of their pockets.

The day-to-day routine quickly became automatic. Small challenges had to be overcome as moccasins, hatches, and even knives were lost. A packhorse went lame and after checking it out, Otis took out a rasp and filed down the hoof. The soft ground of the valley had allowed them to grow. That night all the horses were checked and filed if necessary.

One day Rufus rode back to the camp with a 30-pound beaver draped over the back of the saddle. He pulled the sorrel up suddenly. There were four strange horses at the camp. One with a hackamore had feathers woven into it.

Raising the flap on one of the pistols, he stuck it into his belt. He then took out the second one and held it in his lap. Urging the horse forward, he watched, feeling the tension in his body. Then he saw the Flathead braves. Two were leaning and looking under the fly tarp used by Otis. He could not see their leader Bass anywhere.

One of the braves looked his way and spotted him! Quickly the brave ducked down, saying something to the others. Right there, Rufus decided that he might not be able to win in a confrontation with these Flathead, but by God he would take as many as possible with him for hurting Otis.

Spurring the sorrel forward, he had the reins in one hand and the pistol in the other. He heard a sound of anguish come out of his throat that he'd never heard before. Then Otis stood up, "What the hell, Pike!" he shouted. "You scared me to death with all that noise."

Pulling the sorrel to a stop, Rufus gasped for breath. He swallowed and his throat hurt from the screaming. One of the braves was laughing and pointing at him. "Laugh, you son-of-a-bitch. You don't know how close you came to being dead," he muttered.

Smiling, Otis said something to the braves and then walked toward Rufus. "I think your appearance was a bit upsetting to our guests." Bass told him.

"Not as upsetting as your guests were to me," Rufus said. "I rode in here thinking I was going to die."

A strange look came over Otis' face and then he smiled again. "The braves have beaver they want to trade with us. I was showing them what we had to trade. Come spring, we could end up with 50, maybe 100 extra pelts."

Swinging off the sorrel, Pike asked, "Why wouldn't they trade with Ashley when he gets back?"

Lowering his voice, Otis told him, "Their hunting grounds are far to the north of here and the local Blackfoot are their enemy. They believe that the Blackfoot will attack us at the rendezvous, as well as raid their camps if they stayed. They would prefer to trade with us and be back in their hunting grounds by the time of rendezvous."

Putting the extra pistol back into the saddle holster, Rufus adjusted the one in his belt and followed Bass back to their guests. The braves continued to talk with Otis in Salish. On the blanket in the fly tarp lay several knives, glass beads, hawk bells, flint, lead, and powder. One word that Otis said which Rufus recognized was musket.

Not being a part of the conversation, Rufus went back to the sorrel and got the beaver. They had been using a log to skin and flesh the rodents. Sitting down, he laid the beaver onto the log and began to remove the fur. Two of the Flathead came over and watched.

The taller, and quite frankly more fearsome-looking brave asked Rufus a question. Looking up Pike said, "I don't understand."

"He wants to know if you will give him the beaver meat," Otis called to him.

"Does that include the castor glands?" Rufus asked.

He heard Otis laughing. "I don't believe he'd mind if you took out the glands."

With the pelt removed and then a few quick cuts of the knife removing the castor glands, Rufus lifted the beaver carcass and offered it to the braves. The fearsome one nodded and took the animal. For good faith, Otis gave them a knife. Then all four of the Flathead got on their horses and rode to the north.

"Sharing the meat was a powerful gesture," Bass told him. "They will appreciate that even more than the knife I gave them. You took food from your mouth and shared it with them."

Looking up at his friend, Rufus said, "I thought they had killed you."

"It is a damn good thing you didn't fire the rifle at them before riding in," Otis said. "It would be damn hard for us to say we didn't mean to shoot them."

The camp was moved several times while trapping the valley. It was over 30 miles-long and got wider as they went southwest. Otis did not let them trap out a pond before moving. He said that they could come back in two years and the area could be trapped again.

It was early November when they searched out a new area. They went to the south, into what was Mexican territory. There was little worry of running into any Mexican authority. In 1824 they pretty much ignored the area.

The first valley had been good to the trappers. They had a total of 241 pelts. Shorty was the champion as far as the number of beavers caught. Everyone else paid their bets off with him with tobacco. Rufus was hoping to win some of the tobacco back playing cards, but so far the playing hadn't gotten him ahead.

They worked the ponds seven days a week, not wanting to leave their traps idle for any amount of time. On Sundays Otis would read the Bible, often letting one of the team choose what they wanted to hear. Rufus enjoyed hearing stories that his mother had read to him.

The weather had gotten colder and the mountain tops were snow-covered. Quite often they checked the traps with snowflakes coating their heads and beards. By the time they had checked their traps the men's legs ached with cold. Some mornings the ponds had ice along the shore.

Once the sun was higher in the sky, the temperatures became tolerable. It made the task of skinning their catch more comfortable. Otis talked of having to warm beaver near the fire to thaw them out enough to get the skin off.

After a Sunday reading Otis asked Rufus to check his traps. He said he'd be gone for two days. Pike wondered if he was making a trip to the company cabin. Rufus was sure that they were over a two-day trip back to the cabin, but asked no questions and told his friend he'd check the traps.

At the end of the two days, Otis hadn't returned. Johnson had even raised the question of who would be in charge if Bass didn't return. None of the men sitting around the fire wanted to address that possibility. Rufus sat finishing his coffee. He was sure of two things. One was that Otis would return, and the other was that he'd miss having a chew after losing the last of his tobacco to Shorty the night before.

Rufus was up at daybreak on the third day. Relief flooded over him as he saw Otis' horse picketed near the camp. Nobody asked him why he'd been late getting back. The fact that Otis was back was enough.

The Flathead braves came back in mid-November. They were about to head for their winter camp. They had 85 pelts with them. Otis went through them quickly and realized that several beavers had been caught in early August, and of lower quality, and wouldn't bring them the best price.

A blanket was spread out and the items of trade were placed onto it. Rufus was shocked to see a musket as part of the trade. Somewhere Otis had gotten a musket. The braves looked over the knives, flint, powder, lead, and the foofaraw. A Flathead brave who seemed to be the leader picked up the musket and looked it over. After placing it back onto the blanket, the brave nodded.

The trappers and the braves then smoked a pipe of friendship. Rufus took a deep draw on the pipe, enjoying the first tobacco he'd had in some time. After Otis and the braves spoke for a while, the Flathead got up, folded the blanket around the smaller items and then, taking the musket, they mounted their horses and rode off.

All of the team knew that the items Otis had traded would have to be taken from the 85 pelts before the money was split. The men had pulled their traps that morning and had one more place Bass wanted to work before heading back to the cabin.

Rufus and Johnson finished first and the smoky-eyed man went to get the horses. Standing and watching Otis pack, Rufus asked, "You got any more muskets hidden in your gear?"

Otis looked up and rubbed his balding head. "After you been trapping for a while, you do things for the next season. One of them is finding a good, dry place to cache some items that might be needed, like extra traps, hatchets, axes, shovels, and maybe even a musket or two."

"That's were you went for the two days," Rufus said.

"Yes, that's where I went," Bass told him. "It is a cave with the opening well-hidden. If we were attacked and lost everything but our lives, there is enough powder, lead, flint, and the other items that we could survive the winter. We might be eating porcupine and bobcat, but we could survive."

The rest of the day Rufus pondered on what the old, balding man had told him. Back in New Orleans or St. Louis, a person didn't have to think too far ahead. Here in the mountains, those who don't have a plan end up walking hundreds of miles for help, or slowly starved while the cold took them.

By the end of November, ice covered the ponds. Slower streams had mostly frozen over and the snow had closed most of the passes. They had managed to trap 218 beavers, plus the ones gotten from the Flathead. They also had muskrat, otter, mink, martens, and fishers taken with single-spring traps. Their furs had been stretched on planks.

Otis led the way along ridges and through valleys as the men headed to build their winter camp.

The gear and pelts were divided among the four packhorses and led by the others, leaving Bass to break trail with his horse.

When they finally reached the cabin, they were coming from the south. It surprised Rufus. When they had left, they'd gone northwest. He felt sure that he'd kept track of their location in reference to the cabin. Somehow they had worked their way well south. Rufus vowed he'd not be surprised again. He would pay more attention to the direction they moved when setting the traps.

About half of the men had already returned and were working on some type of shelter for the winter. Most were crude shanties with a door opening to the south. The source of heat would be a fire right outside the doorway. Most had built a low wall beyond the firepit to reflect the heat toward the shanty.

The men would need to build a structure around 16-foot by 8-foot to have room for the five men and their gear. Their furs had been checked in at the cabin, relieving the men from having to store or carry them any further.

After removing the snow from a large area, the men began to cut logs. Two sides were flattened enough to fit them a little closer together. Moss or shredded bark were collected to put between them as caulking.

The back wall was notched to fit the logs into the side walls. This offered a degree of stability to the structure. The roof was only six feet-high and covered over with spruce poles and a layer of boughs. The front wall was vertical poles, leaving an opening for the doorway. A buffalo hide was hung in the opening to keep the weather out.

While Johnson and Howard collected cedar boughs to put onto the shanty floor for sleeping on, Rufus and Shorty shoveled snow onto the roof and around the sides for insulation. Otis fashioned a reflecting wall for the fire pit and stacked pieces of flattened logs to make benches at the front of the shanty to sit on.

All of the scrap wood had been saved to be burnt in the firepit. One of the chores for the coming winter would be cutting and hauling firewood. Harold would kid that every armload of wood warmed you twice. Once making it, and once burning it.

By the end of the second day, the men had a fine winter shelter. Most of the time the buffalo hide door was tied open to one side to allow heat and light from the fire into the shanty. In the open area there were dozens of shanties some better than theirs, and many that were much worse. It didn't matter though, all of them would be abandoned come spring.

It would be four to five months before the spring trapping started. Other than making wood, moving and watering their horses, and cooking their own meals, the men had plenty of idle time. Johnson liked to wander up to the cabin and visit with the company men. Shorty was doing well moving from one card game to another. Otis loved to work with wood and could most often be found with an axe or hatchet building some kind of item that would make life more comfortable.

Harold and Rufus decided they would go hunting. Saddling the sorrel, and selecting one of the packhorses, Pike waited near the shanty for Jones to return. "Where would you recommend we go to find elk or buffalo?" he asked Otis.

The old balding man looked up at the eager hunter. "They have come out of the mountains and headed toward the foothills and the sheltered valleys. A few of the buffalo might still be on the plains, but that would be a long haul from here."

"Unless we find a herd, I figure we'll just get one animal and then head back," Rufus told him.

"Keep an eye on where you are," Otis said. "Use the mountain tops to keep you straight."

Laughing, Pike replied, "I'd hate to end up in Mexico while looking for the cabin."

Bass set his hatchet down and stood up. "One other thing. Watch for wolves. If . . . no, when you kill the elk or buffalo, they'll smell the blood and follow you."

"Don't worry," Rufus said. "I'll hang the meat out of reach at night."

"Don't forget," Otis warned him. "You are meat too."

The sound of Harold coming with his horse and the pack animal gave Rufus a reason to swing into the saddle. He didn't like hearing about the wolves. With the Hawken and the two pistols, he'd be able to keep them back.

"I'll be back in five days," Pike promised. "If we get two buffalo, it will be more like six days," he added, kidding.

Going back to working on his project, Otis waved to the hunters. The frozen breath from the horses rose in the sky as the animals broke through the thin crust of the snow. They rode past the hole where the Popo Agie disappeared into the sink. Over the years it had washed a deep cut, which would make a fine late summer shelter when the water was down.

They rode less than a half-mile and saw the river again. Rufus figured that someday he'd follow the river back up and find what was called the rise where it resurfaced. The two men started watching for game as soon as they left the camp. There was always a chance that the wolves would chase elk back into the hills while attempting to kill them.

Even though Rufus was hunting for elk, he would not pass up a whitetail or mule deer if they came across one. He had taken the Hawken out of his scabbard and held it across his saddle. He had the packhorse's lead rope tied near his blanket roll.

Harold carried a Kentucky Long Rifle, and when they'd emptied the rifles by firing them, they had always chosen a target and he'd proven that he could hit what he shot at. Rufus had given him one of the pistols to wear in his broad belt on the outside of the hair-lined buckskin coat. Both of the men had purchased coats before leaving St. Louis.

Otis and Shorty had buffalo skin coats, and Johnson had a thick, wool coat. Much of the winter the men would just have wool shirts over the long johns and that would provide adequate warmth while staying active. The heavier coat would have caused them to sweat and then get chilled, which was life threatening.

They rode the first day without seeing any game. Several times they had seen deer tracks or wolf tracks. Rufus and Harold had talked of traveling away from the camp for two days. At that point, if they did not see sign of elk or buffalo they would return and try to find a place where the deer were yarded up, and drop a couple of them. It would be less meat, but it could be dangerous with winter weather being too far from the camp.

The two men spent the night in a grove of balsam trees. The night was clear and frigid with little wind. The winter sky was filled with twinkling stars. He noticed one star that looked kind of red and wasn't twinkling. He figured it must be one that was burning out.

On the second day they found sign of elk near a wide stream. One group of tracks appeared to be an elk that was being chased by wolves. Seeing that brought back the warning from Otis. "I'll watch," Rufus mumbled.

The two men stopped midday and drank from their canteens kept under the coats. Movement caught Harold's eye. "I see something near the ridge."

The two men sat, squinting due to the glare of the snow. Then they both broke into a smile as a small herd of elk came out of the evergreens. The herd was walking east along the ridge that sloped down toward a bend in the stream.

Whispering, Harold said, "We can ride to the east and set up ahead of them in the aspen above the bend."

Dismounting, the men led the horses into a swale that ran to the east. They walked near cattails that grew at the swampy bottom, taking care not to step on any ice that would make noise and possibly turn the elk.

They came up behind the aspen and tied the horses. The animals immediately reached up to nibble on the tender ends of the branches. "Eat all you want," Rufus whispered as he started climbing out of the swale through the aspen.

Clutching their rifles and taking care not to snap any branches, the two men worked their way into positions. They had a clear view of the ridge meeting the bend. From the aspen they could not see the elk, and had to hope what little noise they had made didn't turn them over the ridge.

There was as snap of a twig and both men held their breath. At first it looked like shadows in the pines, then three females came out of the evergreens and stood staring in the direction of the two men. Both of the men froze, fearing any movement would send the herd crashing back into the pines.

After what seemed like an enormous amount of time, the cows started down to the stream. Behind them came three calves. The young elk acted playfully as they followed their mothers. Rufus figured that when the female elk reached the stream, they would take two of them. The young elk were old enough to live on their own.

Just as the lead female reached the stream, there was more movement in the pines. Two bulls came out. Both supported a medium-sized rack. Rufus guessed that they were two to three years-old. The meat would be tender.

The cows began to look around nervously as the bulls came down the ridge. Something was bothering them and it wasn't the bulls. The rut had been over for two months. The two male elk were standing and looking somewhere to the men's left. They were about 150 paces away and it was time to take the shots.

Harold was looking at Rufus. Pike nodded and slowly brought the Hawken to his shoulder. When they had reached the aspen they had pulled the rifles to full-cock so they wouldn't make a metallic noise once the elk came into range. Jones watched Rufus pull the set trigger. They were ready to fire.

"Now," Rufus breathed as he touched off the hair trigger. The lead cow was most alert and jumped at the flash, the young bulls were not and stood as the rifles fired, sending the deadly balls in their direction.

The bull Rufus shot at collapsed from the ball's impact and rolled down towards the stream. The cows and calves broke into a run. The bull Harold shot wheeled and ran back toward the pines. "I hit that son-of-a-bitch good," Jones shouted and leaped up, running to follow the elk.

He headed across the ice just before the bend. As Rufus shouted, "Don't cross there!" Harold broke through the ice to his armpits.

"I can't reach bottom!" the man shouted.

There were several dead aspens standing with most of the branches gone. Leaving his Hawken on the bank, Rufus hit one of the dead aspens with his shoulder, snapping it at the stump. Shoving the tip out on the ice in front of him, he pushed it to Jones. "Grab the end!" Rufus shouted.

Grabbing the aspen with one hand, he slid his rifle on the ice toward the shore. As he gripped the aspen pole, more of the ice broke around him and he went underwater. Rufus pulled on the aspen and the struggling man clung to it with a death grip as he appeared above the water.

It felt as though Harold was stuck. "Your possible bag! Get it off!" Rufus shouted. Clinging to the aspen with one hand, Jones tried to get the strap over his head, but couldn't.

"Cut the strap," Pike shouted. He had a sinking feeling inside. He was not going to get Harold out and if the man lost hold and went under . . . then he saw the knife in Jones' hand. He cut the strap and dropped the knife. Once again, he had both hands on the aspen. At first the ice broke as Harold was pulled toward the shore. Finally, Rufus got him onto the ice and dragged him to safety.

Harold was drenched and shaking from the icy water. Rufus had heard that a man could die within minutes if they broke through the ice of a pond and couldn't get out. Jones might be out of the stream, but he was wet through and the temperature of the air was below freezing.

Blankets! He needed blankets. Running through the aspen Rufus got to the horses and grabbed both blanket rolls. Slipping and sliding, he climbed the hill through the aspen and got back to Harold. "We got to get the wet clothes off you," Pike told him.

The pistol, hatchet and belt came off first. When removing the saturated buckskin coat, Rufus found that it was difficult to get the wet sleeves off the arms. The pants were beginning to freeze as he removed them. Stripped to his long johns, Rufus had

Harold sitting on a blanket and had another wrapped around him. The chilled man could not stop shaking.

There was an abundance of broken branches below the dead aspen. Frantically, Rufus collected a pile and crushed some bark for tinder. Pouring some gun powder on the tinder to make it light more quickly, he struck his flint with steel and the powder flashed. The tinder was burning. Rufus continued to feed sticks to encourage the flames and soon had a life-giving fire.

Positioning Harold near the burning branches, he had him open the blanket to capture the warmth. Using his hatchet, Rufus chopped the aspen he used to pull Harold from the water into smaller pieces and added them to the fire. One advantage of aspen was that it burned fast and hot.

He looked at Jones. The mans face was deathly pale. The shaking was less and his long johns and woolen socks were steaming. "Harold," he said, "I have got to take care of the elk. I've got enough wood to keep the fire going for a while. Do you think you can turn to warm all sides?"

The man nodded, and said, "I'm sorry. I didn't think when I ran out on the ice."

"You just hit a thin spot," Rufus said. "It wasn't your fault."

Seeing his hunting partner's condition, Pike felt dread. He had no idea how he'd get him dried off along with his clothing in this snow-covered forest. Glancing at the downed elk, Rufus knew the hide would quickly freeze and he had no idea how far the other elk had run.

Looking at his shivering partner, Rufus knew the elk would have to wait. "The rifle," he told

Harold. "I best get your rifle off the ice." It had slid near the shore, so he grabbed the barrel and put it near the fire. Rufus knew he had to prioritize his next moves.

First things first, he thought. *Harold needed something warm to drink.* Heading back through the aspen, Rufus got the horses and brought them to the stream near his partner. Grabbing the coffee pot, he used the hatchet to break a hole in the ice and filled it with water. Setting it next to the flames, he added more wood.

"Let me help you turn around," he told Jones. "We'll get your back warm while I make you some coffee."

After managing to turn the man, Rufus removed his own coat and draped it over Harold's legs. "We need a shelter don't we?" Pike said, more to himself than Jones.

Cutting some saplings, he made a frame and lashed the ground cloth to it. It would catch more of the heat. Rufus then moved Harold enough to put the second ground cloth on the snow-covered ground for him to sit on. His partner felt like dead weight as he moved him and he could still feel him shaking.

The coffee pot was steaming. "I'll get some coffee for you and it will help to warm your insides," Rufus told him.

Once he had a mug of coffee in the man's shaking hands, Rufus took the sorrel to get the elk lying on the other side of the stream. Just below the area that Harold had gone through was a rapid that was open and only a couple of feet deep. Spring floods had probably washed out the area his friend had went in, creating the deep hole.

After putting the stiffening front legs into the elk's rack, Rufus tied a rope from the horns to his saddle. He led the sorrel, dragging the elk to the rapids. Climbing into the saddle, he pulled the animal across the stream over to where Harold was sitting. He noticed that the hands holding the cup were still.

Swinging off the sorrel, he refilled the mug. Trying to raise the mood, he said, "You can admire this one while I go and get yours."

He heard Harold whisper, "It ran. I think I missed."

"No, you didn't," Rufus told him. "It was running dead. It is probably just over the ridge."

Coiling the rope back up, he turned to get back onto the sorrel and track the other elk. Suddenly, he swore. He hadn't reloaded the Hawken.! Then he had another thought. He took the pistol from his belt and placed it next to Harold. He knew the long rifle had gotten wet and would have to be thawed near the fire before it could be loaded.

Once back across the stream, the tracks of the second elk were easy to follow in the snow. Rufus saw where blood had sprayed out. The elk had been hit. He was disappointed when he didn't see the animal laying just over the ridge. The tracks and signs of blood disappeared into the pines.

He had barely ridden into the pines when Rufus heard the sounds of wolves fighting. They had gotten to the elk first. Turning the sorrel back towards the fire, Rufus hoped that one elk would be enough to keep the wolves busy. It would be at least a day before he'd get Harold ready to travel and he didn't need wolf trouble.

Shock went through Rufus as he got back to the steam. Harold was lying on his side and the fire was dying down. Leaping off the sorrel, he hurried to the man. He lay with the blanket around him and his eyes were closed.

"Harold!" Rufus said raising his voice. "You need to put wood on the fire."

Helping the man to sit up, he felt the cold on the side that had been down. Rufus knew he needed to put something under the ground cloth to insulate against the snow. After adding wood to the fire, he went downstream to a grove of cedar. Cutting several boughs, he dragged them back to the fire.

"I got to move you enough to put the cedar under the ground cloth," he told his hunting partner.

"My bottom got cold and I laid down to let the heat get to it," Harold explained.

"That was good thinking," Rufus told him. "Now I got to move you to put these under the cloth. It will keep you warmer."

The blanket that Harold had been sitting on was cold and wet. Rufus removed it and added it to the other soaked items. "We got to start drying some of this stuff," he told Jones.

"Did you find the other elk?" the man asked.

"I did, Harold," Rufus said. "But not before the wolves got there."

"Damn," Jones said. "It was my shooting."

"You hit it good," Rufus told him. "The animal had lots of heart and made a break for it."

Using the hatchet, he cut several more saplings and built a frame most of the way around the fire. Rufus then draped the frozen, wet clothing and blanket onto the frame, creating an open top lodge. Soon the frozen items thawed and started dripping. He had also put the pistol that had been in Harold's belt and the Springfield rifle near the fire to dry.

With the sounds of the wolves over the ridge, Rufus turned his attention to the elk. The hide was stiff, but the core had not frozen. He gutted the elk, setting the liver and heart to the side. He then removed the tongue and put it with the liver.

As he removed the head, he placed it onto the pile of guts. He looked over at Harold, who was now sitting with only his long johns on. Taking the liver, heart, and tongue, Rufus got his pan and placed it onto the fire.

"I am going to make us something to eat, and then, wet clothing or not, we are going to have to move," he told Jones.

Wearing only his wool shirt and long johns on top, Rufus had felt the chill as he worked on the elk. It felt good to be near the fire as he fried the meat. While it was sizzling in the pan, he went to get more water for coffee.

Placing it near the flames, he turned the meat to brown the other side. It was also time to turn the clothing. Returning to the fire, he moved the meat with his knife. "Almost done," he told Harold.

Noticing his coat, he checked it. Laying it on Harold's legs had only created a little dampness on the inside. With it being warm enough in the enclosure, the man was not using any blankets, so Rufus hung the second one onto the frame to dry.

He knew his hunting partner was feeling better when Harold said, "I feel damn foolish sitting here in my long johns."

Putting the mixture of liver and heart onto two plates, he handed one to Jones. "After we eat, I'll check to see if your pants are dry enough to put on."

With the meal finished and another hot cup of coffee in Harold's hands, Rufus went back to the elk. He caught a glimpse of movement in the pines across the stream. The sorrel snorted. "Yes, I know," he told the horse. "I saw them too."

With the pistol in his waist band, he worked quickly with the knife and quartered the elk. Bringing the pack animals over, he loaded the meat onto them. There was more movement on the other side of the stream. One wolf was brave enough to come out and stand in plain sight.

The Hawken was within reach in the scabbard on the sorrel. Rufus thought for a minute about taking a shot at the wolves. If the clothing was dry and Harold was ready to go he would have, but until then, and as long as they stayed near the pines, Rufus figure it was best to leave them alone.

Leading the horses close to the enclosure, he looked back at what remained of the elk. The bloody guts and the head would be damned tempting to the wolves. He felt the items drying. The coat was still very wet. The trouser cuffs and waistband were damp. To his pleasant surprise the blankets and the shirt were dry to the touch.

Harold had stood up and looked at the wolves near the pines. "They're getting up their nerve to come over."

Picking up the boots near the fire, he felt the insides. They were still damp. The wool socks in their packs should solve this. It took almost an hour to break down the makeshift camp and get everything onto the horses.

He had Harold wear the dry coat, and the wet one was tied with the bedroll. Rufus figured he could wrap a blanket around his shoulders and be warm enough. A large, black wolf walked out onto the ice, only a hundred feet from the men.

Standing behind the sorrel, Rufus pulled the Hawken. Patting the animal on the shoulder, he said softly, "Get ready. This will be loud."

Laying the rifle over the saddle, he put the sights on the black wolf. Firing, the horse's head came up and it stepped back. The wolf spun and slipped on the ice as it cried out. It then lay still, its blood spreading on the crystal surface.

Sitting on his horse, hunched over, Harold smiled. "Good shot, Rufus."

"It will give the others something else to chew on and maybe we can get some distance before they start hunting again," Pike replied.

As the remaining wolves howled and growled in the pines, unsure if they should come out, the two men, leading the packhorses, rode through the aspen and back up the swale.

CHAPTER TWELVE

It was April 1825 and the spring thaw had opened the ponds. The water rushing down the Popo Agie was too much for the sink and now flowed along the surface before rejoining the river beyond the rise. After the long winter months sitting around the shanties, the trappers were anxious to be back on the ponds.

The tobacco was gone, as well as the coffee. It would be late June before more supplies came out with Ashley and Henry. The flour, corn meal, salt, and beans were divided so all the groups had some. The company was abandoning the cabin and would be packing the fall furs back to St. Louis. Each man was given a slip of paper with his tally of pelts and furs. They were also given an account of what they owed.

The official ledger would be carried back to St. Louis and then returned to the rendezvous, where the men would be paid. Rufus was the first of their team to be packed and ready to travel. Otis had talked of good trapping to the southwest.

It was mid-morning when the team rode away from the shanty. Johnson appeared to be in a low mood. He had spent most of the winter visiting the company men in the cabin and had hoped that Philo Becker would ask him to help pack the furs east.

The company was interested in only one thing: Getting all the men on the ponds trapping. That suited Rufus just fine. He was on his way to see new places. Remembering Otis' advice, he watched the mountain tops and other landmarks, creating a map of the areas in his mind.

It took a week to reach the first valley they would trap. Rufus felt excitement as he placed his traps. Even the icy water in the pond couldn't dampen his spirits. For most of the last month the men had lived on beans or gruel made with cold flour. Come tomorrow they should have fresh beaver meat for their supper.

Harold and Shorty came back to camp after setting their traps. Rufus had been thankful that Jones had had no effects from his plunge into the stream. Their laughter had been heard even before they came into sight.

Looking at the two men, Rufus said, "You sure are a happy crew."

"We should be," Shorty said. "I got something to show you all tonight."

Johnson had guessed that they had found something good to add to the bean pot. Rufus hoped that they had left a deer hidden or some other kind of meat to surprise everyone. The only one who wasn't guessing was Otis. He said that he liked beans and nothing could make the meal better.

That night, the beans could have used a little more cooking. They had a slight crunch to them. Once the meal was finished, the men sat looking at Shorty. "Well," Johnson said, "What is the surprise?"

Reaching into his possible bag, Shorty brought out a partial twist of tobacco. Everyone broke into a cheer. "I saved it to celebrate our return to the ponds!" Shorty shouted.

Soon everyone was sitting back with a cheek filled with a chew. Nobody spoke and the only sounds heard were when they spat. Everyone saw that the ponds in this area were well-stocked with beaver and they should have a great start to their spring trapping.

Rufus enjoyed being busy again. Each morning they checked their traps. The afternoon was spent fleshing and stretching the pelts. They had plenty of beaver meat or tail for their meals. While they hadn't seen any Indians, the men kept their rifles at hand at all times.

The next valley that Otis took the men to had both bank beavers and some in ponds. Rufus was looking for new challenges and offered to go after the bank beaver. He had gotten good at figuring where the rodents came out of the river or ponds.

As they worked, the valleys came alive with flowers and song birds. The snow receded on the mountains around them. One morning, after checking his traps, Rufus hung the two beaver he'd caught on the sorrel's saddle.

He was walking back to the camp, leading the horse, when he stopped in mid-step. A small herd of deer were grazing about a quarter-mile away. While Rufus had learned to like the taste of beaver, broiled venison steaks sounded a lot better.

Looking around for any cover he could use to get closer to the deer, he frowned. The only cover was beyond the animals and it made little sense to ride miles to come from that side. The deer might even be gone by the time he got into position to shoot.

Tying the sorrel to an aspen, he pulled the Hawken and checked the powder in the pan. He decided he would stalk the deer. Walking slowly, he headed across the valley toward the herd. He hoped to close some of the distance before he started to crawl. As he walked he watched the deer. He froze when one looked up in his direction. He had covered about a third of the distance.

Slowly he went to his knees and waited. After about 20 minutes the deer had turned slightly away from him, but continued to graze. Lying on his belly with the Hawken out front, he crawled using his elbows and toes to move forward. Foot by foot, he worked his way closer.

Tired from the effort, he stopped and rested for a while. Rufus debated if he should try taking a shot. He was now in range of the Hawken, but it was still a long shot. He continued to move forward. The deer were slowly walking as they grazed and keeping the distance nearly the same.

Craning his neck to look back at the sorrel, he realized that he had stalked well over half the original distance. "Come back this way you damn deer," he muttered.

Suddenly the heads came up on the herd. They were looking to the right. Some of them trotted a few steps and stopped. Rufus knew that the time had come. They were still a long shot away, but he'd have to take it.

Slowly getting to his knees, he brought the rifle to his shoulder. Pulling the rear set trigger, Rufus waited for one of them to turn a bit sideways. Then there was a shot and the deer were off, their white tails waving like flags.

"What the hell!" Rufus exclaimed.

"There's one down," someone hollered. "You can bring it to camp."

Standing up, he saw Otis waving at him. "They were my deer!" Rufus yelled.

That night the broiled venison was enjoyed along with Otis' story of watching the great stalk. "I do have to thank you, Rufus," he said, "you drove them right to me."

The first two weeks of May were cold and wet. The trappers searched out a place to dry their catch and chose a rock cliff with an overhang that prevented the rain from reaching the inner wall. The damp weather made drying the pelts a slow process. At one point they built fires along the base of the cliff to raise the temperature around the stretched pelts.

Rufus and Johnson managed to keep their gear dry in the troop tent. They did suffer with the damp, cold feel of their blankets and extra clothing. They had set up camp not far from the overhang in a dense growth of pines. While Otis preferred to keep the cook fire modest, they chose to burn a larger fire in the evening and often late into the night.

In June, when they were taking the tally of their catch, it was down from the fall season. They had dozens of hides still drying and doubted that any beaver caught at this late date would have time to dry. A green pelt would rot if packed for transport to the rendezvous.

Their supplies were all but exhausted. The men hunted every day for something to put on the cook fire. Rabbits, porcupines, grouse, and even snakes were brought back for the cook pot. Otis shot a young buck that had started to fatten on the spring grasses.

Rufus and Shorty were hunting along a river when they flushed some ducks from a pond. Pike drew the pistol and fired from the hip. The ducks continued to fly and he heard Shorty laughing.

"Did you really think you could hit one of the ducks with the pistol?" he asked.

Smiling, Rufus said, "I did not, but it still felt good to try."

"We won't be going hungry tonight," Shorty said. "The pond is surrounded by cattails. Get your knife out. We're going to dig some roots."

Confused, Rufus followed Smith down to the pond's edge and watched him dig near the base of a cattail. Bringing up a root, he tossed it on the bank. Looking up at Rufus he said, "I ain't going to dig by myself. Get on down here."

They came back into camp with a game bag filled with cattail roots. Harold and Johnson wondered what they were. The old, balding man said, "Nice haul. Get them cleaned and I'll fry them. We got fat left from the deer."

While the times were lean and trapping was over, even though they heard beaver tails splashing on the ponds every day, Rufus did not mind it one bit. He loved the life in the mountains. Early flowers were blooming, the days were comfortable, and he had even found some strawberries on a sunny hillside and spent hours enjoying them.

He felt a bit of disappointment when Otis announced that the pelts were dry enough to pack and the group would be breaking camp in two days. They had over a week's travel to the rendezvous site at the confluences of Burnt Fork and Birch Creek.

They had 161 pelts on the packhorses. Otis had hoped that the Flathead would show up again with furs to trade, but it did not happen. He still felt good about their season. Counting the pelts that were sent east after the fall season, they had a total of 474 pelts. If Ashley and Henry paid an average of $2.50 per pound, each man would make $232.

The old trapper knew that if they had been free trappers, they would have each gotten $464 trading at the rendezvous. If they chose to pack them back to St. Louis they would have gotten even more. But as company trappers the men did not have to worry about supplies and packing traps from the east. They were also given packhorses to haul the pelts.

One thing that Otis was thankful for was they had not lost any packhorses. The one going lame had worried him. Should that have caused them to lose the horse, the group would be docked $30 from the pelts. He led the four men with him, feeling good about their year. This was the first rendezvous in the Rocky

Mountains and Otis saw a great benefit not having to pack their catch east.

* * *

It was the June 26, 1825, when Otis and his men rode along the Henry's Fork toward the Creeks. They passed a few groups that had arrived early and made up temporary quarters while waiting to see where the company set up. They saw teepees, tents, and a few quickly assembled shanties.

The men found others from the company near the Birch Creek. Otis chose to camp there. There were a lot of questions about what would happen at the rendezvous. There was a lot of talk about the wet weather in April. Most of the groups trapped less beaver during the spring season.

After the tent was set up Johnson asked, "What do you want first when Ashley gets here?"

Rufus said, "I am looking forward to coffee."

"Do you owe the company a lot?" the smoky-eyed man asked.

"Not much," Rufus said. "Andre set me up pretty good before I left St. Louis."

Johnson stared into the distance for a while and then said, "I think I owe around $90. Everything is damn expensive out here."

Shorty came by, grumbling, "The company train should be here already. I been out of tobacco for a month."

Once their sleeping arrangements were set up, Rufus collected wood for their evening fire. Harold and Otis had been fishing in the creek and had several cutthroat trout lying on the bank. They would be enjoying fish tonight.

Rufus noticed some Ute women picking flowers. As he walked back towards their camp a lean, bearded man caught up with him. "Do you know why the women are picking the heads off the flowers?"

The lean man glanced back at the women and replied without waiting for Rufus to answer. "They brew them for a tea." He then asked, "Did you come in with Otis Bass?"

"I did. The name's Rufus Pike," he told the man.

"My moniker's Walter Gray," the man told him. "I trapped two years with Otis. He knows where the beaver are."

"He led us well this season," Rufus said.

Suddenly the man shouted, "Hey, Otis!" Walking quickly, he headed for the men fishing.

Dumping the arm load of wood, Rufus watched the two old friends get reacquainted. He smiled and thought, *That would be like me and Damas.* The only problem was that Pike could never go back to New Orleans. One quick reaction had changed his whole life. Looking at the mountains around him, Rufus couldn't complain about the change.

Curious, Rufus headed back to the meadow, where the women were picking the yellow flowers. Collecting a large handful, he headed back to the camp. "I am going to make some tea," he announced.

"We got no tea," Johnson said. "Now if you could make some coffee beans appear, I'd like that."

Having caught extra fish, Otis invited Walter to join the camp for supper. Rufus poured the yellow flower tea into the mugs. The taste was not unpleasant, and it was better than drinking hot or cold water with the meal. The only one who complained about the hot brew was Johnson. He said, "It don't taste like tea and it sure as hell ain't coffee."

Once the meal was done, the two old friends went back to the river bank to talk. Rufus joined them, interested in hearing about any adventures. He soon learned that Walter was the son of an eastern banker. His father had lost everything for supporting the Federalists, who were against the War of 1812.

The war ended in 1815 and Walter had been 16 years-old. He had traveled west to the Mississippi River and managed to make a living working on the boats. To make extra money in the winter when boat traffic slowed, Walter had started trapping the tributaries flowing into the river.

Four years ago, he'd met Otis in St. Louis. Liking the idea of trapping in the Rockies, Walter joined him and the two men had trapped together for three years. This past year, Walter had missed the fall trapping due to illness and had traveled out for the spring season. Having no one to partner up with, Otis had joined the Ashley as a company trapper.

Later that evening, Rufus got to talking with Walter about working on the river and found out that the man had spent time in New Orleans. Walter was even familiar with the La Maison but didn't admit to spending much time there. It was full dark and the fire had burned down to coals, when Gray left to head back to his camp. Rufus crawled into his blankets thinking, *What a small world.*

Word came from trappers arriving at the confluence the next day that Ashley's caravan was still two days out. When the rendezvous had been announced, the trappers had been told that the event would happen on July 1st. Those waiting were glad to hear that they would arrive a couple of days early. Everyone started to sort through their packs of furs, wanting to be ready when the trading started.

Some Arapaho and Cheyenne had come to see what the rendezvous was all about. Another group were a mix of French and British. Word was they had left the Hudson Bay Company as deserters. Rufus thought of those who had signed up with Ashley and Henry for three years. If they were to leave and not complete the term they would be considered deserters.

Walter Gray had begun to visit several times a day. If Otis was gone, he would sit with Rufus. Pike liked the man. He was about seven years older than Rufus and had the same love of the mountains. He told Walter about the season's trapping and wintering near the Popo Agie. Rufus told him of the elk hunt when Harold had gone through the ice. He talked of the wolves getting one of the elk. Walter himself had had more than one run-in with wolves after killing an elk or deer.

"It is almost like the sound of the rifle brings them around," Gray said.

On June 29th the caravan with supplies arrived. Ashley noted that some of the men with the company had not come in yet. As those leading the pack animals started to pull the supplies off the animals, several of the trappers came up with their furs, wanting to be the first to trade.

Rather sternly, the general told the men that supplies would not be available until July 1st. He did not want those who got to the rendezvous in the next couple of days to find all the supplies gone. There was a good deal of grumbling as the men disbanded. From a distance they watched as the tents went up and then they caught a glimpse of coffee, tobacco, beans, flour, cornmeal, and side meat being unpacked.

There were also traps, lead, powder, and knives. The men were sure that trade goods like glass beads, hawk bells, ribbon, and cloth were packed in some of the boxes. What nobody had spotted was alcohol. The men had hoped to purchase whiskey or rum and celebrate a little before heading back into the mountains.

One of the large tents was empty except for a crude table made with planks and some kegs that stood out front. The ledgers filled out after the fall trapping would be opened at the table with the number of furs each group sent back east. Additional furs from the spring trapping would be added to the totals, and after supplies bought on account were subtracted, the group would be paid in silver and gold, or by chit if the group planned to spend it all on supplies.

Company trappers were the first to bring in their furs. They in turn would have first choice of the supplies. Next were free trappers, and then the deserters and Indians. Men had lined up before daylight to sell furs. Some boasted that they would have coffee with their breakfast. It was estimated that there were just over 120 attendees at the rendezvous.

Otis and his trappers followed Alfred Wood's group to the table. The ledger listed each man and their share of furs. Rufus heard some muttering that Woods had taken a bigger share for himself. The men with Otis would have to compensate him for the goods used to trade with the Flathead. They had settled on $10 for the musket, $2 for each of the five knives, and another $5 for the foofaraw. These prices fell somewhere in between the St. Louis and the rendezvous cost.

Rufus had few items on account and was paid just over $200, which was the average annual pay for a man working on the boats or in one of the mills. That amount, plus supplies that had a value of $60, was a good year's wages. Rufus also considered that the loan of traps and a packhorse had been included.

He hadn't meant to watch what others had gotten, but he noticed that when Johnson was paid he received $136 after subtracting what he had on account. As Rufus turned to head for the supply tents, a man at the end of the table told him that he was wanted at Ashley's tent.

A feeling of frustration went through Rufus. He wanted to get to the supply tent before all the good stuff was gone. He was most worried about coffee and tobacco. Walter was waiting with some of the other free trappers and called him over.

"Did you have a good year?" Gray asked.

Smiling, Rufus said, "Good enough. I could have earned more dealing faro in New Orleans, but that can be a deadly game."

"I heard the man tell you to stop at Ashley's tent," Walter said. "Did you sign up for more than one year?"

"I figured I better check this trapping out first, so I only signed up for one," he told Walter.

"They are going to ask you to sign up for another year," Gray said, "maybe two. I am looking for a partner to free trap with this fall. I hoped Otis would be the one, but he signed up for two years in St. Louis. If you are interested in partnering up, tell them no."

Rufus thanked him for the offer and headed for Ashley's tent. The truth was, he had planned to trap the coming year with Otis and his group. While Johnson hadn't said anything, Rufus had the feeling he'd signed up for more than one year. If he didn't go with the company, he'd lose half the tent.

When he got to Ashley's tent, he found Philo Becker sitting in front. "Looks like the trading is going smoothly," the man told him.

"They know their business," Rufus said. "It didn't take no time to sell the furs."

"Did you have a good year?" Philo asked.

"I can't complain," Rufus said, realizing that he had nothing to compare it to.

"Ashley believes in paying his company men a fair price," Becker said, "and he needs men like you to stay with the company. I think I can get you some discounts on your supplies if you sign up for two more years."

"I been thinking of maybe one more year," Rufus said.

Shaking his head, Philo said, “I can’t do much for just one year.” Handing the pencil to Rufus he said, “Go ahead and sign the book for one year and I’ll check with Ashley and see what I can get you. I know he’ll be disappointed because he has heard good things about you, but you can always extend another year if you want the best discounts.”

Pushing the book towards Rufus he went into the tent. It was flattering that General Ashley had heard good things about him. He held the pencil and looked at the page. There were several names on the page. None that he was able to read.

He thought about Walter’s offer. Rufus knew that free trappers got more for their furs, but being free meant you were responsible for everything you needed. Becker came back out of the tent with a frown on his face. Rufus noticed he glanced at the book.

“A few others already signed up for one year and they are paying regular prices. Like I told you, the general is a fair man and it wouldn’t be right if he gave you money off for one.” Then Philo lowered his voice. “I’ll talk to the supply chief and tell him to give you extra powder and lead when he weighs your order. Unless you have decided on two years. Hell, I’ll make sure you still get a good weigh on powder and lead plus your discount.”

Rufus’ head was spinning. He felt that if he put down the pencil and did not sign, he would lose all the extras that he’d just negotiated for. He wished he could step away for just a second and ask advice from Otis. He’d be able to tell him what to do. He also knew that Walter was waiting for an answer.

He needed time to think. He needed to decide on one or two years. If Otis was staying only one year, that is all Rufus wanted to sign up for. If Otis was staying two years, then he'd be throwing away all the great discounts by signing for one.

Taking a deep breath, Rufus said, "Give me a few minutes to think about it and I'll be back to sign."

"I got to warn you, Pike," Philo said, his voice having an edge to it. "There are a limited number of slots to fill and if others sign up first, you won't be able to come with the company this year. Also, every hour that goes by there are less and less items to choose from and any discount offers will be gone."

Setting the pencil down next to the book, Rufus thanked Philo and told him he'd be back in just a little bit. He hurried away to find Otis. The supply tents were filled with men grabbing up the goods. The trade tent was now buying free trappers' furs.

Rufus had a feeling of panic. He had messed up. He had been offered a good deal and hadn't signed. Otis was nowhere to be seen and Walter was trading his furs. He felt the amulet under his shirt. Grabbing it he said, "You damn voodoo queen, tell me what to do!"

Walter was coming from selling is furs and had heard Rufus. "Where the hell is the voodoo queen?"

Embarrassed, Rufus took a deep breath. "Do you know where Otis is?"

"Are you going to tell him you're going free trapping?" Gray asked.

"They are offering me a great deal to sign up for two years and I want to make sure Otis will be staying with the company," Rufus told him.

"You know they mark the prices up as much as five times what they cost in St. Louis," Walter told him.

This Rufus did not know, but he wasn't about to admit that to the free trapper. "I just need to check with Otis."

"Well, I am going to buy a little tobacco and coffee from the supply tent," he told Rufus. "Come tomorrow I am leaving for St. Louis with the caravan."

"They're leaving tomorrow?" Pike asked.

"The trading will be over and they want to get the furs back to St. Louis. Company trappers will be heading back into the mountains. It appears you will be one of them," Walter said.

Rufus walked back to his camp, still hoping to find Otis. After six months of trapping together, the group felt like family. That was something Rufus had never expected to have again. Johnson was sitting in front of their tent looking very disappointed. A pile of goods lay next to him including tobacco.

He looked up as Rufus came. He held up a twist of tobacco. "Want a chew?" the smoky-eyed man asked.

Using his knife, Rufus cut off a piece and shoved it into his cheek. He rolled it to get it wet. "Have you seen Otis?"

"After getting what he needed, he went up the river to do some fishing." Johnson said.

"They want me to sign up for two years," Rufus said. "If Otis isn't going for two more years, I only want to sign up for one."

"What the hell do you mean?" Johnson demanded. "We signed up for three years in St. Louis."

"I had never trapped, so I signed up for one in case I didn't like it," Rufus told him.

"Well, you sure as hell better go and sign up for two more years. You own half of the tent," the man said.

He would have thought Johnson was kidding him, except for the bulging veins in his forehead. He wasn't asking Rufus to sign for two. He was demanding it. Rufus felt his hackles rising at the challenge. Suddenly, he realized that he'd looked at the smoky-eyed man as a leader of the two, but he had really been a pain in his behind since they'd gotten off the boat in St. Louis.

Appearing to be a beaten dog as he left the camp, Rufus knew what he had to do. Rather than being beat, a weight had been lifted. He had to find Walter and partner up with him. More than Otis, Rufus suddenly realized that he had felt he owed Johnson from the day he had taken him under his wing on the steamboat. For a year he had been overlooking things the smoky-eyed man had done. He now knew that the smoky-eyed man had been a "hooray for me and the hell with you" kind of friend.

The next morning, Rufus had his gear packed onto the sorrel. The only things he'd purchased at the supply tent was tobacco, side meat, and coffee. Walter was pleased that he'd chosen to partner with him and Otis seemed happy with his decision. Philo ignored him, as he would a bug, and Johnson sat glaring at him even though Rufus had given him his half of the tent.

Harold and Shorty stood waving at Rufus as he rode away with the caravan. As free traders, he and Walter rode at the end of the caravan with a few others. Overall, the first rendezvous had been a success. The trappers liked the fact that they did not have to pack their furs east, and could head straight to the mountains and prepare for the next season's trapping.

Rufus and Walter would not be going all the way to St. Louis. Walter had a supplier in Franklin, Missouri, a week closer than St. Louis. After a couple of weeks in Franklin, they would be heading back to the Rockies. They would not be taking the North Platte route, but rather the Santa Fe Trail.

Rufus couldn't believe how good he felt becoming a free trapper. On the way to the mountains with the company, he had looked back and felt that free trappers were rabble following the caravan. Now he felt like he was somehow better. Not better than the company men, but better off.

On the trip back east, Rufus learned a lot about Walter. He also shared some of his life, but told little of New Orleans. Walter had been trapping for over eight years if he included the time on the Mississippi. Every year he put money aside with a goal to purchase a business in Franklin. He had sold 96 furs at the rendezvous and had received $464 for them.

While Rufus couldn't read, he was good at math and saw a definite advantage in being a free trapper. He knew he'd have expenses for a packhorse and traps the first year, but after that, figuring $100 for supplies, he'd have a good amount of money to enjoy on whiskey, women and cards.

CHAPTER THIRTEEN

Franklin, Missouri was located in an area called Boone's Lick due to salt deposits that made a spring very saline. Evaporating the liquid resulted in excellent salt. The town consisted of 200 buildings and was close to the Missouri River. To say Rufus fell in love with it the day he rode in would be an overstatement, but it did have saloons that served good whiskey and warm women that offered comfort.

As they rode up the dusty main street past a two-acre square, Walter told Rufus that they would need $100 each for supplies, and a horse and traps would cost near $50. Listening to his new partner, Rufus nodded and thought about the money he had to spend on the town's pleasures.

Fully aware of his weaknesses once he started drinking, Rufus made a request that surprised Walter. "Would you mind holding the $150 for me?"

"I can," Gray told him, "but you haven't known me that long."

"No, I haven't," Rufus said, "but I have known me all my life. You'd be doing me a great favor."

That left $41 in his possible bag. If he paced himself, that should offer many evenings of enjoyment. Rufus vowed he would not play cards. He was thinking about the fun he would be having as he handed the holding money to his partner, when Walter said something that wasn't expected.

"There were some buffalo a day's ride out of town. If we shoot one and jerk the meat, we'll cut our supplies by almost a third."

"When would we do that?" Rufus asked.

"I was thinking we'd go tomorrow and maybe four days to jerk the meat, we'll be back here in a week," Walter said. "We'll need to get you a packhorse in the morning."

Riding up to the livery, Rufus swung off the sorrel. A stocky man with yellow-stained teeth came out from the back. Walter knew the hostler and made the arrangements to have the horses ready first thing in the morning. Then he asked, "You wouldn't have a good packhorse?"

"I got a strawberry roan that is a little rough," Sal, the hostler, told him.

"Rough how?" Rufus asked.

"It was a little old when it was cut. Still got the stallion in him," Sal said. "The gelding ain't took to the pack saddle really well."

"What're you asking for it?" Walter inquired.

Rufus looked at his partner. It was he, not Walter, buying the horse. He should be asking the questions. "What are you asking for it?" Rufus repeated.

"I heard Walter," the hostler said. "You're a good friend and I figure y'all will lose a pack or two. Does $20 sound fair?"

Before Rufus could speak, Walter said, "Fair and sold." He then looked at Rufus and asked, "Okay to take it out of the money?"

"Yes," Rufus said, realizing that he'd have some problems making the decisions with Walter around. But it was a good price for the horse. "I will be needing a pack saddle."

"It's a pack animal," Sal said. "It comes with a saddle."

Suddenly Rufus thought, *Maybe I should keep my mouth shut.*

Sal smiled when Rufus asked if he could sleep in the hay loft. "I take it money is tight," the hostler said.

"This year it's tight. Next year, maybe not," Rufus said.

Walking out of the livery, Walter said, "I will be staying at Sal's house if you need me. See you at daylight."

"Damn," Rufus muttered. "Hardly time to unwind."

Of the five saloons in the town, the nearest was called the Frontier House. The front porch had clods of mud left from the last rain. It had all the smells that Rufus loved: Spilt rye, cheap perfume, and a stout ale. The floor was covered with sawdust from the mill just up the river and a long, scarred bar ran along the left wall. Several tables for playing cards or entertaining ladies stood empty at this time of day and to the back was a faro table. In the dim light he could see a short hall with four doors to the back, no doubt where the ladies worked.

The bartender had a square jaw, broad shoulders, and two muscular arms that could take care of trouble. His pride was that he brewed his own ale kept in a cellar below the bar and drawn up with a hand pump.

Seeing the mountain man walking into the saloon, he took a glass and drew a foaming glass of ale. "Welcome to town," he said. "Try some of my best."

Rufus tilted the glass up, covering his moustache with the head. The ale was full-bodied and had a fruity flavor. He liked it and told the owner so.

"My name's Telly, and I own the place. What's your pleasure?" he asked.

"The name's Rufus Pike, and I'll have whiskey," Rufus replied. "And one more thing. I got to be up at daylight to go hunt buffalo."

Laughing, Telly said, "I will send you to your bed before you pass out."

The whiskey was smooth and without pepper. He was taking his second drink when Telly came over with a thick ham sandwich. "You'd best line your stomach with some food first."

* * *

"Your horse is saddled!" a voice shouted.

Moving sluggishly, Rufus pushed the hay away from his face. "I'm awake, Damas," he called back. "Damn," he swore. "I got to get the La Maison."

Sitting up quickly, his head spun and his stomach lurched. Looking around the dim interior, he realized that he was not in Damas' loft and . . . he might still be late.

Crawling over to the ladder, he grabbed the top and swung for the rungs. His boot slipped from the rung and suddenly Rufus was hanging, his hands sliding on the time-polished side rails while he thrashed to find footing.

"Having a little trouble there?" the voice behind him asked. It was Walter.

Finding the rungs, Rufus climbed down. His partner was sipping hot coffee from a tin mug. Steadying himself by holding the ladder, Rufus croaked, "I could use some of that coffee." His throat was dry and his head was pounding.

Sal came over with another mug to help sooth his misery. "I left the roan for you to saddle. He'll wake you up."

Parched with thirst, Rufus drank the coffee too fast and the hot brew tore at his throat. He stood refusing to show any reaction that might give the others pleasure in his discomfort. Out front of the livery was a water trough for the animals. It had a pump at one end.

Working the complaining handle, he filled his mug a couple of times and drank down the cool water. He then used water in the trough to wash his face to help with the cobwebs in his head. Walking back into the livery he asked, "Where is the pack saddle for the roan?"

As Rufus walked toward the animal, the gelding's head was high and it snorted and bared its teeth. "You bite me and I'll bite you right back," he warned.

Setting the pack saddle down, he held the blanket out for the animal to smell. Shaking its head, the horse moved away in the stall. Taking the lead rope, Rufus stepped into the stall, talking softly to the roan. As he talked, he placed his hand on the horse's shoulder, while the horse had the look that it was about to explode.

Sal and Walter stood back watching. There was a tightness in Walter's stomach, fearing that Rufus could very well get hurt. "He's got a way with horses," Sal whispered.

As the roan seemed to settle down, Rufus put the lead rope onto its halter. Thinking the better of it, he walked alongside the animal as he led it out of the stall. There was no way he was going to give the horse a chance to bite him. After tying it next to the water trough, Rufus noticed that the horse settled down when outside.

As he talked softly to the animal, and put the blanket onto its back, he heard Walter and Sal coming. Looking over, he saw that his partner was carrying the pack saddle. "I see you got a way with horses," Walter said.

"The roan probably noticed I was hungover and decided to take it easy on me," Rufus said, making light of the compliment.

As he took the pack saddle and placed it onto the animal's back, he asked Sal, "Where did you get this horse?"

"It came with some I bought from an outfit in Memphis," Sal told him.

"The horse was abused or hurt at some point while in the stall," Rufus said. "I am betting it will be just fine out of the livery."

As he secured the saddle onto the roan, it dipped its nose in the trough and drank. Then it looked back, water from its muzzle dripping onto Rufus' shirt. Leaving the animal near the trough, he went to the sorrel tied up just outside the bay doors. He saw that his blanket roll and the Hawken were next to the wall.

Figuring he'd gotten a good price on the packhorse, Rufus asked Sal, "You wouldn't happen to have some saddlebags that you'd sell?"

"Why, hell," the hostler said, "you just bought a packhorse to carry your things."

"Yes, and I realize you gave me a good price on the animal," Rufus told him, "but my possible bag is getting awful heavy with all the things I have to carry."

"I saw the double saddle holster inside," Sal said. "It had no pistols. Is that why the bag is so heavy?"

Smiling, Pike said, "That and a few other things I like to keep handy."

Heading into the livery, the hostler returned, knocking the dust off a set of saddlebags. "These are better than they look," he told Rufus. "How does $10 sound?"

"It sounds okay, but not as good as $5," he told the hostler.

Sal held the bags up and shook his head, "Any less and I am losing money, but you did take the gelding off my hands. For you $7."

Walter stood by, smiling. His new partner had just dickered himself a good price for the saddlebags. Rufus secured them behind the sorrel's saddle and then tied on the blanket roll. While Walter talked with Sal, Rufus transferred a pistol, his tobacco, the lead and things needed to make balls for the rifle and pistols, and other lesser used items from the possible bag. Giving it a lift, he was pleased with the much lighter bag.

Slinging the possible bag and powder horn over his shoulder, Rufus put the other Kentucky Flintlock into his broad belt with the hatchet and skinning knife. Then, taking the rifle leaning against the livery wall, he slid it into the scabbard.

He led the sorrel to the water trough to let it drink before he tightened the cinch, and then swung into the saddle. Quite satisfied with himself, Rufus watched as Walter led his dun and buckskin with packs from the livery.

As they rode away from the livery, an hour after daylight, Walter asked, "Do you always take so much time to get going?"

"I guess I do," Rufus told him, "but a partner like me is worth waiting for."

Sal heard the two men laughing as they rode toward the river crossing. He was pleased that Walter had found someone else to trap with. Rufus would be every bit a mountain man and someone to watch his friend's back.

The morning sun was warm on their backs as the two men rode out onto the prairie. Rufus found that the roan tended to ride up on the side of the sorrel. Pike accepted that it would take some time before the animal realized its place and followed behind. He was sure that the sorrel would prevent the roan from trying to take the lead.

They passed some free trappers coming with their furs just after crossing the Missouri River. They'd been without coffee or tobacco since early spring. Sharing a little with the men, Walter inquired if they had passed any buffalo. They had come up the Santa Fe Trail and had seen a small herd about a half-day's ride west.

Feeling good that they might have their buffalo as early as tomorrow morning, the two men set off at a trot. It brought back memories of the first buffalo hunt Rufus had been on. He hadn't realized that part of the trip had been on the Santa Fe Trail.

Mid-afternoon, Rufus put up his hand to stop Walter. "We got a rabbit just ahead of us," he said.

Sliding to the ground, Rufus pulled the pistol from his belt. Slowly he walked ahead, until movement by the rabbits stopped him. Raising the Kentucky Flintlock, he put it to full-cock and aimed at the animal 30 feet away. The sound of the pistol quieted the playful chirping of the birds feeding on seeds and insects in the prairie grass. The rabbit lay kicking its last.

Riding up on the dun, Walter said, "That was a damn fine shot."

Laughing Rufus replied, "Just another stump to me."

The sun was getting low in the western sky when the riders spotted some buffalo. A stream lined with cottonwood wound toward the south. Walter knew it would supply the wood they'd need to build the drying racks.

After pulling the gear off their horses, Rufus skinned the rabbit while Walter put together a fire. Once Rufus had the rabbit impaled on the forked stick, he stuck it into the ground over the fire and got out his pannikin for the coffee Walter had started.

As they waited for the meat to get done, they poured some coffee and watched the blazing red sunset in the west. "One thing the big sky of the prairie has is beautiful sunsets," Walter commented.

"It sure does," Rufus replied. "It lasts, unlike disappearing quickly behind the mountains."

The men figured they would have to move the next day to the area where the buffalo was shot, so they just rolled their blankets out under the cottonwoods. The roan was slowly familiarizing itself with the sorrel. After a few snorts and nips from the mare, the gelding recognized its place in the pecking order.

When Rufus sat up the next morning, he saw that Walter had already gone to relieve himself. The sound of sticks cracking alerted Pike that his partner was returning. "We got to get ready to shoot," Gray whispered.

Looking over, Rufus saw that several of the buffalo were at the stream drinking. It made sense to shoot the animal near the stream where the wood for the racks was, rather than killing it on the prairie and having to drag it back.

Pulling his boots on, Rufus took the Hawken from the edge of his blankets and checked the pan for prime. He then asked Walter, "Did you want to shoot the buffalo?"

"You go and knock one down," his partner said. "I'll get some coffee ready."

Weaving his way through the trees along the stream, Rufus stalked the wooly beasts. He worked his way along a cut that led to the river and froze when he heard the deep grunts of the buffalo. Peering over the bank, he caught his breath. Not a hundred feet away were three animals.

One of the females had this year's calf with it. The other would be his target. Slowly he pulled the Hawken to full-cock. The slight metallic sounds would have sent a whitetail bounding away. The buffalo did not even look his way.

On his previous buffalo hunts, Hank Hanson had told him that the best shot was a ball through both lungs. Lining his sights on the buffalo's shoulder just behind the front leg, he pulled the set trigger and then touched off the hair trigger. The .54 caliber rifle slammed against his shoulder as fire and smoke belched out of the barrel.

The buffalo sidestepped and then lurched forward, collapsing onto the prairie grass. The other female raised its head and snorted, as the cloud of spent black powder floated away. It stepped over to the downed buffalo and seemed to be encouraging it to get up. The calf ran a few steps away and stood watching its mother.

After loading the Hawken, Rufus headed back to camp. Walter was slicing some side meat into a small frying pan. "Sounds like you got one."

"Could have had two," Pike replied. "The poor beasts haven't learned to be afraid of the rifle. Makes killing a bunch easy work."

The camp was moved to the downed buffalo. By the time they had reached it, the other animal and its calf had left to join the herd. Walter took his hatchet and started to build the racks to dry the buffalo meat. Remembering the moves from the prior summer, Rufus quickly had the hide skinned down each side.

The main difference was when he went to turn the animal. Now the hide was spread onto the grass to keep dirt off of the carcass. Soon the hide was completely separate from the buffalo. Then the deboning process started. Strips of meat, cut across the grain when possible, were removed.

The drying rack was completed by Walter with several sturdy branches for hanging the meat spanning across two side poles. The side poles were supported by three-foot sticks to keep them above the grass. Using the green branches, Walter built a smoky fire upwind to help keep the flies off the drying meat.

Once the rack was filled with salted meat, the hide was tightly wrapped around the remaining carcass. The two men built a second set of racks and then cut and salted enough meat to fill them. Coarse pepper was also rubbed on the second rack of meat. Rufus had the tongue and liver set aside for their meals. He hung a couple of pieces of the backstraps above the smoky fire to broil for midday.

It took four days to process the meat. The men tested the first rack of meat after 10 hours in the sun. As they chewed the dried buffalo they smiled and nodded to each other. The jerky was wonderful.

The buffalo hide had been fleshed and staked out to dry. They could get $5 for it back in Franklin. Walter had brought leather bags to pack the jerky in and three bags were filled with about 50 pounds in each.

As they rode away from the stream, Walter said, "If we see a young buffalo, Sal would like us to bring the meat back for his wife to can."

"With our gear, we have 100 pounds on each pack animal," Rufus said. "A year-old buffalo would weigh 300 pounds once gutted and the head removed."

Impressed with the knowledge of his new partner, Walter said, "We will keep our eyes open for a year-old buffalo."

They had hardly left the stream when Walter saw some dark clumps moving across the prairie. "We may find our young buffalo right over there."

If they quickly found and shot a buffalo and quartered it for transport, they would arrive at Franklin just after dark. If they spent too much time hunting, they would have to spend another night on the prairie. Rufus really did not care. He did not mind being away from the towns, although, he did miss the whiskey and the companionship it provided.

As they drew closer to the dark masses Rufus spotted a young buffalo grazing away from the herd. Pointing he said, "There's your buffalo. Take your shot Walter."

They were still an eighth of a mile from the animals. That was well within range of the men's Hawken rifles. "Would you like to take the shot?" Walter asked his partner.

"I think it is your turn," Rufus replied. "I'll be ready in case you miss."

Rufus smiled when Walter snorted, "Miss my . . ."

Swinging off the horse, Gray took his Hawken and resting the rifle over the saddle of the dun, he cocked the rifle. The shot thundered across the prairie, flushing two grouse nearby. The buffalo ran a few steps and then stopped, standing with its head down.

"Take your shot," Walter called to Rufus. He then looked at his partner still sitting on the sorrel with his rifle in the scabbard. "What the hell?" he exclaimed.

"Don't worry, Walter," Rufus said. "It is dead on its feet." Just as he finished saying it, the animal sunk to the ground.

It was near midnight when the men rode into Franklin, the pack horses heavily loaded with the meat. Sal had a two-story house a quarter-mile from the livery. Pounding on the door, Walter woke his friend and announced, "We got your meat."

After moving the meat and jerky into a shed in the back, Sal offered to let Rufus stay at the house. "I thank you, but I would prefer the hayloft," Rufus said. "I would like to put the roan in the corral."

"You can put both of your horses in the corral. Give them some hay and grain," Sal said. "There'll be no charge."

Rufus led all four animals to the livery. After pulling the gear off the horses and watering them, he set them loose in the corral and pitched them some hay. It had been a long week and Rufus was looking forward to curling up in the loft. He washed up as best he could in the trough and then looked at the open doors of the livery. In the distance he could hear the music from the Frontier House.

"Damn," he muttered as he strode toward the music.

* * *

Two days later, Rufus was invited to have supper at Sal's. Knowing that he was far from presentable, Pike visited the barber. His shoulder-length hair was again cut above the ear. The beard was gone and an impressive moustache remained. The barber recommended a bath and laundry two miles away near Boone's Lick.

The mineral water used in the bath had a hint of salt to the taste. There was ample hot water that was heated in a large cauldron and Rufus took advantage of it, taking a long soak in their copper tub. He had purchased new clothing at the mercantile, so he left the dirty ones to be cleaned and headed to Sal's.

The hostler's home was located on higher ground than the livery. It was a two-story clapboard home, with a full-length porch on the west side. His wife, Tiny, was a petite, rosy-cheeked woman who carried a few extra pounds, showing her good health. They had one child, a son, who had joined the army and was stationed in the Washington area.

All of the windows were open to let the heat from her cook stove escape. With it were the wonderful smells of a roast and on a window sill sat two apple pies cooling. As Rufus was introduced to Tiny, she gave him a tall glass of sweetened tea that had been cooled in the hand-dug well behind the house that was now used for cooling the milk or, in this case, the tea. The kitchen had its own pump.

Rufus sat in a parlor off the kitchen with Sal and Walter. The conversation tended to lean towards the price of horses, and cost of grain. With little to add to the discussion, Rufus sipped his tea and looked around the home. It was unlike anyplace he'd ever lived. The first floor had a kitchen, parlor, and living room. There were three bedrooms on the second floor. It was smartly decorated, including flowers on the dining table located on one side of the parlor.

The closest Rufus had ever come to this degree of comfort was the cabin he and his father had rented from Camille. Even that didn't begin to compare with the hostler's home. When they sat down to the meal, Sal said grace and then cut slices of the buffalo roast, serving a portion to each person.

Tiny, being rather talkative, told Rufus how much she appreciated him and Walter bringing back the meat. The roast had been saved aside from the other meat that had been canned. She also talked of having pickles, beans, and peas canned. Rufus listened politely as he wolfed down the roast that had been baked with new potatoes and small carrots.

Another thing that Rufus had had little of was the cool, creamy milk served with the meal. When he'd been younger there had been a woman working in one of the saloons who had kept two milking cows. She had always said milking them kept her hands soft.

With the meal finished, hot coffee was served with the apple pie. She had used the last of the prior year's dried apples. Within another month she would be picking this year's crop and promised to make them another pie if they were still around.

Thanking Sal's wife, Rufus and Walter joined the hostler on the porch. They could see the Missouri River and the prairie beyond. "We built up here to make sure nothing could block our view of the river," Sal told them.

As the sky turned red and the sun slid toward the horizon, Tiny joined the men on the porch. "This is my favorite time of day," she told them. Then to Rufus she said, "You must stay the night. Sal said you were staying in the dusty hay loft."

"I thank you for the offer," he told her, "but I need to leave for St. Louis early tomorrow."

"You could leave from here," she replied. "I'll make you a hardy breakfast before you go."

It took some convincing to get her to agree that it was more practical for Rufus to leave from the livery. He would be taking the roan and purchasing his traps and other items from Andre. He expected to be on the Boone's Lick Trail well before daylight.

The next morning, Rufus saddled the roan. After a little crow hopping the horse settled down, accepting the rider. Soon Rufus rode away from Franklin, leading the sorrel. He wanted to give the older horse a break going to St. Louis.

His plan was to make the four-day trip in three days. That meant riding near 50 miles each day. The return trip with his supplies would take four days. His partner Walter was getting anxious to head back to the mountains. He wanted to improve some winter quarters that he'd stayed in during prior years.

After three long days on the trail, Rufus rode up behind the trading post. It was obvious that the shack was vacant, so he put the animals into the lean-to and gave them some of the hay he found there. After using the little house, he went into the back door of the business.

Andre was pleased to see Rufus. He had not expected Pike to come after he hadn't shown up with the other mountain men. Over a mug of coffee, the two men caught up. Rufus told him he was now a free trapper and had partnered with a man named Walter Grey.

"I know Walter," Andre said. "He used to trap with a man named Otis."

"I met Grey at the rendezvous," Rufus said.

"The rendezvous," Andre said. "It will take business from me. Already less trappers have come east to sell furs and buy supplies."

"The price they sell things for is very high," Rufus told him. "Ashley and Henry mark things up four or five times what they buy them for."

Laughing, Andre replied, “If I had to drag the supplies almost 1,000 miles, I might also take that kind of markup.”

The two men had a late meal of stew and fresh bread from a new bakery just up the street. Rufus did not worry too much about his friend’s business. Every year, new men hoping to become trappers came to St. Louis and needed to be outfitted. Mountain man gear from Andre and rifles from the Hawkens would continue to be in demand for years to come.

It was late when Rufus headed for the shack, carrying a candle. He drew water out of the well for the thirsty horses and then gave them more hay. “Tomorrow I’ll get you some grain from Billy,” he promised.

The shack was as he’d left it almost a year ago. Dust from the street had drifted in and settled on the table and other fixtures. He gave the blanket a quick shake, removing a cloud that settled elsewhere in the shack.

Remembering the finished walls covered with pleasing designs in Sal’s home made the rough walls of the shack look crude and anything but homey, but Rufus didn’t mind. The bed slept well and it kept the weather off him. Blowing out the candle, he crawled under the now less dusty blanket.

CHAPTER FOURTEEN

After a strong mug of coffee the next morning, Rufus began to pick out the things he'd need for trapping. Having been in the mountains the year before, he found the task simple, with few decisions to make. Realizing he didn't have the company to lean on for lost items, he did get an extra knife and hatchet.

He also picked up traps, castor, glass beads, hawk bells, trade mirrors, some trade silver, rope, flint, steel striker, a roll of leather, trousers, shirts, wool socks, long johns, low heel boots, moccasins, oilcloth poncho, twists of tobacco, coffee beans, corn meal, white beans, flour, salt, pepper, and several other items needed to survive in the mountains, such as buckskins.

Walter had asked him to pick up a few things for him that included a scythe blade, extra powder and lead, a short handle shovel, and an axe.

Just before midday, Rufus headed over to the livery to say hello to Billy and get grain for the horses. Walking over, he passed as sweet of a girl as he'd ever seen before. She gave him a big smile and got him thinking about this evening. The old hostler was busy cleaning stalls when he got there. "I need a bag of grain for my horse's," Rufus called to him.

Walking out smiling, Billy said, "I see the mountains ain't killed you yet."

"They are as peaceful as a church yard," Rufus said. "A man can get killed on the waterfront in St. Louis quicker than in the mountains."

Scooping some grain into a sack for him, Billy said, "You are right about it being easy to get killed. Over the winter two men got themselves killed in knife fights."

"What were they fighting over?" Rufus asked as he took the bag and gave Billy two bits.

"From what I understand they had scars on their necks and the man challenged them. Claimed they was a murderer from New Orleans." Billy said. "He was mighty good with that knife. Looked like he'd been cut himself at one time. Had a scar down his cheek that went through one side of his nose."

Rufus felt a flash go through his body. Those in New Orleans were still looking for him and it was getting innocent folks killed. "Did they run the man out of town?" he asked.

Shaking his head, Billy replied, "No reason to. They was fair fights." Then he suddenly looked at Rufus. "Damn. You best be careful. Ain't you got a mark on your neck?"

"That I do," Rufus said. "Some time back I was hunting and the horse got startled and ran through some trees. A branch damn near took my head off."

"I wouldn't be hanging around St. Louis if I was you," the hostler said. "That knife-happy bastard cuts first and asks questions later."

Thanking the hostler, Rufus headed back to the shack with the grain. His mind was pondering what he'd just heard. His trading was about done and he could leave for Franklin at any time. His plan was to spend some of what was left from the supply money on whiskey and comfort tonight.

After giving the grain to the sorrel and roan, Rufus headed back into the trading post. Just as he entered the back, a man in a dark, long coat was leaving from the front. He heard Andre say, ". . . and I haven't seen anyone with a scar on their neck in my place."

"Is the man looking for someone?" Rufus asked innocently.

Staring after the man, Andre said, "That man has killed two men who just happened to have scars on their necks. Now he comes in here asking if I'd seen anyone new with a scar."

"I have a scar," Rufus said, realizing that Andre already knew that.

"That I know," LaRue said as he busied himself straightening items on the shelves.

Rufus went to the potbelly stove and poured a mug of coffee. "Did he say why he was looking for a man with a scar?"

"He said a man named Tom Wallingford killed a man playing faro in cold blood," Andre said. "He also said the brother-in-law of the dead man has offered money to anyone that finds this Wallingford."

"I could use the money," Rufus said. "Maybe I will run into this Wallingford."

Andre gave Rufus as stern look. "You must take your things and leave St. Louis. As long as there are men looking for a man with a scar, you are in danger."

The emotion that went through him upon hearing these words from his friend saddened Rufus. The wound had still been new when he had first met Andre, and without question the man had supplied him with some salve and bandages.

Suddenly, Rufus began to speak. He heard the words and they seemed to be coming from someone else. "I was dealing faro in New Orleans. A man at my table was cheating and I called him on it. He pulled a boot pistol and shot me. I had my pistol and fired back, hitting him in the stomach. It was him or me."

As though he hadn't heard the confession, Andre added some cigars to the order and told Rufus, "You are all settled up. It is time for you to go. Say hello to Walter for me and be safe in the mountains."

Leaving by the back door, Rufus went to the shanty and put the pack saddle onto the roan. Leading it back to the trading post, he loaded the packs onto the horse with Andre's help. The men heard thunder in the distance. A storm was coming in off the prairie.

Slipping the Hawken into the scabbard and the extra pistol into his saddlebag, Rufus was almost ready to go. He had the knife, hatchet, and additional pistol in his broad belt around his waist. The horses were aware that they would be traveling and stomped their feet in anticipation.

The two men realized that this was truly goodbye. Rufus would never be coming back. Andre looked at the lean, tall mountain man. "I worked the waterfronts," LaRue said, "and they believe in a life for a life, no matter what the situation was. Some day when the brother-in-law is dead, they will stop looking."

"I will see you again, Andre LaRue," Rufus said as he climbed onto the sorrel.

Drops of rain began to hit Pike and he slipped on the oilskin poncho. It was somewhat stiff and had a strong smell of linseed oil. The rain would keep the animals cool along the Boone's Lick Trail. Rufus didn't plan to push them as hard as the trip to St. Louis. As it was, he was leaving a half-day earlier than he'd planned. Smiling, he figured with more money left also.

As he rode, the stress of the past few hours in St. Louis faded away. A steady drizzle was falling and Rufus was dry under his new poncho. He wished he'd gotten a bottle before leaving the city. It would have been nice to have a few drinks during the evenings on the trail.

Suddenly his thoughts were interrupted by a man on the side of the trail, kneeling next to his horse. "You got a problem with the horse?" Rufus asked.

"I don't know," the man said. "It seems to be limping, but I don't see anything wrong with the shoe or hoof."

Swinging off the sorrel, Rufus said, "I'll take a look."

As Pike was walking toward the horse, the man stood up. He was wearing a long, black coat. "I believe I have been looking for you," the man in black said.

"I don't believe we've met before," Rufus replied, acting confused.

"A little gal had told me she met a man a year ago that had a fresh wound on his neck," the man said. "Today she came and told me she saw the man walking from the trading post to the livery."

Feeling a chill go through him, Rufus asked, "How are things in New Orleans?"

"You'll know when I get you there," the man snarled. "Then again, you are going to be dead."

The sadistic man pulled out a knife with a razor-sharp 12-inch blade. "I think you killed my friend on the water front. I will enjoy watching you die."

Rufus reached under his poncho. "Good luck with that skinning knife. I was hoping you'd put up a fight," the man said, noticing the move. He began to circle Rufus, no doubt fancying himself as the better man with the knife.

Pulling the Kentucky Flintlock from under the poncho, Rufus coldly looked at the man. As he pulled the trigger, he saw the man's eyes grow large. The pistol recoiled in his hand, and the .54 caliber ball, struck the knife wielding man in the center of his chest.

Feeling no remorse, Rufus watched him fall to the muddy trail, the knife still clutched in his hand.

* * *

The sky was blue, with white, puffy clouds drifting past, casting shadows on the prairie grass as Rufus and Walter rode away from Franklin, Missouri. They were full from the breakfast of fried potatoes and eggs that Tiny had made them earlier.

Walter looked over at his friend. "I been meaning to ask you about your trip to St. Louis. I tend to get busy just before heading west, trying to make sure I have things we'll need."

"I had a good visit with Andre," Rufus said. "Did you notice I came back with some money?"

"I did at that," Walter replied. "You sure made up for it, the night you got back. The Frontier House will never be the same."

"It took a lot of whiskey to get me thinking straight," Rufus told him.

Laughing, Walter said, "Telly said you were with two women."

Smiling at the memory, Rufus said, "I also needed a lot of comfort."

They were riding along the Santa Fe Trail rather than following the Platte River. The men would be trapping south of the Wind River Range in Mexican territory. There wasn't any conflict between the United States and Mexico at this time. The only worry the two men had was the Apache or Comanche tribes. When not fighting each other, they took offence to travelers on the Santa Fe Trail crossing their lands.

Walter wanted to trap an area south of the rendezvous. He was aware of a marshland that had a good number of beavers. Rufus was half listening to his new trapping partner as they rode. Walter talked of knowing when an area became less profitable and the need for finding a new one to trap.

The trapping season was relatively short in the mountains, providing prime pelts for only a couple of months. Days wasted at a depleted area would cost them money. While Rufus didn't recognize it, Walter's thinking came from the influences of his father being a banker.

Rufus was slapping at a deer fly buzzing around his head when he heard his partner say, "We are being watched."

"What?" Rufus asked. "Where do you see . . ."

When Walter kicked the dun he was riding and took off, Pike sat low in the sorrel's saddle, clung to the gelding's lead rope and followed his partner away from the trail. He could hear the shrill yells of the Comanches who had been watching for travelers.

Walter had caught sight of movement in some boulders further up the trail. There was little cover in the area and the riders were thankful to find a dry riverbed. The two men entered it at a full gallop in a cloud of dust. Pulling up at the bottom, the partners pulled their rifles and slapped the animals, heading them further down the wash.

Scrambling back to the bank, they could see eight braves bearing down on them. Walter was the first to fire, hitting the lead horse and causing it to veer, spilling its rider. Rufus sighted on the riders with his Hawken and fired. He didn't watch to see if he'd had any success, but rather began to reload the rifle as the smoke from his first shot drifted away.

With the sun burning down on them, the two men continued to fire. Their first shots had split the band of Comanches and they rode wide before turning back toward the riverbed. Rufus fired at those on the left, managing to inflict enough damage to force them to dismount. Walter had brought down two horses from those to the right and at least one brave lay in the open, either wounded or dead.

They had succeeded in stopping the Comanches before they reached the riverbed, and the braves were now dismounted, working their way closer. "It's time to run," Walter said.

The horses were 50 yards down the riverbed, having been stopped by a tangle of debris. Clinging to their rifles and keeping low, the two men headed for the animals. The sound of arrows clipping the cottonwoods lining the riverbed, and an occasional musket shot from the braves spurred the partners on as they ran for dear life toward the horses.

Scrambling onto the saddles with their packhorses' lead ropes in hand, they urged the horses up the far bank and were soon galloping across the buffalo grass. Other than another musket shot and some shrill cries, the two men quickly put distance between themselves and the Comanches.

A mile from the riverbed they slowed the horses to a walk, and Walter led the way west along a boulder strewn valley. They stopped near some cottonwood that shaded a small pond. Since leaving the dry riverbed neither man had uttered a word. Swinging out of the saddles, the men loosened the cinches and let the horses drink sparingly from the pond.

Adrenaline was still coursing through Rufus' veins and his hands were shaking. Tilting his hat back, he splashed water onto his face. "I'd say we came out of that scrap quite well," he heard Walter say.

"I didn't see them up the trail," Pike admitted.

"Luck was on our side," Walter told him. "One of the braves decided to get in a better shooting position as we rode toward them. It was a quick movement, but it didn't fit. I figured it wouldn't be healthy to get any closer."

"You say it didn't fit," Pike replied. "It could have been a cat or even a bird. How did you know we needed to run?"

Smiling, Gray said, "I didn't know, but a short run away from the boulders would let us know if it was danger or not, and as it turned out it was. We also had a good jump on them, allowing us to get set up in the riverbed."

"It was a good thing you saw the riverbed," Rufus said.

Chuckling, Walter replied. "I didn't see the riverbed until we got to it. We were damn lucky it was there."

* * *

Other than spending a night in a Cheyenne village and sharing meals with a few freighters, the rest of the trip toward the mountains was just the two riders on an open trail. As they approached the mountains, they traveled through heavy cloud cover and periods of rain for several days.

The inclement weather continued as they reached the foothills. Rufus shot a mule deer on a pine-covered hillside. While Walter scavenged for dry wood to build their evening fire, Rufus skinned the animal and cut some steaks for their meal. It was after dark by the time they'd eaten and did a final check on the horses.

"We head north come morning," Walter told him.

"How many more days before we get our traps wet?" Pike asked him.

"We should be knee-deep in beaver ponds by this time next week," Gray replied. "If the rain lets up, we should make it to my cache in three days. Maybe a day or two to get my traps oiled and then to the ponds."

"There are a few stars peaking out of the clouds," Rufus said. "My guess is it will be clear tomorrow."

Just in case the good weather prediction was wrong, the men set up a fly tarp to store their gear and sleep under. Well after Walter crawled under his blankets, Rufus remained near the dying fire. He breathed deep. The smell of the air had changed. He was sure the rain was gone. Above him, more and more stars appeared between the clouds.

Rufus woke to the sound of his partner breaking up sticks for their morning fire. The air was cold and his blankets were warm. Groaning, he rolled over and crawled out from under the tarp. "My God," he breathed.

To the west rose a 14,000-foot mountain. As if by magic, it appeared on the horizon once the clouds and haze had blown away. In late summer the top remained snow-covered and glistened in the morning sun.

"That's Pike's Peak," Walter called to him. "It was named after Zebulon Pike. Maybe he was kin of yours."

His hand went to the amulet under his shirt as Rufus recalled Camille holding it up and declaring that his name would now be Rufus Pike. "We're not kin, but we do share last names," he told his partner.

The two men spent an additional day in the camp, drying out their gear and admiring the mountain. They moved the horses several times, putting them on fresh grass to graze. Walter got out a file and worked on the animals' hooves while Rufus washed a few items of clothing in a nearby stream.

It felt exhilarating to be back in the mountains. Pike hung the clothing on some nearby bushes and went to collect some additional firewood. The air was fresh from the rain and the sunshine warmed the body and soul.

Dropping an armload of wood near the fire, Rufus looked over at his partner tending to the horses. This was his second trip to the mountains and he had always depended on others to guide him to the ponds. Rufus wondered how long it would take before he had the knowledge that Walter and Otis had. His thoughts were interrupted as Walter finished with the horses and tapped the file against a stump.

"The hooves are in good shape," Gray announced. "This evening we can give them a good brushing and we will ride out of here looking right smart."

"You are going to make a damn good hostler once you get your livery," Rufus remarked. "I swear you're happier with horses than with people."

Without comment, Walter smiled as he stuck the file into his packs and commenced making some afternoon coffee. Rufus assisted by stirring the coals and adding wood to the fire. The two men seemed to anticipate what the other needed, and without a word pitched in to do it.

The next morning the packs were loaded onto the horses and the men rode north toward the South Platte River. The region they were heading for was a territory inhabited by the Ute tribe, as well as some Cheyenne and Arapaho. At this time there was little hostility between the trappers and the Ute, but their horses would still be looked upon as a prize.

Walter's first objective was his cache. Their stay there would be short, due to Gray having trapped the area the year before. Rufus followed his partner, paying special attention to the landmarks and mountain peaks. He was determined that a time would come when he'd be the one leading others into the mountains in pursuit of the beaver pelts.

As they followed streams and rivers that flowed through the mountain valleys and meadows, Rufus marveled at the beauty of the green hills and wild flowers, with their color splashed across the grass-covered knolls.

Several times he saw beaver lodges in dammed-up streams and wanted to ask Walter why they didn't stop and set traps? While he had a year of trapping behind him, Rufus still realized that he was still somewhat of a greenhorn, and with luck time would make things make sense.

The two men were riding abreast of each other across a wide valley with several ponds and a fair amount of beaver activity. Rufus was sure this had been his partner's goal. Walter pulled up and pointed to a rock ledge with a tangle of windfalls.

"That there is where I have my cache," he told Rufus. "I figure we will winter in this valley."

Somewhat skeptical, Pike stood in his stirrups and squinted at the ledge, expecting to catch the outline of a cabin. "Are you talking about a cabin in the trees to the right?" he asked.

Grinning, Walter replied, "Nope. It's right under all them dead trees against the ledge."

Leading the way, Gray rode toward the rock ledge. They were only 100 feet from the tangle of evergreen poles and Rufus still saw nothing. Walter swung out of the saddle and walked up to the base of the ledge. He took hold of one of the weathered spruce poles and pulled it. On the far side it was connected to a half dozen others and it swung back, exposing an opening into a cave.

Dismounting from the sorrel, Rufus looped the reins and lead rope of his horses on some small bushes. "I'll be damned," he said. "How did you ever find this place?"

"It was just a cave in the rock ledge the first time I come here," Walter told him. "To the east was a stand of spruce that a windstorm had taken down. I spent a summer limbing and dragging the spruce over here and piling them in front of the cave opening.

What you see is the result. A perfect cache that can't be spotted by anyone riding by."

"Where do you keep the animals in the winter?" Rufus asked.

"Just beyond on the other side is a fine meadow with plenty of grass for grazing," Walter said. "I haven't spent a winter here yet, but if the weather got too bad, the cave has room for the horses."

His partner led the way into the cave. The opening in the spruce provided some light to the dim interior. The cave was cool and had plenty of height. Rufus noticed that there was an opening in the ceiling of the front room that exited somewhere in the rock ledge and he could see light toward the top.

There was the sound of water dripping, and Rufus mentioned it to Walter. "That's water running into the pool a bit further back. I store my cache just beyond the pool. The cave gets a little lower as you go back. I never explored beyond that to see how far it goes."

Rufus stumbled on some rocks just below the ceiling opening. "What the hell?" he said. "Do you build a fire right here?"

"I spent a rainy week in hear a few years back and tested the vent in the ceiling. It drew smoke like a fine chimney," Gray told him.

The cave impressed Rufus. It would make a good cache for their extra supplies and concerns about winter quarters were gone. The next couple of days were busy. Their extra supplies for spring trapping were moved into the cache and Walter got the traps and other gear he needed for the fall season. Once they were finished, the spruce pole opening was closed, making the cache invisible.

CHAPTER FIFTEEN

As the two men rode down the valley, leaving the cave behind, Rufus' thoughts were swirling with questions. Walter had not been very forthcoming about the areas they would be trapping. He had also given Rufus very little information about the cave he used as a cache.

Other than what little he mentioned about building the enclosure, he never spoke of others who might know of the cave or whether he'd originally planned to spend winters in it. The nights that the two of them had spent there gave Rufus the feeling that it had been inhabited before.

The fire pit in the cave was perfectly positioned to take advantage of the vent in the ceiling. In the light of their evening fire, he could see crude furniture that would make an extended stay more comfortable. The area around the vent was blackened by previous fires. It could have been from prior residents, but if it had been tribes in the area, they would have used hides and furs to sit on and would have had no need for the furniture.

"You mentioned that we would be trapping soon," Pike said as they passed a pond with three lodges.

"We'll be at our first location by noon tomorrow," Walter informed him.

"You wanted to leave this pond for another year," Rufus said. "What if someone else comes in and traps it while we are gone?"

Staring straight ahead, Gray replied, "We don't own the ponds or the beaver. If this place is trapped, we will find another area. There is always another place with beaver."

The next day, when they crested the ridge above their destination, Rufus caught his breath. The valley below had several streams coming down from the mountains lining the sides. Several had been dammed up by the beavers. The valley had a good growth of aspen that the beaver used for dam building and food.

Walter said that the valley was all of five miles before it turned to the north. How far it continued would be discovered as they worked through the ponds. Walter led the way about a mile into the valley and stopped at a dilapidated lean-to.

Noticing the look of confusion on Rufus' face, Walter said, "It don't look like much right now, but with a little fixing up it will work out well until the snow flies."

"It won't take much to prop it back up and add poles to the roof, but it is kind of small," Rufus pointed out. "Where do we dry and store our pelts?"

"There is an overhang on the ledge behind the lean-to that is dry and has plenty of room for our catch," Walter explained.

The afternoon was spent making the necessary repairs to the lean-to and cutting stakes to secure the traps. A fire crackled in the new firepit located in front of the opening and was boiling a pot of beans for their supper.

As he passed the fire, Walter gave the pot a stir and said, "We need to set some traps before dark. With luck, we'll be eating beaver meat tomorrow."

With the lean-to finished and the last of the stakes peeled, Rufus looked at his partner. "It's time we got some traps wet."

With nothing left to prevent them from heading into the ponds, the two men got their traps and hung them from the sawbuck saddles on their pack horses. Leading the animals to the nearest pond, they soon had their first traps set.

That evening, while sharing a meal of beans washed down with coffee, Walter told Rufus about trapping this valley with Otis. They had had some bear trouble and had finally had to suspend trapping and devote time to hunting the grizzly. Their conversations were still somewhat general, having only known each other since June. By the time they'd spent the winter together in the cave, there was little doubt that they would know most details about each other's lives. Maybe it would take more time for Rufus to talk of New Orleans.

The valley proved to be a bonanza, keeping the two men busy setting traps, skinning and fleshing the beaver pelts, and making additional hoops for stretching the furs. By late October they were riding four miles to set their traps. Walter talked of moving to a new base near the bend in the valley. They had over 87 pelts dried and folded for transport. They also had a dozen stretched on hoops in some stage of drying.

The overhang would be a good place to cache the processed pelts until they were ready to ride back to the cave. "We'll pull the traps today and make our move tomorrow," Walter said.

Rufus felt excitement run through him. For almost two months he had gazed in the direction of the bend and wondered if it had the same bounty of beaver as this end. Tomorrow he would find out.

* * *

The two men rode away from the lean-to to check the traps and pull them. Rufus walked into the pond and felt the slick bottom slide under his moccasins. Taking care, he moved through the water and suddenly smiled as he noted that the stake was leaning. He had another beaver.

The two men had three beaver to process when they got back to the lean-to. Riding the sorrel and leading his roan, Rufus talked on about the number of beavers they had taken so far. Water was still dripping from his buckskin pantlegs when Walter suddenly pulled up. He raised his face up and sniffed the air.

"What is it?" Pike asked.

"Bear," Walter growled. "There is a damn bear in the area."

"How do you know?" Rufus asked.

"Can't you smell it?" Walter asked. "The stink of it is in the air."

There were always various scents in the air. Rufus could smell the rain coming, or if a polecat had been in the area, or even a hint of smoke that didn't belong. But it wasn't until they got closer to the lean-to and the smell was stronger before he picked it up. The horses had become noticeably nervous.

The men's eyes grew wide as they arrived at the lean-to. Their packs of supplies were ripped open and scattered in front of the structure. The left wall of the lean-to had been pushed out and the roof was sagging. There were piles of scat and some vomit in front, near the pot of spilt beans.

Leaping off the sorrel, Rufus ran, stumbling through the trees to the ledge. Their pelts had not been touched. Relieved, he walked back to the lean-to and heard Walter say, "Our damn tobacco made the bear vomit."

As the two men cleaned up the camp and salvaged what they could from their supplies, the smell of the bear was indelibly etched into Rufus' brain. The only tobacco they had left was that in their possible bags. A partial bag of cornmeal and some beans were all the supplies that were left. Their side meat, cold flour, and jerky were gone. Being late in the season, the amount was not that much, but without it, beaver meat and little else would have to sustain them until the two men went back to the cache.

Rufus joined Walter to follow the tracks out of their camp. By the size, his partner estimated that the bear was full-grown and something more than 400 pounds. They stopped at the pond that the bear had drank from before it went north toward the pine covered foothills.

"We may have to leave this area," Walter said. "The damn bear won't forget the easy meal it got at the lean-to."

"I'm going after the bear," Rufus declared.

"Do that and you'll become its next meal," his friend warned.

"We have a short time to finish the fall trapping and good trapping left in this area," Pike said. "Looking for another area will cost us pelts and the damn bear might just follow our trail to get the last of our beans."

As they walked back to camp, the two men debated the risks and benefits of going after the bear. At one-point Walter said the he was also going to go after the bear if Rufus went.

"We both can't go," Rufus argued. "One of us has to keep trapping. In a couple of weeks, we'll be busting ice to get into the ponds."

"Then I should go," Walter said.

Smiling, Rufus said, "You don't have a charm to protect you from the bear and I do."

"And what would that be?" Walter demanded.

Pulling the amulet out from under his shirt, he showed it to his friend. "This here was made by a voodoo queen and protects me. It will prevent the bear from getting its teeth in me."

Snorting, Walter replied, "I'll end up finding that damn charm in the bear scat along with what is left of your bones."

As Rufus put a few things together, his friend continued to grumble as he began to skin the beaver. Suddenly he hollered, "If you get yourself killed, I ain't going to carry your furs out for you."

"Well I don't care if you do or . . ." Suddenly he realized what his friend had said and began to laugh. "I guess I best not get killed then so I can carry them out."

Rufus left his packhorse and saddled the sorrel. If the bear attacked them, he didn't want to leave Walter without enough stock to pack out the furs. If he got the bear, he could lead the sorrel and pack out the hide and some of the meat.

With his horse ready to travel, Rufus checked the load in his Hawken. Walter's face was sober as he walked over to give his friend some final advice. "The bear's been eating whitebark pine nuts. I saw it in the scat. They are partial to them. There is a good stand of white pine northeast of here and the bear will go there to feed. I can't say when, but it will be there."

"I won't take any chances, Walter," Pike promised. "I'll be back to finish the season's trapping."

* * *

The tracks from the pond were easy to follow. Springs kept the ground soft. The satisfied bear appeared to have a destination in mind and walked in a direct route. At one time it stopped, rubbed up against and clawed a tall aspen. Rufus shuttered at the reach of the bear. It was a big one.

After a couple miles, Pike pulled up and noted the direction the bear was heading. It had turned to the southwest. Walter had talked of pines in the northeast. Rufus decided to go to the pines and wait for the bear. If the bear winded him on its trail, it might lie in wait for him and ambush him and the sorrel. As he followed the tracks, he'd felt the tension build inside not knowing how far the bear was ahead of him. As soon as he turned to the northeast, Rufus felt the tension ebb.

A half-hour later, the pine-covered hills came into view. Evidence of scat told him that the grizzly had been this way. The bear was a solitary animal and it was unlikely that more than one would be in the area.

As Rufus slowly rode toward the pines, he searched for a place to watch for the grizzly. He had a high degree of confidence that the bear wasn't back into the pines yet. When it had left their camp, it had a different destination in mind.

Entering the pines, he got his first whiff of grizzly. It was faint, but the smell left no doubt. Evidence of broken branches, claw marks, and an abundance of pine nuts gave Rufus confidence that the bear would be back. He spotted an outcrop of rock half-way up the hillside. Sliding off the horse, he led the sorrel toward it.

If there was a safe place to put the horse, the outcrop would be an ideal place to wait for the bear's return. As he approached it, he saw an open meadow above the trees that would offer grazing for the sorrel.

It was late afternoon and some time was needed to allow the horse to graze.

Taking a quick look at the outcrop, he noticed that the upper side would give him access to the top. Satisfied, Rufus led the horse up to the meadow and picketed it on the golden grass. The tension he'd felt earlier had returned. He was now in the grizzly's lair.

Building a small fire, Rufus broiled some meat from the beaver. What little coffee they had left, he'd let Walter keep. Chewing on the stringy meat, he washed it down with water from his canteen. All the while, Rufus listened for any sounds of the bear's return.

That evening, he brushed the sorrel to help calm his nerves. His thoughts were four miles away at the lean-to. By now Walter would have the gear packed, with plans of an early start to move the camp further down the valley. Rufus also planned an early rising, to be on the rock outcrop well before daylight.

It was still dark when Pike threw off his blankets. The air was brisk and the meadow grass was covered with a light frost. He had chosen a spot to leave the sorrel the night before and, pulling the picket pin, he brought the horse to the grove of spruce.

The sky was clear and the moon had already gone down, so with only starlight to guide him, Rufus headed for the outcrop, the Hawken across his front, ready for any surprises. He knew that it might be days before the bear's travels brought it back to this stand of pine, but whenever it did happen, he had to be ready.

Endeavoring to move as silently as possible, Rufus finally reached the top of the rock. It was not as smooth as he had hoped, and lying on the frost-cracked top wasn't comfortable. He briefly thought about cutting some pine boughs but then scolded himself. *You aren't making a damn bed.*

The chill of the morning was soon gone and the bright sun in the blue sky blazed down on him. Rufus removed his wool shirt and used it to lie on. His eyes grew heavy as he watched the pines and valley below. Twice he had caught sight of movement. Once it was a bobcat and the other was a family of raccoons that had come to eat the pine nuts.

By the third day of watching, Rufus was out of food and realized that he'd have to quit early and do some hunting. He had decided that if the raccoons came back he would shoot one. Rufus had his eye on a squirrel that was making quite a racket as it went from branch to branch, chewing and dropping pine cones. His stomach growled and the squirrel was looking tastier and tastier.

The scream of his sorrel brought Rufus out of his thoughts as he whirled around. He couldn't see the animal in the spruce grove. There was crashing and more screams. Suddenly the horse burst out of the spruce, trailing its picket rope. Close behind it was the grizzly!

The grove was over 300 yards away and the horse was running across the meadow, taking the bear further away. The charging grizzly took a swipe at the rump of the horse and just managed to clip it, turning it back towards the pines.

Wide-eyed, Rufus shouted as he watched the life and death chase, thankful that they were no longer moving away. Sighting in on the grizzly, he said a prayer as he touched off the hair trigger. Smoke and fire belched from the Hawken and a .54 caliber ball streaked across the meadow, striking the bear. The grizzly threw its head up and growled, breaking its stride momentarily. The horse that was just a step or two ahead of the bear managed to gain a few feet before the bear recovered and continued after it.

Nearly in a panic, Rufus reloaded the Hawken and primed the pan. As he brought the rifle back to his shoulder, the frantic horse and angry grizzly were about to enter the pines. With no time to spare, Rufus sighted and fired. He cried out in anguish as he witnessed the second shot having no effect on the bear. Then the bear and horse were gone into the trees, branches cracking and crashing as they disappeared.

Fighting the urge to run carelessly after them, Rufus took a moment and loaded the Hawken. Once finished, he scrambled off the rock outcrop, banging his knees and scraping his right hand as the left clung to the rifle. Reaching the bottom, he ran blindly in the direction the horse and bear had gone. A windfall caught his boot and sent him sprawling onto his stomach, knocking the wind out of him.

Gasping for breath, Rufus regained his feet and continued after the animals. He could not believe the grizzly had come into the pines from the meadow. As he busted through brambles and branches in pursuit of the bear, he scolded himself for not having scouted the area more thoroughly.

Finding where they went through the pines, he slowed to a walk. The last thing he wanted to do was run carelessly into a wounded bear. Memories of the last shot having no effect on the grizzly worried him. Had he shot too fast and missed?

A spattering of blood on the pine needles and branches confirmed that he had hit the bear at least once. Then he remembered the bear clawing the horse. It could be blood from the sorrel. The fleeing horse had entered the pines in a dense area, smashing branches as it went. Rufus saw more blood as he followed the broken branches. He vowed that even if the bear caught the horse, it would never live to eat it.

Other than his own breathing, the pines were silent. The sharp branches tore at his long john top as he pushed his way through. Rufus realized that the wounded bear might lie in wait. He no longer cared. He felt as cold as steel and just wanted to put another shot into the behemoth.

Suddenly, the smell of the bear was strong. He stopped and his heart began to pound. The grizzly was nearby. Fearful of taking another step, Rufus waited and listened. The dense brush in front of him could easily hide the animal. Slowly, he took another step. There was a sound. Fighting to hold his breath, he listened. It was raspy breathing.

It was coming from just in front of him! Rufus saw that there was a depression 20 paces in front of him. The grizzly was waiting in it for him to get close enough to grab. Moving slowly to the side, a branch snapped, almost stopping his heart. His hands were sweating on the Hawken. Rufus no longer felt like cold steel. He found it hard not to flee and feared his legs would give out if he did.

Another sound came from the depression. It was sort of a growl, but with his heart pounding in his ears, Rufus couldn't be sure. All of a sudden, he saw brown hair just above the depression. It moved back out of sight. The bear was waiting for him.

Unable to help himself, Rufus shouted, "Come out of there already, you bastard!"

Silence. All Rufus heard was silence. With the rifle at the ready, he moved closer to the depression. Then he could see the grizzly. It lay in a tangled heap among the broken branches. Picking up a stick, Pike prodded the animal. There was no response. The grizzly was dead.

Rather than feeling excitement over the kill, Rufus felt drained. He sank to the ground, shaking, and stared at the large, male grizzly. He felt the amulet against his chest. "You did it again, Camille," he whispered.

It was several minutes before Rufus regained his feet and continued down the hill in search of the sorrel. He was certain that it would be injured from the chase and his next task would be to put it out of its misery.

Fending off the branches that seemed determined to poke an eye out, Rufus worked his way down the hillside through the pines. Several times he slipped on the bed of needles, or stumbled on the debris beneath the trees. The normally quiet mountain man paid little attention to how much noise he was making.

As Rufus came out of the pines onto the valley floor, he looked back, realizing that the sorrel might have never made it off the hillside and could be lying injured. The picket rope may have snagged and snapped the animal around, bringing it down.

Rufus decided to walk along the edge of the pines and look for any sign that the sorrel might have come out. First, he walked to the east, staring intently at the ground. After going a mile, he felt sure that the horse wouldn't have veered any farther.

Again, he spent time looking out onto the valley. The dense thickets of poplar made it difficult to see any distance. He could see a pond that they had overlooked with several lodges. "There are damn beaver everywhere. Where the hell are you horse?" he muttered.

Walking back toward the west, Rufus could feel the burning in his stomach. Was it hunger, or was he going to be sick? Unsure, he continued. If he did not find any sign beyond the point where he'd come out, Rufus realized he would have to work the hillside in the pines.

"You damn fool," he scolded himself. "You should have started looked for the horse at the spot where the bear went down."

About a half-mile past the point where he'd come out, Rufus finally saw the tracks of the horse. He also saw blood. Dread washed through him. The sorrel might have been severely injured when the grizzly raked its rump with its claws.

The tracks led out toward a stand of aspen. With the trail plain to see, Rufus walked briskly. The horse had still been at a gallop until it turned at the trees. It had stopped at one point and evidence of more blood was found.

All of a sudden, a disturbing thought came to Pike. In his haste to fire the second shot, could he had swung the Hawken too far and hit the horse? The bear and horse had been only a few feet apart.

Angry with himself, Rufus shouted, "That's stupid thinking!"

Then there was a whinny. His heart leaped as he realized the horse had heard him. Forcing himself to walk so he wouldn't frighten the injured animal, Rufus made his way through the poplar. As he came out the other side, there was the sorrel, standing and staring at the mountain man.

"The bear is dead," he said to the animal in a soft tone. "I am here to help you."

As he slowly approached the horse, the sorrel shook its head and started walking towards him. Rufus held out his hand as he reached the animal and carefully took hold of the halter. Somewhere during the chase, the picket rope had broken and only a few feet remained.

For the next hour, Rufus went over the animal, assessing its injuries. The swipe across the back of the horse had bled, but was not deep. With proper care it would heal, leaving scars but no permanent damage. One ear was split, and there were several additional scratches from the muzzle to the tail, caused by crashing through the pines. Again, these were not severe.

Using the grass, Rufus wiped as much blood as he could from the right back leg. Then, taking what remained of the picket rope, he led the horse back toward the pines, leading it well around the bear.

Once he had the horse settled back in the spruce, Rufus took his Hawken and headed back to the grizzly. He had wanted to use the horse to drag the carcass to the valley floor and then skin it out, but it had been favoring the right back leg during the climb back to their camp. It could be due to bruising from the blow of the bear. It wouldn't be right to force the horse to go back near the grizzly that had just hours ago been intent on bringing it down and killing it.

Arriving back at the grizzly, Rufus looked at the large carcass. He realized that it would take a team of horses to pull it out of the gorge it had collapsed in. It was also entwined with trees it had taken down. With regret, he realized that this would be the behemoth's resting place.

"I ain't going to pass up getting a meal out of you," Rufus said as he pulled his knife.

CHAPTER SIXTEEN

It was the next evening when Rufus led the horse into Walter's new camp. He found his friend near the fire, busy skinning some beaver. Walter looked up and smiled. "Looks like you didn't find the bear."

Tying the sorrel to a sapling, he removed a pack hanging from the saddle. Tossing it near the fly tarp, he joined Walter. "I got the grizzly, but not until it damn near killed the horse."

"Where is the hide?" Gray asked.

"Still on the damn bear," Rufus replied.

"Hell," Walter said, pausing from his work. "A grizzly hide is worth as much as 20 beavers."

While sitting and drinking weak coffee that Walter had near the fire, Rufus told him the story of his bear hunt. When he finished, his friend shook his head and said, "Damn."

"Other than some meat, the claws, and grease for the sorrel's wounds, the rest is rotting on the hillside," Rufus concluded.

"You got any of the meat left?" Walter asked.

"I still have one backstrap," Pike replied, "but it tastes a lot like pine nuts."

Over the next two weeks the men trapped beaver, wading in the now frigid water. The sorrel responded well to Rufus' care and was soon as good as ever. The mountains around the trappers were shrouded in snow, and the cold nights made them long for the comfort of the cave.

The first heavy snow came the second week of November. It was time to pull the traps and head for their winter quarters. The first season had been good. Each trapper had nearly 100 pelts. If the spring season was as good, each of the men could make near $600. Once they subtracted the supplies and stock they had purchased, they'd still be better off than the company trappers.

With the pelts on the packhorses, the two men led them up the hill toward the cave. Their horses were pushing through foot and a half-deep snow. Lazy flakes were falling as they tied the horses in front of the winter quarters and pulled the pole closure open.

A puff of temperate air hit the men. While it was most likely in the 50's, the below freezing conditions they had been riding in made the cave temperature feel balmy. The men removed their extra gear carried on their persons and their buckskin coats. Then the packs and saddles were taken off the horses. All this was placed in the larger front room to be moved later.

The horses' breath froze as they snorted and stomped their hooves. "I'm going to picket the animals on the grass beyond the cave," Rufus called to his friend.

"I'll have some coffee on when you get back, if I can find the extra beans we left here," Walter promised.

Slipping his buckskin coat back on, Rufus went out and put halters on the dun and sorrel. He then led the animals to the meadow beyond the cave. He picketed them in an area where the wind had blown some of the snow clear, leaving the brown grass exposed.

They'd had decent grazing in the areas they'd been trapping, so the horses were in good shape. They looked a little rough in their long winter coats. Without hesitation, the animals began to paw the snow and pull on the grass.

Rufus looked around, hoping that there were no wolves or other predators in the area. Riding up to the cave, they hadn't seen any tracks. Enjoying the isolation around him, Rufus sat on a windfall and watched the horses graze. With the longer coat, the scars on the sorrel were hardly noticeable. It would always have the split ear to remind the mountain man of the bear attack.

As promised, Walter had the fire going in the cave and a pot of coffee water heating. It quickly raised the temperature in the cave. With the wind being calm, they left the pole closure open. Rufus lit a candle and placed it toward the back of the cave. He looked at the gear Walter had cached beyond the pool.

The main room was near 20 feet-wide, with the ceiling about 15 feet-high. Toward the back, the ceiling sloped down to about five feet. Rufus was forced to crawl as he moved the packs and gear to the back. He stared into the darkness beyond the packs and wondered how far it went back. Suddenly he felt a gust of breeze from the back. Maybe there was another exit.

With everything stored, the two men sat on crude benches near the fire. A pot of beans was steaming and the coffee was brewed. This would be their home for the next four to five months. With a little hunting to supplement their supplies, they had enough to prevent going hungry.

Feeling restless in the cave, Rufus stood up and said, "I am going to check on the horses. I will also make some more firewood." Without waiting for an answer, he grabbed an axe and his Hawken and headed out into the open spaces.

While the cave was an excellent place to get away from the frigid nights, come daylight Rufus preferred to be outside. The horses were kept in a grove of aspen during the nights. The trees were just west of the cave and provided an acceptable windbreak for the animals.

Each day the two men would take them around to the meadow and let them forage under the snow for last summers grass. Walter would build a fire to make coffee while Rufus cut wood. As long as the weather was fair, they would walk the horses to a nearby pond and chop a hole in the ice to let them drink.

Most of their evening meals were cooked over a fire in front of the winter quarters. Logs had been flattened on one side and dragged to the spot for sitting while enjoying the warmth of the fire. The men were always on the lookout for any game. They would take long rides into the valley hunting. About anything that moved became game.

Walter had made some snowshoes using saplings and leather strips once the snow became too deep, making travel on horseback difficult. In late January, Rufus headed out across the snow in search of food while Walter took the horses to the meadow. The sky was spotted with some fluffy clouds and chickadees sang their songs in the aspen.

After three hours of snowshoeing across the valley floor, Rufus spotted a porcupine climbing a large spruce. The two men had become partial to the meat of the quill-covered rodent. Pulling the Hawken to full-cock, he pulled the set trigger and then touched off the hair trigger, sending a lethal ball at the animal.

The porcupine lurched as the ball struck its neck. A moment later, its grip on the spruce was lost and it began to fall, getting caught well out of reach in a fork of a branch. Rufus tramped up to the tree, the snow crunching under his snowshoes.

"You couldn't make it easy," he said, looking up at his supper.

Removing the hatchet from his broad belt, Rufus took a couple steps back and threw the short axe hoping to knock the porcupine lose. The hatchet deflected off the tree trunk near the rodent and fell, disappearing into the snow. "That was damn stupid," Rufus said, scolding himself.

Leaning his rifle against the evergreen and removing the snowshoes, he pushed through the thigh-deep snow to the point of entry where the hatchet disappeared. Digging into the snow with his choppers, the mountain man scooped frantically, fearing that he just might have lost the hatchet.

Relief flooded over him when his chopper hit the short axe. Pulling it out, he knocked the snow off it. Returning to the base of the spruce, Rufus realized that he was going to have to climb the tree. Setting his possible bag and choppers next to his rifle, he gripped the nearest branch and started the difficult ascent.

Snow cascaded down from the upper branches, pelleting Rufus as he weaved his way up the tree. Finally, the porcupine was just four feet out of his reach. He attempted to shake the tree, but that only brought more snow down on him.

Pulling the hatchet from his belt, Rufus chopped off a nearby branch. Using the branch, he poked at the rodent. After several attempts, the porcupine finally slipped from the fork and fell straight at the mountain man.

Attempting to avoid the quills, Rufus ducked away, losing his hold of the tree. Thrashing and grabbing, he fell through the branches, plunging head first into the snow below. Stunned for a moment, Rufus lay half-buried. As he tried to push himself up, the snow gave way and he floundered, finally managing to lie on his back, gasping for breath.

Struggling to his feet, he swore, “It’s a damn lot of trouble for a meal.”

His bare hands were stiff and cold as he attempted to get his gear together for the trek back to the cave. Snow had gotten down his neck and under the bottom of his deerskin coat. Rufus dug it out as best he could before pulling his choppers on with his teeth.

After a great degree of effort, he finally had his gear together and the snowshoes back on. To avoid the quills, Rufus decided to drag the porcupine behind him using a short piece of rope. The wind had started to pick up and the sun was behind the clouds. Looking down the valley, he caught his breath. Over half of it was obscured by a white wall of blowing snow.

Fighting down the feeling of panic, Rufus realized that he was almost four miles from the cave. The storm would be on him before he could make half of that distance. He needed to find some kind of shelter. To the north he could see a mixture of spruce and poplar. Without hesitating, he headed for them.

Frozen bits of icy snow began to pellet his left side as the storm began to engulf him. He was only 100 paces from the trees. His efforts were making him feel warm, and despite the snow he opened his coat. He began to wish he'd stayed at the big spruce, but all of its lower branches were gone and all he could have done was burrow into the snow for shelter.

The wind-blown snow was almost blinding the mountain man when he finally got to the grove of trees. He spotted a spruce with dense branches buried in the snow. Stopping at the downwind side of the tree, Rufus forced the boughs apart. Using his hatchet, he removed enough limbs to get to the base of the tree. These he wove into the other branches to improve the cover.

Removing the rope from the porcupine, he pulled and tied more branches toward him to make the barrier against the wind even more dense. Huddling in his makeshift shelter, he watched the snow swirling through the grove of trees. The howling of the wind was constant. He thanked God that he'd had time to make it to some kind of shelter.

For the next six hours, Rufus huddled under the spruce, feeling the cold of the blizzard. He had laid the porcupine over his feet, hoping to gain any body heat that the carcass had left. In his solitude, Rufus' thoughts went to his mother. Songs she had sung to him went through his mind. He began to wonder if he was dying. Would he soon be with her again?

Somehow, the mountain man dozed off. When he woke the storm was gone and it was dark. He tried to move, but his feet felt like blocks. Rufus knew that he needed to make a fire. He feared that his feet might be frostbit. Back in St. Louis trappers would come in to the trading post and tell stories of losing toes and ears due to the freezing temperatures.

In the dark, Rufus began to search out dead branches and snap them off, collecting a pile just outside the opening. Unable to stand, he crawled through the snow, feeling for larger wood. Finally, he had enough to start a decent fire. Using the tinder in his possible bag, he placed it near the smaller, dry sticks and struck the steel on his flint, sending a blinding shower of sparks into the collection.

After several tries, Rufus was rewarded with smoke coming from the tinder. He blew on it and encouraged a flame. The snapping sound of the burning twigs was music to his ears. Slowly he fed more wood to the fire, and finally was enjoying the life-giving warmth of the flames.

Struggling to move, he got his numb feet near the fire. Rufus then took his pannikin, filled it with snow and placed it near the snapping blaze. He had not eaten or drank anything since morning. He looked around for the porcupine. He could not see it. Rufus hoped that he hadn't gotten too many quills in his clothes while trying to make the fire. He had probably crawled all over the frozen rodent.

Poking additional sticks into the fire, he kept it burning. Suddenly he felt a tingle in his feet. As he tried to stomp them, the tingle quickly went to pins and needles. The pain almost made him cry out. When he was finally able to move his toes, relief flooded over him.

The snow had melted in the pannikin and Rufus sipped the warm water, relieving the dryness in his throat. Feeling almost human again, the mountain man looked around and saw a dead spruce not 30 feet away. Slowly, he got to his feet and took a tentative step. His feet ached but he was able to walk.

With the added fuel for his fire, he quickly had a large blaze going. The added light of the bigger fire also revealed the porcupine. Taking his time, he thawed it enough to skin and gut it. After fashioning a spit with spruce boughs, he had the animal roasting over the flames.

"You're going to make it," he whispered, and then shouted, "You are going to make it!"

* * *

When Rufus got back to the winter quarters, he found that his worried partner had taken the horses into the cave during the blizzard. While they added some warmth to the dwelling, they also left a pungent smell.

The cave proved to be an excellent place to winter. It provided a place for both man and beast during the remaining winter storms, and kept their gear dry and safe. The smell of spring was in the air by April. Packs of traps and supplies were readied for their trip to the next area.

While the two men sat near the winter fire, they made plans for improving the winter quarters. They even talked of adding a place for the horses in the front. These were plans for the future. It was now time to locate the next trapping area. Taking care to close the pole opening, and removing as much evidence as possible of their being there from the front, the men mounted up and led the packhorses to the southwest.

It was near mid-April when the two men arrived at their destination. The valley was more of a bowl, with several ponds visible from the brim. The snow had just melted and the streams rushed down form the mountains, taxing the beaver dams.

Little was said as the two men rode down into the valley and set up camp. They worked as a team, anticipating the other's moves and needs. By nightfall, they had the traps ready to place and their gear stowed under the fly tarp.

They sat drinking the last of their coffee and made plans for the morning. The spring season would be done with few supplies. The tobacco was gone, they had a few beans, and some rice. Their main fare would be beaver meat. They were both looking forward to the coming rendezvous, where they could replenish some of the most necessary supplies.

This location did not have the quantity of beavers that their fall area had had. In three weeks, they were searching for another place. This year's rendezvous would be in Willow Valley. Word had been passed that it would start the first or second week of June. It would take just over a week to travel from the cave to the Willow Valley, so Walter decided they would finish the season near their winter quarters.

When they arrived back at the cave, Rufus had the good feeling of familiar places. It was even more so than the small shack behind Larue's. The men wasted no time getting traps into the ponds. They had only a few weeks to finish the season before they packed up for the trip to the rendezvous.

* * *

The rendezvous of 1826 started at the beginning of June. Unlike the year before, this one lasted more than one day. This rendezvous also had whiskey and rum. Rufus and Walter arrived fully expecting something similar to the one in 1825. They got there in the last week of June and found the festivities in full swing.

The sound of laughter, firing of weapons, music, and verbal conflicts laced with colorful cussing could be heard well before the two men caught sight of the rendezvous. They found trappers and various tribes camped along Willow Valley as far as they could see. Large tents marked the area where the company had set up to purchase furs, sell supplies, and dispense liquor that had been watered down to prevent the attendees from killing themselves.

Riding past the tents, they led their packhorses along the Bear River until they found an area that offered willow trees for shade and grazing for the horses nearby. Their camp was just under a mile from the tents and far enough from the noise to be tolerable.

"Let's set up camp and git down to the supply tents and buy some coffee," Walter said, swinging off the dun.

"Coffee, hell!" Rufus exclaimed. "It's whiskey that I'm hankering for."

Laughing, Gray said, "Make it both. Come morning you will be needing the coffee to help with the pounding in your head."

Soon they had the fly tarp up and their meager supplies stowed. They had around 350 pelts plus the bear claws on the pack horses. Everywhere they looked there were trappers, Shoshones, Ute, and peddlers walking to and from the company tents. The two men felt uncomfortable leaving their stock and furs unattended.

They finally headed for the trading tent with the furs and their horses in tow. They overheard several men talking of the price of furs being down and the supplies sky high. Suddenly, Rufus saw a familiar face.

"Johnson!" he called. "How was your year?"

The smoky-eyed man had a sullen look on his face and waited for the two men to walk up before speaking. "I made a few dollars. I imagine you two free trappers will be living high after selling your beavers."

Walter kept quiet, giving Johnson a disapproving look. Rufus smiled at his prior partner and replied, "Our fall season was as good as one could hope, but after the thaw things were a bit slow."

"Where'd you trap?" Johnson asked.

"Hell, I don't know," Rufus said. "I just followed Walter around."

After a bit more conversation, the past partners promised to look each other up later.

As soon as they were out of earshot, Walter said, "You did good. We never want to tell others where we have found beaver."

Rufus was surprised how many men were still in the process of selling their furs. It was almost an hour before they opened their packs and began the trade. Most of their pelts were plew, or high quality. They finally settled at $3.50 a pound and the count was 362 furs. Each man walked away with over $600.

Without hesitation, Pike gave half of his to Walter to hold until they got back to Franklin. "Are you sure you want to do this?" Gray asked.

"If I go broke here at the rendezvous, you will have extra for me to enjoy in Franklin with plenty left for next year's supplies."

Walter didn't understand how his friend could spend until his pockets were empty. His father had always taught him to put something aside for the future and then use pocket money on things needed for day-to-day living. Walter didn't mind spending on some pleasures such as whiskey or entertaining a lady, but sitting in a card game run by sharks made no sense.

The two men found that there were some men who would tend to the horses for a reasonable fee. It was not a surprise when they learned that Johnson worked with them. With the ever-present danger of having stock stolen, they decided to leave the animals with the horse tenders until one or the other was ready to head back to camp.

Rufus was anxious to join the merriment that was going on all around them, but Walter reminded him that they needed to purchase enough supplies to get them back to Franklin. Rufus followed his friend to the supply tents.

The two men were astonished at the amount of supplies being offered at the rendezvous. The caravan that had brought them out had been made up of 300 mules carrying everything a trapper would need in the mountains. And this time additional items had been included for the celebration at the rendezvous.

Realizing that there would be plenty of supplies without the worry of the company running out, the two men bought some tobacco and coffee and then headed for the tent selling whiskey. Rufus purchased the first bottle and he and Walter found a place near the water to enjoy a drink and a chew.

For the next two weeks Rufus was like a wild man, rushing from one venue to another. He won money and lost some shooting the Hawken. He also bet on knife throwing, hatchet throwing, arm wrestling, stone throwing, and even on how long a butterfly sat on a flower.

As the sun went down he would wander down to the river, seeking comfort from the maidens. He almost fell in love with a pretty Cheyenne woman, but after too many losing games of poker, he didn't have the extra horse or musket that her father wanted, or the money to continue the courtship.

Hurting and exhausted, Walter dragged his friend away from the rendezvous in time to prevent Rufus from succeeding in killing himself. Hardly able to cling to his saddle, Rufus followed the pack mules heavily loaded with furs as they began the long trek back east.

Riding nearby Rufus, Walter asked, "How much do you have left of the money you kept?"

Looking up at his friend with his eyes barely open, Pike said, "I run out of money two days ago. Some new friends that had won all my money kept me in whiskey. They said I brought them luck."

"Did you ever think they might have been waiting for you to bet your pistols or rifle to try and win some money back?" Walter asked.

"They did offer," Rufus said. "But after I lost my tobacco, knife and hatchet, I got to thinking and told them no."

"Too bad your thinking came too late," Walter told him, chuckling.

* * *

A lifelong friendship was rooted that first year in the mountains together. While it wasn't necessary to travel back east each year, the two men most often chose to do so. Trapping had been good when they arrived at the 1827 rendezvous at Sweet Lake, packing mostly prime pelts. There had been a small skirmish with some Blackfoot braves just prior to the caravan's arrival. Rufus and Walter missed it, but were regaled with the stories about the *battle* by every mountain man who had participated.

That year a wheel-mounted four-pounder cannon was included with the caravan. It was the first wheeled vehicle to make the trip to the mountains. Beaver pelts sold for $3 a pound while supplies were very high. Once again, Rufus thoroughly enjoyed himself, spending much of his earnings on pleasures offered at the rendezvous.

While at the rendezvous there was talk of spring flooding along the Missouri River. Some who had come out with the caravan called it a hundred-year flood. Nothing was said about Franklin, so Rufus and Walter figured they'd been spared. Their arrival in Missouri was greeted with carnage that was difficult to describe.

They found Sal near the site of the now collapsed livery. Much of the structure had been washed downstream. Walter slid off the dun and ran over to his friend. "We heard there'd been flooding, but never expected that the whole damn town would be gone."

The hostler looked at his friend with sad, tear-filled eyes. "My life's work is gone."

"Is Tiny okay?" Walter asked.

"She is," Sal replied. "It was by the grace of God that we wanted a view to the west and built the house on high ground. It was spared, and I got the horses out before the water took the building down. But down here . . ." His voice faded.

Rufus sat on the sorrel, looking in awe at the damage. He wanted to say something that would comfort Sal, but was unable to find the words. There were areas that had been fertile fields but were now covered with boulders and mud. All the bridges that had spanned tributaries flowing into the Missouri had been washed out. Main Street was washed away, along with the buildings that once stood on both sides. The Frontier House had been close to the river and was completely gone, along with Rufus' plans for whiskey and comfort.

While some of the residents gave up and moved away, many remained. The spirit of these people was strong, as they chose a new location on higher ground and began to rebuild. The new location was named New Franklin. That year Walter and Rufus got a late start for the fall season. The two men remained in Missouri to help Sal rebuild the livery a short distance from his house, and it was the first of September before they headed for the mountains.

Due to the success of the Rocky Mountain Rendezvous, additional companies joined in, offering better prices for the pelts, but still selling supplies at prices several times higher than St. Louis. Walter and Rufus continued to purchase most of their supplies during their trips to Franklin.

One summer they chose to stay in the west and improve the winter quarter at the cave. A structure was added to the front of the cave, making room to stable the horses. Once again, the construction resembled a twisted pile of spruce poles and windfalls.

Their cache-cave was in Mexican territory and there continued to be conflicts between Mexico and the United States. Mostly the tension was associated with Texas. Neither country had shown much interest in the northern territory where the cave was located.

In 1829 there were two rendezvous: One on the Popo Agie in early July, the second one was at Pierre's Hole in late August. Walter and Rufus attended the first one and it was all the celebrating that Rufus could handle. They went back with the Popo Agie caravan and, as usual, Walter was carrying his trapping partner's supply money.

In 1832 the rendezvous was back at Pierre's Hole, and was hampered by attacks from the Blackfoot. With the help of friendly tribes attending the rendezvous, the Blackfoot were forced to abandon the fight.

That same year the competition between the Rocky Mountain Fur Company and the American Fur Company was reaching new heights and continued into the fall hunt. The two companies waged an active campaign to spoil the hunt of their competitors.

While the company trappers made things difficult for each other, Rufus and Walter as free trappers stayed clear of the fray. Beavers where still plentiful and they continued to do most of their trapping in the Mexican territory. Each rendezvous there was talk of beaver in the Yellowstone and areas controlled by the Hudson Bay Company. Rufus hoped to see those areas someday, but he and Walter preferred places they were familiar with.

CHAPTER SEVENTEEN

In August 1832, the two partners took the Platte River and Sweetwater River route to the mountains. They wanted to give the area near the cave a year to recover. Rufus and Walter stopped to resupply at a new stockade on the Green River named Fort Bonneville. Captain Benjamin Bonneville had been given a commission to explore Wyoming and west, and had come out with 20 wagons and over 100 men under the guise of being trappers and had built the fort.

As Rufus and Walter rode down from the South Pass, they passed trappers who had visited the fort and were told it would be handy for resupplying during the early winter months and spring. As the 100 ft x 100 ft stockade came into view they felt some disappointment. From what other trappers had told them, they had expected it to be larger. It had 15-foot cottonwood walls and two block houses on opposite corners.

There was evidence of stumps along the Green River where the trees had been harvested. The place looked more like a fortified trading post, having only a few buildings within the walls. One was a long barracks that housed the men who had constructed the fort, and another was Bonneville's headquarters, which included living quarters for the captain and his officers.

The trading post had adequate supplies, but was not set up to buy and trade for furs. Rufus was also disappointed to find that there was no type of saloon or the sale of liquor. He noticed that Walter appeared relieved to learn this.

Setting up camp on the river outside the fort, the two men planned to rest their animals for a couple of days and readied their traps and other gear that would be needed in the next few weeks. They would not be visiting the cache this year and would improvise some type of shanty near the Snake or Green River.

This was the first year that they would be trapping near the Hudson Bay Company. Both the United State and Britain claimed the territory, so they would have to beware of Hudson Bay trappers, as well as Shoshone and Bannock in the area. They also hadn't forgotten the problems with the Blackfoot at Pierre's Hole.

Their plans were to trap tributaries off the Snake River. Walter had been there a couple of years before meeting Rufus and remembered it being thick with beavers. With the camp set up and some time spent fishing, they soon had cutthroat trout broiling over their fire and water heating for the tea they had purchased at the fort.

"It ain't big, but is sure is sturdy," Rufus said, commenting on the fort.

"They talked of it being a trading post," Walter replied, "but to me it looks more like an army outpost. Did you notice that they had an elk hanging near the mess area?"

"That I did," Rufus replied. "I also noticed that the cook was boiling the meat. It reminded me of my first trip into the mountains. Our cook was named Sooky and the man ruined a lot of good steaks boiling them for our meals."

Walter grinned at his partner and said, "That is another sign of the fort being army. They often require all meat to be boiled to get the most of out every piece, both meat and broth. It also insures that meat that might be turning is well cooked to prevent the soldiers from getting sick eating it."

"Hell," Rufus replied, "we just burn it a little longer in the pan."

"I was talking to the man in the supply building," Walter told Rufus, "and he said the venture was privately funded and Astor was one that put up some money."

"If Astor's in on it," Rufus said, "then it's got to be about furs. Maybe the fort will be buying and trading for beaver next year. Next summer's rendezvous is supposed to be held near here."

As the sunset blazed red in the western sky, the two men sat near their dying fire, drinking a last cup of tea and smoking cigars purchased at the fort. The nights were already cold at the 7,000 ft elevation, giving the promise of thick beaver pelts.

Walter led the way to the northwest from the fort. They had swam their horses across the Green River, and knew that the current and depth was much less than they'd find on the return trip in the spring. The Snake River was only about a three-day ride from Fort Bonneville. Once they reached the river, several days traveling north would be needed to locate their first ponds for trapping.

This was the first time Rufus had been in the Snake River area. The mountain peaks on the horizon were new landmarks for him to memorize. They camped near a lake with the Teton Mountains in the background.

"I have wanted to come back here from the moment I left," Walter told the mountain man.

"Why did you leave?" Rufus asked.

All his partner did was shake his head and shrug. Rufus finished slicing side meat into the blackened frying pan and set it onto the fire. He knew that Walter loved the mountains, but his heart was back in Franklin. Each year they returned to the Missouri town, where he spent hours talking with the aging Sal. The time was coming when Rufus would be riding west alone, in need of another partner.

Over the past seven years that the mountain man had known Walter, he had watched his friend go from brown hair to gray. The lines in his face had grown deeper, he got up slower from the fire and complained of aches from sleeping on the ground. None of these ailments prevented Walter from doing his share in the mountains.

The first two areas where the men hoped to trap had been worked hard the year before. One had been all but destroyed by bears tearing apart the lodges. The third tributary had a good beaver population. That evening the two mountain men sat around their fire, relieved to finally have their traps in the water.

The next day, Rufus came back to camp leading the roan and three beavers hanging from the pack saddle. Water was still dripping off his buckskin britches and the water squished in his moccasins. "I must have seen six beavers swimming in another pond," Rufus said. "We'll be here for a month catching them rodents."

Sitting on a log, skinning one of the beavers he'd caught, Walter smiled. "We are only a day's ride from the geysers in Yellowstone. I think you'd like to see them before we leave the area."

"I heard about them geysers," Rufus replied. "Maybe we'd see something to shoot and have a few meals that weren't beaver."

While the mountain man fleshed the pelts, Walter made hoops to stretch them. A pot of rice was steaming on their fire. As always, the blackened frying pan was warming to fry the meat cut from their catch. In the air there was the smell of a storm coming.

"It's cold enough," Walter said. "Could be snow."

"Too early for snow down here," Rufus replied. "The mountains will get some."

As they were finishing the last of the coffee before turning in, a few lazy flakes began to fall. Laughing, Rufus said, "You're right again. We got snow."

They woke the next morning to three inches of snow covering their camp. The world around them had been transformed to a winter wonderland. Rufus headed into the trees to relieve himself and suffered the indignities of snow falling from the branches and going down his neck.

Walter watched him coming out of the trees, brushing snow from his head and digging it out of his collar. "You got to learn to wear your hat after fresh snow."

"I think it just wanted to remind me that you were right," Rufus conceded.

"Let's check the traps and take care of the catch and then ride up to the Yellowstone," Walter suggested. "This snow could be a sign of an early winter and travel could be tough."

Rufus didn't know if it was the snowy night or what, but they only caught two beavers that morning. By mid-morning they were riding north to the Yellowstone. The day was sunny and the snow hanging from the trees was beginning to drip and fall from the trees, making a plopping sound as it hit the ground.

To prevent wasting the trip north, the two men watched for future ponds they could trap. By the time they reached the Yellowstone, the snow had pretty much melted, with only patches left in shady spots.

The first geyser they saw sounded like a tea kettle bubbling. Rumbling could be heard in the distance and several clouds of steam could be seen above the trees. Rufus saw ponds that were blue, yellow, and reddish brown. Then he saw a meadow that was white.

"Looks like all the snow hasn't melted up here yet," the mountain man pointed out.

"It's like that all year," Walter replied. "The steam from the geysers coat them with the white stuff."

The two men stopped near a mound that was emitting steam and an occasional splash of hot water. "Not much to see here," Rufus said.

"Just wait," Walter told him.

For the next half hour, they sat on their horses and stared at the mound. Finally, Rufus swung down from the sorrel and loosened the cinch. "I may as well make the horse more comfortable," he said.

Walter continued to set on the dun and smile. Suddenly the mound became more active with additional steam and water bubbling out. The wind was blowing the steam toward the men. "We best move around to the other side," he suggested.

Leading the sorrel, Rufus followed his friend. Then the mound began to spurt even more. Unsure of what to expect, the mountain man stood anticipating more steam and scalding water to gush out. Then, moment by moment, it became more violent as the roar and tower of water shot up over 100 feet, forcing Rufus to step back quickly.

He hardly noticed when the reins were pulled from his hand as the column of water and steam continued for four minutes. As quickly as it shot up, the spout of water continued to grow shorter, and finally there was just the steam and some bubbling from the mound.

He heard Walter say something, but being in awe of what he had just witnessed, Rufus didn't comprehend what his partner had said. "Rufus! Your horse!" Walter shouted.

Finally hearing his friend, Rufus looked around. The sorrel was gone. He watched as Walter galloped away toward the stand of cottonwood. The mountain man looked back once more at the mound before running after Walter.

* * *

The fall season trapping was cut short by significant early snow storms in the Green and Snake River area. They managed to erect a crude shanty that kept most of the snow out and was heated by a fire just outside the doorway. The fly tarp was used to cover the opening during the worst storms.

Rufus had been a good student over the past years. With the hip deep snow surrounding their shanty, he sat in the open space and made a pair of snowshoes. His objective was a sheltered valley of cedars and spruce four miles away where deer yarded up. He hoped to stretch their supplies by bagging one.

Inside the shanty, Walter was doing the final touches on his snowshoes. Both men would be carrying their blanket rolls and expected to spend at least one night. With the snow too deep for the horses, they had built a rough log fence around a grove of aspen. Within this fence they would have tender branches and bark to feed on.

Each man left the shanty with one of Rufus' Kentucky flintlocks pistols under their coats and their Hawken rifles. The haversack was slung over Rufus' shoulder, carrying enough supplies for a meal and a pan to cook with. Pannikins hung on their possible bags to brew tea with the meal.

The two men kept up a steady pace toward the deer yard. Both had their hats pulled low over their eyes to avoid some of the glare from the sun. Rufus was looking for anything that could provide a meal. They had been eating rice or beans since their last catch of beaver. Any fresh meat would be a treat after the spartan diet.

He mentioned this to Walter. His friend laughed, "Even a porcupine? Remember the one you ate during a storm? You came back with quills sticking all through your buckskins."

Thinking of the event, Rufus replied, "Even a porcupine. I would eat it quills and all right now."

The only signs of any life across the white expanse were the tracks of a bobcat that was hunting for birds or mice. Bigger animals would flounder in the deep snow, making stalking game almost impossible.

It was late afternoon when the two men reached the yard. With all the snow there was little sign of deer coming into and out of the cedars. The valley was all of a mile long and they had hoped to find trails used by the deer to watch and wait.

"I may as well walk to the far end and push them to you," Rufus told his friend.

"You'll look a damn lot like a deer dressed in buckskins," Walter told him.

Laughing, the mountain man replied, "I'll just have to trust you can tell the difference between me and a whitetail, or mule deer."

"We'll be packing it back to the shanty," Walter said. "We should only bring down one."

"Hell, I can eat damn near a whole deer in one meal," Rufus said. "It's been a while since we had fresh meat."

Without waiting for a reply, the mountain man started for the other end of the valley, remaining well above it as not to push the deer in the wrong direction. Rufus was relieved when he came across a trail used by the deer going to drink at a small water fall. It confirmed that they were in the cedars.

Well toward the far side, he went down into the valley and removed his snowshoes. Using a pigging string, he tied them across his back. While there was plenty of snow in the evergreens, the clusters of trees would be difficult to work his way through with the snowshoes.

Moving along the valley, he figured any branches be snapped would help to push the deer to Walter. The first quarter-mile, he saw few tracks and the trees were mostly spruce. Suddenly he heard crashing of a deer ahead as it ran from him. Watching, he saw the flash of its white tail.

"That's right," he murmured. "You just keep moving to Walter."

He held the Hawken, cradled in one arm so that the action was protected from snow falling from branches. Moving through the trees was warm work and he opened his buckskin coat to let body heat out.

All of a sudden, there was the sound of a shot. Walter had had the deer come near him. Smiling, Rufus continued through the trees. Then he froze. A deer that had been driven back due to the rifle fire stood not 30 paces from him, looking back toward the shot.

Hardly breathing, Rufus pulled his chopper off with his teeth. He gripped the Hawken, feeling the sharp cold of the metal. Slowly he pulled the rifle to full-cock and brought it to his shoulder. The whitetail jumped ahead, still looking back. Rufus saw the movement of another deer coming.

Sighting just behind the shoulder, he touched off the hair trigger. Smoke and fire exploded from the rifle, sending the lead ball to its target. The impact caused the deer to leap to the side in an attempt to flee. Crashing into a small cedar, the whitetail collapsed to the ground.

In the distance he heard Walter shout, "If you just got another one, we got two to pack back to the camp!"

"We got two," Rufus called back.

Looking around before moving to the deer, Rufus saw no additional movement. His bare hand used for firing was already becoming numb from the cold. Cradling the rifle, he struggled to get the chopper back on.

Pushing through the snow in the opening between him and the deer, Rufus admired the young buck. Once gutted, he could carry it back over his shoulders. With two deer, and eating the meat sparingly, it would last them a month, maybe more.

As he knelt to gut the deer, he again caught sight of movement. He looked through the trees trying to see what it was. He had learned on the plains when hunting buffalo that the sound of shooting drew the scavengers in.

Removing his choppers, and pulling his knife from its sheath, he quickly cut around the back of the deer and then slit up the stomach to the breast. Then he heard a growl or snarl. Looking up, he saw the wolf through the trees.

"You must be damn hungry," he said. "Just wait your turn and I'll leave the innards and head for you."

Snarling, the animal continued to come closer. Standing up, he shouted, "Damn brave of you, you damn cuss! Get out of here!"

He wished he had something to throw at the belligerent animal. Rufus knew his rifle was empty. Even though his hand had been near numb, he now wished he'd taken a moment to load it. The damn wolf continued towards him snarling. It was now 30 feet away.

Reaching for the pistol in his waistband, Rufus watched the animal. Something wasn't right about it. Wolves could be aggressive, but this one displayed no caution. He was standing a few feet away from the deer and the wolf was coming right at him.

Reaching for his powder horn, he opened the pan and added powder to the Kentucky flintlock. He watched the animal continue closing the distance, head low and snarling. Rufus' heart was pounding. He was looking at a sick animal, possibly rabid. If it bit him, it would be only a matter of time and he too would die.

He had one shot. If the wolf was wounded and came at him, he had the knife to finish it off, but the infected teeth would surely cut him. He shouted one more time in an attempt to scare it off. It was now within range to leap on him.

With a prayer in his throat that the pistol wouldn't misfire, he took aim and pulled the trigger. He felt the recoil and the .54 caliber ball flew at the rabid animal. At the same time, Rufus reached for the Hawken to use as a club if the wolf continued on.

The animal yelped and leaped, falling to its side. Then it rolled to its stomach and continued to crawl toward the mountain man. Rufus watched, knowing he had delivered a fatal shot. Within 10 feet of him, the wolf breathed its last. He could see the now bloody foaming around its mouth.

Then came the shout, "Damnit, Rufus! You didn't shoot another one."

"No, I didn't!" the mountain man called back. "I just killed a rabid wolf!"

After gutting the deer and preparing them for carrying, the two men piled wood onto the wolf carcass lying in the opening and burned it. They did not want other animals feeding on it and becoming rabid. They broiled the deer livers over the same fire for their meal before heading back toward the shanty with the two deer over their shoulders. Some distance away from the wolf and deer yard, they would spend the night.

* * *

The snowy winter finally broke in mid-April, bringing the warmer winds that quickly melted the snow. There was still some ice on the edge of the ponds when they set their traps. The frigid winter had the furs in prime condition.

Enduring hours in the chilling ponds, with supplies nearly exhausted, the two mountain men worked to make up for the early freeze of the prior fall. The work was rewarded with a number of excellent pelts.

Each night they ate beaver meat and drank hot water while talking of the coming rendezvous. It would be held at the Green River and Horse Creek confluence near Fort Bonneville. From the shanty they would reach the rendezvous with a week's travel. The thoughts of coffee and tobacco even overshadowed whiskey.

Rufus and Walter continued to trap until late June and then, bidding the crude shanty farewell, they headed for Fort Bonneville and the rendezvous. Their horses still displayed some long winter hair and had recovered somewhat from the lean winter months. Rufus planned to purchase grain from the fort to build the animals up for the trip east to Franklin.

The water in the Green River was high when they swam the horses across, the pack horses with their loads having the hardest time. With water dripping from the animals, the two mountain men stopped on the east bank near the fort and looked at the early arrivals camped along the river. From high ground above the river they could see the tents of another company several miles south.

They soon learned that there were four companies, including Benjamin Bonneville, offering to purchase furs. The American Fur Company, The Rocky Mountain Fur Company, and The St. Louis Fur Company were in attendance. The 1833 rendezvous was strung 10 miles along the Green River. Nearly 300 trappers joined the celebration and as many, or more Indians, mostly Shoshone.

After a stop at the fort to purchase a few needed supplies, the two mountain men rode along the river in search of an area to set up their camp. They finally found a place almost five miles from the fort, near the American Fur Company. They ran into Johnson, who was working as one of the wranglers for the extra animals used in the supply train.

In the past seven years they had only seen Johnson twice. Once his three-year contract was over he had quit Ashley's company and had only come to the rendezvous as part of a pack train. Johnson had told Rufus that he liked seeing the mountains, but the life in them had no future. His plan was to get rich buying and selling horses.

With the celebration of the rendezvous spread out so wide there was always some kind of action going on day or night. Walter looked for the company that was offering the best price per pound for the furs. He found that they all pretty much stuck together and used other come-ons to get the men to trade, such as cheaper whiskey, deals on foofaraw, or even access to Indian brides. Other supplies that were needed by the trappers remained very high.

Rufus, with his extra earnings in his money sack, ran himself to exhaustion trying to take in all of the rendezvous and attempting to put a dent in the whiskey supply. The celebration would only last three weeks and there was much to make up for the months in the mountains.

One night Rufus came back to their camp, well liquored-up and in a great mood. He woke Walter to tell his great news. "I just beat Johnson with the rifle!" he shouted. "Drunk or sober, I can out shoot that bugger."

Rubbing the sleep out of his eyes, Walter asked, "How the hell did you shoot in the dark?"

Taken aback for a second, his partner stammered, "Well …, it … I, it weren't in the dark. It was this afternoon. I been getting drunk on his money since then . . . 'cause I beat him in the afternoon."

The next morning Walter was on his second mug of coffee when Rufus crawled out from under the fly tarp. "Ohhh," he moaned. "Too much fun. I had too much fun last night."

Handing a mug of steaming coffee to his partner, Walter grinned. "You can thank Johnson for that. He gave you the money."

Wincing as the coffee burned his mouth, Rufus asked, "Johnson bought me whiskey last night?"

"Damn, *you* don't remember?" Walter laughed.

Rubbing his head in an attempt to clear the cobwebs, Rufus said, "I may forget a few things after a bottle or two, but I wouldn't forget Johnson buying me whiskey."

"You beat him in a rifle shooting contest and you used the winnings to buy more whiskey," Walter told him, trying to jog his memory. "You come in last night all excited and woke me from a dream I was having about Franklin."

With his head hanging, Rufus continued to sip the coffee. Then a sideways grin broke out on his face. "I remember. Johnson challenged me to a match and I did beat him. I did beat him!"

The excitement of the memory was short-lived, as the throbbing in his head shut down his jubilation. But, Rufus knew that drunk or sober, he could outshoot Johnson.

While frying up some side meat, Walter asked, "Did you hear about the wolves?"

The smell of the frying meat kind of turned Rufus' stomach. "I didn't hear anything about wolves."

"Several men got bit by rabid wolves," Walter told him. "It might have been only one wolf, but some camps were attacked and a bunch of men were bit. Some animals were also attacked."

"Damn," Rufus said. "The poor bastards will more than likely die. How far was the camp from here?"

"A few miles south," Walter said. "Too damn close for comfort."

Thinking about the wolf that had come at him, Rufus agreed with his partner.

With the meal finished, the two men decided to ride up to the fort and get some additional grain for the horses. After they took care of the animals Pike planned to try and find Johnson and revel in his victory. Maybe he could get a rematch and win some more money.

The normally organized fort seemed somewhat disheveled. Boxes and barrels were stacked in front of the buildings near the wagons, and the furs were being loaded for transport. Rufus saw the man they'd gotten grain from when they arrived at the rendezvous.

Leading the sorrel over, he asked, "Can I get some more grain for the animals?"

"I got about 50 pounds to spare," the man said. "The rest will be needed for the teams heading back with the furs."

"By the looks of it, you're moving out of the fort," the mountain man told him.

"The captain told us just this morning that we was continuing west," the man said. "The winters in this area are too severe. Nothing could be done but sit tight and wait for spring. Captain wants to do more than that in the winter."

"You built a damn fine fort here to just move out," Rufus said, confused.

"We'll build another, maybe a couple more," he said. "I hear we will be going all the way to Oregon territory, or maybe to California."

"Are the Hudson Bay Company or Mexicans going to let you do that?" the mountain man asked.

"We ain't going to ask permission," the confident man told him.

Giving the man money for the expensive grain, Rufus went back to find Walter. His partner was talking with one of the officers. After a moment, Walter came back shaking his head. "You won't believe what they're doing."

"According the man with the grain, they're moving out," Rufus replied.

"They did a damn lot of work to just leave the place," Walter said.

"It's the weather," the mountain man said. "They don't like the snow."

* * *

The rabid wolf, or wolves, struck the next two nights biting at least twelve men as well as a score of animals. The last night was within a mile of their camp. Walter was angry. "I don't know why the damn wolves haven't been shot already."

"Think about it," Rufus told him. "No doubt the men that got bit were drunk and when the wolves come in, they weren't in any shape to draw a bead on them."

"I think we should leave," his friend said.

"Leave when?" Pike asked. "The rendezvous will be in full swing for another week, maybe more."

"There will be whiskey in Franklin," Walter told him. "If we get bitten, there won't be any more whiskey. We should leave as soon as we can break camp."

"I'm supposed to meet Johnson for a rematch at noon," Rufus replied. "If I leave before we shoot, he'll think I was afraid to meet him again."

"After you shoot then," Walter conceded.

"I am going to have a few drinks," his friend warned him.

"If you fall off your damn horse, I ain't picking you up," Walter told him.

As he headed out of camp, Rufus promised, "I won't fall off my horse and if I do, I'll climb back on myself."

Walter still had Rufus' second Kentucky pistol and he had it loaded and primed in his broad belt. If he saw a wolf anywhere, he sure as hell was going to take a shot at it. He watched Rufus with his Hawken, heading out, with a bit of a bounce in his step. His friend was looking forward to the match.

Rufus found Johnson near the company tent. "You ready to get beat?" the smoky-eyed man asked.

The mountain man looked at the crowd near Johnson, waiting for the contest. All had been drinking for a while and were loudly supporting one contestant or the other. A bottle was thrust into Rufus' hand by one of his supporters.

The firing range had been set up. Several 3 to 4-inch blocks of wood had been placed on a log out at 100 paces. Each man would fire five shots. If each knocked down the same number, they would continue until one of the men was successful knocking more down.

The crowd was growing and the betting was brisk. Rufus took another drink and then handed the bottle back. The raucous mountain men began to chant, anxious to start the contest. Johnson's face was tight. He hadn't expected that many trappers watching.

Unexpectedly, Johnson told Pike, "We will be shooting for bragging rights."

"You don't want to lose more money to me?" Rufus challenged.

"I got a coin," the smoky-eyed man said, ignoring the comment. "You want to call heads or tails for who shoots first?"

Smiling at the man, Rufus said, "You set the terms, so you just choose who's first."

Without answering, Johnson stepped up to the line and commenced to load and fire. As each shot scored a hit, the crowd got louder and louder. Again, the bottle was thrust into Rufus' hand. Taking a drink, he passed it back.

Johnson knocked down five of the largest blocks with his first round of shots. He turned to Rufus with a smile that was almost a sneer. "You're up, Pike."

Looking at the remaining blocks, the mountain man went up to the firing line. He could feel the glow of the whiskey. Rufus methodically knocked down five of the smaller blocks. As the crowd cheered, several men ran down to put blocks back up onto the log.

For the next hour the two men continued shooting, with a delay to cut more blocks due to the lead balls splitting some into pieces after a couple of strikes. Bets in the crowd were won or lost, the money going back and forth.

Sweat was breaking out on Johnson's forehead. Each time he missed one or two blocks, Rufus would also miss. He suspected that Pike was toying with him. "I want you to shoot first this time," he told Rufus.

Stepping up to the line, Rufus began to load and fire. Taking his time, he knocked the first four blocks down. His fifth shot was a clear miss. The noise of the crowd was deafening. Those backing Johnson figured they were coming into some money.

Rufus could see the gleam in Johnson's eyes as he pushed by, rushing to the line. The smoky-eyed man hit with the first three shots. He narrowly missed with the fourth shot, rocking a block but not knocking it down. Rufus saw the mans hand's shaking as he loaded the final shot.

Taking aim, Johnson fought to control his breathing. If he hit the next block, he would still have a chance to put his past trapping partner in his place. Rufus watched the man, half hoping he would knock another one down so he could continue to torment his old friend.

Johnson fired and there was dead silence as the crowd watched the blocks remain standing. Then those backing Pike erupted. Their champion had won the contest. The smoky-eyed man began to shout, claiming that the one he had rocked should count. His protesting went for naught. The contest was over.

Surrounded by those betting on him, Rufus accepted the bottles and took a drink from each. The victory of beating Johnson one more time was very sweet and he didn't want the party to end. Someone tapped him on the shoulder. Looking back, he stared into the proud eyes of his friend, Walter.

"We have to be going," Gray told him. "That was some fine shooting, but I can't say it was wise to intentionally miss your last shot."

"Did you see him shaking?" Rufus asked, grinning.

Thanking the supporting crowd, Walter managed to get Pike to head back for the camp. Everything was ready to be put onto the horses. Rufus saddled the sorrel, feeling regret that the 1833 rendezvous should end so suddenly for him. He did agree with Walter that the rabid wolves were a real danger, but under the influence of the whiskey, it was difficult to leave.

With the horses ready, Rufus climbed into the saddle and looked around at the celebrating men up and down the river and shouted, "See you next year!"

CHAPTER EIGHTEEN

Rufus rode alongside his partner listening to the clink of two more bottles in his haversack. Generally, Walter was against drinking when traveling, or even when trapping. In both cases he believed a man needed a clear head. As part of the concession of leaving the rendezvous early, Walter had agreed that his friend could take the two bottles given by admiring fans of his shooting skills.

The two men were heading for a fort recently built on the Laramie River. William Sublette had his men construct the fort on their way to the rendezvous. It had been named Fort William in his honor. It would take them 10 days of steady riding to reach the fort.

They rode through the South Pass on their way to the Sweetwater River. When they reached the river, the two men set up camp. Rufus enjoyed the first bottle of whiskey. Walter did have a measure in his evening coffee and another taste while enjoying a chew at their dying fire.

The next afternoon Walter spotted some braves hunting buffalo. The two men remained out of sight in a grove of alder along the river until dusk. The sounds of the hunt could be heard with the firing of muskets and the high-pitched cries when a buffalo fell.

Under the cover of darkness and leading their horses, they continued well into the night, putting distance between themselves and the hunters before making a cold camp. At sunup, they rode away with their Hawkens across the front of their saddles, avoiding high ground.

They were crossing one of the bends in the Sweetwater River when the sorrel mis-stepped. An instant later there was the sound of a musket! As the horse went down, several Blackfoot rose from the sage-covered ground, on the north side of the river, sending arrows their way.

Rufus kicked his boot out of the stirrup, his hat flying as the sorrel hit the ground. He heard Walter fire behind him. Using the dying horse for cover, Pike sighted on a brave and fired the rifle. Pulling the pistol out of his belt, he fired again, spinning one of the Blackfoot.

Two horses ran past, splashing in the river as Rufus hurried to reload the Hawken. There was a cry downriver and then a muffled shot. Suddenly, one of the braves came at him with a raised knife. Stepping back from the dead horse, Rufus swung the rifle, striking the Blackfoot across the ribs. As the brave tried to get up, he hit him on the temple with the barrel.

The world became very small and focused as Rufus fought for his life. The dead horse, the downed brave, his rifle and the cries of the Blackfoot were all he was aware of. He knelt behind the sorrel, loading the Hawken and firing. Another musket ball hit the horse and arrows flashed by, narrowly missing him.

Then all was quiet. The amulet felt heavy against his heaving chest. He loaded both the Hawken and Kentucky pistol. "You okay, Walter?" he called. There was no answer. Again, he called, "Walter!" Nothing. Fear for his partner began to well up inside him. Maybe his friend had worked his way out of hearing range during the fight.

Then there was the sound of running horses. It was coming from the northwest. Could it be their horses? No, he thought. Their horses had run behind him, going southeast across the river. It had to be the Blackfoot leaving. Then he heard a groan. He looked at the motionless brave next to him. The sound had come from behind Rufus.

Keeping low, he made his way along the river. His breath caught as Rufus saw Walter lying on his back, his legs in the river and a dead Blackfoot lying across his unmoving body. His partner's bloody head told him that Walter had been scalped.

Splashing through the shallows along the river, Rufus dropped the Hawken near Walter, then threw the brave off his friend. The discharged Kentucky flintlock lay on Walters chest, and the Blackfoot still had his friend's scalp in his hand. Both the brave and Walter were covered with blood from the ragged hole in the Blackfoot's chest.

Kneeling next to his friend, he lifted him, cradling him close, and whispered, "Walter, I'm sorry. I led you right into the ambush."

Fighting back the tears he felt welling up in his eyes, Rufus carefully lay his friend back down. Then there was a groan. It was Walter! His eyes were open. "Keep still," Rufus said. "I'm here to take care of you."

With all the blood that was covering his friend, as well as being scalped, Rufus could not believe he wasn't dead. One thing that the mountain man knew for sure was that he had to move from this area. Shortly the Blackfoot would be back for the two dead braves.

Then Rufus caught some movement across the river. The dun had come back and stood with reins trailing on the far side of the river. "Walter," Rufus said, "I'm going for your horse. I will be right back."

Splashing across the river, Rufus prayed that the horse wouldn't run. The dun reached his nose out and walked toward him. Then Rufus saw the roan grazing less than a quarter-mile away. Leading the dun back across the river, he tried to move his friend.

Walter cried out from the pain. "My leg," he said.

Not only had his friend been scalped, he had somehow injured his leg. "I got to get you on the horse," Rufus told him. "We got to move from here."

With the horse standing in the river below them, Rufus managed to get Walter into the saddle. His friend lay over the horse's neck, fighting to hold on. Picking up his friend's hat, he put it on the bloody scalp to keep flies off. Slipping Walters Hawken in the scabbard, and hanging his possible bag off the saddle horn, he led the dun to the dead sorrel.

He got his saddlebags and the haversack and hung them over his shoulders. Cradling the loaded

Hawken, and with the two Kentucky pistols in his broad belt, he was ready in case the Blackfoot returned. Rufus led the dun carrying his injured partner away from the scene of the ambush.

As he passed the roan, he called to the horse and, not wanting to be left behind, it came to him. Walter was sagging to one side of the saddle and would soon fall. Rufus got some rope from the pack horse and used it to tie his partner into the saddle. Each time he went near the left leg, Walter would cry out.

"Just a little farther," he told his friend. "I'll check the leg and try and clean you up."

A mile along the Sweetwater, Rufus found a sheltered area with cottonwood that would offer some protection in case the Blackfoot came back. His heart ached at the cries of his friend as he got him off the horse and onto the ground.

Rufus had no idea what he should do first. While Walter was the priority, the horses had to be tied and some of the gear taken off. There were items he needed in the saddle bags and packs. After spreading the ground tarp and blankets onto the ground, Rufus was as careful as possible getting Walter onto them and putting the hat back on his head. A quick look at the leg told him it was broken.

Fearing that his partner would slip to the other side at any moment, Rufus searched for dry branches to keep smoke to a minimum, then built a small fire to warm some water. Then he cut some saplings to make a splint for the broken leg. He slit the buckskin pant leg to get a better look at the leg. Rufus was relieved that the bone had not broken through the skin. If it had, Walter would have lost the leg.

Doing his best to align the leg, Rufus attempted to immobilize the limb with the splints. While Walter continued to cry out, Rufus didn't think his friend was fully conscious. With the splint installed with strips of cloth from Walter's spare shirt, Rufus moved to take his first close look at the scalp. He wondered if he should have taken the bloody piece of scalp from the brave's hand.

Moving the pot of steaming water next to his friend, Rufus slowly removed the hat. His jaw quivered at he looked at the blood matted hair and the angry area where the brave had removed the scalp. It was less than a three-inch patch, but to Rufus it looked like half of Walters head.

Trying to clean as much of the blood from the hair as he could, the pot of hot water became bright red. His friend's hair kept falling across the head wound as Rufus worked at cleaning the blood. He took his skinning knife and cut the hair short around the wound.

Needing another shirt to make a bandage for the scalp, Rufus opened his haversack. The bottle of whiskey had been broken when the horse had gone down. Everything in the haversack was saturated with the liquor. Thankful that his shirt had been shielded from the glass, he cut it into strips inhaling the smell of the whiskey.

As he wrapped it on his friends wound, Rufus told him, "This shirt has the last of my whiskey in it. I hope you're dreaming that we are sharing a bottle."

He looked at his unconscious friend, and Rufus was filled with worry. There was so little he could do, or even knew how to do. There was another hour of daylight and he needed to look for Walter's packhorse and go back to get the saddle off of the sorrel.

All of a sudden, the memories of the horse being killed by the Blackfoot rushed back. The pain of the loss was added to his concern for Walter. The sorrel had been with him for years. Leaving his injured friend, Rufus stripped the remaining gear off the roan, then he led the dun out of the trees, taking a moment to look for any movement.

Arriving back at the site of the attack, he found that the brave he had clubbed was gone as well as the saddle from the sorrel. There was no sign of the packhorse. The animal had probably been found by the Blackfoot. Other than Walter's traps, there had been little of value on the horse.

Being back at the sight of the ambush brought tension back into Rufus' body, and he was anxious to get away. Riding the dun, Pike stayed close to the river as he went back. Arriving at the shelter in the cottonwoods he could see Walter lying where he'd left him, looking more dead than alive. A quick check confirmed that he was breathing.

Adding some more wood to the coals, Rufus rinsed the bloody pot and put more water on to heat. Using jerky purchased at the rendezvous, he shredded it into the pot. He hoped to get Walter to swallow some of the broth. Moving back to his friend, Rufus checked the leg for swelling and his head for fever.

Suddenly he reached into his shirt and brought out the amulet made by Camille in New Orleans. Carefully lifting Walter's head, he placed it around his neck. "She told me it would protect me and now I hope it does the same for you," Rufus said.

Once the broth was hot, he took a mug and poured a few drops onto Walter's lips. The first attempts ran down the side of his friend's face. Parting the lips a little with his finger, he again poured a few drops of liquid. Relief washed over Rufus when Walter swallowed.

After a half-hour, Rufus managed to get half of a mug into his friend. After taking care of the horses, he fried up some side meat for his own meal. He was just about to eat when he heard his name. "Rufus," Walter said, his voice weak and raspy.

Setting down the frying pan, Pike went over to his friend. "I'm here, Walter."

His friend lay with his eyes open, staring at the sky. "Water," he said.

Filling the mug from the river, Rufus held his friend up a bit as he gave him a drink. Walter pulled his head away and coughed. "I let you have too much at one time," the mountain man told his friend. Taking his time, Rufus managed to get Walter to drink the full mug.

Placing his head back down, Rufus said, "We'll rest here for a day and then I'll get you to Fort William. They should have some kind of doctor."

Then he heard his friend speaking. "The brave came at me from the side and rolled me on my back," Walter told his partner. "He hit me with something as I got the pistol out. That's the last thing I remember."

"You killed him," Rufus told his friend. "He lifted some of your hair, but you killed him."

"My hair?" Walter wondered. He attempted to move and groaned. "My leg. I twisted it when I jumped from the horse. Right now, it's hurting like hell."

"You broke it," Pike said. "I got a splint on it."

"It is aching something awful and my head hurts," Walter told his friend. Then he said, "I need you to take the money belt and what's in my possible bag."

"You hold on to it," Rufus told him. "I won't need any until we get to the fort."

Straining to speak, Walter said, "I want you to carry our money."

Removing the belt from under his friend's shirt, Rufus put it around his own. He then sat watching his partner, hurting and lying with his eyes closed. Walter's face was deathly pale. The sun would be going down soon and they couldn't risk having the fire spotted by Blackfoot in the area.

Moving to the fire Rufus saw the frying pan with the side meat. It sat with the grease thick around the meat. There were only a few coals left and he couldn't add more wood. Rufus thought about setting the pan on what was left of the coals, but the burning hunger in his stomach made him decide to eat the tepid, greasy meat.

The blankets from Walter's dun had been used to make a bed for the injured man. Rufus had lost his blankets and coat when the saddle was taken, so he huddled on a bed of leaves with the saddle blanket off Walter's horse to cover him.

The next morning, he checked on his partner and found him running a fever. Alarm went through Rufus. Had there been more injuries that he hadn't noticed? Was the scalp wound becoming infected or even the leg?

He sniffed the scalp and only smelled the whiskey on the cloth. Rufus grabbed a piece of shirt and soaked it in the cool Sweetwater River. Folding it, he placed the damp cloth on his friend's forehead. Other than shallow breathing, Walter showed no other sign of life.

Getting the fire going, Rufus put a pot of water to heat. Then, taking his skinning knife, he cut strips of the cottonwood bark. He knew that the Indians boiled it to help with fevers. Filling the pot with the strips, he then added more small branches to the fire.

While waiting for the concoction in the pot to boil, Rufus chewed on some hard bread and sipped cold water. He refused to allow himself to make any coffee until he got the liquid into Walter. Rufus continued to bathe his friend's forehead, uncertain that it was doing any good to curb the fever.

Twice he had tried to wake Walter, without success. Thinking back about the prior day, Rufus remembered that his friend had said he was hit with something as he pulled the pistol from his belt. If the brave had struck him with a tomahawk or a knife butt, there could be damage to Walter's brain.

The pot came to a boil Rufus poured some of the liquid into a mug and set it to cool while going to check on the horses. Returning, he tasted the brew to see if it had cooled enough. It was unpleasantly bitter. He remembered his mother telling him that medicine tasted bad and that's what made it good.

"This damn stuff must be great," he muttered.

Kneeling next to his friend, he raised Walter's head and let some dribble onto his lips. He got a reaction of the lips parting. "Good," he whispered.

Then he said, "Walter, this will be awful, but it will help with your fever and maybe with the pain."

Unsure that his friend was fully awake, Walter gagged and coughed as he drank the liquid. During the whole ordeal, his eyes never opened. Rufus only gave him one cup, not knowing if it was enough or too much.

Rufus knew they had to move on. They were in the middle of the Blackfoot hunting area and in constant danger. They were still a week or more from Fort William. The mountain man knew it wouldn't be good to move his friend, but it was only a matter of time before their camp would be discovered and another attack would come.

While he was able to get Walter onto a horse moving from the ambush site to their camp, there was no way that he'd be able to ride for days on end. Taking his short axe, Rufus cut some trees to make a travois. He would be able to secure it to the packs on the roan.

Once he had the travois completed, he checked on Walter. His friend was covered with sweat. The brew had broken the fever. He fed another cup to Walter. He was rewarded during the process with his friend opening his eyes. It was only for a short period of time and Rufus wasn't sure he was focusing on anything.

After hearing some shooting in the distance, Rufus decided that they would need to leave as soon as the sun went down. The sound of the shot would only travel about a mile during the summer warmth and breezes, so the braves were within the distance to spot the smoke from their fire.

He made more broth for Walter and coffee and rice for himself. He put the remaining bark liquid into a canteen to use if the fever came back. After feeding the broth to his friend and eating the rice for his meal, Rufus readied the camp for their departure.

It was an hour before dark and he decided to go back to the ambush site one more time to look for anything of use. Maybe he'd find his hat. The mile to the site took almost a half hour due to caution needed. The first thing he heard was the sound of flies buzzing around the sorrel.

Moving past it, he went to where Walter had been attacked. The blood covered grass was coated with flies. He saw maggots crawling on something not far away. It was Walter's hair sticking out of the slimy mass. Rufus smiled, and whispered, "At least they didn't get to keep your scalp, Walter."

There was nothing of use left at that spot. Moving back to the sorrel, he got the reins off of the bloated carcass. Then he noticed the brim of his hat protruding from under the horse. Pulling it loose, he pushed the crown back out. Placing it onto his head, he caught the odor of the rotting horse. He knew it would disappear soon enough.

Heading back for the camp, he had a crawling feeling up his back, expecting to be jumped on at any time. The reins he'd taken would be useful to make the travois sturdier. All was quiet when he got back to the camp. The sun was going down and it was time to move.

He picked up his friend and placed him on the tarp stretched between the poles. Walter was dead weight and didn't even groan from the leg during the move. Rufus left the camp leading the two horses and the travois on the roan. He kept to low ground and within the trees whenever possible.

At one point he had to wade through the river, or go over the rise. Due to Walter being on the travois, Rufus chose the rise. At the top, he spotted Blackfoot fires in the distance. It gave him some comfort knowing where they were camped and that it was unlikely that braves would be wandering across the plains during the night.

While traveling in the dark, Rufus went back several times to check on Walter. One time he heard his friend say something. Leaning close he asked, "What do you want, Walter?"

"Got to pee," was all Walter said. The challenge of helping a man with a broken leg, plus being unsteady from head trauma, was time consuming. It was over a half-hour before Walter was back on the travois. His friend was warm again, so Rufus gave him the rest of the bark water.

Retying the ropes that prevented Walter from falling out of the travois, Rufus looked at his friend in the pale moon light. His eyes were open. "Tomorrow I will make you some rice for your meal."

He heard a weak, "Thanks," before heading back to lead the horses.

After a couple of nights, putting distance between them and the Blackfoot, Rufus began to travel during the daylight hours. While making a fire for their supper, the mountain man heard his friend call. Hurrying to his side, Rufus asked, "What's wrong?"

"I need some paper and a pencil," Walter said.

"I don't know if we have any," he told his friend.

"In my saddle bags," Walter told him. "Get it for me."

Finding a tally book and a stub of a pencil, Rufus brought them to Gray. His friend looked pale and his eyes appeared sunken. Despite these, Rufus was thankful that Walter was talking more. After telling him about being attacked, he had hardly spoken.

Returning to making their meal, Pike looked over and saw Walter writing in the tally book, his hand shaking. Rufus had noticed that his friend had felt warm when he'd taken him from the travois. They were in a grove of aspen and he planned to boil some more bark to break the fever.

Rufus mashed some beans in the jerky broth for Walter. Slowly, he managed to get the man to finish the brew. While the bark boiled on the fire, he helped his friend drink some coffee. As he held Walter's head up to sip the coffee, he again felt the heat of the fever. He said a silent prayer that the bark water would work.

Walter held his hand up to let Rufus know he'd had enough. He then handed the tally book to the mountain man. "I wrote my will in the book, just in case I don't make it."

Feeling fear mixed with anger, Rufus said, "You are going to make it."

Ignoring what Pike had said, Walter continued. "I have money in the bank in Franklin. If I don't make it, I have left it to you."

"I don't want your money," Rufus said. "You need it to buy Sal's livery. Hell, I would just waste it on whiskey."

"I'd like to think you'd need the whiskey to get over my dying," Walter said, giving a weak chuckle.

"Nobody is dying here," Pike said, turning away from his friend and busying himself at the fire.

The greatest difficulty during the trip was when they forded the North Platte River. Rufus had thought about building a raft to float Walter across, but finally found a way to get his friend onto the dun, having to endure Walter's cries every time the leg got bumped. Twice he changed the bandage on the head and almost got sick at the appearance of the ugly wound. Each time the whiskey-saturated cloth was used.

After eight long days of slow travel, they reached the fort. Rufus was exhausted. He had only managed to sleep a few hours each night, between taking care of Walter and tending to the animals. Little had changed with his partner. He would wake for short periods of time and then be back out. Wet cloths seemed to take care of the temperatures, plus Rufus boiled up some more bark when camped near poplars, just in case they lasted.

The bruising on his leg had changed from blue to greenish-yellow. It remained swollen when compared to the other leg. Rufus noticed that he hadn't gotten it as straight as he had hoped when applying the splints.

The fort had a wooden palisade around the perimeter. It was larger than Fort Bonneville and had two buildings with plenty of room for additional buildings that could be used for fur storage and supplies. It was fortified more for the protection of the furs and supplies rather than for defense.

The main gate stood open without any guards. Unlike Fort Bonneville, which gave one the feel of a military operation, this had all the earmarks of nothing more than a very large trading post. One of the trappers noticed him come in with Walter on the travois.

He came running over. "Can I help ya? Looks like ya got a wounded feller. Indian trouble?"

"Is there any kind of a doctor in the fort?" Rufus asked.

"If'n anyone needs doctoring they go to Freeman," the trapper said. "He was in the army. Learned his doctor'n fight'n the Brits in 1812."

"My friend was attacked by Blackfoot," Rufus told him. "Can you show me where this doctor is?"

"Blackfoot!" the trapper exclaimed. "We ain't got no Blackfoot around here. Fought them myself at the rendezvous of '28. Foller me. I'll take ya to Freeman."

Rufus led the horses and followed the man to the large building toward the back of the fort. On the left end was a door that opened into the medical man's quarters and office. The trapper yelled, "Freeman! Got some business for ya."

The door opened and a white-haired man with an impressive moustache came out. Looking at the trapper and Rufus, he asked, "Which one of you two need fixing up?"

"It's my friend on the travois," the mountain man told him. "His name is Walter Gray and we were attacked by Blackfoot."

"He got money to pay?" Freeman asked as he went to Walter.

"We got money," Rufus told him, feeling a little burn from the question. "His leg is broken and he was scalped. He may have gotten a hit on the head also."

While the man looked over Walter, he mumbled things that Rufus couldn't hear. Turning quickly, he said, "Bring him into the office and be careful with the leg. Could end up having to cut the damn thing off."

At this point, Rufus would have pounded the man into raw meat if he didn't need him for Walter. The trapper helped him carry his friend into the office. There was a cot toward the back of the room that had a piece of tarp nailed to the rafter above. It offered some privacy for the patient.

Rufus helped get his friend's clothing off. He then went to the front of the office. The trapper was standing near the horses. From behind the tarp the doc continued to mutter and did not sound happy. Feeling angry at Freeman and worried for Walter, Rufus stepped outside to get away and cool off.

"Don't take Freeman too personal," the trapper said. "He knows his doctor'n and will do his damnedest for your man."

"I been trapping with Walter for a lot of years," Rufus told him. "I don't . . ."

The trapper interrupted him, "It don't do no good to worry about things that might happen. Let the doc do what he does. Tell ya what. Once a week they sell whiskey out of room they call the post. They figure one night won't turn this place into a rendezvous. After ya get word from Freeman, come on by and I'll share a bottle with ya. The name's Hubert. They call me Hube."

Thanking Hube, Rufus watched him walk away. The thought of a drink, in fact many drinks, was strong in the mountain man. Anything to make the tragedy go away, even for one night. Right now, he had to take care of the horses. They had had little time to graze over the past eight days, and it showed. They stood with their heads hanging.

He'd seen a couple of corrals next to a low building that might be a livery. Leading the tired animals out of the fort, it was confirmed when he saw a crude sign with 'Livery' on it. A young man with a dirty white shirt and suspenders holding up his baggy pants stood near the building.

"Need a place to keep your animals?" he called.

"You got some grain for these tired horses?" Rufus asked.

Quickly he made arrangements for the animals and his gear. The travois was left discarded near the corral. When Rufus got back to Freeman's office, he glanced into the room. Activity was still going on behind the tarp and so was the constant muttering of the old doc.

There was a bench in front of the building and Rufus took a seat. He was hungry, but was determined to wait for word on Walter. Rufus still feared for his friend's life. He thought about when Walter had complained about his leg and told him to take the money belt. Then came the fever. He had spoken less often after that.

Looking toward the doorway, he wondered if Freeman was taking so long because he was removing Walter's leg. His friend was weak. Rufus doubted that he could survive the amputation. Finally, the old doc came out and sat on the bench next to the mountain man. He still had his apron on and it was not covered with blood. That was a good sign.

"You done good on the scalp," Freeman said.

"I'm guessing you didn't take the leg," Rufus replied.

"The leg ain't out of danger yet, but putting the whiskey on the bandage on his head prevented infection from taking hold," the old man said. "It will be some months before he is back on his feet, that is, if he has feet to stand on."

"Can I see him?" Rufus asked.

"It can't hurt, but he is weak," Freeman said. "I got some coffee and beans on the stove. You're welcome to have some after you talk to your friend."

As Rufus walked into the office, he was struck by the change in the old doc. While he still looked gruff, his attitude had changed. The anger was gone. Stepping around the curtain, he saw that Walter was sleeping. The dirty long johns had been replaced with fresh ones. His head was covered with clean bandages, the leg had proper splints and was wrapped with wide strips of cloth.

He saw that the amulet was lying on his chest. "Camille, I need you to work your voodoo for Walter. He is a good man and has lots of beavers to catch yet."

Rufus' jaw dropped when he heard, "What I need is you to go out and have a drink. I am finally comfortable after a week in that damn travois."

The grateful Rufus replied, "I see you are awake. I couldn't get hardly a word out of you coming from the Sweetwater."

"That's 'cause I was gritting my teeth against the pain in my leg from bouncing along the trail," his friend said. "By the way, I am trusting you not to spend all our money. Tomorrow we got to talk about what I wrote in the tally book."

While Rufus was about to respond, Walter drifted off to sleep. The mountain man came around the tarp to take advantage of the coffee and beans. "He doesn't seem to be able to stay awake," he told the old doc.

"That's because I gave him laudanum," Freeman said. "It makes him sleepy, but helps with the pain."

After the meal, Rufus spent another couple of hours watching and talking to his sleepy friend. By that time, it was dark and the old man had gone to sleep. Rufus planned to sleep on the bench he'd been sitting on. Stepping outside, he heard the voices coming from the trading post. Several men were enjoying the night out.

Hube saw him walk in the door and called him over. "You come for that drink?" he asked.

"Maybe a few more," Rufus told him.

* * *

The next morning, Freeman found Rufus sleeping on the bench. "That bed looks damn uncomfortable," the old doc said, waking the mountain man.

Sitting up, Rufus rubbed his beard-covered face. "After the long trip and a few drinks, I could have slept on a pile of rocks."

"Coffee's on the stove," Freeman said. "Walter was asking for you."

After pouring himself a steaming cup of coffee, Rufus went around the tarp to see Walter. His friend was propped up with pillows and eating hot porridge. "I heard your snoring out front," Walter told him. "Did you enjoy your night at the post?"

"I did, and you would be proud of me. I stopped after one bottle," Rufus said.

"See anyone we know?" Walter asked.

"As a matter of fact, I did," the mountain man replied. "Harold Jones came here to get supplies. He came with a caravan that included Johnson."

"What are your plans?" Walter asked.

Furling his brow, Rufus replied, "What do you mean, plans? I will stay here until you are ready to travel and then we will go trapping this fall."

"I'm done," Walter told him. "The doc said that the leg is crooked and while I will be able to walk on it in time, it won't be in a beaver pond. My trapping days are over."

"What the hell!" Rufus exclaimed. "Freeman ain't no doctor. He don't know how things will work out. You will be up and around in no time."

Looking at his upset friend, Walter said, "He knows these things. I knew the time was coming. If possible, I will go back to Franklin and try and buy Sal's place. Maybe hire a young lad to do the heavy work."

"I'll go back to Franklin with you," Rufus said. "We lost two horses to the Blackfoot. We got the dun and roan left. After you are strong enough, we'll buy a couple more horses and go back to the mountains."

"You are a good man in the mountains," Walter told him. "You wouldn't be happy in Franklin and I must admit that your abilities in the beaver ponds are better than I've ever been. It's time you find another trapper to partner up with."

Things were moving too fast for Rufus. He did not understand his friend being so calm about stopping trapping. Though flattered by Walter's comments, he felt that there was nobody more knowledgeable than his friend.

Grasping for something to convince Walter to change his mind, Rufus said, "How about the cave? You have a lot of stuff there that I could never afford to buy. We were going to trap the Yellowstone. I know nothing of the area and will need you there."

"The horses, the cave, and the challenge of trapping the Yellowstone are all yours," Walter said. "If you come back to Franklin each year, you will always have a place to sleep. I'll even hang on to enough of your money to make sure you can buy supplies."

They seemed to be at an impasse that was finally broken when Freeman called, "I got some porridge left if you want a bowl."

Rufus looked in the direction of the voice. He began to stand up when Walter stopped him. "We got to talk about one more thing. I wrote the will when I thought I was going to die."

"I know that," Rufus said. "It looks like you ain't going to die, so you can just rip up that page."

"That is not what I'm saying," Walter continued. "This here will leaves everything I have to you when I do die. I hope that is some years away, but the time will come."

Getting up, his eyes stinging, Rufus said, "I got to get the porridge before it gets cold."

"I will be making it official and keep it in the bank in Franklin," Gray called after him.

For three weeks, Rufus stayed around the fort, hoping that things would change and Walter would decide to trap. While at the post one Saturday night, he noticed a red-headed man who looked familiar. It was Wally Talbert. The wiry frame and freckled covered face couldn't be mistaken.

As the man walked by, Rufus said, "You come one hell of a long way to hunt buffalo."

Wally stopped and stared hard at the bearded mountain man. "That gravely voice is familiar, but I'll be damned if I recognize the face. Are we friends?"

"We sure as hell are," the mountain man said. "The name's Rufus Pike."

"Well, I'll be damned," Wally said, reaching out to shake his hand. "I still ain't forgotten you outshooting me and taking my money."

"Is Hank here with you?" Rufus asked.

"No, he isn't," Wally said, his face falling a bit. "The Lakota got him while we was after buffalo. I managed to get him back to St. Louis, but the wounds went bad on him."

"I'm sorry to hear that," Pike replied. "What brings you this far west?"

"For years I have watched trappers come and go from St. Louis, and always had a hankering to try it," Wally said. "I was told caravans stop here before heading to the mountains. I figured I could sign up with one of them."

For the next hour, Rufus and Wally talked of old times over a bottle of the post's best whiskey. A thought started formulating in his mind. His plan had been to find an experienced trapper to go west with. Wally knew buffalo hunting and was a fine shot, but he knew nothing about trapping.

What Wally did have was frontier savvy, and if trouble came he would be a good man to have his back. Before they had too much to drink, Rufus told him, "My trapping partner got hurt pretty bad fighting some Blackfoot. He had to give up trapping. I was wondering if you'd consider partnering with me this season."

"How many years have you been trapping?" the redhead asked.

"Well, since I buffalo hunted with you and Hank," Rufus said. "That would be nigh on to seven years, maybe eight."

Wally tossed down a shot and smiled, exposing his missing teeth. "Well, I figure you've learned a thing or two about trapping by now. Course, I was planning on using company gear to start out."

Laughing, Rufus replied, "I know a whole lot about trapping, and it sure beats skinning buffalo. I also know of a cave that should have all the gear you'll need. You do have horses, don't you?"

That evening, over another bottle, the two men finalized some plans for the coming year's trapping. The Yellowstone would have to wait for another year, but beaver should be back in the ponds near the cave.

With a true feeling of loss, Rufus went one last time to see his friend. "I will be leaving come morning with a buffalo hunter I knew in St. Louis. We're going to trap the area near the cave."

"What the hell does a buffalo hunter know about trapping?" Walter asked.

"I figure about as much as I knew back in '26, when I quit buffalo hunting," Rufus said, smiling.

"I believe you'll need this," Walter said as he began to remove the amulet.

"No, it's yours," he said. "You have a long trip east and it will help keep you safe."

"Did you get a good price on supplies?" his friend asked.

"Better than the rendezvous, but not as good as in Franklin," the mountain man told him.

After some final goodbyes, Rufus left the doc's with a hollow feeling inside. While he was happy that Wally would be going with him, the security from looking to Walter for all the major decisions was gone. Up to now, Rufus had had little responsibility other than doing his share in the ponds. Walter had always carried the burden of planning a successful season.

His partner had had lots of rules. These rules guided their lives and, in some cases, prevented them from losing them. No whiskey was a rule that had always bothered Rufus. He remembered that Hank had also had that rule when hunting buffalo. It must be a good rule, Rufus figured, and he'd have to mention it to Wally.

He found the redhead at the livery, checking his packs. "This is a hell of a lot harder than planning a two-week trip hunting buffalo," Wally told him. "What do you do after you run out of beans?"

"Just like buffalo hunting," Rufus told him. "You eat what's available. We'll be eating beaver. When we run out of tobacco, coffee, beans, rice, and side meat, if we do it right, we will always have beaver."

"I hear there are deer with antlers wider than a man can reach," Wally said.

"That would be elk," Rufus told him. "There are also grizzlies in the mountains. Good money in them, but they're damn dangerous."

The new partner's eyes lit up at the thought of grizzlies. It was after dark when they finally finished checking the packs and the horses. The hostler had gone to sleep, but had left some coffee from supper. The two men sat in front of the livery drinking the stale brew and having a chew. They'd be sleeping in the loft tonight, and come morning the young hostler had promised to have some porridge for them.

"Will you be stopping in on Walter before we leave?" Wally asked.

"Nope," Rufus replied. "We already said our goodbyes. No sense dragging them out."

After a bit of a pause, with each in their own thoughts, Wally said, "You know you'll have to show me how to set a beaver trap."

"Yep, that and a few other things," Rufus replied.

Suddenly he realized that he, Rufus Pike, was now the leader and was looked upon as a mountain man.

www.ingramcontent.com/pod-product-compliance
Lightning Source LLC
LaVergne TN
LVHW020525100826
845148LV00010B/1339

* 9 7 8 1 7 3 4 0 0 2 1 4 0 *